# That Mad Game

AJ Hodges

# That Mad Game

AJ Hodges

ISBN 978-1-941266-24-3

ISBN 978-1-941266-24-3

Published by: Trenchant Publishing

PO Box 21

Gilbertsville, PA 19525

Editing by Diane Moser and Zak Frey

Cover Design by Sherwin Soy from 99designs.com

# Tweet This Book!

Please help AJ Hodges by spreading the word about this book on Twitter!

The suggested hashtag for this book is #thatmadgame.

Find out what other people are saying about the book by clicking on this link to search for this hashtag on Twitter:

#thatmadgame

*War: that mad game the world so loves to play.*

*– Jonathan Swift*

*For Captain Donald MacIntyre, RN*

# Chapter I

## May 26th, 1940

Smoke from the oil refineries and God knows what else hung like a pall along the horizon. All of Dunkirk had to be burning. But even so, what was left of the French army and the British Expeditionary Force were moving toward it because they saw that French port on the English Channel as their last hope for salvation. And they were moving fast, pushed hard by German Panzers, leaving in their wake a vast, stinking wasteland of dead men and horses, abandoned and burning vehicles, overturned wagons, field guns with barrels blown and peeled back, looking like partially-eaten overripe bananas, rifles and paper – incredible amounts of paper.

After the corpses, it was the paper that saddened Hauptmann Hans Richter the most, not the cases of files and orders that would interest German military intelligence, but the papers that were mute evidence of individual men dead or lost in terrified flight, letters and pictures from home, children's drawings, bills, and on and on. It all blew in the breeze, spilling from bundles dropped by the sides of the road, fluttering to a stop against any obstacle in its path.

He was facing a lone tree, relieving himself against it, and wondering why men so often looked for a surface to christen. Why it made a difference, he couldn't have said, but it seemed to. A man was vulnerable at that moment and it gave him some cover? Maybe that was it. Or somewhere in the dim dark distance of his genetic past, he was related to the dog? The instinct certainly was the same.

Bemused, he buttoned his fly buttons, then turned and opened his mouth to give the order for his Panzers to move out. It was then that the bullet hit him, slamming into his shoulder and spinning him around just enough to make the second one miss. He landed hard, unaware that the wild scream he heard was his own. The light seemed to be fading and he lay there, gritting his teeth against the waves of nausea and pain engulfing him, struggling to hang on to what was left of consciousness. He had to move, to get to cover, to get behind the ruins of the stone wall, to get that wall between himself and that rifle.

And so he tried to clench his left arm to his side to ease the pain, tried to turn, to roll over enough to get some purchase with his feet, concentrating on all of that so hard that he was oblivious to the fusillade of shots passing over his head and the explosions of incoming artillery fire that had just begun. He was aware of nothing but himself and the wall until suddenly there was the sound of heavy breathing in his ear and he heard his own grunt of surprise and pain as his upper body was lifted. He was being dragged toward the wall.

There was another sharp grunt – this time not his own – and as a great weight fell on him, he lost awareness of anything.

Dieter Bergmann had seen it all and so he ran, diving into the tank through his driver's hatch as Schuster scrambled up through the loader's side of the turret. Schmidt was already at his gun. Dieter started the engine and the turret turned. CRACK! His ears rang from the concussion of the gun firing almost over his head and he slammed on his earphones. The radio wasn't on but they were the only protection his ears had.

Schmidt had waited for nothing, no one. His was a cold directed fury and his big gun was the perfect vent for it, to shoot the son-of-a-bitch who had shot the Hauptmann.

The shooter had to be in the barn. As if in confirmation, a man raced from the back towards a stand of trees, followed by a veritable river of tracers that were converging on him from several directions. It caught him and Schmidt felt a flash of satisfaction. CRACK!

The other tanks of their squadron were fanning out, heading for cover in the few copses and folds the flat terrain had to offer, so they could shoot it out with the artillery that had already found their range without unduly exposing themselves. For once, Dieter didn't even think about that. His whole being was focused on that barn and that low stone wall.

CRACK! The last shot was point blank and the barn caved in.

Schuster reloaded the gun, then shifted to Bauer's assistant driver's seat and began spraying the ruins of the barn and the copse beyond it with machine gun fire. Damn. Damn. Damn! His breath was coming in a choking fury.

There was a large explosion behind them. Dieter couldn't see what it was but it made him aware at last of the incoming artillery fire. They needed to get under cover and fast. He pulled the tank in behind the small stand of trees close to the end of the wall, grabbed the first aid kit and was out and running, staying low. Schuster tried to follow but his hatch was blocked by the gun, so he slid back into the turret only to find Schmidt blocking his way.

"Stay here," he told Schuster grimly. "There may be more snipers around." He looked out, the Hauptmann's machine pistol at the ready while Schuster waited, his heart pounding.

"All right," Schmidt said finally. "Dieter's with them and he hasn't been shot yet. Go. I'll cover you."

Dieter had seen the hole in Bauer's back at once but there was no time for niceties and so he rolled him off Richter as gently as great haste permitted. Bauer gasped in pain and a froth of bright red blood came from the exit wound in his chest. His lungs. Bauer was done for. Dieter's heart fell. Bauer's lips moved and Dieter used a precious moment to put his ear close. The whispered words came out separately and with great effort. "Take care of the Hauptmann, I'll be alright."

Dieter was nodding as Schuster came pounding up and then he heard himself saying, "Compression bandages back and front. I'll see to the Hauptmann."

Schuster whipped his knife out of his boot and cut away Bauer's tunic and undershirt as Dieter bent over Hans Richter.

Then Schmidt was there, helping Schuster. Their eyes met. It was hopeless and they both knew it, but that didn't stop Schmidt from tearing the woolen undershirt into long strips while Schuster applied pressure back and front. They had just finished wrapping his chest when Schmidt saw a feeble gesture. He hunkered down.

"Is ... the Hauptmann ... alright?" The words were barely audible.

"Sure, Hermann." Schmidt nodded vigorously. "Bergmann's taking good care of him."

There was a wisp of a smile, a grimace and then Bauer's eyes were vacant. Schmidt had never watched a man die before, but he knew. It was like walking past a house, day after day, never noticing that it was lived in, and then going by one day and realizing that it was empty. There was no discernible difference. One just knew.

He felt for a pulse, even though there wouldn't be one. There wasn't. And so he just knelt there for a moment, head bowed, before reaching out and closing Bauer's eyes.

Schuster turned away. "I'll ... I'll see if I can help with the Hauptmann."

Schmidt didn't hear him. He lifted Bauer and carried him back to the tank, walking as though through a bad dream, then laid him carefully on the back deck before climbing up himself. So young, he thought angrily, as he dug into the storage box. And so small. Nothing to him at all. Bauer's blanket had a tear in one corner. When he found it, he hauled it out and wrapped the body in it. Poor little sod.

With that he turned away, jumped off, and walked toward the wall without looking back. "Well?" he asked Dieter when he got there.

Bergmann didn't raise his head but he sounded almost cheerful when he said, "Nasty break. High on the arm. But he's still got his reflexes."

"Is he ... conscious?"

A vigorous shake of the head. "No. No. Not yet. But he will be." He looked around. "I need something..." Apparently he didn't see what he needed because he looked directly at Schmidt at last without releasing the pressure he was applying to the wound. "Get me ... a barn door? Something big enough to use for a stretcher."

Schmidt was off and running.

"And Schuster, you're going to have to help me. We need to get this arm stabilized."

Finally the arm was bandaged and stabilized and Hans was lying on the remains of a barn door, which was barely big enough, lashed to the back deck of the tank next to Bauer.

"Get on the radio set, Schuster. Find Lieutenant Wagner. Tell him Richter's been wounded and that our gun is jammed and we have to go back for repairs. We've got to find a field hospital." Dieter was in command now and no one was questioning that fact.

Schuster spoke, even as he was putting on the earphones. "There was a British field hospital in the church in the last village we went through. Some of our medical people ought to be there by now. They're bound to be using it." He turned on the radio.

"My gun is not jammed." Schmidt was annoyed.

"Then jam it unless you have a better excuse for leaving the battlefield. I don't relish having a court martial convened, even if you do. Or maybe you'd rather have Schuster call up a medic and have him jolt the Hauptmann back to the field hospital in a motorcycle side-car?"

"No. Certainly not." said Schmidt indignantly. "Just so you know my gun is not jammed."

"Of course I know! I made it up, didn't I? Good grief!" Dieter started the engine and drowned out the sound of Schuster droning into the radio. It was ridiculous. Bauer dead, the Hauptmann badly wounded and we're sitting in the middle of a battlefield arguing like school boys.

The intercom came on and he was able to say, "One of you get out and see that the Hauptmann stays put. I'm going to get there as fast as I can."

There was no discussion from anyone this time.

\*     \*     \*

Hans could hear voices from far away, coming and going. One was familiar. Why? Who was it? He tried to think about that but it was too hard.

A face peered into his and broke into a delightful grin. He knew that face. Whose...?

"Well, well, if the great Panzer hero, Johann Richter, boy Hauptmann hasn't just returned to the land of the living. Welcome!"

His lips seemed to be moving but he couldn't hear the "Who?" that he uttered.

"It's Georg, Hans, Georg Brandt, your old drinking buddy from Munich and Prussian summers. We've just finished fixing you up and you're going to be as good as new. The Good Lord does indeed watch over fools, children and drunks, especially when He has a superb surgeon at His disposal."

Georg saw the wisp of a smile and the attempt to focus the eyes. Hans' lips moved again and this time he managed a hoarse "Crew?"

"Ah, yes. Your crew. They're fine, all three of them. A real special delivery package, you were, and properly trussed up, too. Whoever did that knew what he was doing. You came in just like tales of the American Wild West, a cloud of dust and out of the sunset rides our hero, tied to a door on the back of a tank. The only problem was that the sun wasn't setting at the time and you came out of the north.

"That driver of yours is something. Looks tough as nails, but he hovered over you like a mother hen. Raised one hell of a row with our poor triage man. Said no one was going to touch you but an orthopedic surgeon or, failing that, a neurosurgeon. My, my, where does he think we are?

"But it seems he had a machine pistol in his hand at the time. Never threatened anyone with it, mind you, but just the fact that he had it and looked so sinister in the bargain was enough to ensure prompt service. So I was rousted out of bed, taken from the first honest sleep I'd had in days. Called in on consultation so to speak. And what did I find? Johann Richter, boy Hauptmann.

"And was I surprised? Of course I was surprised. I laughed. Amazed at the coincidence, you understand. But he didn't understand and apparently didn't like what he didn't understand.

Whoever sewed up that long cut on his cheek botched it. The scar gets livid when he's angry." Georg was helpless to stop his prattling. It had been a shock to find Hans there, needing his attention so badly.

"I explained and that mollified him a bit, considerably when I commented on the ingenuity and sensical nature of your bandage. And he was properly astounded by the coincidence. So was I."

He moved around the bed and Hans felt his legs being handled, then a tap on his knee. There was a mumbled "Fine. Fine." But why couldn't he seem to move himself?

Georg was still rattling on and Hans was grateful that no reply seemed to be expected. "I have the distinct feeling that they won't find a field repair unit nor will that gun be cleared by their own efforts, for all the work they're supposedly doing on it, until I tell them that you really have survived my ministrations and let them see it for themselves."

He came back around to where Hans could see him again and nodded. "They should be impressed with the results. I certainly am, if I do say so myself." And he was, especially since, initially, it was very difficult to forget whom he had under the knife.

Hans gave him a little nod and closed his eyes. But then his brow furrowed and he made the effort to look at Georg again. He'd said something that wasn't quite right. What was it? Oh, yes. "Four." It was a parched croak.

"Four what?"

"Crew of four."

"Well, I saw only the three." Then he remembered the bundle tied so carefully onto the back of the tank. Hans wasn't ready to hear about that. Not yet. "The other one must have been minding the store."

There was something about the way that Georg had said it that Hans didn't like. "Are ... they ... here?"

"They can't be far. No one's run them off. They're supposed to be working on that gun, and besides, I don't think anyone would want to tangle with that driver of yours. I know I wouldn't."

"Bergmann."

"Yes, yes. That's his name."

Hans was able to focus his eyes now and he was becoming aware of the fact that he hurt somewhere. His chest. No, it was left of that. His shoulder. He tried to turn his head to look.

Georg stopped him. "Don't try to move too much yet. You were shot in the very upper arm. The bone stopped the bullet and in the process got a rather nasty break just under the head. You're lucky. The wound was lateral. No nerve damage to speak of. Your middle deltoid isn't what it used to be, though. May never be."

He turned to go out of the tiny room, then thought better of it. "If you find you can't move, it's because you're in a massive and rather confining cast, so don't worry about it. But if you need something for the pain, let me know.

"I'll bring in Bergmann, if he's around, but not the others. You shouldn't be seeing even him right now." With that he was gone.

Hans found he could lift his head, helped by the fact that the head of his bed was elevated slightly. God Almighty! His arm was in a huge cast that covered his torso then stuck out straight to the side from his shoulder before bending at the elbow. He tried his fingers. They worked. The effort exhausted him and set up a fierce ache in his shoulder. He let his head fall back.

Georg spoke from the doorway. "He's here. He was waiting outside. They all were, but I told them only one and he was elected. Five minutes. That's all. Then I'll have to give you something for the pain."

Then Hans saw Bergmann's worried face bending over him. It was an effort to keep his eyes open.

"Are you alright, Herr Hauptmann?"

Hans managed a weak grin and gestured toward the cast.

Dieter gave a nervous little laugh. It was hard to see the Hauptmann lying there looking so... fragile. "Sorry. Of course ..."

"Who was it ... fell on top of me?"

"Bauer."

"Is he all right?"

The answer came slowly. "No. No, he's not." Then Dieter straightened up and his words were direct and to the point. "He took a bullet in the back just as he got you to the wall. He ... he's dead."

Hans was silent and Dieter stood looking down at him anxiously. "There was nothing I could do. Nothing anyone could do."

"If there had been... you would have done it."

He sounded so utterly weary that, despite the words, Dieter's heart fell. "Thank you, sir."

"He took that bullet instead of me." It wasn't a question.

Dieter looked out the small window. It was dirty. "If he had to die when he did, that's the way he would have wanted it. When I got to him, all he wanted... He wanted me to take care of you. Said he'd be all right." There was a pause before he went on. "It was Bauer who did your laundry that one time. He was... always doing things for you. We all knew but we never said anything, even to him. It would have embarrassed him. He..."

"Out, man. Out!" Georg's harsh voice came from the doorway. "He needs sleep."

"Just one more thing, please, sir."

"Make it quick."

Dieter turned back to Hans, speaking quickly. "Herr Hauptmann, the tank's all in one piece but it is a command tank. So someone else... it wouldn't be the same, you see, even if there were... replacements." He drew in a long breath. "So if, when you're better, when you're out of here... You're going to need a driver, someone to look after you. If you want me to, I'd be glad to do it."

Hans found there was a lump in his throat that made speech even more difficult.

"You're sure to be offered a tank of your own."

"I don't want one." He shook his head for emphasis. "I never have."

Hans nodded slowly. "But look, I ..."

"Please, at least consider it." Bergmann's face had hardened and the words were said as a formal application.

"It's what you really want?" He found it hard to believe.

"Yes, sir." He was almost at attention, his eyes fixed on the wall somewhere over Hans' head.

"All right, then, Bergmann, I'll try to arrange it."

"Thank you." He had turned to leave but was stopped by the sound of Hans' voice, stronger now.

"Don't thank me. I should thank you. Any commanding officer would be lucky to have you. And besides, I wouldn't have much of an arm left if it weren't for you. Georg told me about the bandage. And you were the only one there who could have done it."

Dieter looked at his boots.

"I always knew I could count on you, and when the chips were down for me... You... All of you... I'll miss you. Schuster and Schmidt, too. Tell them ... thank you. And if you'll get Bauer's address to me, I'd like to write to his mother."

"Of course. But I don't think they were very close. It was only his grandmother who wrote him, and sent him packages."

"Both addresses, then."

Dieter nodded then slipped by Georg who was still in the doorway, and disappeared.

Georg looked after him. "Odd," he said softly, "not one salute or Heil Hitler in the bunch." He shrugged and moved back into the tiny vestry that was to have been his own room and began checking Hans' cast which was, at last, beginning to feel dry. "It's remarkable, really. I've rarely seen such devotion to a commanding officer. They all risked courts martial or at least severe disciplinary action to bring you here. If they hadn't, I don't like to think about what might have happened. And not only to your arm. You lost a lot of blood."

Hans didn't reply.

Georg looked up sharply. "I'll get you something for the pain."

"You can't give me anything for this sort of pain."

"Why?"

"One of them died. Took a bullet that was rightfully mine."

"The fourth man."

"Yes, the fourth man."

"I was right about the devotion, Hans." He disappeared though the doorway and came back almost at once, needle in hand. "You need sleep."

He nodded as Georg swabbed his arm with anesthetic. The needle slid in and it was a relief to slip back into nothingness.

*　　*　　*

He couldn't move! Everything was black and he couldn't move! He struggled, trying to sit up, to get out, but he couldn't. Why? Oh, God. And what was wrong with his arm?

Still in a panic, he reached across to touch it with his right hand. Something hard. A cast. The cast. He sank back sweating, his heart gradually slowing as he remembered. All of it. Bauer. Especially Bauer.

At least Bauer was out of it, well out of it. No more killing for Bauer. No more anything. Stupid to think that way. It was just ... This damn cast. He was trapped in it, stuck. No way out. Not now. Not while the British and the cream of the French army had their backs to the Channel at Dunkirk. Belgium and Holland had surrendered and France was bound to fall. Their army was too demoralized for anything but defeat. And the people... His eyes screwed shut against the vision of the hordes of people fleeing, clogging the roads. All sorts of people. Luxury cars in line with horse-drawn wagons. Old men bowed in the traces of farm carts piled high with possessions, followed by old women dressed in black. Children peering at them from behind their mothers' skirts, wide-eyed and solemn, sensing the fear in their parents. The victims of strafings pushed off into the ditches. It was all so futile. There was nowhere to run. The Wehrmacht had come too fast.

Four years. Four... goddamn... years. And for what? For four years he had sent it all to Michael. Tank types, number, and specifications, strategy, the development of the tactics the world was now calling the Blitzkrieg. He'd warned Michael about Poland and told Michael about France. About the invasion. Over and over. The general plan. Even the approximate date. And what the hell had it been for? All the risks. Jesus. The risks.

He remembered the day clearly. The place. Even the date. The office of Captain Michael Compton, D.S.C, RN(Ret), in the Foreign Office, Whitehall, London. August sixteenth, nineteen thirty-six. Two days after his father's funeral. When Michael had rung up the day before, to ask him to come by, he had thought that it was simply to express godfatherly concern and to offer to help him in any way he could. And indeed, at first that was just what it seemed to be, even when Michael urged him to go back to Munich as his father had done shortly before he died.

"Do you know what it is like there?" he had snapped at Michael. "Those brown-shirted bully-boys strutting around, burning books and stomping people in the streets just for the fun of it. And most of the best professors were Jewish, so they're gone, kicked out by order of the 'beloved' Fuhrer." He shook his head. "I'm not going back to that."

"In one more year, you will finish your degree." He said it mildly.

"I'll finish it somewhere else. There's ... " He stopped, slumping back into the chair on the other side of the desk and rubbing his neck wearily. "I'm sorry. I was rude just now. Tired, I guess. The last few weeks have been ... difficult."

Michael's face softened. "How's your mother?"

"She's doing well, everything considered. But it isn't easy for her."

"And your brother?"

"You know James." John gave a little smile. "He's solid as a rock. When my father first got sick a couple of years ago, he must have seen the handwriting on the wall because he gradually turned the business over to James. And since James was born here before there was any fighting with Germany, he chose to become a British subject. James will be all right."

"And you?" The tone was gentle. "How are you?"

He shrugged. "I'll miss him. He was a tough man, and a good father. I was just really getting to know him." John took a deep breath and it shuddered out as he went on. "I know he wanted me to finish at Munich. And now so do you. But I don't think either of you really know what is going on over in Germany. I don't want any part of it and if I went back, I wouldn't have any choice about that. They'd make me part of it, because some time this year I'll be called up into the Wehrmacht and would have to go the minute I finished my degree. In case you'd forgotten, because my father was German and I was born in Berlin during the last war, I am irrevocably a German citizen."

"I haven't forgotten."

"And I want to do something about that." He went on as if Michael hadn't spoken. "I want to become a British subject – I didn't feel I could while my father was alive, but now there's no reason not to – and I can't do that if I go back to Germany."

Michael began fiddling with a pencil. It was a moment before he looked up. "I'm afraid that I have a vested interest in your going back to Germany, a professionally vested interest."

"Professionally vested? Why the hell would you have a professionally vested interest in my going anywhere, let alone back to Germany? Don't you understand? I'd be called up!"

Michael nodded slowly.

John looked back at him, his confusion growing. "You want me to be called up?"

Another nod.

John shook his head slowly. "No." Then, as Michael's eyes seemed to be boring right through him, reluctantly, "Why?"

"Do you know a man named Heinz Guderian?"

"The general?" What the hell does he have to do with anything? Michael just nodded again.

"Yes, I know him, vaguely," said John angrily. "I met him several years ago when we were in Prussia, at Uncle Karl's. He was out there hunting. What about him?"

"Unfortunately Heinz Guderian is a very bright man. He's

developed an armored force for the Wehrmacht that is going to revolutionize land warfare. And he did it by reading and believing some very bright Englishmen – Fuller, Liddell-Hart, and Hobart – and then testing out their ideas and throwing in a few of his own for good measure. If his book is any indication of what's to come – and since Hitler seems to believe in what he's doing, I don't see why it shouldn't be – Germany's going to have an armored force that's far more powerful and effective than anything the world has ever seen. As I said, it will change the whole concept of the way wars are fought. And with Germany rearming ..." He shrugged. "There's going to be another war, John."

"Jesus, I hope not."

"It's beyond the hoping stage. War is going to come and Britain's not going to be ready for it unless something happens to wake up the powers-that-be and soon."

"But those men you mentioned. Fuller, was it? And Liddell Hobart?

"Liddell-Hart and Hobart."

"Those names sound British."

"They are."

"Then why isn't Britain developing that same sort of armored force here?"

Michael struggled to control his growing impatience. "Their theories are revolutionary. They're going to change everything. And there's considerable resistance to change among Britain's military leaders. They consider these men troublemakers and so they've been shoved out of the way and no one pays any attention to them, at least not on this side of our Channel moat. Our generals are saying that they won the last war, didn't they? So why change anything?

"But what those damn fools don't see is that until those masses of fresh American troops refilled the lines and our tanks scared the Germans out of their wits and got our infantry out of the trenches... It was when our armies began to move that we won. Mobility did it then and mobility will do it again. Mobility will be the means of winning the next war, and tanks are the key to that mobility."

"Well, well," said John drily. "As Buttercup said in *Pinafore*, 'Things are seldom what they seem.'"

Michael's eyebrows rose in inquiry.

"To think that all this time I thought you were slaving away almost unrewarded in the dreary trenches of the Foreign Office civil service."

A small smile played across his face. "And I'm not?"

John gave his head a little shake. He didn't know the name of the organization Michael worked for, but it certainly was not the Foreign Office, or if it was, it was part of the Foreign Office that had nothing to do with diplomacy.

"What is it that you think I do, then?" Michael asked.

"Intelligence." The word came out as if he was reluctant to say it. He was, because he had a strong and not entirely happy feeling that Intelligence was why he was here, was what Michael wanted him to 'do.'

"I knew you'd see to the heart of the matter," said Michael grimly. Then he sighed and reached into his bottom desk drawer and pulled out a sheet of paper. "How do you feel about the Official Secrets Act?"

John took the paper. "I'm not sure. I've never read it."

"It's meant to strike fear into the heart of anyone who would be tempted to talk about things that they shouldn't talk about and impress them with the need for secrecy. Most of the time it works. You're not the sort who needs it but it is required." Michael's pause was barely perceptible. John looked up. "Will you sign it?"

"If I do, will you tell me what all of this is about?"

"Of course."

"All right, then," he said and reached for a pen as Michael pressed the buzzer button on his desk.

Michael's secretary, Miss Trimby appeared. "Sir?"

John rose.

"You've met my godson, John Richter?"

"Yes, sir. He introduced himself when he came in." She flashed John a spectacular smile. He was most appreciative.

"Fine. I want you to witness his signature."

She nodded as John sat down again, signed his name and wrote the date in the appropriate place.

Then Miss Trimby signed, followed by Michael. It was all so quick, so simple. John wondered why he felt a sudden chill. Someone had walked over his grave? Stupid saying. He brushed it aside.

"Is there anything else, sir?"

"Not for the moment. Thank you, Miss Trimby."

She nodded to John as she shut the door after herself.

"She's been here only two weeks and already I wonder what I'd do without her. But one of these days, some young pup will sweep her up and away and that will be that."

John grinned. "You always have had good taste."

"You mean the veritable Cerberus who guarded my portals before the happy advent of Miss Trimby?"

"Scarcely." John laughed.

"I didn't think you did."

Their eyes met and John was suddenly sober. "I meant my mother."

He didn't even try to dissemble. "How did you know?"

"I think I've always known."

"The three of us were good friends, your mother, father, and I."

"I've always known that, too. It all seemed very natural to me. Does Mother know how you feel?"

"I've never told her. It isn't that sort of relationship. She was utterly devoted to your father."

John nodded. "They were happy together. It was a long time before I realized that not all marriages are like that. And it's why I'm especially glad right now that you care so much about her. She's going to need you."

"Thank you." Michael cleared his throat. "I'm sure you know that I won't take advantage of the situation."

John smiled as he waved his hand toward the paper that lay on the desk. "Not even over this?"

"Especially not over this. I'll give you the outline, enough to make a decision. The rest will have to wait until your decision is made."

"From what you've said, you seem to think that there's only one way I can decide."

"I do. At least the part of me that sits behind this desk does. You have a unique set of qualifications for a job that desperately needs doing. The godfather part of me wishes that you didn't, wishes that there were someone else, anyone else who had even remotely similar qualifications. Believe me, if there were, he'd be sitting here instead of you. It's a dangerous business."

He stopped and looked closely at John for a moment before he went on. When he did, he was brisk, business-like.

"First, your father was a German and you were born in Berlin during the Great War, which means, as you said, that you're a German citizen even though your mother is an American and you were raised here.

"Second, you have an uncle, Karl von der Greif, the husband of your father's younger sister and one of his closest friends, who is on the German General Staff, the OKH. Through him you would have a natural entre to Heinz Guderian and almost any other German general you'd care to meet.

"Third, if you go back, a year from now you will have a degree in mechanical engineering from one of the most respected universities in Germany." He stopped and it was obvious that he was coming to the heart of the matter. "With that sort of background, you'd be certain to rise quickly in the Panzer Korps."

There was a long silence before he heard John's hushed and very angry voice. "You want me to join the Panzer Korps."

"Exactly." Michael had always been one for facing issues squarely.

"Why?" It was a whispered shout.

"Because we need the sort of information you could get for us if you were in the Panzer Korps. We need to know what they're doing with armor. About the tanks themselves. Advanced engineering, metallurgy, guns, suspensions, numbers, types, capabilities, and tactics. And beyond that, we need to know strategy. When and where the tanks will be used. That's why your connection with the General Staff is so important."

"Even if I did ..." He bolted out of the chair and started pacing the room. "Do you know what you're asking me to do?" His face was full of anguish as he turned on Michael. "Do you know what that would mean? The lying alone. My God! I have never been a good liar! And even if I could become one... How the hell could I possibly find out all that sort of information and if I did, get it back to you. It's... insane!"

"I wish it were," Michael said softly. "I wish it were insane and unnecessary, that Hitler would go away and leave this part of the world in peace. I wish a lot of things." He was getting angry himself. "But wishes are nothing. Even the wish that there was someone else besides you! There is going to be war, whether I wish it or not and all my wishing isn't going to get us ready for it. Only damn hard patient work and a lot of sacrifice!"

"My sacrifice, you mean," he said bitterly.

"And mine." He glared back. It was more of a sacrifice than John would ever know. "And part of that for both of us would be the fact that neither your mother or your brother could know what you're really doing over there. They'd have to think that you got caught in Germany and had to go into the army before you could get back out. It's dangerous, what I'm asking you to do. Terribly dangerous. Spies are hanged. And part of the smoke screen you need around yourself to protect you, part of your cover, is having your mother and brother uncomprehending and angry. It's part of the lie you would have to live and live so totally that you'd be within a hair's breadth of believing it yourself."

"I cannot play the Nazi." John was still angry, but his voice was calmer and with a hard edge that Michael had never heard before.

"You wouldn't have to." Michael studied the pencil he was holding between his hands.

"Just the loyal German. We want you in the Wehrmacht, not the SS."

"Thank God for small favors."

John's caustic reply was duly noted and a fleeting smile played across Michael's face. "We do try to keep these things as close to reality as possible." The smile faded. "What's your attitude been in Munich, toward the Hitler government?"

"I kept quiet." He was looking out the window, studying the Parliament building. He paused as Big Ben chimed the three-quarters hour. "It was safer that way, and I didn't want to get into the middle of anything. All I wanted was to finish the year and get home. The only person I talked to about it at all was Georg Brandt, an old friend from summers in Prussia, and even we beat around the bush. He's fanatically anti-Nazi but had more to lose by talking about it than I did by far. His father was in the Reichstag, a Socialist, and life is none too comfortable for the former 'loyal opposition' in Germany these days. In fact his father spent time in a labor camp. A warning, I suppose. He was let out considerably the worse for such wear about six months ago, has retired to his estate in Prussia and has been ordered to stay there. Georg has kept his mouth shut tight ever since."

He sighed and looked down, scuffing the edge of the rug with his toe. "But Georg isn't in Munich anymore anyway. He got his medical degree and has gone to Berlin to finish his training. Orthopedic surgery."

Michael said nothing. He wouldn't have been heard if he had. "You're right, you know." John's voice was soft and full of pain. "There is going to be another war." He nodded slowly without looking around. His foot was still fussing with the rug. "Everyone in Germany was so frightened about what the French would do when Hitler moved those troops into the Rhineland. Do you know how weak those troops were?" He turned around and looked at Michael at last and he was angry again.

Michael nodded.

"A half-baked army! My God... They could have been blown out of there by a good stiff wind, let alone by the biggest standing army in Europe. What the hell did the French think they were doing?"

"Preventing a war," said Michael drily. "By letting the Germans have back what was, after all, their own."

"You believe that?"

"No." A pause. "How did you know how weak the troops were?"

"I know people..." He turned away, realizing suddenly that he was proving Michael's case for him with this sort of talk. "I know, too, that if there had been any real resistance from the French, the Wehrmacht had orders to turn right around and march right back out of there. They were scared shitless, or at least those of them that could think about it were.

"And because you all sat on your hands, Hitler got away with it, and now he thinks that he can take what he wants, anything that he wants without interference from the West."

"And right now, he's right," said Michael grimly. "No one is willing to hear about the sort of man he really is. And why the hell they don't ... He wrote it all out, for God's sake! *Mein Kampf.* The trouble is that it's so badly written and such a terrible bore that few people are willing to wade through it. They prefer to hide behind 'good, kind Christian thoughts' and 'no one can really be as evil as that man is supposed to be.' It's really because they're terrified. The last war bled us almost white, cost us almost a whole generation of our very best men. But what these idiots don't see is that unless they stop him now before he really rearms and gets a well-trained standing army... The cost of the last war in human terms will be nothing to the cost of this one.

"But they won't stop him until he turns west, and he's going to have to do that sooner or later, because he'll have to secure his back door if he's going to be assured of holding onto his precious Lebensraum in the east, what he claims is the due of the German people. Only a fool would be willing to fight a two-front war and Hitler may be a lot of things but he's no fool. He knows that the time will come when we realize he's inhaling all of Europe east of the Maginot Line, and we won't sit still for the human and economic consequences. Though probably with this government of ours," he said with rare bitterness, "it will be the economic consequences that tell the most. But Hitler's going to be the one to pick the time and the place. If we know beforehand and if we know what his resources are, even part of that, we may be able to wake up the powers-that-be in the nick of time and find some sort of spanner to throw in his works. That's why ..." He let the words trail off.

"You sound like my father." John ignored the unspoken.

"I'm not surprised," said Michael mildly. "We talked about it often enough. Hitler worried him."

"That's why I was so surprised that he was so adamant about my finishing up at Munich. He didn't know what you... He wasn't in on..." He waved a hand toward the Official Secrets Act that was still lying on Michael's desk.

"No! No! For God's sake... He just wanted you to finish... To be German. He married an American and lived the bulk of his adult life in England, but he was still a German – Prussian really – and that explains a great deal, especially why he went back to Germany and worked procuring supplies for the German army during the Great War instead of following his money to Switzerland."

"Then why did he absolutely insist, make James promise just two weeks ago, that our interest in the Hamburg office would be sold out within the next year? The office is run by his nephew."

"Because that nephew is a dedicated Nazi and so he and your father no longer saw eye to eye. And two, it's amazing what a die-hard Nazi is able to sneak into Germany when he runs a respected import-export firm."

"I see." And indeed John was beginning to and he didn't like what he saw. "If I did do this." He paused, then repeated, "If I did do this, just how long would I have to stay in the Panzer Korps?"

"Right now the enlistment is for two years, but with the call-ups and this Spanish business, that's no guarantee. The problem is, of course, that once you're in, you'd have to stay the term. It would be almost impossible to get you out."

"How would you get the information?"

"I can't tell you that unless you decide to take it on. But it wouldn't be a problem."

John turned his back to the window. "I don't want to do it. Don't want to go back. Don't want... Especially if Mother and James can't know." He looked over at Michael, and the words came faster and with firmness. "But that tells me how serious the situation is. That you'd ask me, that alone would be enough. But that you're willing to put them through anything like that..." He shook his head. "I'll have to do a lot of thinking. Do you need an answer right away?"

"Not today." Michael's voice was gruff. "But say, within ten days. You'd have to go back for the new term in early October and you'd need some training before then. But please, take the time to think about it carefully. If you have any reservations, any real reservations at all, I don't want you to go."

John nodded slowly, then moved toward the door as Michael came out from behind his desk. "I'll let you know within the week."

Six weeks later he had gone back to Germany.

It had all been so simple, just like Michael said it would be. He had finished his degree, had been called up and had gone first into the Wehrmacht then into the Panzer Korps. He hadn't even needed his Uncle Karl's help – Karl had come later. A stint as his aide in Berlin where he had come to General Guderian's attention. After that it had been back to the Panzers under Guderian's eye, then a posting as liaison to the Luftwaffe at one of the secret Russian training bases where the Blitzkrieg tactics had been developed. Then back to Berlin before being sent to Poland as a tank platoon squadron commander.

He had been given every opportunity to advance fast and he had made use of every one of them. The Panzer Korps' "golden boy." Shit. And he even had a Ritterkreuz to show for his pains. And through it all he had sent Michael everything he asked for and more. But what the hell good had it done? None. All the risks he had to take... All for damn-all nothing.

Nothing had stopped the German race across Luxembourg. In fact, that tiny country's police force had gotten out and directed traffic, wanting only to get them through and out as fast as possible. And there hadn't been one reconnaissance plane sighted all the way from the undulating pontoon bridges on which they'd crossed the Rhine to the Belgian border where they had finally met resistance. The columns of tanks and troop carriers had been fifty miles long, for God's sake, and they had moved by daylight as well as through the night, headlights blazing. If even one plane had come, had seen that... There could have been no mistaking those columns for anything but what they were, no possible way that anyone wouldn't have known what they intended to do. That is, if they'd been looking, he concluded bitterly.

But no one had been looking, had they? The bombers still hadn't come, not even when they were well into Luxembourg. What just one well-placed bomb could have done on those narrow twisting roads of the Ardennes where the land fell off steeply on one side and rose just as steeply on the other... Damnable that they hadn't come. Insane that neutrality had been preserved well beyond the eleventh hour, until it was far too late. But if the bombers had come... He shivered. Despite everything, those tanks were his tanks and those men his men.

But now it was all over. Or almost. Everything he had done since 1937 had gone down the drain. What had Michael done with it all? Especially with the whole invasion plan he'd finally been able to send, down to the approximate date?

And what about Mother? She'd gone through it all for nothing as well. She'd been furious and very upset when he'd been called up but it was nothing compared to her anguish in a letter. That letter had finally reached him some weeks after Poland, sent through Aunt Frances and Uncle Frank in the United States because by then Britain and Germany were at war, at least officially. The words had burned themselves into his brain.

My son, I can neither understand nor condone what
you've done, what you're doing. What's happened is
despicable and I cannot bear you having any part

in it. You must know that in the long run Germany
will lose as she did the last time. But you are
my son and I love you. Nothing can change that. I
just pray to God that it's over soon, that you and
Germany come to your senses so that we can all be
together and happy again.

All together and happy again? When? Ever? Especially now? God damn James. He had never written, had he, and he had absolutely refused to come and see him. And now he was a British subject. Had been for two years. Easy for him. He had been born in England, after all. Royal Navy. James in the Royal Navy. A lieutenant serving on a destroyer. James' anger as they faced each other in the Richter import-export firm's Hamburg office the day it was sold, when they had all had to be there to sign the papers...

James had turned his back and walked out. He pushed the vision of that away and another one came, a different one, of James laughing. During the summer they had spent in the United States with Aunt Frances and Uncle Frank and their genial giant of a cousin, Peter, at their summer house on the shores of Lake Erie. Hans could still see the long oar boats silhouetted against the horizon, the swallows soaring above the clay and sand cliffs that rose above the small rocky beach, the slow streams of liquid clay that ran down those cliffs. What hell he'd gotten the day he could no longer resist and had walked down one. The clay had made heavy boots of his shoes and those shoes had never been the same, even after hours of work.

It was the summer that he and James had become friends as well as brothers. They had a lot of laughs that summer, and James could really laugh when he got going.

Then his head swiveled as the door slowly creaked open and he saw the glowing end of a cigar coming toward the bed. "Hans?" The voice was just above a whisper.

"Hello, Georg."

"What are you doing lying awake in the middle of the night?"

"More to the point, what are you doing awake in the middle of the night? You should be in the arms of Morpheus, readying yourself for more surgery on the morrow."

"Surgery waits for no man and the arms of almost anyone would be preferable to what I've been doing. Gangrene. An emergency. Hence the cigar. To wipe out... the memory."

Georg must have heard him struggling to move himself up in the bed, for suddenly Hans found himself engulfed in a cloud of smoke as he was briskly repositioned. He coughed. "My God, that cigar is enough to wipe out more than a memory!"

Georg leaned forward with what was, even in the darkness, a threatening air and waved the cigar under Hans' nose. "Insult my cigar, will you? The anoxia torture for you, my friend. Persist and I shall exhale in your face. Encased as you are, you'd be helpless to resist!"

"Mercy, oh, Gengis Khan, mercy," he whined pathetically. "Take pity on this poor, brave soldier."

Georg had taken the blanket from the foot of the bed and was draping it over the curtain rod. "Brave, hah! I know where that wound came from." Then he was striking a match to light the candle that stood in a holder on the table beside the bed. "From the sword of a cuckolded husband who caught you in the act. Now that's what I call a field of honor." He plunked himself down onto the only chair in the room, a wooden one, and leaned it against the wall on the back two legs, raising his cigar in a mock salute.

Hans heaved an exaggerated sigh. "Sad to say, there are no medals for such conquests."

Georg turned serious. "You were in uniform when they brought you in, of course, and you were wearing a Ritterkreuz. What the hell have you been doing?"

"Poland."

"Ah yes. You've been doing Poland. Charming country. Charming people. Horse cavalry charging tanks with lances, flattened villages, corpses by the mile. It must have been an enchanting trip."

"Enchanting. Yes, indeed."

"You hated this Nazi business once upon a time. So tell me, what are you doing in the midst of this and with a Ritterkreuz no less?"

Hans shrugged. It made him wince. "Sometimes I wonder."

Georg sighed and the front legs of the chair hit the floor with a thud. "Ah, for the good old days when all we had to worry about was whether we'd win the next riding competition or if Herr Reimann would catch us stealing his pears and who was going to get the most dances with Birgid."

"Whatever happened to Birgid?"

"I married her."

Hans laughed, really laughed. "You lucky devil! Think you can handle her?"

"Good grief, no. She handles me, and charmingly so. Ah, Birgid." His tone exuded lasciviousness.

"How long ago?"

"While you were racing around Poland playing hero." He rose. "Now I must play doctor."

The stethoscope was cold. "Do you refrigerate those things?"

"Yes, indeed. Right next to the bedpans." Georg's hands were gentle, probing. "You're in disgustingly fine shape. Now, move the fingers of your left hand."

They moved easily.

"You are also damn lucky, Herr Hauptmann Richter, hero of Poland and France. The bullet missed every major artery and nerve. Just cracked the hell out of the bone and that will heal. It may even prove the perfect barometer. Every cloud has its silver lining."

"How long?"

"Six weeks. Maybe eight."

"Too long."

"It always is."

"The hell of it is that I can't move."

"We're going to fix that right now." Georg bellowed in the vague direction of the hall.

Someone must have understood for after a moment, middle of the night or no, a worried-looking face appeared around the door jam.

"Yes, sir?"

"Help me get our hero out of the sack."

The orderly moved to the head of the bed and Georg to the foot and before Hans knew what had happened, he had been pivoted around and was sitting up, his feet just touching the floor. His head was swimming. "Just a moment, please."

"We aim to please."

Then finally he was standing. His knees started to buckle and he was tipping backward, terrified that he would fall. But hands were holding him, arms pivoting him again on the fulcrum of his rear end. At last he was lying down, wet with sweat, breathing hard.

Georg's voice came through the haze. "Weak as a kitten, eh, Hans? Don't worry about it. Our friend here will be back in the morning with another orderly and the two of them will get you up again. Have to keep the blood circulating. Some doctors, most really, believe in leaving their patients in bed for ages, but that can lead to all sorts of lovely things like phlebitis and pneumonia. It will be easier next time, I promise, and easier yet the time after that."

Hans devoutly hoped so. His shoulder hurt abominably.

"Hans?"

His ears were ringing and he couldn't be bothered to answer.

"You're in pain."

He nodded and Georg disappeared, returning with another needle and a cotton swab soaked in antiseptic. He began rubbing it vigorously on Hans' arm. "You need sleep."

"Wait."

Georg stopped, needle poised as Hans asked, "What about Dunkirk?"

"It's burning."

"I know it's burning, but has it fallen?"

"Not yet. The British and French are evacuating their armies."

"How?"

"Ships. Destroyers, ferries – all sorts of ships."

"Have you seen them?"

"No. But I've heard plenty about it. The brass is in a swivet to say the least. They don't want the armies to get away. On top of that, no one can believe they are pulling it off. Even the Stukas haven't been able to stop it and they're certainly trying hard enough."

Hans shuddered.

"What's wrong?"

"Stukas."

Georg slid in the needle. "You've seen the Stukas in action?" The needle was out and Hans hadn't even noticed.

"Yes." Hans paused when he spoke again, his voice a bit fuzzy. "Destroyers."

"Stukas are destroyers?" Was he delirious?

"No. Are... British destroyers... at Dunkirk?"

George relaxed. "They're there alright."

"Stukas sinking destroyers?" It was getting hard to concentrate.

"I'm sure they are. They seem to be sinking everything in sight. The British must have a bottomless reservoir of ships. Why?"

"James... on a British destroyer."

The last thing Hans heard for quite some time was the sharp intake of Georg's breath.

His last thought was that he hoped James was somewhere else, anywhere else.

He wasn't.

# Chapter II

James stood rooted to the deck, looking up. The Stukas were forming a line. The lead one seemed to pause, then it tipped and was nose down, diving straight at him with an unearthly whistling scream. Oh, God, 'there's no hidin' place down here.' It ran through his brain in an endless sing-song as he willed his legs not to collapse, his body not to fall to the deck, his arms not to cover his head.

He saw the bomb release and suddenly there was no sound, nothing but that large black dot growing, falling, falling, taking forever.

A huge geyser off the port waist, a bucking lurch of the ship and he was breathing again, feeling the vibration of the deck plates, steadying himself against the cant of the deck as the ship turned sharply yet again, trying to run for sea room while the pom-poms and Oerlikons fired their fury skyward.

Unwieldy way to operate a gun, James thought as he saw the pom-pom barrel being elevated toward the last Stuka in line. Rafferty to lay it; Kennedy to train it. They were each the picture of utter concentration. Lucky sods. At least they had something useful to do.

And then the whistling scream came again, and he looked up helplessly. There was nothing to do but stand, wait, and take it. Oh, for a sub attack. Stupid. The last thing they needed. But at least it would have been his.

The captain was looking up as well, totally intent on what was coming, judging the chances nicely. His head bobbed down to the voice pipe. It was impossible to hear anything, but the ship veered again. Another miss. This time to starboard. How long could they keep this up without getting hit?

The sound of an explosion turned every head back toward the harbor.

"Jesus." It was the awed voice of Rigby, the young signal rating.

A huge columnar cloud rose, then mushroomed out. Ammunition? James shuddered.

A sudden sharp gesture from the pom-pom caught his eye and he followed the line of Rafferty's no longer pointing finger, and he saw a Stuka exploding in the water. He laughed. If that was theirs, there'd be no living with Rafferty.

Another explosion, near them again, just off the beach. God Almighty, the bomb must have gone down the funnel. What ship? He couldn't tell beyond the fact that it was another old V and W. It split down the middle as tiny figures cleared the deck, hitting the water with an irregular pattern of tiny splashes, like a handful of gravel thrown into a pond.

The sky was screaming at them again. How much more could they take? Would they ever get used to it? Could they? Could anyone? At least the *Vectis* was loaded and on her way home. But most of the nearly 600 troops on board were jammed in below. If one of those bombs hit... Being on the bridge was heaven compared to the hell of waiting for death below.

He saw the captain watching, watching, then bobbing down to the voice pipe yet again. How could he stand there, seemingly unmoved, almost serene? It defied credulity. James couldn't know that Rigby was wondering the same thing about him.

The ship was heeling over more sharply this time. Thank God the Old Man had jettisoned the torpedoes and depth charges that were always stored on deck. Packed as they were, top to bottom with troops, they would have been far too top heavy to maneuver otherwise. As it was, the Old Man was cutting it fine. It suddenly occurred to James how incongruous it was to call Lieutenant Commander Fredericks 'the Old Man'. He couldn't be much over thirty-five if he was that.

They had been working since the first sign of dawn. Only when the sun had finally appeared over the horizon had he realized that the odd blackness of the beaches was caused by the men, thousands and thousands of men, black masses of them on the beaches, black lines of them on the eastern mole and the rocks below, waiting. Thank God the sea was calm. It would have been impossible otherwise.

He had cursed the slow, back-breaking hours of loading men off the beaches, hauling them over the rails on either side as they scrambled up nets from the whaler, the motorboat, and one or two other smaller boats that had appeared from somewhere. It had been exhausting, tedious, but at least they hadn't been trapped in the harbor. He looked back but couldn't bear the sight of smoke and flames, and so he turned away again. All sorts of ships had been packed in there along the jetties like sardines in a can, sitting side by side as they loaded troops. They had no chance to get away. He sighed. Backbreaking work was infinitely preferable to that. But it was slow, far too slow. What was needed was more small boats to ferry the troops out, to speed up the process. But where the hell would they come from?

The harbor drew his eyes back like a magnet, and it hit him again, the magnitude of the defeat they'd suffered. The evidence was everywhere: in the wreckage of the harbor and the beach, the masses of men and their individual faces as they staggered on board and all but fell into a heap on the deck. The Germans had come too fast. What were they calling it? The Blitzkrieg. The lightning war. Appropriate. It had hit like lightning, and it had moved like lightning. And somewhere out there, in one of the Panzers that had caused it all, was that shit of a little brother John, fighting his fucking heart out for the Nazis. Odd to think that once he'd hated hunting, refused to go despite Father's anger, because there he was now, off in a goddamn tank in the fight of his life, hunting what James had once heard called the biggest game of all. Serve him right if he got his head blown off.

That sound again. His head jerked up. Oh, God, it wasn't fair. Just when he'd thought they were well out of it.

The signal rating backed up and stepped on James' foot. "Sorry, sir."

James caught him just in time and bit off an angry retort. The boy's voice had trembled. In fact he was trembling all over.

Another miss.

"You all right, Rigby?"

The boy drew himself erect and tried to look indignant. "'Course, sir!"

"Those things give an unearthly scream, don't they." He managed to keep a purely conversational tone.

James saw the boy sigh. It was impossible to hear much of anything again. They both had to shout.

"Yes, sir. They do." James leaned closer and so could hear him as he went on. "Like nothing I ever heard before. If they just didn't do that."

James smiled and shouted back, "I imagine that's why they do. One of the soldiers told me that they sounded worse here, that they must have put something new on the planes."

The tag end of the sentence caught them in a momentary oasis of quiet and heads on the bridge turned. James gave a nervous little laugh and nodded an apology which was met with sympathetic grins.

The two lookouts never took their binoculars from the sky.

*      *      *

They were back again, taking men off the beaches at dawn. But now there were improvised piers spilling off the beaches into the water formed by trucks driven out at low tide and parked side by side parallel to the beach, with boards laid across the beds so that men could walk along them to the end without having to climb painfully in and out of each one. And a miracle had occurred. The whole inshore area was full of little boats and more were coming in all the time. It was unbelievable, heart-stopping. It choked the captain's voice and brought tears to James' eyes.

"Bloody fools." Stillson, the First Lieutenant, was being true to form. "What business have they got crossing the Channel? We'll be hauling them out of the drink all the way home."

The captain's voice held more than a hint of reproach. "It's those 'bloody fools', Number One, who are going to save us hours of work and a lot of lives."

And they had. There were sailboats, yachts, Thames River barges, lifeboats, fishing boats, more types of small boats than James had ever dreamed existed on the face of the earth. He would have sworn that one tiller was manned by a gentleman of eighty at the very least. Another small yacht had gone by, the captain, in the complete regalia of the London Yacht Club, thumbing his nose at the Stukas assembling overhead.

And still the BEF was queued endlessly on the beach. It reminded James of the myth of the couple who had given one of the major gods – was it Zeus? – the last of their bread and milk when he appeared at their door in human form, tired and hungry. In return, whoever the god was had decreed that no matter how much they sliced it, their loaf of bread would never be consumed and no matter how much they poured from their milk pitcher, it would never be empty.

But at least the beaches were better organized now. No more were men rushing and broaching the small boats in a frantic attempt to get aboard. They were lined up and waiting patiently, despite strafings and bombings, often going down on one knee to fire rifles at the oncoming planes, occasionally even hitting one, then rising to fill the places of those who had fallen. Damn the idiot who had ordered the destruction of the army's anti-aircraft guns to keep them from falling into German hands. He might have waited a bit.

By the fourth trip, they were ready to drop in their tracks. James was seeing faces in his sleep, what little he'd managed to snatch. Tired faces, worn, dirty faces, faces of men so exhausted and in so much pain that they couldn't comprehend anything beyond the fact that they were on a British ship at last. In his dreams he would see the explosions all over again, see the sea coated with oil and heavy with floating bodies and hear the Stukas and the bombs until he woke, sweating and shaking.

This time *Vectis* had come in by night, working her way through the harbor entrance, easing in between a wreck and the end of the east mole where they were to pick up the waiting troops. Only God alone knew how the Old Man managed to do it by the flickering light of the still-burning harbor – what could there be left to burn by now? – with almost nothing to guide him but his own senses and a hooded light held on the stern of the ship berthed just ahead of where they were to be. Fredericks edged the ship in, bow first. Heaving lines were thrown to the exhausted and inexperienced soldiers who hauled away, awkwardly but with a will, until they finally managed to slip the wire eyes of the headrope and spring over the bollards, all to the accompaniment of instructions shouted through a megaphone wielded by Stillson, who was standing in the fo'c'scle. Gunner had another on the afterdeck and, despite the confusion, they were finally in and made fast. Amazing. Fredericks had made it look like a training exercise.

Heavy planks were slid up both fore and aft to the wooden walkway on the mole just above them – the regulation bows were too heavy and took too long to rig – and at once there was the sound of boots clomping down onto the deck.

The men looked at James, who had managed a clean shirt and a shave, as if he were a creature from outer space. He was standing at the aft plank, moving the men on by rote, almost as exhausted as they were, concentrating on his French, for this was a load of French soldiers. Amazing what some of them were trying to bring on with them. That hadn't been a problem with the men coming off the beaches. They had dropped everything, almost. But here there were suitcases, great bulging sacks and on and on. Didn't they know that there wasn't the space, that men were infinitely more important? "No room! No room!" He shouted it over and over in French as most of the baggage was thrown over the side. It wasn't easy, but he made himself be ruthless. There was no time for anything else.

They had just pulled in the planks when James heard the drone of high-level bombers, and the night erupted into a curtain of tracer fire. The pyrotechnics were spectacular; for a moment James was able to forget the reason for them and he was an awe-struck boy again. He'd never seen anything like it.

It was the vibration of the deck plates under his feet that brought him back to reality. The spring had been cast off and the screws were churning the water under the stern into a ferocious foam as the ship strained to back out and away from the mole in time. They were almost clear when the first bombs fell, shattering their way through the walkway and the men left standing on it to explode below, sending stone shrapnel raining into the port bow.

James was sweating as he grabbed the rail and leaned out to watch as *Vectis* slid astern, well clear of the wreck and now the mole. The ship in front of them had just begun to cast off. They had been missed entirely, the lucky bastards. If *Vectis* had been holed below the waterline...

It seemed an eternity before they cleared the open arms of the harbor. Fredericks was almost yelling his orders so he wouldn't have to bend down to the voice pipe as he judged the distance, the end of the two moles, the wrecks, and other shipping. It was incredible the way the Old Man could take it all in, organize it, and spit out the right orders without hesitation. Seamanship of the first order. Oh, God. More flares.

"Half astern port."

"Half ahead starboard."

"Hard aport."

The orders went on calmly, relentlessly, as the bombers came overhead once more. They had almost completed the turn when suddenly the stern bucked, the ship canted to starboard and a flood of water poured over the afterdeck. James grabbed the rail to keep from falling and was sickened by the waves of screams and terrified shouts coming from the soldiers packed onto the deck as they slammed into each other and anything else in their way, including the starboard rail.

"Richter, go down and lend a hand." The harshness of Fredericks' voice was the only thing that betrayed his agony.

It took a bit of doing, but James managed to break through the ranks of terrified men, oblivious to the still-falling bombs until the night was lit even further by a huge explosion and a flash of fire. God in heaven, what had been hit now? And then there was no time to wonder or even think before an appalling sight greeted his eyes as the mass of troops untangled, leaving men writhing on the deck and others ominously still. Blood showed itself dark in the white light of the flares, streaming from wounds, pooling next to prostrate bodies in the few open spots where men weren't huddled together.

Harvey, the gunner, had wrapped a strip of his shirt around his forehead but blood was already soaking through as he knelt over a motionless form. One of the ratings was standing there, watching him, apparently too stunned to move. James shouted for him to get Doc and all of the splints and bandages he could carry and then started clearing what space he could.

Splints. There weren't enough splints in all of England for this job, or room either. Was there ever enough room for anything anymore? Or time?

At least he'd forgotten that he was tired. His sweat flowed in rivers, and a certain kind of chaotic order began to appear.

He would never know how magnificent he was, that he had a knack for doing the right thing at the right time, the bearing and assurance to give comfort to the wounded and the terrified. He simply did what had to be done and kept doing it until the end of the task was in sight and there was a void in his ear and a tug at his sleeve.

"Sir! Sir!"

The voice was anxious as was the tug, an unusual occurrence. James looked up. It was Rigby. "Sir, the first lieutenant wants you to pick up any men you can here and some off-watch stokers and shore up the tiller flat bulkhead. That last one flooded the tiller flat and the pumps can't compete."

James looked around and shouted for the first four men he saw, then turned back to Rigby. "How bad is it?"

"Some hull plates stove in and the port plumber block is running hot. They may have to stop the port engine."

"And the first lieutenant?" He was the damage control officer.

"Rocks from the mole holder in the port bow just below the waterline, sir, and he says he can't be at both ends of the ship at the same time."

Leave it to Stillson to say that. "Thank you, Rigby; I'll tend to it."

The boy nodded and backed off, watching James as he did, thinking that it was too bad about his brother. He hadn't believed it when he'd first heard about it, but it was true. Rafferty said so and Rafferty knew everything. Terrible to have a brother who was a Jerry, especially now. Some of the men were looking at him again and muttering, especially that bully Briggs. But then the lieutenant had sat on Briggs hard and more than once – time someone did – and that had to be the reason he'd started... saying things again.

Rafferty had said that there'd been a lot of trouble when the lieutenant had first come on board. What did they think he'd do? Report on his own ship and get it sunk? But that Richter had been smart, kept his mouth shut, just did his job and ignored everything else, "Even that ass of a Number One who still rides his tail." Rafferty had shaken his head over that. But then Number One rode everyone's tail. He was just nasty. To everyone. He seemed to like making people feel stupid. Now the lieutenant, he never did that. Well, hardly ever, and when he did, there was a good reason for it. He was a good officer, the lieutenant was, and he'd like to hear anyone to tell him different, even Briggs.

He shook his head in indignation and started up the ladder to the bridge. If Briggs had his way, he'd have everyone believing that Richter had brought on the Stukas and the high-level bombers and the whole German army all by himself. He almost laughed at the thought then struggled to compose himself as he came to attention beside the compass platform where the captain was standing.

"Everything all right, Rigby?" he asked the boy gently after a moment.

Rigby flushed, only then realizing that he hadn't spoken when he should have. "Yes, sir. The lieutenant ... He said he'd take care of everything, sir." And he would. Yes, sir, the lieutenant was a bloody good officer.

The captain just nodded and bent to the voice pipe.

*       *       *

James and the men moved fast, collecting two off-duty stokers and timber shores from their stowage on the way down to the steward's mess. He left three men and some shores there under the direction of a leading stoker and went down with the other three to the storeroom below where the bulkhead would be under the greater pressure by far. They were soon wet with sweat as they struggled to get the shores in place in the cramped, badly ventilated space. But at last it was done and they were climbing back up to the steward's mess, having left one man behind on watch. The men were at their ease, finished and waiting.

He looked everything over carefully. "Good job, Riley."

James left a watch there as well, and as he went out into the flat, he heard "...bloody picnic up here while we were sweating away like lascars down there." They had indeed. James pulled his shirt away from his back. It would be good to get on deck.

He hauled himself up to the bridge to make his report, damning the Germans for taking Calais so they were having to take such a roundabout route back. If they'd been able to head straight for Dover... But there was no use thinking about it. At least the bulkhead seemed to be holding.

The first rays of the sun were coming over the horizon, making the white cliffs guarding Dover a ghostly line separating the Channel from the sky. He'd never been so glad to see anything in his life.

"Well, well, Richter." Stillson's acid voice broke through his thoughts. "You look like the last rose of summer."

Ignoring Stillson's remark, James made his report in the precisely correct manner.

*       *       *

Anne Richter was pacing the floor of her bedroom. The sun was shining through the trees leaving dappled shadows on the floor and flowers were blooming in the window boxes. But she saw none of it.

Where was Michael? She had told Miss Trimby it was urgent. Didn't she understand? She sighed. Of course she'd understood. Miss Trimby had known she was upset, had been kindness itself, saying that she would try to contact the Captain at once.

Where was he?

John. Precious John. Wounded. His arm. Oh, God. Three days ago. She looked at the telegram again. No, four.

The doorbell rang and she rushed to the landing, looking over the railing as Hannah, her maid-of-all-work, opened the door.

Michael! Praise God. Her heart lifted, and she relished the top of his head for a brief moment before she rushed down the stairs. Hannah had discretely disappeared by the time she reached the bottom. He took her hands, concern written all over him. "Anne. What is it? Miss Trimby said that you sounded frantic." It had terrified him. Anne had never sounded frantic, even when Gerhard had been dying. "Not James..."

"No." She took a deep breath. "It's John. He's been wounded."

Michael stiffened, his heart pounding. "How badly?"

"The telegram says it's his arm, that he's recovering and doing 'as well as can be expected.'" Her voice caught.

"Whatever that means."

"How did you hear?"

"The Red Cross."

"Let me ring them up and see if I can get them working on it to find out more."

"Would you? Oh, please, Michael."

"Of course." He hesitated. "But it sounds as if he's been lucky."

"Lucky? Lucky?"

"Darling Anne, it could have been a very different sort of telegram."

She was quiet for a moment and when she spoke, she was subdued. "You're right, of course. I hadn't thought of it that way."

He put his arms around her and held her gently, his heart twisting. She shouldn't have to be going through this. John on the other side. Information about him so difficult to come by. And she was so small.

"You know, Michael," her voice was muffled against his jacket, "it's quite remarkable how much better you make me feel." She gave him a little laugh. "Even over this." Then she pulled back and looked up at him. "You're such a good friend and you make me feel so well cared for."

He looked down at her. "I'm glad."

She had never seen quite that expression on his face and it puzzled her briefly before she forgot everything else in remembering John again. "You will call the Red Cross, won't you?"

"Of course."

Later, after Anne had played for him – she had been a promising piano student at the London Conservatory when Gerhard Richter had swept her off her feet and married her – while he had tea and some of Hannah's marvelous scones, as he was being driven back to Whitehall, the pain of it swept over him again. John. Still over there. Wounded now. God knows, all the information he'd sent to England had been valuable, perhaps even invaluable, but who the bloody hell had listened? Either to him or to the several other sources spewing out essentially the same information? Not the Belgians, certainly. They'd been warned and warned and warned – even had the German plan drop from the sky into their laps, for God's sake, when that courier plane had crashed – and still their collective head stayed in the sand and they'd refused to let the French army and the BEF in to take up defensive positions until the German army was halfway across Luxembourg, when it was far too late. John had sent the whole plan and the approximate date. The trouble was that there had been so many alarms and postponements by then that people were worn out and so inured to alarms that they refused to believe what should have been the evidence of their own eyes.

If after all that, and after no one listening, for God's sake, John didn't live through it... He shuddered. Come home, damn you, John. You shouldn't have been in France in the first place. I told you to stop, to come home a year ago, before Poland. But you refused, saying you were too well placed, that what you were doing was too important. You were right, of course, but that didn't make your refusal any easier to take then, and it certainly isn't making it any easier now.

If only you weren't so damn good at it, cutting to the heart of the matter, sensing what the heart of the matter was, then sending the information in a clear, concise fashion. And when you couldn't send it directly, there were those marvelously inventive love letters, perfect in tone, concealing the coded messages they contained. They must have taken hours to compose. Exquisite love letters from someone called Siegfried – and we certainly should have thought of a less dramatic code name – to his English sweetheart, 'Darling Julia', sent through a postal forwarding service in Portugal after Poland. Julia, the roommate of the redoubtable Annabelle Trimby and the perfect cover for any supposedly lovelorn man; a Junoesque, seemingly scatterbrained female with a mind like a steel trap who left men wallowing in her wake like the veritable destroyer she was. My God, the woman had to be a heartbreaker. She must get 27 love letters a day. One more or less wouldn't make any difference. And she was Tommy Markham's secretary in the Admiralty and so would know how to keep her mouth shut in the bargain. But even if she should slip, she had no idea who Siegfried really was. Michael was the only one who knew and it was he who answered these passionate letters himself. Actually, that part of it had been rather fun.

Captain Michael Paul Cosgrove Compton, DSC, RN (Ret.) sighed and contemplated the vagaries of life. There were too many, and his thoughts turned idly to love letters again.

He had never written Anne a letter. Oh, there had been postcards from far away places, but never a proper letter. Maybe it was because he couldn't say the only thing he wanted to say. A friend.

Gad. That was galling. But at least she had tempered it with the fact that he made her feel well cared for because that was precisely what he'd tried to do since Gerhard died.

It was getting harder and harder not to tell her how he felt. Lord knows, he'd wanted to, had wanted to for almost four years. But how could he ask anything of her, expect her to trust him, hope that she could love him in return when he bore the cancer on his soul of having sent her son, the godson with whom he had been trusted at birth, into the deadliest possible situation, one that was not only dangerous for John but caused her great pain as well? And now that he had been wounded... How could she love him if she knew and how could he even contemplate marrying her without telling her?

"We're here, sir."

Michael sat up. "So we are. Thank you."

\*        \*        \*

James lay staring at the ceiling. The bed was far too comfortable for him to even contemplate moving. Certainly the bed wasn't moving, and what bliss that was. No, there was no good reason he could think of for moving, especially since every time he did, he found that he ached in a place he hadn't known about before.

The sound of the traffic on King's Road came through the open window and he could hear the sounds of children playing in the small park below. What time was it anyway? The rays of the sun were playing through the leaves on the trees outside but it was impossible to tell just how high it was in the sky.

If he wanted to know what time it was, he was simply going to have to turn his head. But was it worth the effort? He laughed. This was an absolutely ridiculous conversation to be having, even with himself.

He turned his head. It was 10:29.

Turning his head worked out so well that he made the mistake of stretching. He seemed to hurt everywhere. Another hot bath and some aspirin, that's what he needed. But Hannah would think he was sick, taking another bath this morning. She had never gotten over the fact that she virtually had to dump him into the tub when he was young. And he was still Master James to her. Thirty years old and still Master James. He laughed himself into resignation. He'd be Master James when he was sixty. Master John, too. If he lived until he was sixty, James thought sourly. God damn wound. The bastard deserved a little pain. No. A lot of pain. It wasn't too bad, just his arm.

James struggled to his feet and moved in a gingerly fashion into the bathroom. When he got there, he started running his bath, took two aspirin, and sat on the only seat available, watching the water swirl into the tub, his mind a careful blank.

It wasn't until he'd sunk into the blissful luxury of hot water up to his neck that he permitted his brain to function again and then it was Hannah he let back in. He laughed. The expression on her face when he'd walked through the door had been priceless.

Granted, he'd looked anything but his best. With workmen swarming all over the ship almost the minute they'd docked, he hadn't had time for a shave, just a quick wash and a clean shirt. And they'd all been bleary-eyed and staggering after keeping the ship going all night by hard work and sheer effort of will as she'd crept from Dover to Portsmouth, almost the entire way on the starboard engine alone.

Every ship that could float and fight was needed desperately and here he was, sitting in London for six days with his ship laid up in dry dock. He felt a pang of guilt, even though poor old *Vectis* had been barely afloat and so was certainly in no shape to fight. Six days for repairs. He doubted that they could be done by then, but that's what he'd been told, and by no less that the infallible Stillson himself.

Stillson. Number One. The ubiquitous Royal Navy term for the first lieutenant of every fighting ship. The only way that Stillson was really Number One was in Aunt Frances' loo talk. Aunt Frances, bless her. Ever the lady. What one did in the toilet was never anything – if indeed it had to be referred to at all – but Number One and Number Two. He laughed. Well, for once Stillson just might be right. Maybe it would be done in six days. He'd never seen so many workmen moving so fast in his life. It was unbelievable.

There had been a veritable stampede for the London train. Even with their First Class travel warrants, he and Colin had been lucky to find seats. Almost every passenger carriage in Britain had to have been shunted off to the Kentish ports to haul away the soldiers pouring in from Dunkirk.

Hannah had been putting up the blackout curtains when he'd arrived and had waved out the window as he'd paid the cabbie, obviously delighted to see him, that is until she actually saw him face to face. Then she was all for rushing him upstairs and into a hot tub. It was even worse when she heard where he'd been. Her eyes had rounded and filled with tears, and she had done an astounding thing. She had thrown her arms around him and given him a real hug. He couldn't remember her having done that ever, even when he was a child.

When she'd realized what she'd done, she'd drawn back, embarrassed suddenly, covering it by wiping her eyes and saying harshly, "Hot bath and bed."

But brandy was what he wanted before he had anything else, brandy and a comfortable chair, and that was what he got along with Hannah fluttering all the while.

"Where's Mother?" he'd asked when he was settled down and ready to notice things.

"Out for dinner with Captain Compton... again."

James' eyebrows flew up. "Oh?"

"It's been more often these days," said Hannah smugly, "and the last two nights in a row, since she heard your brother was wounded."

His heart had fallen. "John was... wounded?"

Hannah looked horrified. "You didn't know?"

"No. How bad is it?"

"But she left you a message. In Dover. At your ship."

"How serious is it?"

"His arm. She had a telegram. It said he's doing as well as can be expected. Captain Compton is trying to find out more about it."

He slumped back in the chair. Stupid little shit. Jesus. That tears it. Then he looked back at Hannah and saw her anguished expression. "I'm sorry I snapped at you, but things have been frantic in Dover, and we weren't there long enough to get any messages. How is Mother taking it?"

"She's all right, now."

James looked at her closely. Something was going on. He could hear it in her voice, see it in her attitude. "What do you mean, 'now'?"

"Well..." Her expression was sly. "I think that the captain has been some consolation to her. She's singing again."

Well, well, well. That was interesting. James hadn't heard his mother sing in the house since his father died. Hannah, the incurable romantic, rides again? Better humor her. "What's she singing?"

"That daft song about the range and the buffalo that's all the rage."

James laughed. "She is doing well, then."

"And she looks bloody marvelous."

"Hannah!" said James with mock severity.

"Well, she does!"

"She must or you wouldn't say so."

He looked around. The bath water had cooled and the aspirin seemed to have done its work, thank God. He climbed out of the tub and took his time shaving.

A little later he came down the stairs to be greeted by the strains of 'Home on the Range' wafting, appropriately enough, from the music room. He went to the open door and saw his mother, her back to him as she shuffled through what had to be a stack of music on the table. That pleased him as much as her singing for she had played all too rarely in recent years.

"How about a tune, Mother?"

She started, then turned quickly, her smile dazzling. "James, darling!" She hugged him hard, then looked up at him critically. "You look fine."

James grimaced. "I'm sure Hannah had me at death's door." Then he smiled. "But why shouldn't I look fine? I've slept for twelve hours with a long hot bath at each end."

She laughed. "You're right about Hannah and death's door." But then her face saddened and she spoke hoarsely. "But where you've been..." She turned away and her face was momentarily muffled by a handkerchief, the only words coming through clearly were, "I'm glad you're home." She had found his note when she came in, a brief "I'm home, James," with Hannah's addition at the bottom, "From Dunkirk. He looks awful."

She had stood in the doorway of his bedroom watching him sleep by the light from the hall, grateful just for the sight of her elder son, home, safe. And then, as she hadn't done since he was a baby, she had gone in and placed a hand on his chest to make sure that he was still breathing, wanting desperately to put her arms around him, but knowing she'd wake him if she did, and that he needed sleep more than anything else. It was a long moment before she was able to go out and softly shut the door. She had slept fitfully until dawn when she had checked him again. Then she had fallen into a deep sleep, not waking until shortly before nine.

When she turned back to James, her eyes were suspiciously bright. "Why are you home? From what I can gather, every ship in England is hauling troops across the Channel."

He avoided her eyes. "*Vectis* is in dry dock."

"Then it was very bad, indeed."

"I shouldn't have told you that, so please don't mention it to anyone." But then he managed a grin. "Look at it this way. At least I have six days at home."

"And we'll make the most of them. Come into the dining room and start. Hannah will be having a fit. She heard you stirring around earlier and has been fussing in the kitchen ever since. Seems that nothing is too good for you this morning. And it's still breakfast."

"Bless her and I hope it's a 'Hail to the conquering hero' breakfast." He paused. "I just wish that we were conquering..." It was hard to go on, to say it, but he knew that he had to. "Hannah told me about John."

He hated the bleakness in her face. "Yes... Yes... I'm glad she did. I tried to let you know, but..." she shrugged helplessly.

"There was too much confusion," he finished the sentence for her. The bitter edge to his voice was inescapable. "At least he's conquering, wounded or not."

Anne looked at him sadly. "Darling, I know he makes life difficult for you sometimes. And I know that there's no sense to what he's doing, that it's hateful, awful." She turned back to her music and picked up the pile, tapping it on the edge to neaten it. "Obscene." She sounded angry suddenly and when she put the music back down, she leaned on the table on her hands. Every line of her back was taut. "But I cannot have... I will not have... He is your brother!" She turned on him in anger. "No matter what he's done, you must never ever forget that."

He sighed, thinking, you remember it, mother, for both of us. I manage to forget it for longer and longer periods of time, and I'm happiest when I do.

Fortunately, before he had to answer she had turned away again, her voice brisk, matter-of-fact as she said, "Come along. We can't spoil Hannah's breakfast."

Obviously the subject was closed.

She left him to the morning paper, shaking his head over the concept of the evacuation of Dunkirk as a real victory as he worked his way through four rashers of bacon, a rack of toast, and the best mushroom omelet he'd had in years, for once unaware that it had to be the food ration for a week. It wasn't until he was stirring his third cup of coffee that his mother came back in and he managed a casual, "How's Michael?"

"Fine, just fine. Tired, of course."

Was she a trace self-conscious? "No wonder he's tired." Suddenly he was self-conscious himself. "You kept him out late enough last night."

My God, she was blushing.

True to form, she accepted her confusion. "James, you're impossible."

He bore in. "That late on other nights?" Then he leaned back, enjoying watching the emotions play across her face, thinking that if this was what he thought it was, Michael was a lucky man.

"I can see Hannah's been talking again. No. And I wasn't really that late last night. Lately we've just had the occasional brief dinner because he's been terribly busy."

"But it's fun?"

"We always have a marvelous time," she said archly.

"Often?"

"Only lately." She cast him a baleful eye. "Are you checking up on me?"

James ignored the question. "Why so much more lately? What's happened?"

She looked surprised. "Why ... nothing."

"I don't call the way you looked when I came down this morning nothing."

"What on earth do you mean?"

Amazing. Maybe she didn't know. "You look..." He was momentarily at a loss, "...radiant. That's the word." And it was.

"Goodness, James." She smiled. "What a delightful thing to say! You should come home more often."

"And you're singing again."

"I feel like singing."

"That's just the point. You haven't felt like singing in years. Why now?" Especially with you, bastard brother, he thought with a flash of anger that died as quickly as it had been born, lying there in some godforsaken field hospital gangrening your arm to death.

She sat back, considering that. James was right. Why now? Why especially right now. No answer came so she shrugged and changed the subject. "What are your plans?"

"I haven't had a chance to think about it yet."

"No girl?"

"When have I had time to find one?"

"You never had time even when you had time. Whenever I thought 'maybe', it was, boom, off with the old, on with the new."

"The trouble is that I'm looking for a girl just like the girl who married dear old Dad and I can't find one."

"Excuses, excuses, but it's delightful to hear all the same." Her smile belied the words that came next. "I'm serious. When are you going to settle down?"

"Now you're sounding like a mother."

"Maybe that's because I am one."

"Yes, but you haven't sounded like one in ages."

"I haven't needed to."

"There's no need to now. There's a war on, you know," he said, pretending grave severity. "One hasn't time for such frivolous pursuits."

"James, what am I going to do with you?" Then her face brightened. "Come to think of it, I know precisely what I'm going to do with you."

He looked at her fondly. This was one of her most delightful moods, the perfect antidote for bleak memories. "And precisely what is that?"

"Never you mind." She was positively smug.

"All right. I'll wait, but just to humor you."

"Meantime, why not come to dinner with Michael and me tomorrow night?"

"You're going out to dinner again?" he asked, rolling his eyes in mock horror.

"Oh," she said casually, "he hasn't asked me yet."

"Will he?"

"I'll see to it. But he may have to put it off for a day or two. It depends on how much he has on his plate. Never mind that." She flapped a casual hand. "Will you go? He'd love to see you, I know. It's been a long time."

"And I'd be glad to see him. Any time. Just give me twenty-four hours notice."

# Chapter III

Georg didn't like it, didn't like it at all. "Damn it, Herr Major, he could have lost his arm. He's not ready." That was an exaggeration but the major wouldn't know that and Hans wasn't ready. Oh, physically he could probably go, but mentally... There was something eating him. Georg couldn't put his finger on it, but it was there. Besides, he didn't like the looks of this man.

"You mean he's physically incapable of traveling to Dunkirk by car. We'd make sure that his billet was comfortable, that he was well cared for and that he'd have to spend only part of each day interviewing people, if that was all he could do."

"He would need help," Georg snapped. "And a lot of it. Is this really important?"

"Very."

"Why not someone else?"

"Because Hauptmann Richter was requested specifically." The major was getting restless but he tried to conceal it. Admiral Canaris' order had been most definite. And with Richter's uncle being on the General Staff — He had to get Richter, physical difficulties or not. That meant that this Dr. Brandt, Hauptmann Brandt, he corrected himself, had to sign the release papers; these damn doctors were a law unto themselves in that regard. No doctor could be ordered to release Richter if, in his 'best medical judgement', it was inadvisable to do so. Bah! So Major Minten oozed condescending politeness. "It seems that his background is unique."

Hmm, thought Georg. The unique background has to be the English part. And interviewing people... in Dunkirk? Thousands of British prisoners in Dunkirk. POW interrogations? This Major Minten wasn't going to say. And why can't the pompous fart look me in the eye? Piggy little eyes with jowls to match. And those pudgy hands. Manicured. Clear nail polish. It fit. Nasty-neat customer. He rose.

"Wait here. I'll talk with him."

"I'll talk with him, if you don't mind, Doctor." Now why did he have trouble remembering that this man was a Hauptmann? Because in this case it didn't matter? Because Hauptmann or no, he couldn't order a doctor to release a patient?

"But I do mind, Herr Major." Georg's gaze was steady. He was throwing caution to the wind. "He's my patient. I'll have to see if he's ready."

Minten gave in with poor grace. "I have some business at division headquarters. Please be through by the time I get back." With that he stalked off, furious. Damn these doctors. He had to bring Richter back, and he'd do it even if it meant getting another doctor to sign those papers. This Richter, whoever he was, certainly had the right connections. Asked for by the head of the Abwehr at the suggestion of a member of the Wehrmacht General Staff. He'd have to tread carefully, cultivate him, keep a close eye on him. Richter needed someone to help him, didn't he? Yes indeed, a close eye would be kept.

*       *       *

Hans knew that something was wrong the moment Georg walked through the door. "Why the long face?"

"There's a Major Minten here to see you. He wants to get you released for some sort of special duty."

"What the hell kind of special duty? I can't even dress myself, let alone get into a tank while I'm wearing this contraption."

"I think they want your English."

"What for?"

"POW interrogations?"

Hans sighed.

Georg waited but when Hans still didn't speak, he asked something he had wanted to ask since the day Hans was brought in. "Why did you come back to Germany after your father died?"

He looked up sharply. "What's that got to do with anything?"

"Answer me, please."

"Why do you want to know?"

"Because I have to sign the release papers that would send you off with that bastard to do something I'm sure you can't want to do. Because when I last saw you in Munich, you'd had this Nazi crap in spades and I can't believe you've changed that much. So your being here now doesn't make any sense at all." Georg was leaning over the bed, talking very softly.

Hans looked at him angrily. "I had only one more year at Munich and it was my father's wish that I finish there. So I went back and got called up before I could get out."

Georg nodded slowly. It made a certain kind of sense, not enough, but still... And if there were something more, Hans wouldn't dare talk about it anyway. Well, Hans, he thought, you're just going to have to pay the piper. Neither of us has any real choice about that. Not with the major... "Minten's a nasty customer. You'll see what I mean when you talk with him. And he's going to take you with him if he has to do it over my dead body."

"We won't let it come to that, Georg." Hans felt the cast closing in around him. He was trapped in it, locked into serving Nazi Germany, a hostage no better off than Georg or Bergmann. In fact in a way it was worse. He had walked into his trap all by himself and with his eyes wide open.

Georg was watching his face. "Look, Hans," he said slowly. "I don't have to sign the papers. I could say..."

"How's your father?" Hans interrupted harshly.

Georg turned and looked out the window.

"He's home."

"Doing what?"

"Just... home."

"Is he being... shall we say... 'protected'?"

"You might call it that."

Georg and Bergmann. It was ironic. Both fathers were Socialists, Bergmann's in Austria, Georg's in Prussia. And both were virtual hostages. At least he had only himself to worry about, thank God. "Sign the papers, Georg. I'll go. Just one thing. How the hell will I manage in this cast?"

"They'll have to find someone to help you."

Hans paused, considering that. "Will they let me have anyone I want?"

Georg smiled at last. "Bergmann."

Hans laughed. "How did you know?"

"I heard him ask you to send for him and because you have good reason to like and trust him. With the good major around, you'll need someone like that. In fact, I'll insist on it. Has he had any sort of medical training? The way you were bandaged..." His voice trailed off.

Hans nodded slowly.

Georg was looking at him carefully. There was something about this... "What sort of training?"

Hans drew a shuddering breath. "Medical school. Two years."

"Where?"

"Vienna."

"Then why the hell is he a tank driver? He was exempt from call-up!"

Hans regarded him steadily.

"I shouldn't ask," said Georg flatly and turned away. "What the hell are we coming to when I can't ask a simple question like that?"

"You know what we're coming to." It was an effort for Hans to keep his voice low. "And you shouldn't ask for precisely the same reasons you wouldn't want him asking about you."

"Then his father was a Socialist. In the Austrian Parliament, I take it since that's where he's from?"

Hans nodded.

"Probably even worse than having been a Socialist member of the Reichstag. Something about the need to 'subdue the colonies'." His voice was bitter.

"At least his father was never in a labor camp."

"Lucky him. And his non-arrival in such coincided with his son's enlistment?"

"Precisely."

Georg's face was grim. "He must trust you a great deal if he told you about it."

"He didn't exactly tell me. I guessed."

"Don't blame him then for asking to stay with you. It makes things easier, serving under someone who knows."

"And the man over you?"

"He knows. That's why I'm in the boondocks, heading a mobile field hospital. Keeps me out of the way." He grinned. "And out of trouble, for the most part." The grin faded. "I just hope I can do that for Bergmann. But if he's been reassigned... The army's already moving south."

"Yes, but everything's happened so fast that they'll have a hard time catching up with the paperwork. They'll have to have replacements for Bauer and me."

"Damn army moves on paper," Georg said gloomily. "Let's just hope it's working for us, for once. All I can do is back you up with the major, but he'll have to agree to do it. He's the only one who can give the order." He turned away. "I'd better see if he's back."

"From where?"

"Headquarters."

"Don't. Not until I'm up. I'd be at too big a disadvantage with him if I were lying in bed. I'll go outside and see him there."

"Your chaise awaits, monsieur."

"Merci."

And so when Major Minten did return, he found Hauptmann Johann Richter waiting for him, ensconced on an oddly colorful chaise lounge that had been set in the shade of a huge chestnut tree. The Hauptmann was regarding him steadily as he approached.

Hans couldn't believe it. The man was a caricature, of what he couldn't say, but a caricature, nonetheless. He was of medium height and squat, with a jowly, moon-shaped face. Only one deep-set piggy eye was visible. The other was obscured by a monocle set

so deeply into the fat cheek below his left eye that it looked as if it
grew there. And this apparition was supported by ridiculously short
fat feet that were encased in gleaming black boots. Hans agreed
with Georg. He was a thoroughly nasty looking customer.

At last the major was standing before him, clicking his heels and
throwing himself into a paroxysm of a Nazi salute. "Heil Hitler!"

Most unusual, thought Hans. Not only shouldn't the Major have
saluted first, he shouldn't have saluted at all since Hans couldn't
rise and so couldn't return it. So his "Heil" in return was especially
perfunctory. "Sit down, please, Herr Major." He gestured toward the
chair that Georg had put there for that purpose. "And excuse me for
not rising."

"No apology necessary, certainly. And thank you, but I prefer to
stand. I've been sitting most of the morning." But really the major
was rather enjoying the feeling that standing over this man gave
him.

He was still at attention and Hans wondered if he was ever
really at ease. Probably when he made love, that is if any woman
would have him. But on second thought, he probably approached
even that as a formal, technical exercise, to be completely correct
in every detail.

The major didn't like being scrutinized in such a fashion. This
Richter was cool, far too cool, and contained. "The doctor has talked
with you? Told you that the Fatherland has need of your services?"

"Yes, sir, he has, and of course I am at the Fatherland's disposal.
But as you can see, I'm scarcely fit for combat."

"Combat is not my concern."

Hans believed him. It couldn't be. The gleam from those boots
alone would be a sniper's dream, to say nothing of his girth. And
then he had the sudden vision of Major Minten stuck half in and
half out of the commander's hatch of a tank, his legs churning
helplessly, creating an interior breeze, much like Winnie-the-Pooh
stuck in the entrance to Rabbit's hole after he had eaten too much
honey. He covered his laughter with a choking cough.

"Are you all right, Hauptmann Richter?"

"Yes, Herr Major. Thank you. Just something caught in my throat. What is required of me?"

The major didn't appreciate Richter's driving to the point at once since it gave him no chance for a pretty speech about heeding the call of the Fatherland and a man's higher duty. "Your unique background and a facility with the English language."

"Yes?" Hans was looking at him steadily, willing to give no quarter. Minten's annoyance increased.

"Abwehr needs your services in interrogating British prisoners."

Abwehr. German Military Intelligence. He should have realized. His heart started pounding, but his voice was calm, level, as he said, "I've had no experience interrogating anyone, or with military intelligence either, for that matter." Then the irony of it all began to strike him.

"That is obvious from your record."

"Then why me?" How had Abwehr heard about him, for God's sake? Uncle Karl? But it was Abwehr who wanted him. The irony, and that was the only word for it, was delicious. It was all he could do to keep from laughing.

Minten controlled his impatience with effort. He must remember this man's connections. "Because you have lived in England and will understand the nuances of what is said."

"I haven't lived there in quite some time."

"But you did as a child." Minten looked at him sternly. "Are you saying that you refuse?"

"No, certainly not." Hans' voice was heavy with sweet reason. He could see that he had gone far enough. "What sort of information would you expect me to get?"

This was more like it. Minten felt that he was finally getting the upper hand. "Home defenses, armament, weapons, troop morale and so on."

"Why do we need that? Isn't Britain going to be beaten along with France?" Hans just couldn't resist.

"We are sure that they will capitulate when France falls. But we feel we must be prepared for any eventuality."

"Invasion?" He had to work to keep it a casual question.

Minten's mouth became a tight line. "I cannot comment on that at this time."

"Tell me, just how do you plan to conduct these interrogations?" An ugly thought had crossed his mind. "I heard some nasty rumors from Poland."

"Gross exaggerations, I'm sure. And we are under strict orders to be more correct with the British prisoners, to show the British our good will. That will make it easier for them to accept the inevitable and surrender to us. Much of their army got away but without their weapons. They are lying staked out and naked before us." The analogy pleased Minten no end.

It was an effort to keep still, but Hans managed. If he played his card right, he might be able to stay with Abwehr, might even be able to get in on the planning for the invasion, if there was to be one. His English background would be useful to Abwehr for that, too, wouldn't it? By God... but he'd have to be very careful not to appear too anxious and he'd need Bergmann more than ever. He couldn't very well afford to have one of the major's men looking over his shoulder. "Herr Major, I will be glad to serve in any way I can. But there is one problem."

"And what is that?" Minten was almost purring. He was going to have Richter right where he wanted him.

"The doctor has said that I must have someone to help me. With this," he gestured toward his cast. "I can't even button my own pants."

"Of course." Minten beamed. "I have the perfect man for you." He hadn't decided who it would be yet, but whoever it was it had damn well better be perfect.

"Thank you, sir, but I would prefer to have my own man if possible."

"You have one already?" Minten wasn't entirely successful in hiding his disappointment, and he was surprised. It was most unusual for a Hauptmann to have his own man, especially a combat Hauptmann.

"Not my man exactly. My Panzer driver. A sergeant named Dieter Bergmann. He's had some medical training, so he'd know how to cope with my situation. Can you get him for me?"

"I can try," Minten snapped. There was nothing else for it, especially if Richter got the backing of that damn doctor. It might take days to get someone who could sign Richter out if Brandt refused to do it. It seemed that the good doctor was head of the hospital, and that it was all up to him. Headquarters had told him so, very firmly. Damn them. "He might not be available. Do you know where his unit is?" If only this Bergmann had already headed south or his records were so tied up in red tape that no one knew where he was.

"Last I heard, the battalion was bivouacked just west of Er-inghem. I'm sure that HQ" – he gestured toward the building across the square from which Minten had come – "would contact them for you."

Damn. And probably that great fucking divisional commander would be only too glad to help Richter out. One of his fair-haired boys. Shit. But he'd have to put a good face on it. "I'll see what I can do." Then he brightened. "But what if he doesn't want to come?"

There was something odd here. Minten wasn't happy about the prospect of Bergmann. But why should he care, beyond the trouble it might be to find him? "He and I will discuss it if he's available. I wouldn't keep him if he didn't want to stay." And pray God that he does, that he hasn't changed his mind.

"Of course not. Of course not." He paused. "I'll see what I can do," he repeated. "I would have preferred to leave today, but I can see that it will have to be tomorrow. But we must leave tomorrow, regardless. So I'm afraid that if your sergeant hasn't arrived by then, we'll have to find someone for you in Dunkirk."

Hans' heart sank. "Of course, Herr Major. That's understood. But I'll appreciate anything you can do to get hold of him." It was terribly important that he have Bergmann and no one else. But if Bergmann had changed his mind, or if Minten couldn't find him right away... And would he really try?

Minten nodded absently and said yet again, "I'll see what I can do." He'd have to try, at least half-heartedly. Damn.

"Thank you, sir." And then it was awkward. Hans couldn't salute Minten while he was sitting down, but the major obviously expected something. "I'll appreciate that." Inane conversation. They both were repeating themselves.

"I'll let you know." With that Minten finally turned and left, walking briskly back across the square toward divisional headquarters.

*       *       *

It was almost supper time and Hans was back out on the chaise lounge. There had been no word from the major. Probably... And then he saw him, Bergmann, striding toward him, grinning, duffel bag over one shoulder, machine pistol dangling from the other hand. By God, it was good to see him. It was all Hans could do not to whoop his delight. If he was going to beard the lion in his den, there was no one he'd rather have at his back than Bergmann. Dieter stopped as he got to the chaise, lowered the duffel bag, then clicked his heels and made a formal bow. "Herr Hauptmann."

Then they were grinning at each other and it was hard to stop.

"Sit down, Bergmann."

"Thank you."

"How did you get here so quickly?"

He laughed. "That part of it was easy. I was fixing General Wegmann's staff car when the call came through from HQ. When he heard it was you who wanted me, he came out himself and told me to get my tail over here. So here I am."

"Why on earth were you fixing the general's staff car?"

"Well, it was broken." He smiled. "Actually, I'd transferred to a field repair unit."

"Why?"

Dieter shrugged. "They were short of mechanics and asked for volunteers. I volunteered."

Hans studied him as he shook his head slowly. "It's never made any sense to me why you won't take a command." He'd turned one down after Poland, after asking Hans if he could stay on as his driver. Hans had been surprised, but, he had to admit, touched as well. And Bergmann was the best damn driver-mechanic in the division in the bargain. But now he'd been offered one again and to turn down a command twice? It made even less sense than it had then. Still, if he'd wanted one, he wouldn't have offered to come, wouldn't be here now. He'd have been on his way south. The whole division was pulling out.

Dieter had said nothing, was just sitting there looking at him.

"You're right," Hans said slowly. "It's none of my business."

Dieter flushed and opened his mouth, but before he could speak, Hans waved him to silence. "I'm afraid what I want you for is pretty dull stuff."

"Given the last month, I'm ready for a little dullness in my life. And I asked... I assume you need someone to... help you."

Hans nodded. "They want me to go to Dunkirk to interrogate British POWs. I can do that all right, but I'm as helpless as a baby in this damn thing. Can't even button my own pants. And you'd have to drive me around," he concluded ruefully.

"Driving's no problem. I've been driving you for what, ten months?"

"In a tank."

Dieter shrugged again. "And as for the rest... I've done some of that before, for my father, after his skiing accident."

"And you really won't mind?"

Dieter met his gaze steadily, thinking that even 'nurse-maiding' was preferable to war. He'd seen far too much of death and destruction to want to see any more of it. The command he'd been offered... He didn't want that sort of responsibility for other men's lives, especially since it was on behalf of Adolf Hitler. And since the man asking was Hauptmann Richter... Richter was one of the few things that made war bearable. "When do we start?"

"Tomorrow." Hans' relief was palpable. "Thank you."

*       *       *

Hans couldn't believe what he was seeing.

"It was kind of the British and French to leave so much for us, don't you think?" the major was saying. "Of course most of it will have to be melted down and recast, but never mind. We can always use high grade metal, especially the alloys in that fighter over there." Minten's fat finger was pointing down Dunkirk's beach toward the wreckage of a plane in the distance.

"Isn't that one of ours?" Dieter couldn't resist.

"It doesn't matter," Minten snapped. "We'll use it all."

"It's staggering," Hans said dully.

"So was their defeat." Minten sounded positively smug.

They were standing on the sand at the end of a long wooden ramp that had been built down to the beach over the top of the slanting sea wall. All Hans could see in either direction was wreckage. Dunkirk's beach was one vast junk yard which didn't stop at the water's edge. Makeshift piers made of trucks stretched out into the Channel. The masts of wrecked ships canted at odd angles above the water and there was even one huge ship beached high and dry.

In one way it defied credulity. But in another, it all looked so ordinary. Men working under the sun, shirts off, sweating, a Thames River barge lying sideways to the water's edge, lifting and falling with each gentle swell. But the sense of the ordinary vanished when he realized what one group of men was dragging from the water. Bodies. They were being stacked like cordwood on a flatbed trailer. Several must have been there for quite some time, for the hair was dry enough to be riffling in the breeze.

Off to his right, Todt Organization men were pushing wheelbarrows along makeshift board sidewalks. Building fortifications. And anti-aircraft guns were already well dug in up and down the beach. They weren't wasting any time.

And to think he'd been part of what had caused this beach. Suddenly his cast seemed to weigh a ton, his shoulder hurt, his mouth was dry and he wanted to go home, to get away from everything and sleep for days on end in his own bed. He wanted to see his mother sitting at the piano, playing, to laugh with James and eat Hannah's scones. He wanted not to have to be careful about what he said, not to have to play games with that anymore, not to have to try to notice everything and piece it all together. The sun was shining and the Channel waters were calm. He could swim home from here, almost, or sail home on something, anything... if it weren't for this damn cast. A string of expletives ran through his brain.

He turned away, catching his toe on something buried in the sand. Dieter braced him before he could fall and set him back on his feet. Hans was too frustrated and infuriated even to thank him. He was so goddamn-ably, knee-buckling, ass-dragging tired.

"Herr Hauptmann," Dieter's voice was full of concern. He had never seen Richter look this way, ever. "We'd better get back to the car. You need to get out of the sun." He turned toward Major Minten. "Is it all right to take him back now, sir?"

"Certainly. Certainly. He's seen what I wanted him to see. Can't have him wearing himself out." Minten didn't even look up as Richter and Bergmann moved away. He was studying the pearl-handled .45 that his driver, Corporal Kugelmann, had picked out of the sand and was handing to him, using a stick through the trigger guard. It was that on which Hans had tripped.

"Kugelmann, there is romance in someone's soul. I wonder how he could bear to leave it. Clean it up for me. It will make a superb trophy."

The corporal took the pistol gingerly and with great distaste. He disliked firearms intensely and this one in particular, since it was covered with sand and grease and was a thoroughly messy proposition. He carried it with two fingers, away from his body, as he followed Minten up the ramp.

They were well down the Avenue de la Mer, Kugelmann steering the car carefully through the wreckage, before anyone spoke, and then it was Minten who said, "I wanted you to see the beach so you'd have a better appreciation of the frame of mind of the men you'll be interrogating, know something of what they've been through."

Hans' voice was hoarse. "How many got away?"

Minten jerked his head around to look at him, setting his jowls aquiver. "Not as many as they would like us to think but far more than we would have liked."

"How many prisoners?"

"The count is not complete as yet, but with the wounded still in hospitals in the area, it should be over sixty thousand."

"Well then, we'd better get on with it." Hans said no more.

Dieter was watching closely as they turned right onto the Rue de la Republique, still picking their way through the junk left by the departing armies. He would need to get oriented if he was to get the Hauptmann to the places he needed to go. And he'd need a map.

Just beyond where the Rue Albert Camus and the Avenue Adolphe Gaert – funny name, that, wonder who he was – came together, Kugelmann made a U-turn and stopped before a group of three attached houses that looked totally undamaged. They were far from prepossessing.

"It's a fairly straight shot out to the Fort des Dunes from here. That's where the interrogations will be conducted." Kugelmann was speaking with great precision. "It would be more convenient for you to be staying out there, but with so many prisoners, the guard staff has to have priority. However, this should be satisfactory."

He reached into the glove compartment, took out a map and handed it to Dieter. "I marked all the places you'll need to know, at least for now. The rest you'll have to find for yourself."

"He'd like to get out now." Minten's tone was acid.

"Of course, sir." Kugelmann was unperturbed. His eyes were caressing Dieter's face. It was all Hans could do not to laugh. So it wasn't only women who were attracted to Bergmann's sinister good looks and magnificent build.

Dieter caught his eye and reddened slightly.

"Sergeant Bergmann," Kugelmann went on, oblivious to the by-play, "the officer to be billeted with you will bring the car when he comes this evening. He'll also bring further instructions and see that you get where you need to go in the morning."

Minten wondered what Hans would think when he found that the man sharing the house with them was someone who knew him and didn't like him at all. Odd that Lieutenant Kramer disliked the Hauptmann so much. Richter seemed pleasant enough but of course first impressions could be deceiving. Still, it had to be one of those childhood things. They hadn't seen each other in years. And Kramer did tend to hold grudges. But thank God it had been Kramer who'd brought Admiral Canaris' orders back from Berlin. And thank God he'd been able to get through to Kramer last night. Kramer had been anything but pleased at being told he'd have to move out of that cushy seaside villa he'd managed to get himself assigned to, to move into this little house in town, that is until he'd been told that it was so he could keep an eye on Richter. Kramer's laugh at that little bit of news had been positively vicious. If anyone could turn up dirt on Richter, it would be Kramer, even more because he'd so enjoy finding it.

And Kramer was bright. He'd notice things that got by other men. Bright and discrete. That scrape in Hamburg. Minten shuddered. That had been a close call, a very close call – he should never have been so careless – and he might not have survived if it hadn't been for Kramer. Good man, Kramer. He nodded. And when this business was over here in Dunkirk, and he was made chief of the Hamburg Abwehr station, Kramer just might be the perfect assistant. Bright. Loyal. God knows he'd need someone like that. A lot went on in Hamburg. Too much for the man currently heading the station, he thought sourly. A lot of clean-up work that needed doing, especially in the Codes section. Dead wood at the top. Several heads would roll. There was that young upstart Fenstermacher. He might do. A real comer. Good man. Like Kramer.

"Thank you, Herr Major."

The words intruded on Minten's thoughts and he saw that Bergmann was helping Richter out of the car. "You're welcome, Hauptmann Richter. And don't bother to report until 1030 tomorrow. You need time to get settled. We'll be working you in gradually."

"Thank you, Herr Major," he said again, "but I'm glad to do all that's required of me."

"Just so. Just so. But we dare not wear you out. At least not right away." He managed a little high pitched laugh. He'd have to be careful about that or Canaris or that damn general-uncle of Richter's would have his head on a platter. "Consider that an order." His voice had turned stern, fatherly.

"Yes, sir. Thank you, sir." Hans struggled to hide his amusement.

Minten nodded and gave the apparently obligatory, "Heil Hitler."

Hans' brief "Heil" in return was lost as the car pulled off.

# Chapter IV

James knew that his mother had something up her sleeve but it wasn't until they were in the cab on their way to the Savoy two nights later that he realized what it was.

"By the way, James," her tone was far too casual, "Michael is bringing his secretary along. She's had her nose to the grindstone and he said that she needed a night out."

James snorted. "Whose idea did you say this was? Michael's?"

"Of course." Sweet innocence.

"Of course, my foot. Who's being incorrigible now?"

"Whatever do you mean?" Her eyes were wide.

"I mean that this is what you meant the other day when you said, 'I know precisely what I'm going to do with you'."

She tried to look puzzled.

"Come on, Mother. 'Fess up."

She laughed, "She's really a remarkable girl."

"Who looks like a horse. I've heard what a paragon of efficiency she is. It couldn't be any other way."

Anne was genuinely amused. "You've never seen her?"

"Never."

"Then I won't spoil it for you."

She settled back in the seat and, refusing further comment, retreated into her own thoughts. Michael had been entertained by her matchmaking efforts and a little leery of bringing his secretary to a social occasion.

"But Michael, she's perfect for James, and I want him to meet her. Besides, she's more than presentable."

"You're right, but I wonder if it's wise to mix business with pleasure."

"Then I'll make sure it's no pleasure for you. We can leave before dessert."

"At the Savoy? Not with their strawberry tart!"

At that moment she'd known she had him. "After dessert, then."

"All right. All right," he'd grumbled. "I know when I'm beaten."

Why had she done it? She never meddled in James' love life and ever since she had, she'd been uncomfortably aware that she had an ulterior motive beyond having him meet a very attractive woman. That was the trouble. Miss Trimby was far too attractive. Anne had finally met her the night James had come home from Dunkirk, when Miss Trimby had brought Michael an urgent message while they were dining at the Connaught.

That was the reason she'd come home as early as she had. It had been most disconcerting to see Michael and Miss Trimby go off in the car together after he'd arranged for a cab to take her home. He'd been most apologetic, of course, but still... Miss Trimby was gorgeous. Michael had never mentioned that. Hadn't he noticed? That was ridiculous. Of course he'd noticed! Any man would notice and at once. Why hadn't the fool woman found a man to marry? They ought to be lined up outside her door in droves.

"Mother!"

She startled.

"We're here. You've been gathering enough wool to open a mill."

James paid off the driver as he got out of the cab and then turned to her. "All right." His voice was full of resignation. "I feel like one of those sheep you just sheared who's being led to slaughter."

At that she laughed, a big full laugh and as they came through the door, they were laughing together, enormously pleased with each other.

Annabelle Trimby was walking out of the hallway leading to the ladies' room and saw them come in. Not realizing who they were for a moment, she was struck by what a marvelous and happy-looking pair they were as they struggled to suppress their laughter and walk with some measure of decorum across the lobby. She smiled. They weren't entirely successful.

It was only as their paths converged at the door to the dining room that she said with surprise, "Why, Mrs. Richter, it's so nice to see you again."

Anne put out her hand and as Annabelle took it said, "Miss Trimby! How lovely you look." Her eyes were sparkling and she glanced at James with anticipation. "This is my son, Lieutenant James Richter. James this is Michael's secretary, Annabelle Trimby."

It was all James could do not to laugh again. It was unbelievable. Certainly not what he'd expected. He took her proffered hand saying, "Miss Trimby," all the while thinking that no one so efficient had a right to look as she did. He continued looking at her and answered that enchanting smile with one of his own. Then, unable to suppress it any longer, he laughed his pleasure out loud.

She wasn't offended. How could anyone be offended in the face of such delightful good humor? And then she was laughing herself. "I've never caused quite this reaction before."

"It's just..." James was at a total loss for words.

"He was thinking of the secretary who preceded you, Miss Trimby." Michael's deep voice finished the thought. He had come up to the group entirely unnoticed, and had been watching the proceedings with considerable amusement.

He shook hands with James. "Good to have you back."

"Good to be back, sir."

"Anne, my dear, shall we go in?"

She looked up at him happily. "Of course, Michael."

James and Annabelle fell in behind them as they went down the steps and across the main dining room to the smaller one beyond, and the table waiting for them by one of the huge windows overlooking the Thames.

"Is he right, Lieutenant?"

"About what, Miss Trimby?"

"About my predecessor?"

She had lovely eyes. It was all very disconcerting. "In a way."

"She was a dear woman under all of that, you know." A little smile played across her lips.

"And are you?"

"Am I what?"

"A dear woman under all of that?"

She caught her breath. "You'll have to judge that for yourself."

"Will I have the opportunity?"

Annabelle stopped, studying his face. His heart gave a lurch. What a cool, level gaze she had. None of that idiotic saccharine female coyness here, thank God. He was surprised by how anxious he was to hear her reply.

"Possibly." A full blown smile took the sting from her words.

"A definite 'possibility'?"

She gave a little laugh and turned to follow Anne and Michael, unwilling to say more. It was a relief to have the waiter standing behind her chair, holding it for her, to have the fuss of getting settled and the pampered feeling of having her napkin put in her lap for her. She needed the time to compose herself.

He was too attractive and almost too charming by half. And to think she'd hesitated about accepting the invitation because she'd known he'd be there and hated having an escort arranged for her. But curiosity about Captain Compton and Mrs. Richter had gotten the better of her and she was beginning to be very glad that it had.

And they were talking, relaxed easy talk, the war pushed to the background for the time being. For the most part, Annabelle was content to watch and listen, to let it all ebb and flow over her, talk of music, books, theater, ideas, people both famous and infamous and all of it spiced with wit and considerable good humor. It was a marvelous change from the usual inane chatter she'd been subjected to so often lately.

But even more, Annabelle had never seen this side of the Captain and it fascinated her to find that he was a bit boyish and could be utterly relaxed and happy. She'd seen how exquisite Anne Richter was the night she'd taken the message to the Connaught and she'd wanted to know if there was anything to go with it.

It had amazed her to discover how many bright and capable men were married to frivolous women. She was rapidly becoming reassured about Mrs. Richter and she was glad, thinking with a rising protective ferociousness, that he deserved the best and that this woman had better be the best since, at this moment, the fact that he was in love with her was written all over his face.

"You look like a thunder cloud."

James' voice startled her, but she managed a smile. "It's been a difficult week."

"For us all."

"But at least the evacuation was a triumph." She paused, resettling her napkin in her lap. "I envy you being there."

He studied his coffee cup for a moment, and when he finally looked up at her she was deeply moved, for his face was bleak. It was another moment before he spoke. "It's difficult to know what to say to that. I'm glad you weren't there."

"Why?" Her voice was gentle.

James let out a long breath. "The papers show the romantic side of it. There was something magnificent about all the little boats and the men struggling to get the troops off the beach, and the way the troops came and waited through everything. But I saw too many ships go down, too many men die, a town burning, a junkyard of a beach and harbor." He was sweating and his hands were trembling.

Impulsively she covered his hand with hers. "I'm sorry, Lieutenant. I wasn't being flip. It's just... well... Everyone in England who could think and feel wanted to be part of it. We snatched the whole army out from under Hitler's nose, and he can't be happy about it. It's the first thing that hasn't gone his way. So it's a victory of sorts and I would so like to have seen it."

He started talking, slowly at first but then more quickly, barely seeing her anguished face as he told her about it: the Stukas, the ships, the men on the mole and the beaches, the lack of anti-aircraft guns, all of it. It all came pouring out as if a dam had begun to overflow.

Anne became aware that something was happening and touched Michael's hand so that she could listen. At first she was simply surprised. James never talked like this, at least not when it was something that had obviously affected him so deeply. But then there were tears in her eyes for what he had to bear, and she thanked God that Miss Trimby was such a good listener and that she seemed to care about what he was saying.

Michael touched her arm and gestured toward the dance floor. The band had started playing without her noticing. She nodded dumbly, and they moved out onto the parquet floor, leaving Annabelle and James totally engrossed in each other.

As he pulled her close, he could feel that she was trembling. "What is it, Anne?" He had never seen her like this.

She looked up, her face white, strained. "Take me home, please?"

"Of course. If that is what you want." He took her hand and led her back to their table.

"I'm taking your mother home, James. She's worn out."

James rose. "We'll go with you, of course."

"Of course," echoed Annabelle and reached for her purse.

Anne had herself under control now, but her smile was forced. "Please don't. It really isn't necessary. I just need some sleep. Stay and enjoy the band. It's such a good one."

James looked down at Annabelle.

"It's up to you," she said, hoping against hope that he would want to stay.

"Are you sure, Mother?"

"I'd feel much better if you would." And then, to give them no time to change their minds, she rushed on. "Miss Trimby, it's been such a pleasure seeing you."

"Thank you, Mrs. Richter. And Captain Compton, thank you for including me."

"It was my pleasure. I'm glad you'll stay. Enjoy yourselves."

"Thank you, Michael," James said. "It was good to see you again. And take care of her, please."

Then he leaned over and kissed his mother's cheek as Michael said, "I'll do my best."

Anne was surprised and touched. That was the sort of thing James so rarely did, especially when anyone else was around. Her lips trembled. She couldn't trust herself to speak and so confined her farewells to a brief wave as they hurried out.

"Are you sure she's all right, Lieutenant?"

"Please, call me James. No, I'm not. Something is bothering her, but whatever it is, I think Michael's the one to take care of her right now." Then he made a formal little bow. "Miss Trimby."

She smiled. "Annabelle."

He bowed again. "Annabelle." He liked the way her name rolled off his tongue. "The band and I are at your disposal."

She took his proffered hand, and they moved out onto the dance floor. He was such a good sort, and he had been through hell. But then she forgot everything in the pleasure of discovering that he was also a superb dancer.

*     *     *

A cab was waiting. Michael asked no questions. It wasn't the time. All during the drive home she sat stony-faced, staring fixedly out the window at nothing, clutching his hand.

When they got back to Eaton Square, he refused to leave her, grateful that it was Hannah's night out so he could insist on staying, saying she was in no condition to be left alone. He poured a brandy and settled himself onto the sofa, watching her as she paced.

Finally he said, "All right. Out with it."

She turned on him, her face contorted. "Why did James have to go through all of that? Why did any of them have to? Why didn't the French squash that obscenity of a man – that... Hitler – when he moved troops into the Rhineland years ago? They could have then, before..." She turned away but he knew better than to try to comfort her or to say anything at all. She needed to get it all out and right now. "Why did those damn-them-all-to-hell politicians let it come to this? The French... Chamberlin... All those good boys, dead. All those ships sunk. The terrible waste and destruction. For what? Greed? Power?

"That James should see... He looked awful when he came home. Hannah told me. I know she exaggerates, but if he looked even half as bad as she said he did, it was just that. Awful. And to hear him talk like that! Michael, I've never heard him talk like that about anything. Ever. He's always kept everything to himself and suffered in silence, no matter what I did or how hard I tried to get him to tell me."

"Thank God that girl's a good listener," Michael said. "And she seems to care about what he's been through."

"But is anyone listening to John and what he's been through?"

Pain stabbed through Michael's heart.

She went on relentlessly. "And why the hell is he going through it? What possessed him to stay there? He's not a Nazi. I know that. But there he is," – her face was bright red and viciously angry – "over there fighting hard for the Nazis and winning medals! He should have come back. Here. He still should. And when he does get back, finally, I'm going to kill him!" And then her face started to dissolve and her voice broke. "Kill him? Oh, no. Please. God. I'd just hug him so hard."

Then at last she was crying, speaking between sobs, leaning over slightly, holding her arms over her stomach. "I can't stand another war. I cannot stand it. I thought I could, but I can't."

Anne sank to her knees on the rug before the fireplace, weeping, her face in her hands.

Michael burst to his feet in a fit of agony, pulled her up and held her to him as she wept. He did it as much for himself as for her because it was the only way he could bear the pain. Finally he lifted her in his arms and carried her to the couch, settling her across his lap, cradling her as one cradles a child. So consumed was she with her own grief that she didn't see the tears streaming down his cheeks.

At last she was quiet, and he heard a shuddering sigh. "It's all James and John, really."

His grip tightened involuntarily.

"I can't bear the thought of what they've gone through and what they'll have to go through before this is all over." She paused "That is if either of them survives."

He crushed her to him until he heard a breathless, "I can't breathe."

She went on as if nothing had happened.

"If only they were on the same side, on this side. It would be so much easier to bear because at least they'd both be fighting for the same thing, the right thing, and I could see John from time to time. It's wrong what he's doing, wrong. James isn't sensible about it. He hates John or at least he thinks he does. What that does to him... It wasn't easy for him when people found out, especially in the Navy... It's been hard enough for me. The looks... Oh, God. But I don't care about that. I care about John. I want him back. That's all. And his wound. I know you're trying to find out more about it, but I want to know now.

"It takes so long for his letters to get here. I haven't heard for weeks and I probably won't for weeks more. They must have stopped them all writing before the invasion." She took a deep breath but he said nothing. He couldn't. It was as if she had stuck a knife in him. He couldn't bear it.

"I'm all right now, Michael." She stirred in his arms. "I didn't mean to burden you with all of this, but I'm selfish enough to be glad that I did, because apparently I had to say it to someone." She tried to sit up.

His grip tightened again. "Don't. I like having you right where you are."

She settled back gratefully, looking up at him, and she was beautiful. He thought that no woman who had been crying as she had could be beautiful but she was. The pain of what he had done consumed him all over again.

Anne was studying his face and finally she saw it all, the pain, the infinite sadness and oh my God, the love. Her heart filled to overflowing. How could she have been so blind? New tears filled her eyes and she put her hand to his cheek, too moved to speak.

He couldn't breathe. Something had happened, but he didn't dare think what it might be. He just looked down at her, waiting, and the waiting had a fearful urgency.

Her words came slowly. "Why haven't I seen it before now?"

"Seen what?" His voice was a hoarse rasp. He was still waiting.

"That I love you with all my heart." And now it was she who was waiting in absolute stillness, all breath and thought suspended.

She felt him start and then he was trembling. She tried to see his face but he had raised his head. Could she have been wrong? Her voice was anxious. "Have I offended you?"

Again, there was no breath or thought, only a wild joy as she was engulfed in his arms, his mouth hard on hers. When he finally released her, they were both trembling. He breathed in the fragrance of her hair, forgetting everything in an agony of happiness. "I have waited forever to hear you say that."

"Why didn't you tell me before?"

"I didn't feel I had the right to."

Before she had time to think about that, he was kissing her again, gently this time and with infinite tenderness. When he pulled back to look down at her, he was smiling, and all the deep-etched lines of pain and fatigue had been erased from his face. "But I still haven't told you."

"Told me what?" She was nestled in his arms, completely content.

"That I love you."

"Do you love me?" Anne knew the answer but she wanted to hear him say it.

"Utterly."

She smiled up at him. "But you did tell me."

"When?"

"A few minutes ago."

"I hadn't said a word about it."

"But you told me all the same."

"Can you read my mind? Now that would not bode well for the future."

"Have you felt this way for long?"

"For more years than I care to remember. But it became acute this spring."

"Then no, I can't read your mind, because I didn't know until just now."

"Perhaps you weren't ready to know before now."

They talked on, his hand brushing her hair from her face where it was falling in a marvelous disarray; she pulling his head down to kiss his eyes, his chin; lifting her hand to trace his lips with her forefinger until he could stand it no longer and caught it gently between his teeth.

But finally she knew it wasn't enough. He felt the tension as she looked at him, searching his face for something. For what?

"Will you come with me, Michael? We have wasted so much precious time."

He couldn't take his eyes from her face, couldn't believe what she was saying, what she wanted to give him, what she was asking to give him. Michael had wanted her so much for so long that he suddenly feared that if he moved or even spoke, she would evaporate and he would be left holding nothing, even worse off than before because he had come so close to his heart's desire. But... John. Oh God. No. He loved her so. He couldn't. But he couldn't not. "Is this what you really want, my darling?" His voice was hoarse.

She nodded, too moved to speak. Her stomach was full of butterflies, and she realized again how much she loved him and how long it had been.

They untangled themselves and rose, Michael taking her hand and leading her toward the steps, still not quite able to believe what was happening. So it was no surprise when she pulled him to a stop.

"You're worried about James coming home," he said, his voice so full of pained resignation that she had to laugh.

"No, I have faith in him, and if I can read anyone's mind..." She wrinkled her nose at him and he pulled her into his arms. It was a long moment before she could go on. "As I was saying before I was so rudely interrupted, if I can read the signs, he'll be very late. It's just..." She hesitated, not quite sure how to say it. There had been his slight hesitation. She took a deep breath and looked at him squarely, thinking, don't feel sorry for me. I couldn't bear it.

It has to be because you love me. "I need to make sure that this is what you really want."

"Anne, I have yearned for you, ached for you, loved you, desired you until I thought I couldn't bear it. You are for me, my darling, the pot of gold at the end of the rainbow."

"Pot indeed!" She snorted. "I'll beat you upstairs."

She almost did. They bumped each other through the door to her bedroom, Michael slamming it behind them before collapsing with her on the bed, laughing, until he rolled over and pulled her under his chest, studying her face yet again, wondering if he would ever get enough of looking at her, especially as she looked at this moment.

Then there was no time for tenderness. They were together, still half-clothed in their urgency. Even when they were spent, she held him to her. "Now that I know this, know you, how can I let you go?"

"I hope you won't." He bent down to kiss her.

A bit breathless, she said, "If we're going to do any more of this..." And then she moved away from him and stood.

"We can't if you're... Where are you going?"

"I'm just taking these things off."

He laughed his delight. "I'll help you."

"All right, but turnabout's fair play. If you help me, then I get to help you."

He rose from the bed and began helping her. He helped her and she helped him and they both helped each other at the same time. It was a long, delightfully complicated process.

Michael woke later that night, totally disoriented in the blackness of the strange room. He reached out blindly until his hand touched the warmth of her. Then, flooded with happiness, he lay back, content, wondering why he felt no guilt over John. It would come later. It was bound to. But right now it didn't matter. Nothing mattered except the fact that she had made herself his and that somehow, he would make sure that she stayed his. The Lord alone knew how, but he would. He had to.

Then he was sitting up, listening. There was a step on the stairs. My God, they had forgotten about James.

"What is it?" Her whisper was urgent.

His hand covered her mouth as he leaned down, hissing in her ear, "James!"

The whole bed shook with her silent laughter.

How could she laugh at a time like this? "Anne!" It was an angry hiss this time as he heard James shut the door to his bedroom. At least they were safe so far.

But she hadn't stopped laughing and suddenly he was laughing with her. They were having a terrible time keeping quiet. Gasps were smothered with pillows and he had to grab her to keep her from rolling off the bed. But the touch of her wiped away the whole ridiculous situation and before he knew what he was doing, he was on her, in her, her warmth welcoming him, enveloping him.

Afterwards he lay on his side, holding her back against him, his mind able to work only in slow motion. He had been celibate for so long. How was all of this possible? His voice was a gentle whisper in her ear. "What sort of magic do you possess to get such a performance out of a broken-down piece of machinery like me?"

She turned and stretched luxuriously, whispering back, "You'll never get old, my darling, no matter how old you get. And as for your being broken down... It seems to me that your machinery is in very good working order, indeed."

"Just very good?"

She gave a throaty laugh. "Excellent."

"That's better." He sounded smug.

They lay in contented silence for a moment before he turned back to her. "How are we going to get out of this?"

It set them both off laughing again. The idea of James catching him in flagrante delicto with Anne was more than Michael could bear. "Sir," he intoned in a deep whisper, mentally taking on the classic Victorian hero's outraged stance, "how dare you lay hand on my mother?"

"Oh Son," she squeaked, "he laid on a lot more than that!"

That was the end of sense for a time, but finally she composed herself and put on her robe. "I'll see about James."

She turned the knob of James' door cautiously, grimacing as the latch clicked. But all that greeted her was the sound of his deep, even breathing. Satisfied, she carefully pulled the door to and padded back, shutting her bedroom door behind her.

"We're safe. He's dead to the world." Anne sat on the edge of the bed, reaching for him.

He took her hand, kissing the palm gently. "I can't bear to leave you."

"And I can't bear to have you leave. May I come with you?" she teased. He chuckled. "It might be worth it just to see the expression on Carter's face. The man's a bit of a prig, I'm afraid. I can just hear his quivering tones, 'Sir, in all the years I've been in your employ... Well, sir, you leave me speechless.' His wattles flapping all the while."

"Would he really say anything? I can't imagine. He's so... proper."

"Prig is the word, as I said before. No, I doubt that he would actually say it, but he'd certainly think it. And disapproval would be written all over his face. It just isn't done, my dear." The last sentence was said in an impeccable falsetto.

"Oh yes, it is," she said happily. "over and over again, all the time."

"You're incorrigible."

He couldn't have been more delighted.

# Chapter V

Hans woke to find the sun streaming in the window. The watch he picked up from the table beside the bed told him that it was 0815. He'd slept for almost twelve hours. Luxury. He felt like a new man. There was a tap on the door. Had there been one before? Was that what had awakened him?

"Come!"

It was Dieter, smiling from ear to ear as he whipped a peculiar looking tunic out from behind his back. "Voila!"

"Voila?"

"The lady of the house and I have been hard at work. The tunic you were wearing was unraveling where they had to cut it for your cast. Madame Richard fixed that one and I took care of the other two you had."

"My God!" Hans said in falsetto. "He sews, too. Will you marry me?"

"Not on your life. You're not buxom enough. I'm saving myself for that American, Mae West."

"She's far too old for you."

"Never mind that. She has everything else I'm concerned with. Besides, older women are so appreciative."

Hans raised an eyebrow. "And how would you know that?"

"You'd be surprised what I know," came the airy reply.

"Never again." He grinned. "Come on. Help me up. We'll shave, then I'll put on the tunic, and we'll see how good you really are."

They struggled through the shaving with only a slight nick on Hans' chin. The tunic fit perfectly. Dieter stood back, admiring his handiwork.

Hans smiled. "An improvement?"

"Thanks a lot!" He laughed. "Has our star boarder arrived?"

"Late last night and with supplies."

"Who is it?"

"I don't know. I didn't see him. But he sounded put out about being in the back bedroom."

"What happened?"

"I'm not sure. My French is rather sketchy but I think that Madame told him about you. He seemed to know that already, though. But then she told him about me and I think she said that because you were so incapacitated, I had to have the other front room, next to yours, so that if you needed something during the night, all you had to do was pound on the wall."

"True enough. Did he give her any trouble about it?"

"Just some grumbling. Then he slung his stuff into the back bedroom and followed after it. I didn't hear any more out of him."

"Did he bring a car?"

"Yes. A Kubelwagen. Standard issue. Scarcely what we were in yesterday, but it will do." He paused, clearing his throat. "We'll have to hurry, I'm afraid. I told Madame Richard that we'd be down by 0900 and it is nearly that now."

"You must know more French than you are letting on."

Dieter shrugged. "An innkeeper's son picks up a bit of every-thing. No English, though. Our village is outside Innsbruck, a bit out of the way for very many Englishmen. And I took French in school. That and Italian were the only languages offered besides Latin. But I could use some help with my French, so if you don't mind, Herr Hauptmann, I would appreciate the loan of your French-German-English dictionary." He held it up.

Hans started. That dictionary? His and Michael's last resort, to be used only if all else failed. To write letters to 'Darling Julia.' Well, all else certainly had failed. He thought it had been lost. If there was only a way to mail the letters without them taking weeks to get there. "Of course. Where did you find it?"

"In the storage box on the tank. It was in the bottom. I cleaned it out before I left."

"Then be my guest. Just don't lose it. I may need it myself." And it had to be that precise edition. He and Michael had to have exactly the same edition if the letter code were to work.

"I'll leave it here, at the house. It's only when I talk with Madame Richard that I have any problem." He opened the door and bowed from the waist. "Your morning repast awaits."

Hans managed to put a bit of a mince in his step and they were still laughing when they got to the bottom of the stairs. Dieter went on into the kitchen, leaving Hans to walk through the sitting room into the small dining room. He saw the curtain-covered frame that held the pull-down bed on which Madame Richard was sleeping. She would have to move the table to get it out. He sighed. There was nothing else for it with all the bedrooms full. But at least she had a bed and it was inside her own house, which was more than a lot of people had these days.

What did her husband do? They certainly weren't poor. A shop of some sort? Whatever it was, he wasn't here to tend to it, even if the business were still standing.

The voices coming out of the kitchen told him the Bergmann had been far too modest about his French. True, he had a pronounced German accent and it wasn't colloquial, but he spoke it very well indeed.

Chickens. He looked out the open window, watching as eight or nine strutted and pecked at a sprinkle of grain in a small run next to the ruins of their hen house. Madame Richard had saved her chickens by hiding them in the attic. Resourceful woman. Messy attic. He gave a short, sharp laugh.

"Ready, sir?"

Hans turned and nodded, then let Dieter help him into the chair facing the window. The table had been set for two. "Join me?"

"Thank you, Herr Hauptmann, but I ate before I got you up. The other officer should be down soon. Madame Richard said she heard him stirring around. His bedroom is right over the kitchen. I'll go up and finish the unpacking."

They heard a step on the stairs and then a voice came across the sitting room. "Good morning."

Hans cursed the cast that prevented him from rising or even turning around.

"Good morning, sir." It was Dieter who spoke first. "Your breakfast should be right out." And then he left.

Finally the man was standing where Hans could see him. "Good morning, Lieutenant. I hope you slept well."

"Well enough, thank you. That is until that fool woman started banging around in the kitchen at some ungodly hour. This was the only morning I've had to sleep in in weeks."

"A rare luxury these days," said Hans drily.

"Yes, it is." There was a pause. "I'm Walther Kramer."

"Hans Richter. Have a seat."

"Thank you." He took the chair opposite, remarking that after all that racket, he certainly hoped breakfast would be something worth eating. Then, as he put his napkin into his lap, he asked "Where did you pick up that unwieldy thing?"

"A sniper."

Kramer snorted, relieved that Madame Richard had appeared and saved him the necessity for a sympathetic reply. How like Richter not to remember him even after he'd heard his name. Richter and that older brother of his had always thought they were too good for everyone, especially the likes of him. They and that precious Georg Brandt had made that abundantly clear.

"Sir!" The woman's nervous voice broke into his thoughts. She was standing beside him, a jam pot in one hand, butter dish in the other.

"Yes?" Kramer snapped, switching to French.

"I'm afraid..." And it was obvious that she was just that. It gave Kramer a certain vicious pleasure. "I'm afraid," she said again, "that there is no coffee. I only have tea."

"Tea will be fine, Madame," said Hans gently, "and these croissants look marvelous." They did. And his were already pulled into conveniently-sized pieces and filled with butter and jam. She had to have made them herself, undoubtedly from the supplies that Lieutenant Kramer had brought along, which was probably the reason she had been 'banging around the kitchen at some ungodly hour'. It had to have been at least as ungodly an hour for her as it had been for Lieutenant Kramer. And the poor woman seemed to be scared out of her wits. What could the lieutenant have said to her last night? She hadn't been that way before Kramer came.

"Tea will not be fine." Kramer was saying as he fixed her with a malevolent glare. "Why isn't there any coffee?"

"Mine ran out a week ago and there wasn't any in the box, sir."

Kramer's jaw tightened. Bitch probably stole it and sold it. At least she was near tears.

"There's no sense harassing the poor woman," Hans said in German, not bothering to hide his annoyance. If this was any indication, life with Lieutenant Kramer was going to be no bed of roses. Then, switching back to French, he said to her, "We'll find some coffee for the lieutenant later today. In the meantime, tea will be fine. Please don't concern yourself further."

"Of course, of course," mumbled Kramer, backing off as Madame Richard fled back into the kitchen. Minten had stuck him in this pest-hole to get on friendly terms with Richter so he could keep an eye on him. Besides, Richter was a superior officer with impeccable connections and it never hurt to be on good terms with well-connected people. "I brought the Kubelwagen assigned to us."

The slight emphasis on 'us' didn't escape Hans. "Sergeant Bergmann said it would be quite a letdown after Major Minten's staff car."

"You've already seen the major, then."

"He came to the hospital to collect me."

Kramer managed to hold his surprise. So that was where Minten had gone. Most unusual for him to do anything like that himself, especially if it meant driving around the backwaters of northern France. But the 'suggestion' to get hold of Richter had come directly from Admiral Canaris, and the admiral didn't usually bother about that sort of detail either. Was Richter slated for bigger things in Abwehr? If he were, all the more reason to keep an eye on him. If Richter tried to get in the way... No. He wasn't going to let that happen, not now, not when he had Minten right where he wanted him.

Of course Minten had no idea of that, not yet, and he wouldn't, not until he had made Hauptmann, which should be soon, and the time was ripe. When that happened, Minten would be out. The Hamburg station needed a major, at least, in charge, but a Hauptmann would do, on a temporary basis, and when he showed them how well that place could be run, he'd make major and get the job in the bargain. But if Richter were around... Richter was already a Hauptmann. Due for promotion to major soon, unless he missed his guess. And so Kramer's smile was a bit forced as he said, "Then you have to be some sort of VIP. He rarely runs errands for himself, especially when he has so much else to do."

"It's nice to know that someone thinks I'm a VIP..."

Hypocrite, given the connections Richter had to have to the General Staff through that damn uncle of his... He thought about that. Did Minten think Richter was a ringer, sent to keep a close eye on things? The General Staff's own man in Abwehr? Political intrigue was bread and meat to Minten, and he was damn good at it. He'd hand Minten that, along with an appalling native shrewdness that seemed to bring him through almost anything. But not this time. He was going to beat that fat ass at his own game, and Richter as well, whatever his game might be and despite his connections. In fact, those connections were all the more reason to get and stay on his good side, if he had one. "Anyone with a Ritterkreuz is a VIP. There aren't many of those around."

Hans didn't know what to say, so he just shrugged, wishing he could put his finger on what it was he found odd in Kramer's attitude. It was almost as if he were waiting for something. But what?

"Where did you get it?

"Poland."

"Then you've been in for a while."

"Since 1937." And why all the questions? "What were you doing before the war?"

"I went straight into the Abwehr from the university, just before Poland. Herr Hauptmann," he paused briefly, "you look familiar.

Did you ever spend any time on an estate near Stettin?"

"As a matter of fact I did. Why?"

"I thought so. We met one summer, years ago. Birgid Brandt, nee Flade, is my cousin. I spent the summer with her family because my mother was ill. I remember you, Georg Brandt, of course, and your brother... James, isn't it?"

Hans had a feeling that he knew damn well it was James. "That's right."

"Yes." Kramer nodded, apparently satisfied that his memory had served. "The three of you used to ride over occasionally."

"More than occasionally. But you must have a remarkable memory. You'll have to forgive me, for I'm afraid I don't remember you at all."

"I'm not surprised." The words were bitter in his throat. "I spent most of my time with Birgid's younger brother Uwe. We're the same age." And none of you had time for either of us. "But I remember you because you had such an unusual accent, which you seem to have lost, by the way, and because you'd been so many different places." And because, you bastard, of the day when the three of you sat high and mighty on your horses laughing down at me as I sat in the mud puddle where my horse had deposited me. Uwe had been solicitousness personified, the fool. But stupid, kind Uwe was a Hauptmann already. A field promotion. He'd gone into the infantry. Ridiculous. It took years to build a power base in the infantry, if you ever could.

"Lieutenant Kramer?" What the hell was wrong with him?

"Sir?" He looked up. "Oh, sorry. Seeing you reminded me of that summer..." His voice trailed off.

"I said it was Georg Brandt who put this cast on."

"Georg? Where is he?"

"South of here. He heads a field hospital."

"Amazing coincidence."

"I thought so and so did he. But it was good to see him again."

"I was surprised when Birgid married him."

"Why?"

"His father. It wasn't politic."

"Since when was Birgid Flade ever concerned about doing the politic thing?"

That got an honest laugh. "You're right. But tell me, Herr Hauptmann, where is your mother these days? I remember her well. She came to Flade's for tea several times, and, forgive me, I thought she was the most beautiful woman I'd ever seen."

"You'd probably still think so. She's living in London." He sipped from the mug of tea that Madame Richard had brought in.

"London? What the hell is she doing there? She should have gone to her family in the United States, should go while she still can."

What was it about Richter's father? He leaned forward, speaking with condescending urgency. "Britain will have to capitulate when we finish off France and that shouldn't take long. Even if the British are stubborn and refuse...," he shrugged. "We'll simply finish them off as well. And when we do, it will be a bloody business and very dangerous for her." He leaned back and picked up his tea cup. "She's got to leave."

Pontifical ass. "She makes up her own mind. And anyway, I don't see what I can do. My letters take weeks to get there. They have to go through my aunt and uncle in the U.S. now."

Kramer thought about that. With Abwehr's connections, a more direct route shouldn't be too difficult to arrange. And if he could arrange it himself, before Richter thought to ask someone else, he could also arrange to read the letters, couldn't he? And if those letters happened to prove of interest... Besides, arranging it would put Richter in his debt and that in itself would make it more than worth the minimal trouble involved. "I'll be glad to see if I can arrange something more direct for you." His voice oozed importance.

Hans just looked at him thinking, and aren't we the lord of the manor, conferring special privilege on his minions, even if in this cast the minion happened to be a superior officer. "I'd appreciate that." He even smiled to hide his rising excitement, as it occurred to him that if by some odd chance Kramer could indeed arrange such a thing, he might be able to use the same pipeline for letters to 'Darling Julia,' as well. "But how could I hear back from her? Her letters would still take weeks" Could Kramer do it, or was he just trying to make himself look more important than he really was?

"I'm sure they could come back the same way." Good. Richter was pleased at the prospect. But wouldn't he be writing his father as well? Oh. Yes. "Birgid told me about your father. I'm sorry." That had to be why the mother had stayed on in England. Otherwise the whole family would have come back to Germany.

"Thank you. He had been ill for a long time."

"What's your brother doing?"

"Fighting in the Royal Navy." It still cost him to say that.

Kramer gave a low whistle. Better and better. That hadn't been in Richter's file. Didn't they know? "When did he join?"

"Last fall, after Poland."

"Fascinating. It wasn't too common for brothers to be fighting on the opposite sides during the American Civil War, but I can't imagine it in this one." He shook his head. "I'm glad that you at least chose the right side." He considered that for a moment. "Why did they let him join? He's German, isn't he?"

"Not now. He was born in England and that seems to have made a difference to him. He became a British subject several years ago."

Kramer snorted in disgust. "Weren't you born there, too?" He already knew the answer but it wouldn't do to let Richter know that.

"No. My parents came back to Berlin before the last war. I was born in Berlin."

"So you had no choice." Now what would he say to that?

"Even if I had, I'd have done nothing differently."

Clever reply.

Hans had had enough of this. "If you'll excuse me..." As he tried to push himself away from the table, the rear chair legs caught in the carpet and the chair tilted back. In his surprise, Hans overbalanced and had a moment of sheer panic before he came to a sudden stop, legs in mid-air, head against a firm stomach.

"It seems I came down just in time." There was relief in Dieter's voice.

"I seem determined to make rescuing me your life's work." There was a trace of nervous laughter.

"It's just that you haven't learned to live with that cast yet, sir."

"I wonder if I ever will. Lieutenant Kramer, this is Sergeant Bergmann."

"Sir." Dieter jerked his head into a stiff nod. They were indoors, so no salute was necessary, and besides, he had his hands full.

Kramer nodded back. "That was quick thinking, Bergmann."

"Thank you, Herr Lieutenant. That's what I'm here for."

"Just so. Just so." He rose. "Are we ready to leave? The Major wants us there by 1030, at the latest."

It took nearly a half an hour to work their way through the chaos of the war-torn roads, but finally the polychromatic brick Fort des Dunes was visible across the fields. The fields... Hans' heart was in his throat and he had to struggle to keep his face a mask as his eyes swept across the acres and acres of prisoners, a veritable sea of prisoners on both sides of the road, confined in open compounds by barbed wire and guards. Oh, God. It would take forever to get through all those men, and he didn't have forever if he was going to...

"It's a glorious sight, isn't it, Herr Hauptmann." Kramer was reveling in it. "And all of them to do with as we wish."

"Within the limits of the Geneva Convention, of course." Hans' tone was acid.

"Of course. Of course," he said in hasty agreement.

Hans was grateful when they arrived at the gate of the fort and he was spared the necessity of further conversation. The buildings and walls were pockmarked by shells and bullets and most of the windows were out. They were already being replaced.

They were through the gate and pulling up in front of what had to be the commandant's office. Dieter helped him out and he stood there waiting – for what he wasn't sure – dreading what was to come.

*   *   *

Hans looked gratefully around the small office assigned to him. It was a corner room and away from the wall around the fort, which meant that there were windows on two walls. And the west one was shaded by a tree that had miraculously survived, so he wouldn't have to contend with the afternoon sun. Despite a gentle cross breeze, sweat was pouring off him, and the skin under his cast itched unmercifully.

And it wasn't going to be as bad as he feared. The prisoners were being pre-screened, thank God, so it would be three weeks, four at the outside. Without that it would have been more like four months. Even the questioning he had to do sounded simple enough. Talk to them, simply talk, so that the important questions could be insinuated at the natural moment. They wanted him to get information about anything and everything, methods and sources of supply, home defenses, morale, tactics, order of battle, new weapons that hadn't been used in France, conditions and terrain in the area to Britain's south coast.

"We're hoping you can give us some useful information about that yourself, Richter," Minten had said. Hans had nodded, his heart pounding. He certainly could tell them a great deal about the south coast, the eastern section, anyway, and it was the southeast coast of England that should interest them the most. If he could just find out where they intended to land an invasion force...

Minten's wattle had flapped happily as he said, "Play on the theme that they were left behind, abandoned so that others could get away, especially their general officers. And while we're reasonably sure they left everything they have in the way of weapons on the beaches, we need to be certain. That's the priority. Home defenses are the second. But almost anything will help. You never know what will be important, the one piece that's the key to making the rest of the pieces fall into place."

The briefing had been something of a surprise, actually. Minten had conducted it himself, and though he tended to go on and on, he was an excellent organizer. A shrewd mind lurked behind those piggy eyes. Amazing. He really would have to be careful, far more careful even than he'd originally thought.

Thank God Dieter had agreed to act as guard in the room instead of the man Minten had wanted to foist on him. This was going to be difficult enough without having to worry about whether or not one of Minten's lackeys was reporting his every word. Minten had given in with bad grace, but he had given in. He'd had no choice, not after Hans had told him that he needed Bergmann close at hand to help him in case he had any physical problems, and since he was capable of acting as guard, as well, there was no sense wasting an additional man.

It was bound to be tedious for Bergmann, though, since he didn't speak a word of English. But he'd shrugged that off, saying he'd learn. He probably would, too, and fast.

There was a knock at the door. "Come!"

It was Dieter and he was carrying the machine pistol.

"Just keep it on single shot." Hans laughed. "In this room..." He waved his good arm in a sweeping gesture to emphasize his point. It was a small room.

It was then that Kugelmann came bustling in, carrying a holstered pistol in one hand and a clipboard in the other. He couldn't salute, but he tried. Hans was amused by his efforts.

"Good morning, Herr Hauptmann." He peered fussily at his watch. "I'm sorry. Actually, it's 'Good afternoon'." He looked up, satisfied. "Major Minten asked that I come in and take notes for you since your cast would make that difficult for you to do it yourself."

Hans all but groaned. So he was to have one of Minten's lackeys after all. "Thank you, Corporal. That will be a great help." Unfortunately, it would be.

"You're welcome, Herr Hauptmann. And Sergeant Bergmann, this is for you." He handed Dieter the pistol by the belt. "The major sent it in since you're to be our guard, and he wasn't sure you'd been issued a weapon. It's loaded, and you can pick up extra ammunition on the way out." He paused for a moment as he caught sight of the machine pistol in Dieter's hand, but then plunged on. "I trust you know how to use it."

Bergmann glanced down at it. "Of course. It's standard Wehrmacht issue. But I have this." He lifted the machine pistol that was in his other hand before giving the pistol back. Kugelmann took it with obvious distaste, went to the door and gave it to the guard in the hall.

In the meantime, Dieter had retired to a wooden chair in the corner, tilting it back as he checked the machine pistol, making sure it really was on single shot. Could he use it if he had to? This or any other weapon in a closed room, face to face with an unarmed man? He hoped he wouldn't have to find out. Surely just the threat would be enough.

"You speak English then, Corporal?" Hans broke the silence as Minten's driver pulled a chair up to the end of the table.

"Yes, Herr Hauptmann, along with French, Russian, and Italian."

Supercilious little ass. But he must have had an education. Then why wasn't he an officer? Hans shuddered at the thought. Kugelmann would be a disaster as an officer. But he was the perfect driver-clerk, a non-descript man of medium height with medium brown hair and gold-rimmed glasses that seemed a part of his medium face. "Doesn't the major need you?"

"Not this afternoon, Herr Hauptmann. But if he does, someone else will be sent in." Kugelmann was arranging the pens and paper to his liking and going about that simple task with such grim determination that Hans realized that he didn't want to be here anymore than Hans wanted him to be.

There was a knock at the door.

"Come!"

A bedraggled-looking man was propelled through the doorway, followed by a helmeted German soldier who saluted smartly. "I'll be outside if you need me, Herr Hauptmann."

"Thank you."

The soldier shut the door while the prisoner brought himself to rigid attention and stared out the window at a point over Hans' head.

Hans looked at him carefully. He was obviously exhausted and could be recognized as a British officer only by the tabs left on the shoulders of his filthy uniform. But at least he was clean shaven, or relatively so. The blue shadow on his jaw was balanced by a thatch of black hair and heavy black eyebrows.

"Name." Hans was startled to hear how harsh and guttural the single word sounded. It had been a long time since he had really spoken English.

"Henry Lloyd Kilpatrick, Captain, serial number 87468."

"Regiment?"

The man paused, collecting himself. "Henry Lloyd Kilpatrick, Captain, serial number 87468."

Hans glanced at a paper which Kugelmann slid in front of him. "It says here that you were one of the Royal Fusiliers captured at Nieuport."

The man said nothing.

"Nice to be left here so that the others could get away. What happened to your commanding officers?"

The man continued to stare out of the window, saying nothing, his mouth a set line.

Hans tried cordiality. "Sit down, Captain Kilpatrick. You look as if you're about to fall down."

He looked at Hans for a moment and then glanced around hesitantly, saw the chair almost behind him and sat down. "Thank you."

That was something at least. Hans reminded himself that the first one was the worst. There was nothing to compare it to. And there had been very few guidelines. "Now," he started again, "you are a Royal Fusilier. How long have you been in France?"

"Kilpatrick..."

"Look," Hans broke in, "let's make this easy for each other. We have to talk for a time. You're not delighted about it and neither am

I. It's hot in here, and this damn cast itches."

Kilpatrick sneered. "You have my heartfelt sympathy."

Hans refused to be offended. "Where are you from? Liverpool? Manchester?"

The man was surprised, caught off guard for a moment. "Bolton."

"Not too far off."

He looked at Hans closely. "How did you know that?"

"Your accent. I've been there, or close to there."

Kilpatrick drew himself to attention in the chair and stared past Hans' left ear, out the window again.

"Most of the BEF got away. You were abandoned, left here while almost everyone else went home."

"Someone had to hold the line so the rest could get away. We were elected, that's all."

"How lucky for you." It was Hans who was sneering now. "That's bloody marvelous."

He had the man's interest again. "Where did you learn to speak English like that?"

"I studied in England."

"Where?"

Hans told him and they were talking at last. Once Kilpatrick started, it was easy, at least in part. They talked about schools, food, football teams, film stars, but when it came to weapons, training, how and when he came to France, he said nothing. Hans got nowhere except for gaining a sense that morale wasn't low, at least this man's wasn't, despite his appearance. There was an element of pride that he had been part of helping to snatch the BEF from the closing jaws of the German juggernaut.

After about twenty minutes, Hans gave up and had the next man brought in. He was a tall, imposing-looking Scot who gave his name, rank, and serial number in a magnificent, unrestrained burr. He too refused to say anything beyond the fact that the bulk of the BEF had indeed gotten away and that they would be back to have another whack, sometime, somewhere. It was obvious that defeat rested uneasily on this man's shoulders and that he was supremely confident that both he and the British army would win in the long run.

In the brief interval between the time the Scot left and the next prisoner was brought in, Hans felt compelled to venture the opinion that he was likely to try to escape. Kugelmann nodded his agreement.

It was the third man who was nearly his undoing. He looked like trouble the moment he came through the door. He was tall, spindly, immaculate, arrogance personified, with a tight little mouth set under the pencil line of a moustache. He didn't even deign to even glance at Hans, preferring to stand at stiff attention, staring out the window. Damn that window anyway, thought Hans. They'd have to change the room around so that the prisoners were staring at a blank wall. But would it be worth it? If they did, he'd miss the cross breeze, faint as it was.

"Name?"

"George Ferraby-Smith, Major, serial number 27983."

Major. God. Either he'd been in longer than it looked as if he could have been or he had political clout. What a pleasure it would be to make this bastard spill his guts. The discovery that he felt that way didn't please him at all. "Sit down."

Not even his eyelids moved. "I would rather stand."

"Very well, but if you change your mind, the chair is there."

Curiosity must have gotten the better of the prisoner, for finally his eyes flickered over Hans, then moved left to Bergmann and right to Kugelmann before resting on Hans a second time. After a moment, he raised them and looked out the window again.

"Is something the matter, Major?" Hans made his voice ooze with solicitousness. "We like our prisoners to be... comfortable."

"That's a laugh. If that were the case, we wouldn't be out in an open field surrounded by barbed wire with no sanitary facilities and very little food."

"Give us time, Major. There are a lot of you."

"May I ask one question?"

Odd. Have to be careful not to lose the upper hand. But if he were given enough rope, he might hang himself. "Why not?"

"You know my name. What's yours?"

Kugelmann sucked in his breath between his teeth. Hans ignored him. "Richter, Johann, Hauptmann, serial number 337669"

There was a short nasty laugh. "I thought so." He sounded almost jubilant.

"Thought what?" Hans was genuinely puzzled.

"You know bloody well what. That that's your name. Don't play games with me. And why are you talking with that fake German accent? You speak the King's English at least as well as I do."

Dieter sat forward in his chair and fingered the machine pistol carefully. Something odd was going on here and he didn't like it. He didn't need to understand the actual words when the tone of voice was so clear.

Hans' reply was calm, even. "It isn't a fake accent. I've spoken very little English for almost four years."

"I think I shall sit down after all."

Kugelmann was startled. It was almost as if the prisoner was in control of the situation. He didn't like it, but at least it was interesting. The last two interviews had been deadly dull, and he cursed Minten again for getting him into it, and with barely five minutes warning. It seemed that the English-speaking guard who was to keep an eye on things had been replaced by Bergmann, and Minten had only just thought of this note-taking business. He should have thought of it at once. Richter obviously needed someone to do it but it should have been someone else, anyone else. This was a stenographer's work, and he'd be here tomorrow over his dead body.

Hans and the prisoner stared at each other until Ferraby-Smith broke the silence. "You traitorous little bastard."

Hans had to work hard to stay looking relaxed and amused in the face of such an onslaught.

Ferraby-Smith was openly sneering now. "You're a disgrace. I heard that you were in the German army, and when I heard it, it really made me laugh. You and that sanctimonious brother of yours always thought that you were too good for everyone, even though you were a snot-nosed little prick. But at least you've been paid off a bit." He made an obscene gesture toward the cast.

"You don't have your facts straight, I'm afraid, Major. I'm a German citizen and always have been. I'd be a traitor if I were fighting for your side. And listening to you and seeing you right now makes me very glad I'm not." For the moment that was perfectly true. "Just who are you, may I ask? And where am I supposed to have had the dubious pleasure of your acquaintance?"

Kugelmann watched avidly, all pretense of notetaking forgotten.

"Your brother and I were in the same form when you came up from the Lower School. You might remember me as Potter."

"Well, well. Potter Ferraby-Smith. How could I have forgotten. My, how you've grown. No wonder I didn't recognize you. And just how long have you been gracing the British army with your presence?"

"I went straight on into Sandhurst."

"And right into a cushy office job, I'm sure."

Ferraby-Smith reddened, for that's precisely what had happened. He denied it vehemently, saying that Ordnance was scarcely cushy.

"But if you were in Ordnance, how did you manage to get captured? You should have been retreating well ahead of the units you were supplying."

"Part of the unit got caught in a pocket. The colonel waited too long to move."

Hans looked at the information sheet. Amazing how efficient someone had been in the midst of the chaos of huge numbers of men surrendering. But the circumstances were a bit unusual. Ferraby-Smith had been caught in a Bedford truck along with two enlisted men and a whole load of objects d'art and antique silver. Where did he think he could go with that? "How many in your unit were caught?"

"Just the three of us," came the sullen reply. "The rest got away by leaving everything behind."

"And so you were caught because you were 'rescuing' silver and paintings. Just what an army needs. Your soldiers could always throw silver platters and candlesticks at us instead of shells. Did you plan to use the paintings for target practice?"

Ferraby-Smith looked positively apoplectic. "We were rescuing it, preserving it for posterity."

"The hell you were." Each word came out with studied venom. "You were looking out for your own posterity."

Dieter sat forward in the chair, his feet well under him, ready to move.

"You're the traitor," Hans went on. "You were derelict in your duty. You left the basic supplies an army needs for survival, abandoned them to the enemy, imperiled men in your charge just so you could make a financial killing. And on top of that, you fed on the misery and misfortune of others to rob them blind. No wonder the BEF was ill-prepared. With officers like you in charge of their weapons and ammunition, it couldn't be any other way. You haven't changed at all. You were always out for yourself, always got others to do your dirty work and then made them take the blame when something went wrong."

Hans was remembering it all now, how Ferraby-Smith had hazed him, had physically humiliated him in front of his friends and how glad he'd been to see James appear and beat Ferraby-Smith within an inch of his life. After that he'd been left alone, except that his clothes had been slashed and a dead rat left in his bed. The thought of that rat still got to him, even after all these years. He'd known who had done it, but he had no proof and even if he had, he was no squealer.

The prisoner was on his feet now, leaning on the table, almost screaming, not even hearing the click as Dieter released the safety on the machine pistol. The action had been automatic, and it didn't occur to Dieter to be surprised that he was ready and indeed willing to shoot this man if he so much as laid a finger on the Hauptmann.

"You're scum, Richter! Scum! You turned your back on the country that raised you and you call me a traitor and a crook? Just wait. We'll make mince-meat out of you yet and it would give me a great deal of pleasure to deal with you myself. We have weapons coming along that you've never dreamed of in your wildest imaginings."

It all came pouring out. Kugelmann was scribbling furiously thinking that these were scarcely weapons beyond anyone's wildest imaginings but still... Details of tanks under development, new types of artillery and on and on.

How had this man come by so much valuable information? Hans was appalled. But he sat there and listened in stony-faced silence until finally Ferraby-Smith stopped abruptly. Was he tired or had he finally realized what he was saying? "It's good to know that we may eventually have an enemy worthy of our mettle," he said with a little laugh. "But I can't imagine that it could be soon. You stripped yourselves for France and then had to leave it all behind on the beach. We'll use what we can and recover the metal for the rest, then run it or throw it right back at you. And even if you do indeed have anything left, let alone any of these new weapons coming along, I can't imagine where you think you're going to use it."

Ferraby-Smith tried to put on a knowing smile. He succeeded in looking sick. "You'll see." And then he tried to get off onto another track. "Why the black uniform? Are you SS? Can I expect to face the rack? I hear you boys are experts at that kind of thing."

"I'm in the Panzer Korps when I'm not in this cast. Our uniform is black, but it's not SS. And no, you don't have to worry about the rack. We don't need that with you. You've managed to give us everything we could hope to have without it."

Ferraby-Smith reddened visibly, and then, before any of them could move, flung himself across the table, grabbing Hans by the throat as they fell in slow motion toward Bergmann's feet. They landed in a heap, the prisoner on the floor in front of Hans who was on his right side with his cast both protecting his arm and rendering him helpless to defend himself.

Ferraby-Smith reached out, his fingers tightening around Hans' throat. He couldn't breathe. His ears were ringing and a grey mist was descending over his eyes. But then, suddenly, it was all over. The hands were wrenched from his throat and he was hauling air into his lungs in agonized gasps. There was a thud followed by an ominous crack, but he didn't hear it. All he heard was Dieter's frantic voice crying, "Herr Hauptmann! Herr Hauptmann! Are you all right?"

He could only nod as Dieter hunkered down, watching him anxiously, then relaxing a bit, content to let him recover himself for a moment.

A guard had burst through the door and was standing there, looking at the chaos in the room, dumbfounded. It was a moment before he saw the prisoner slumped against the wall, totally out of commission.

Kugelmann's eyes were glittering with pleasure. Now there was a man. What power! My God, it had been beautiful to watch. Bergmann had looked for all the world like an avenging angel, his face contorted with rage, the long scar on his cheek livid as he hauled that madman off Hauptmann Richter, turning the table over in the process. And then he had literally thrown the man in the opposite wall. Magnificent! Bergmann was just the sort... He shivered with pleasure and so it was a moment before he remembered himself enough to yell at the still dumbfounded guard.

"Get a medic and some stretchers!"

Kugelmann studied Ferraby-Smith critically as the guard rushed out. The man hadn't moved and he had the feeling that he never would again. His head was canted at a most peculiar angle. Messy business. He was glad that he didn't have to deal with that.

Dieter tried again. "Can you talk now, Herr Hauptmann?"

"I think so." Hans' voice was a croak. His throat was burning.

"Your shoulder."

Hans moved the fingers of his left hand experimentally. Odd. His shoulder didn't hurt. Of course he'd fallen on his right side but still, he must not have hit the floor very hard, or maybe he was just numb. "It's all right." He still couldn't recognize his voice as his own. "... sit up."

Then Dieter's hands were under his right side and he was being pivoted into a sitting position, leaning against the wall directly opposite Ferraby-Smith. Something about him looked odd. "See to him. I'm all right."

Kugelmann was busy gathering up his papers which were scattered all over the floor. "I don't think he needs to bother, Herr Hauptmann."

But Dieter was already on his feet. It was then that the medic rushed in and they all stayed silent as, guided by Kugelmann's pointing finger, he knelt by the prisoner. Dieter was holding his breath as the medic looked up. "He's dead. His neck's broken."

Kugelmann nodded, satisfied with his diagnosis. Too bad. The man had been a veritable gold mine.

Dieter turned away, looking out of the window without seeing anything. It had been so easy. He hadn't thought, just grabbed and threw. He'd never killed anyone in cold blood like that before. It had been bad enough in battle, but this...

"Up."

He looked down, and Hans saw that his face was bleak.

"Help me up, please."

Kugelmann was watching them with interest. Apparently this was the second time that Bergmann had saved his commander. Was there something in their relationship that could be used? He doubted it. Neither of them seemed the sort. But appearances could be deceiving. No, for once Minten was probably telling him the whole truth and it was just that he was worried about what Richter might be up to. With his connections... And that Bergmann of his...

He brushed the thought aside. Interesting, this British business. That would have to be looked into. There had been no mistaking Richter's flash of fury at the prisoner's vitriol. But then, no one likes to be called a traitor, even if it in no way applies.

Ferraby-Smith's body was on a stretcher and halfway out the

door. Hans concentrated on Dieter's face, not wanting to watch.

"Let's get out of here. I need some air."

Dieter looked back at him anxiously. "Are you sure you are all right?"

"Right enough for that, at any rate."

It was even odds who was helping whom the more when they walked down the hall. Major Minten bustled out of his office just in time to urge Hans to take the rest of the day off, to go back to the house and lie down. But that was the last thing Hans wanted to do. It would have given him too much time to think.

"Thank you, Herr Major. I just need to sit outside for a bit. We'll go back in when things have been put right."

The major nodded slowly then turned to Dieter, saying "I can see the Hauptmann knew what he was doing when he asked that you act as his guard. You did well."

"Thank you, sir." Dieter's voice was flat, his face set.

"Go. Go and sit. I'll have some beer sent out."

Neither man spoke until they were in chairs that had been set out under the tree next to their office window.

"You all right, Bergmann?" Hans kept his voice low.

"Yes, Herr Hauptmann." He was looking at the ground.

"That was close. I'd have been done for if you hadn't acted so quickly."

Dieter didn't look up. "It's different with a man you've seen, when he's not fighting you."

"Too personal," said Hans sadly.

Dieter went on as if he hadn't heard him. "Your face was turning blue and I couldn't shoot. You were too close together." He gave a great shuddering sigh. "I was afraid he was going to kill you."

"So was I."

They sat in silence for a moment before Hans cleared his throat and said, "He was a school classmate of my brother James."

"A friend?" Dieter was horrified.

"Scarcely. But I didn't realize... It was a long time ago. I must have been about ten. James beat the hell out of him in front of a group of my friends when he caught him hazing me unmercifully. I was in a very bad way at the time."

"Then he'd spent his life asking for it."

"Yes, he did, and I'm afraid that he got it this time. I'm just sorry that you were the one to give it to him. Helpless people were his meat. He always picked on Lower Formers. The last time I saw him was in 1936, just briefly before I came back here. I'd forgotten about it until now. He was just as nasty then, but I thought it was because he was drunk. But he couldn't have been that drunk if he recognized me in a place like this. I certainly didn't recognize him. A major." Hans shook his head. "No wonder Britain's in trouble."

Dieter took a deep breath. His hands were shaking and he crossed his arms to hide it. "Kugelmann was writing furiously. I assume he had a lot to say."

"An amazing lot. It's hard to believe that someone like this was trusted with that kind of information."

Kugelmann's head appeared out the window. "We'll have everything ready in a few minutes, sir. Are you sure you want to go on?"

A guard appeared with two bottles of beer. "Yes. As soon as we're done with these." He turned to Bergmann. "All right?"

He nodded.

"You're sure?"

"It'll be good to have something to do."

They drank the beer in silence and were walking around the corner of the building when Dieter collided with a hurrying figure.

"Out of my way, dammit."

Dieter jumped back and snapped to attention. One didn't often literally run into a general. "Excuse me, sir."

"Uncle Karl! This is a surprise!"

"Oh, there you are, my boy. Just arrived. Wanted to see you. Major Minten told me what happened. Frantic. Had to see if you were all right." He turned to Dieter. "Sorry, Sergeant."

"That's all right, sir."

"General von der Greif, may I present my... aide, Sergeant Dieter Bergmann."

Bergmann delivered a smart salute which the General returned before offering his hand, shaking Dieter's warmly. "So you're the one. Quick action. Thank you."

"There was nothing else to be done."

"But you did it. That's what counts."

"I didn't mean to kill him."

"Yes. That was unfortunate. Apparently he had a lot to say. Too bad. But as you said, there was nothing else to be done." He turned back to Hans. "Are you all right?"

"Fine. Just a little sore in the throat."

"Lucky if that's all, under the circumstances. Everything else all right?"

"Except for this." He gestured toward his cast.

"Very sorry to hear about that. But Wehrmacht's loss is Abwehr's gain. I dined with Admiral Canaris the night I heard about it and he was most interested in you. Despite the cast, you're going to have an important and continuing role to play."

"I'm glad to hear it."

"I thought you would be."

Hans hesitated, then asked, "Admiral Canaris. Is that how I got here?"

"The major didn't tell you?"

"No, sir, he didn't." Interesting. So he'd been right. It had been Uncle Karl's fine hand. Uncle Karl and Admiral Canaris. The General Staff and Military Intelligence. And the only continuing way in which he could be of help to Abwehr was with information about Great Britain. Continuing. That was the word. If he really could continue with Abwehr... If they wanted the information he could give them about the southeast coast and a great many other things, then there was bound to be some way he could find out what they were planning vis a vis Britain. And if he could get that information to Michael, the damn cast might prove to be worth its weight in gold.

"... all right?"

"I'm sorry, Uncle. What did you say?"

"I asked if you were sure you're all right. Not like you to drift off like that."

Hans smiled wanly. "It's been a difficult day."

"Too tired for a little dinner out?"

Little dinner? Hans almost laughed. Uncle Karl liked to dine well, very well. "Not at all."

"2100?"

"I'll be there. Where?"

"Seaside villa. Escaped the onslaught. Lovely place. Only here a couple of day, so glad we can have dinner together tonight. I'll have my driver give the sergeant a map."

"I'll look forward to it."

"So will I, my boy. It's been too long. Anxious to hear the details of the campaign. It's going very well in the south. Should be all over before too long." He shook his head in wonder. "Never would have believed we could do it so easily."

"Neither would I."

"Well, we are." They shook hands and the general returned Dieter's salute once more. "Thank you again, Sergeant Bergmann."

"Certainly, sir." He didn't know what else to say.

Uncle Karl turned and left, almost as rapidly as he had come.

# Chapter VI

James caught himself humming. Ridiculous. Here it was, middle watch, the black of night and he was conning the ship and humming that idiotic ditty. The trouble was that the fool thing kept running through his brain and wouldn't leave him alone.

> *A capital ship for an ocean trip was the* Walloping Window Blind.

Preposterous name for a ship. The whole song was preposterous.

> *No wind that blew dismayed her crew nor troubled the Captain's mind.*

Whoever had written that had certainly never been in a North Atlantic gale, especially during the winter.

> *The man at the wheel was made to feel contempt for the wildest blow-oh-oh.*
> *Though it often appeared when the gale had cleared, he was down in his bunk below.*

Even bunks weren't any help. If, by some miracle the ship didn't broach without someone at the wheel, the man wouldn't have got much rest. He never had in a blow, half soaked, lashed to his bunk.

He checked the gyro-compass. On course.

The song continued to run mercilessly through his brain, on into the chorus:

> *Then blow ye winds, hi ho. A roving I will go. I'll sail no more from England's shore.*

That part seemed true enough for the moment. No more Atlantic, at least for now. They were escorting convoys and patrolling the Channel off Dover. That was England's shore in spades. It was the English Channel, after all, and he really was English now, thank God, both by birth and now by choice. Officially. He sighed.

But it would never be official enough in some quarters, would it. Not as long as this war lasted anyway. It had been pretty grim when he'd come to *Vectis*. The knowledge had preceded him. Knowledge about John. Stillson, of course. And was it Stillson who had heated everything up again at Dunkirk? His hands tightened on the binnacle and he forced himself to check the compass even as he encouraged the song to run on to its illogical conclusion.

> *So let the music play-ay-ay. I'm off on the morning train*
> *to cross the raging main*
> *I'm off to my love with a boxing glove, ten thousand*
> *miles away.*

Was that the line he had been waiting for? If it was maybe the fool song would leave him alone. But was she his love?

Ridiculous again. After only three evenings together in London, how could she be? He smiled. They had been marvelous evenings. Late. They had danced and laughed and talked on and on, talked in a way he'd never been able to talk to anyone before.

She had been so... what was the word? Upset? Not quite right, but close. The best he could do. She had been upset about John. He didn't know why he'd assumed she had to know everything about him, including where he was now, where he'd been for the past four years, but she hadn't known, and it had obviously been a shock. But there had been none of the condescending pity that made it so difficult to say to so many people. And certainly none of the self-righteous sneering. Stillson... Jesus.

The scene flashed before his eyes with the same nightmare quality it had at the time. A Liverpool pub. Stillson's face red, sweating as he told James with malicious pleasure about a 'Dutch-boy' friend of both of theirs who had run into John in Berlin a few months before. "You have a brother to be proud of, Richter. He's a Hauptmann now." He spat out the German word gleefully. "And he's wearing a Ritterkreuz. You know, Richter," he had leaned across the table at this point, unctuous in the extreme, "they don't hand those out to just anyone. Your mother must be so proud of her baby boy."

That had done it. James had risen and reached across, grabbing Stillson by his lapels, almost dragging him onto the table, sending drinks flying. If Colin hadn't stopped him, he'd have been for it. Striking a superior officer was a court martial offense. But what pleasure it would have been to have shoved those big white teeth right down Stillson's throat. Almost worth it.

The next day, when he'd been called into the captain's harbor cabin, the Old Man had been kindness itself but firm. There was to be no more of that sort of thing. He would not have his officers engaging in barroom brawls, especially with each other, no matter what the provocation. They had Germans to fight, and they couldn't do that effectively if they were fighting each other, as well. Besides, what kind of example was that for the men? He was right, of course.

Then Fredericks had gone on. "I can only imagine the hell you've been through over this business with your brother. It can't be easy, having him on the other side." Then he had stopped, tapping his fingers on his desk before he finally went on. "I was curious." He looked and James squarely. "About your brother. About the sort of person he was, about why he would have chosen to fight for Hitler."

James stood, stony-faced, looking out the scupper over the Old Man's head.

"And so I asked some people I thought might know, but all I got for my pains was a lot of head shaking." He said it angrily.

"No one understands it. No one who really knew him, that is. They all say he's not the sort."

"He's not, sir?" James' voice was tight. "Then why the hell – begging your pardon – is he doing it?"

Fredericks ignored that. "Is he the sort to fight for Hitler?" His voice was still angry. "Be fair. Is he?"

"I wouldn't have thought so." James had turned sullen. "But as I said, that's what he's doing, and the thing speaks for itself."

Fredericks gave up at that point and let him go, but the question the Old Man asked and his own answer had run on and on through James' brain. John wasn't the sort to fight for Hitler. He had almost never fought, but when he did it had always been for the underdog, and, he admitted grudgingly, he had fought hard, tenaciously and without consideration for the odds, which were too often against him.

Because of that, as much as for any other reason, he had hated what was happening in Germany. Those brown-shirts stomping Jews in the streets, literally stomping people with those damn jack boots they wore. Did John wear jack boots himself now? The mental picture of John in Hamburg, in his uniform, came to his mind's eye. No. Jack boots had to be for enlisted men because John wore a different sort. But then John's uniform wasn't the standard field grey, was it. No. It was black. It would have been bad enough to have seen him in a Wehrmacht uniform, but to see him in SS black... He had been prepared to be civil for Mother's sake, but that had torn it. Jesus.

Mother. It had been Stillson's mentioning Mother that had done it and she was the worst part of it all. Rather what John had done to her was. First Father dying, then John going off like that...

Annabelle had met John. Just once in Michael's office right after Father had died. And because she had, somehow he'd started talking about John, about the good times, remembering him as he hadn't remembered him in a long time. Those summers in Prussia with John and Georg Brandt, when they'd ripened like wild men. And Birgid Flade. He gave a little laugh. What had happened to Birgid Flade?

The laugh turned to a sigh. What had happened to all of them? But especially what had happened to little brother John of Prussian summers, Lake Erie summers, the Isle of Wight, school days when he had to fight that ass Ferraby-Smith, who'd had John as close to tears as James had ever seen him. John never cried. As little as he'd been, John had been tough, and he'd never let anyone know how rough things were for him. But James had known. James had always known.

Stop it, he told himself. It's no use. That John is gone. This John is SS, and SS bastards don't have a rough time. They only give them.

He came back to himself and looked around. This was no time to be standing around wool-gathering. He had a ship to conn. He checked the gyro-compass and then his watch. Course change in two minutes. This was so much easier than keeping station on a convoy in the Atlantic at night. Any convoy anywhere at night. But a convoy would be coming through their sector soon. It should be starting through in about twenty minutes, if they were on schedule. But there'd be no station-keeping, even then. *Vectis* was to sweep ahead, to make sure there were no U-boats lying about. Not that they'd seen any yet.

But he was sure to see Annabelle. Tomorrow. She was coming down to Dover with Michael. He frowned. Was she seeing him because she happened to be in Dover or because she really wanted to see him? It was hard to tell. Letters were so damn unsatisfactory. At least she'd signed the last one 'Yours'. Progress of sorts.

But was she his? Could she ever be? Did he want her to be? Or was that 'Yours' simply convention. 'Yours Sincerely' was the way business letters were signed and American business letters were often signed 'Yours Truly'. Powerful declarations, if you took them literally, which no one ever did. Ridiculous to think this way. It was getting him nowhere. And he'd know more tomorrow, when he saw her. No. Today by now. His heart gave a lurch.

Why was Michael coming to Dover anyway? It was a restricted area. People were leaving Dover, not coming. And what would the foreign office want in Dover anyway? Unless... The labyrinths cut into the chalk under that ancient castle? But that was Intelligence. Scarcely Foreign Office. So unless there was more to that job of Michael's than met the eye...

James checked his watch then bent down to the voice pipe. "Starboard 20."

"20 starboard wheel on, sir," came back the hollow-sounding voice of the helmsman and the ship started to turn.

He watched the compass carefully. "Midships."

"Midships," came back the faithful echo.

There was a flash. James swiveled as Riker, the port lookout called, "Star shell off the port quarter, sir."

James bent down to the voice pipe to the captain's tiny sea cabin just below the bridge, where Fredericks was sleeping.

"Captain, sir."

"Yes?"

"Star shell off the port quarter. Has to be trouble with the convoy."

"Sound the alarm. I'll be right up."

James released the alarm button as the captain appeared, then stepped off the compass platform to make way for him. The captain's mouth was at the voice pipe even before he was set and the ship began to turn. The rest of the signal contingent was pounding onto the bridge followed by Hicks, the ASDIC rating. James had retreated to his action station at the side of the bridge next to the ASDIC cabinet, hoping it wouldn't be the inaction station it usually was.

The engines were throbbing and the deck plates vibrated under his feet as they raced back and forth toward the convey. More star shells had appeared on the horizon; faint lines of tracer were visible, and there was the dull boom and flash of guns firing.

"Must be those damn E-boats we've been hearing about." Fredericks' tone was casual. Maddening the time it took to get there. The rigging was singing now as they rushed to come up southeast of the convoy and cut off the line of retreat for whoever and whatever was attacking the convoy.

There was an explosion and a sheet of flame added its orange light to the brilliant white of the star shells. Someone had got it. James cursed under his breath, hoping against hope that it was an E-boat.

"They're laying smoke." Fredericks adjusted the course, then spoke to the lookouts. "Watch carefully. There are some of our motor gun boats with the convoy. Don't want to shoot up our side if we can help it." The captain's brain was racing. The first ones out of the smoke would undoubtedly be German. It had to be E-boats, and a lot of them, to create all of this.

They were running northeast now, just south of the smoke-screen and parallel to it, wary of entering it unannounced, planning to use the element of surprise as the E-boats came out, running for home.

Fredericks looked into the smoke, willing something, anything to appear. Don't give it away by firing a star shell. Damn E-boats were fast and maneuverable and there were the torpedoes they carried. He shuddered. What just one torpedo could do to this precious old ship of his... Caution. Caution. The trouble was that there hadn't been too much opportunity to drill for action against small boats. It hadn't been necessary in the Atlantic and there had been so little time since. But two days ago they had taken the time. He prayed that they all remembered their lessons well.

The arc was almost complete when Riker, the port lookout, sang out, "Bow wave. Red 3-Oh. Range 1,000."

Fredericks let the turn continue until they were headed to intercept. Then he shouted, not bothering to bend down to the voice pipe again, "Wheel amidships!... Meet her!... Full ahead together!"

The E-boat was silhouetted against the glow of the convoy's star shells made of the smoke screen. Why hadn't they been seen? Was the E-boat's night vision still affected by the star shells? Or was *Vectis*' silhouette obscured by the black gloom of the night sky? No matter. Whatever it was, it was Jerry's tough luck. Close enough.

"Guns! Fire as you bear!"

Had he left it too late? The E-boat was veering away. And then the ship lurched as both fore and aft 4.7's fired. Deafening. If it weren't for this fading light of the star shells, the muzzle flash would have blinded him. More light. They needed more light. "Star shells!" No need to worry about the element of surprise while their guns were blazing away. There was a sharp bang and the shell was away, followed a moment later by a white brilliance lighting the night.

Then the continued muzzle flash from the 4.7s was accompanied by strings of tracer from the starboard pom-pom and Oerlikon.

The E-boat was weaving, running hell-bent for home, not even bothering to fire. Out of torpedoes or just cautious? It didn't matter, for suddenly there was a powerful explosion, a yellow flash, and the E-boat was gone, blown out of the water.

"Cease fire!" Fredericks shuddered in the midst of his elation. It would be a miracle if they found any survivors after that.
But there was no time to think about it, for Riker was shouting, "E-boat bearing Red 9-5." Thank God Riker hadn't yielded to the temptation of watching the E-boat go up.

James froze. The E-boat was coming right at them. Nothing he could do but stand there and watch as *Vectis* strained to turn stern to, the fastest way to comb the tracks of the torpedoes James knew would come. There was no other reason for the E-boat to charge and charging she was.

"Guns! Fire as you bear!" The ship was running straight now. Bow to would have meant presenting *Vectis* broadside to the E-boat for a time during the swing. But stern to... Harder to see. Harder to judge. But by damn, if anyone could do it, Fredericks could.

X and Y guns and the Oerlikons, the only guns that could bear, were firing furiously, but James didn't even notice. All he saw were the V-plume splashes made by two torpedoes as they were loosed through their bow tubes. He was sweating despite the breeze. Oh, God, for something to do. Anything.

He heard Frederick's shout "Hard aport!" The waiting... But that was all any of them could do for the moment, except Colin, lucky Colin, in the gun control tower. This was his show, his and Gunner's and the men manning the guns. They wouldn't have time to think about those white foam trails in the water.

The ship was turning sharply now. Sharply enough? Oh, God. Frederick's hands were wet as he leaned forward on the gyro-compass. Why couldn't he have been bow on? It was all he could do to stand there. Would they make it?

Even as he shouted, "Wheel amidships!" the port lookout's

voice rang out. "Two torpedoes passing close off the port quarter."
Fredericks almost laughed with relief.

The E-boat was gone. "Cease fire!" They had been extremely
lucky to get one; two would have been a miracle. There wasn't
much chance of hitting such a small, maneuverable, fast-moving
target, especially at night. Gun control on these old ships was far
too primitive for night gunnery to be anything but a very chancy
proposition.

"Corvette coming out of the smoke screen, red 1-4-5."

"Challenge." Better let them know who *Vectis* was right away.
God knows what could happen in this melee with the smoke still
obscuring everything. He didn't want to be the victim of an itchy
trigger finger.

The corvette winked a reply and then turned to starboard as
*Vectis* continued on, putting them on diverging courses, parallel to
the dissipating smoke screen.

"Two E-boats, dead ahead!" Riker and Aiken spoke almost as
one.

"Star shell! Guns! Fire as you bear!" My God, were there no
other orders to give? At least they were running towards the boats
this time.

Only the forward 4.7's could bear and they were fairly spitting
shells off into the gloom. But the E-boats had turned stern to and
were weaving as they ran for home and mother, shells nipping at
their heels until finally they disappeared into the darkness.

"Cease fire!"

Incredible. The smoke was clearing and there was the convoy,
steaming along peacefully, creating the illusion that they had been
oblivious to the chaos that had surrounded them. But Fredericks
knew how deceptive that was and wondered, not for the first time,
how the merchantmen could do it, convoy after convoy, holding
formation and keeping speed as if nothing was happening. Waiting,
just waiting for it to be their turn while they could do little to defend
themselves, except make sure that they stayed on course and held
position so their defenders would know where they were.

*Vectis* ran back to check for survivors among the wreckage of the E-boat, but a trawler was there ahead of them.

"Thanks for the timely assist and congratulations," flashed from the bridge of the escort commander.

"Glad to be of service and thanks," flashed back and they were gone, sweeping ahead of the convoy again as more ammunition was brought from the magazine.

It was near dawn before the convoy was out of their sector and they were able to secure from action stations. Time to go home. Fredericks considered that. How many "homes" had he had since he'd been in the Navy? And now 'home' was Dover, at least for the time being.

*     *     *

They entered the harbor with a flourish and securing to the buoy was a study in perfection. The buoy jumper didn't even get his feet wet. It was that sort of morning.

James studied the small stones that made up the walls of the ancient Dover Town Hall, wondering how on earth long it had taken to build it in such a fashion. Time and patience. That's what the builders had had. Both were in short supply these days, especially patience. His most of all.

He consulted his watch. Five more minutes until...

And then he looked up and saw her coming toward him. How could she possibly be more beautiful than he remembered?

Finally, she saw him as well and smiled. His knees turned to jelly.

Despite her smile she was dismayed. What had the navy been doing to him? He looked so tired. And then he was smiling back and she forgot everything but her pleasure at seeing him again.

Damn it, he thought, I don't know what to say.

"James, it's so very good to see you."

And it was easy to reply, "You have no idea how good it is to see you. Where shall we go?"

"How long do you have?"

"Until nine tonight. And you?"

"I'll have to ring up Captain Compton after tea to see if he needs me for anything more. He doubted he would. And if he doesn't... It would depend on when the evening train leaves for London."

"Then we have time. We could go up to the Grand but I don't think it's much of a place for a tete-a-tete with the Navy in town."

"Is that what we're to have, a tete-a-tete?"

"I certainly hope so."

"Then why don't we just walk until we find a place that suits? I've been sitting all day."

He nodded and they started down the street, a careful foot apart. She cast furtive glances at his profile. Why doesn't he look at me? What's happening to us? "A bad night?" Oh, why did my voice have to sound so shrill?

"Bad enough," he snapped. "Let's not talk about it." That was the trouble. Not only can't I tell her what happened last night, but I can't even ask her what she's been doing all day.

But somehow, finally, they were talking, even if it was only the aimless chatter of two acquaintances who had been thrown together after not having seen each other in a long time.

But even that failed them when they'd found a place and were settled at a small table across from each other, staring at their respective menus in silence.

After a moment, she shut hers and put it carefully on the table. "James... how are you?

He was annoyed by the concern in her voice. "Fine. Why?"

"You seem... You look a little frazzled," she said carefully.

He studied her over the top of his menu, really looking at her for the first time since they started walking. "This war is enough to frazzle anyone. But it doesn't seem to have frazzled you." He gave a nervous little laugh. "You look bloody marvelous." With that his face turned bright red.

She was enchanted, both by the compliment and the blush that went with it. "Thank you."

James shook his head. "You're absolutely maddening. The Wicked Witch of the West. You've cast some sort of spell that has turned me into a blushing school boy."

"Oh, yes, that new film, *The Wizard of Oz*." She paused, eyes twinkling, then, "Goodness, James, she was a very wicked woman who caused no end of trouble for everyone, if I recall correctly."

"You do." He sat back in his chair laughing. "Just as you seem to be causing me no end of trouble at the moment."

"And am I worth all this... trouble?"

He grinned. "I haven't decided yet."

Her left eyebrow went up. "And just when do you plan to let me know?"

"After I see," he said airily, "just how much trouble you continue to make for me."

And then at last they were laughing and it was as if they'd never been apart. They talked on and on about everyone and everything, barely noticing the arrival of tea and biscuits, consuming everything without realizing they had.

She called Captain Compton and was told that he had left a message for her, saying that she would not be needed and that he would see her in London early tomorrow afternoon.

And so they walked and talked some more, heading slowly for the Dover Priory station to see about train times, not really caring where they were, just caring that they were together.

After leaving the station, they walked up towards the cliffs until the way was barred by a barbed wire perimeter. Even that couldn't spoil the mood. They simply strolled back toward town. As they reached a small copse just above a stone church, he took her hand and pulled her along a path into the overhang of the trees. There were people coming and going along the streets, even up here, and he wanted to be alone with her, really alone without anyone to see them. Someone must have enjoyed this copse regularly because there was a low bench in a little clearing beside the path. He stopped and suddenly it was awkward again. She looked away and was turning to sit on the bench when a small branch snapped under her foot, twisting her ankle just enough to throw her off balance.

He caught her just as she would have fallen and the touch of her solved the problem. His mouth was hard on hers and after the briefest start of surprise, she was kissing him back, relishing the warmth of him, the giddy sense of surrendering to the power of the arms that held her. And then she was rubbing her cheek against the rough wool of his uniformed shoulder, feeling his face in her hair.

"You are indeed the Wicked Witch of the West." His voice was hoarse.

"Am I that evil?"

"No, that bewitching."

She pulled back and looked up at him, smiling. "How could an ugly old witch be bewitching?"

He nodded slowly. "What was the beautiful Good Witch of the North?"

"Glinda?"

"Glinda. Frightful name. But that's the idea."

"What would happen if I were to wave my magic wand?"

"Whatever your heart desires. It's your wand to wave."

"What's your heart's desire?"

"If you keep me trapped in this wilderness..." James gestured broadly toward a house that was just visible through the trees, but he couldn't go on. It was that word, desire. He held her to him fiercely.

The feeling was sweeping over her again, the sense of restrained power, the sure feeling that James was a man to contend with. No one had ever given her that feeling before, and despite her happiness, she was a little afraid.

He felt her tremble and asked with a voice full of concern, "Darling Annabelle, what's wrong?"

Her voice was muffled against his shoulder. "Say that again, please, James."

He released her slightly, but she didn't lift her head from his shoulder, so he had to bend down to her ear. "Darling Annabelle?"

Only then did she lift her head and look at him directly. "Am I your darling Annabelle?" The tone was light, almost bantering. She had worked hard to keep it that way.

The question had caught him by surprise. He brushed a stray hair from her forehead, playing for time, the steadiness of her gaze holding him until there was a sudden realization that there was only one answer. He wouldn't be running for sea room this time. "Yes. Yes you are." He had said it slowly. "Or at least I hope you are." He paused. "Are you?" His heart was pounding so hard and fast that he was sure she must feel it.

"Do you want me to be?"

"Yes, damn it. Yes. You aren't making this easy."

"Why should I? I love you."

He was transfixed. But she had looked away, trembling, terrified that she had ruined everything. Why had she said it? She hadn't meant to, hadn't even known that she loved him until she'd said it. Oh, God, James say something.

"What did you say?" His voice was harsh.

She stared at a twig on the ground and shook her head.

He was almost rough as he took her face in his hands, forcing her to look at him, demanding, "Say it again. I want to make sure... of what you said."

Her tears blinded her to the anguish in his face and it was only the force of him that made her say, viciously, angrily, "I love you."

He held her to him, afraid that the fragile moment would explode in his face. "Annabelle...," he drew a deep breath, "I love you, too." He liked the sound of it. In fact, he liked it so much that he said it again, louder this time. "I love you, Annabelle Trimby." And then he was laughing so hard that he had to let her go and she was left standing there, looking at him, bemused. Who could resist him? She certainly couldn't.

James slumped onto the bench and sat there shaking his head. "It's the war."

That made no sense at all. "You love me because of the war?"

"No, no. Certainly not. That's the best reason I can think of not to fall in love with anyone. It's just that without the war, it might have taken us months to get where we are."

She nodded slowly.

He stood. "In fact it may be one of the very few good things to come out of this whole bloody business." And then he was holding her gently, relishing her face for a moment before he leaned down to kiss her. It seemed as if he would never get his fill as he kissed her again and again.

She was reeling, drunk with happiness.

But finally he stood, just holding her loosely against him, quiet for a time before he took her hand and led the way back to the street. There seemed to be no need to speak and they walked in contented silence down the hill past houses that were shuttered, their occupants evacuated. It was only when they were half way down that he started laughing again.

"James, what is so funny?"

"I was just thinking that I really am my mother's son. If it weren't for this damn uniform, I'd be doing cartwheels down the street."

She laughed at the thought. "What possible difference could your uniform make here?"

"A little matter of 'Conduct Unbecoming of an Officer', even here."

"I think it would be most becoming. But what has your mother got to do with it?"

"It's just the sort of thing she'd do."

"Your mother?" Mrs. Richter seemed the embodiment of fragile elegance.

"My mother, indeed. I'll never forget last summer when she took Michael rowing on the Serpentine, and I mean she did the rowing."

"You saw them?" Annabelle couldn't quite believe it.

"No, but I was home when they got back. Apparently some elderly social lioness saw them and was scandalized by the proceedings. They were still laughing about it."

She tugged at his hand to stop him. Her eyes were shining. "Can you do cartwheels?"

James did not hesitate. "Come on." He pulled her after him up the nearest sidewalk.

"Where are we going?"

"To teach you not to doubt me."

She was breathless, laughing as she struggled to keep up with him. How could she ever have thought him a bit... what? ... staid?

And then they were at the rear of the house, on a brick walkway that surrounded the smaller overgrown garden. James looked again toward the street – no one was in sight – then turned back, trying to be serious as he paced off the narrow strip of tall grass between the house and the weed-filled flower garden. He stopped at the fence on the far side and took off his jacket, carefully hanging it on a post which he then topped with his cap. Neither of them had said a word.

She was waiting, not always able to contain her laughter.

"I'm ready," he said.

"All right."

"Give me the word."

"Which word?"

"There are a great many words I'd like you to give me, but for now I'll settle for 'On your mark'."

She composed herself and tried to look official. "Ready... On your mark... Get set... Go!"

There were two cartwheels in rapid succession followed by a bounding leap into a handspring that brought him up almost before her, teetering dangerously. He was laughing as he recovered himself, a bit breathless, hair standing on end, enormously pleased with himself and therefore utterly irresistible. She was laughing with him as he caught her up in his arms.

"Will you ever doubt me again?"

"Never."

"I really do love you. Can you believe it?" The question was as much for himself as for her. He was having trouble believing the extent of it himself.

"I told you I would never doubt you again, and so since you say you do, I have to believe you. But it's hard."

"It shouldn't be."

"James," she had turned serious. "I wish I could explain it to you, why it's so hard to believe. Maybe it's because everything has happened so fast. Maybe it's the war, as you say. After all, it was only three weeks ago that you dropped into my life, a totally unexpected and wonderful present. I hadn't even expected to enjoy that evening.

"There was nothing else for it, of course. We were together for the next two evenings, wonderful evenings, before you had to leave. And after you left, I wondered if you were real or if I'd dreamed it all. But there were the letters. They had to be coming from someone, but it was still hard to realize that you weren't just a delightful figment of my imagination.

"And the letters were a problem because I wasn't sure how I felt and I certainly didn't know how you felt. When Captain Compton asked me to come down here with him... It's really all his doing that I'm here. He didn't really need me. Any clerk could have done what I did for him." She smiled.

"I think he wanted me to see you."

"I'll send him a dozen roses."

"After this, I have no doubt you will."

"I'm glad to see that you've learned your lesson so well. Go on."

"And here we are. You're real, very real indeed, and I suddenly find that I love you, love you as if I never knew the meaning of the word before.

"That's astounding enough. But to find that you love me..."

He was holding her to him. "I know. I know."

"Do you really?"

"Of course. You're telling my side of it, too."

"And then to have you turning cartwheels over me." Her smile was a bit wicked. "Now, that is beyond a girl's wildest dreams."

He was laughing as he hugged her, hard. "Cheeky. That's what you are. Damn cheeky. Making light of my valiant efforts on your behalf."

"Make light of your magnificence? Never."

He grinned. "I was magnificent, wasn't I?"

"Absolutely."

"But it was 'Conduct Unbecoming an Officer'." He shook his head in mock solemnity.

"I think it was very becoming."

"Then you really are an evil influence. Cartwheels, trespassing, kissing you in broad daylight? Definitely 'Conduct Unbecoming an Officer'."

"Wicked Witch of the West?"

"Definitely."

"Not Glinda?"

"Definitely not. She wouldn't lead me astray."

"You're right."

"I'm always right."

"And the sooner I recognize that fact the better?"

"Absolutely."

"My lord and master?"

"Absolutely. Now that's the way I like to hear you talk. It's good to be given my proper due at last." They walked over to the post where he had left his cap and jacket.

She stopped him as he reached for his cap. "Wait, oh 'lord and master'. Your handmaiden is here to serve you."

"Blessings on thee, oh lovely handmaiden."

She stuck his cap on his head at a rakish angle and then helped him into his jacket.

"The cap. Adjust the cap. Good grief, woman. I can't walk down the street like this!" He managed to look horrified.

"Aye, aye, sir." She adjusted the cap, eyed it critically, adjusted it again then walked around him twice before pronouncing him, "Lovely."

"Lovely? Lovely? A 'lord and master' is scarcely lovely!" He was looking down at her, and the sight of her face put a lump in his throat. "No.

"You're the lovely one." And then he was holding her yet again. "How did I ever get so lucky?"

"Oh, James." Her smile was luminous. "You really are the answer to a maiden's prayer."

\*　　\*　　\*

Michael paced slowly along the tower battlements. The view was spectacular. Below him the green downs rolled toward the Channel, cutting off abruptly mid-rise to form the famous cliffs. The radar towers on the cliffs behind him, to the east, were unseen reminders of the war, of the reason he was here. As he turned at the corner and walked along the west wall, the town appeared, laid out before him, tucked into a break in the cliffs, its buildings funneled back along the approaches to the harbor, and all of it set in a countryside that rolled back again to the horizon.

But Michael was too sunk in gloom to appreciate the view. How could it have happened? And all in less than six weeks? That was what had made it all so hard to comprehend. Six weeks for Luxembourg, Holland, Belgium, and finally for France to fall. His mouth tightened and he stopped pacing and stood, hands clasped behind his back, eyes straight ahead, blind to what was in front of him.

Today. They were signing the bloody surrender documents today, the 21st of June, 1940. At Compiegne. Diabolical, those Germans. To complete the French humiliation, they were to sign the surrender in the same railway car in which the Germans had surrendered at the end of the Great War, and the car was set in the same spot where it had stood that day. It was a park now. Was this seen as wiping out the last vestiges of the German humiliation? Undoubtedly. Hitler was a great one for symbolism. Easy to know what he was thinking now, but what about Petain? What could he possibly be thinking? Heading a puppet French government based in Vichy, the capital of the 'free' zone, the unoccupied zone. God...

At least Britain wouldn't be wasting any more of her precious fighter planes and her vastly more precious fighter pilots in a vain battle over France. What Britain had, she had, and now she knew precisely what she could count on. No more having to consider, thinking she could rely on what had turned out to be the illusion of an ally, which was far worse than no ally at all.

How had it happened and why? Those were the questions that simply wouldn't go away. How had the French, with the largest standing army in Europe managed to fall within six weeks? It shouldn't have happened, couldn't have happened and yet it had, and partly, at least, because the powers-that-be had refused to listen to him, listen to what his spies were saying to them through him.

Appeasement. Chamberlain and appeasement. 'But Herr Hitler is an honorable man.' That's what had been listened to. And so all the intelligence he'd given them had been thrown away as meaningless, used for toilet paper, for bumf. Bumf bought with the lives of good men. And now more of that same bumf was wanted. After that, why the bloody hell should he give them more, even if he could? And he couldn't, of course. At least not right away. All his spy networks were shot to hell, most of them literally. Oh, yes, he was starting over, but that took time – especially now that the Germans were swarming all over the continent – and time was something the British didn't have.

But Britain did have Winston now, didn't she. He sighed. If only he had been made prime minister earlier. Winston would have listened because he was able to see the evidence of his own eyes and hear the evidence of his own ears. And he would have made others listen as well, while Chamberlain...

Stop it, Michael, he told himself. There's no sense in crying over might-have-beens. That's the stuff of which insanity is made. They will listen now, the powers-that-be. Things can be made to move now, and you have to help find the right direction for that movement. Somehow. There was Ultra, the most closely guarded secret Britain had, the secret weapon that was beginning to let them read, very sporadically, all the German military transmission to and from OKH and OKW and so know their plans, including orders, logistics, and troop dispositions. What more could the army want? Except for an improved Ultra, of course, and Ultra was improving all the time.

Not that many of them knew where this first-class information was coming from. He was getting credit he didn't deserve. Only about twenty-five men in England knew, other than the men who were working on it directly. Yes, improvement would come but it would take more of the precious time Britain didn't have, and meantime he was supposed to be filling in the gaps. Even though they would be listening at last, where in the bloody hell was he going to get anything for them to listen to? Photo reconnaissance and radio intercept were about all he had for the moment, along with reports from refugees who were coming in ever smaller numbers now.

He started pacing again. There was only one man left who could give him even a bit of the information he would need and why he'd want to bother to do it, even if he could, Michael couldn't imagine. Things were different in England now. He would be listened to. But how could he know that? You saw four years of work go down the drain, John, and all you've gotten for your pains is an outsize plaster cast.

At least you're getting better. Odd coincidence about that Brandt boy being your surgeon. His letter cheered up your mother to no end. Thank God. And that other letter from one of your tank crew. Bergmann. Another crew member died to save you, old son.

His mother. That Anne loved him as she did was almost more than Michael could comprehend. Never, even in his wildest dreams, had he imagined being loved as she loved him. She even knew when he needed to be alone, and her silences were a gift. To come home to her every night, even to leave her in the morning... That was all he wanted.

That and the laughter. There were times when she saw life as one vast joke, with herself as the punchline, saying that life had become really good only after she'd realized the idiocy of the human condition and how ridiculously insignificant she was in the vast scheme of things. Insignificant... She was the significance of life for him. He wanted to marry her, give her his name, love her, laugh with her, be warmed by her and warm her in return. And just talk. About anything. Anything but the most important thing of all, the fact that he had thrown away her son. How could he marry her with that hanging over his head? Someday she'd know. She'd have to know and he'd have to be the one to tell her. How could she love him then? It was a vicious circle. He and John, trapped in the same vicious circle.

Lucky James. He and Miss Trimby had no terrible secrets that had to be hidden from each other. All they had to do was to find out if they loved one another, and if they did, get married whenever the time was right. For that they needed time. He'd managed to give them some of that time today, and he'd do it again when he could. At least he could do something positive for one of Anne's sons.

He paced on for a few moments, sunk in gloom, until finally he straightened up and saw the radar towers as he forced his mind to begin dealing with the problems that the powers-that-be had dumped into his lap. It was almost a relief.

# Chapter VII

The fox in the hen house. Hans was all but laughing as he leaned back in his desk chair and ran the fingers of his right hand through his hair. The thought wiped away all consciousness of the oppressive heat and the sweat trickling down inside his cast which ordinarily would have had him willing to give a month's pay for a bath.

He was conscious of nothing but the stack of folders in the middle of his desk. Sea Lion folders. Sea Lion, the whimsically ineffective code name for the proposed German invasion of England. And he had it all. All of it. Right here in front of him. Oh... my... God!

He laughed out loud. And to think how depressed he'd been after France had fallen. That had been the lowest day of his life. The 18th of June, the day that Petain had requested an armistice.

But instead... A slow smile began. Minten hadn't wanted him to stay on in Abwehr, that had become obvious. And so he felt that all that lay ahead was a long tedious convalescence cooped up with Aunt Gretl on Uncle Karl's estate in Prussia. And then what? He would have been trapped into serving the Nazis in a manner of their choosing, and for a long, long time.

But Major Minten notwithstanding... Why had the good major been so anxious to get rid of him? Scared of his connections? Worried that he wanted the job that Minten had just claimed as head of the Hamburg Abwehr station? He needn't worry. In fact even if he wanted to, he doubted he could take it. Minten was doing a superb job, surprisingly enough. In just two weeks under Fenstermacher, the efficiency level of the Code Room had risen sharply, and liaison with the transmitting-receiving station was never better, according to Jensen, who couldn't quite believe what was happening. Yes, indeed, Minten was doing very well. The thought made Hans shake his head. Somehow Minten both looked and seemed as if everything could go wrong, but apparently it rarely did.

No. He didn't want Minten's job. He didn't need Minten's job. He had everything he could use and more without it.

But whatever the reasons for his feelings, Minten had done an about face, had been all deference suddenly when, as the POW interrogations were winding down, he'd asked Hans to come to Hamburg as part of his staff. Uncle Karl had said he'd have a continuing role to play, that he and Admiral Canaris would see to it. The major had had no choice but to comply?

And Hamburg was the ideal place. It was the Hamburg station that ran the radio contacts and saw to the intelligence for all of Great Britain and North America. Radio messages poured into and out of a secluded mansion north of town through the huge radio antennae and receiver that stood off to one side. And because of this, it was the Hamburg station that was primarily responsible for analyzing raw data and using it to make comprehensive reports and suggestions regarding the proposed invasion. It was unbelievable that he was here. The perfect place at the perfect time. Muck it up this time, Michael... Muck it up this time and there'll be nothing left. If Britain fell as France had... It didn't bear thinking about.

He leaned his head back against the top of the chair, realizing suddenly how tired he was. There was too damn much to do now that the agents-in-training to go to Britain had come. During the day he had to be here, at the Abwehr offices in the Military District Headquarters, analyzing data, studying reports, often being questioned in minute detail about sections of the southeast coast with which he was familiar, aided by aerial maps and tourist guides. He'd never realized how much simple tourist guides gave away, and the industrial guides were even worse.

Abwehr was learning a great deal from him, but he was learning even more from them. The invasion was being planned all right, but the Wehrmacht and the Kreigsmarine were arguing ferociously, the Kreigsmarine insisting that they didn't have the capacity to provide both the transportation and route protection necessary for the broad front landing the Wehrmacht wanted and the Wehrmacht saying that landing on the narrow front the Kriegsmarine wanted would be tantamount to running their men through a sausage grinder.

The only thing both sides could agree on was that the RAF had to be smashed before a landing of any sort could take place. Goering had bombasted, of course, saying that there'd be no problem about that. Oh, God... save the RAF. He sighed.

And after dealing with that for most of the day, he had to spend the late afternoon and early evening with the agents-in-training at the School House, as they called the mansion that had become both training school and billet. He was responsible for teaching them English conversation, manners and customs, the political system, recent history and on and on. Since their papers would say that they had been in England for three months, they were also reading the British papers, as was he, both to clarify them for the 'students' and because he supposedly could understand the nuances and so understand what was really being said. They were his agony as well as his joy. So near and yet so far. And what must the agents-in-training think about them? British news was a far different matter from the propaganda-loaded pap that passed for news in the German papers. But they probably thought the British papers were spewing out propaganda as well. Still, how did they account for the letters to the editor and the anti-government editorials? In Germany everyone loved the government whether they wanted to or not.

But soon there would be more than papers to read. There would be letters. From home. He grinned. And it was Minten himself who had not only seen to it that he was beautifully placed to get all the information he needed, but was also making it possible for him to get that information to England. Apoplexy wasn't the word for what Minten would have if he knew.

Major Minten and Uncle Karl. The thought sobered him instantly. How Karl would hate what he was doing, hate him if he knew. Uncle Karl had always had a soft spot for Mother and it was he who'd suggested to the major that it would be a nice thing if Hans had a way to write to his mother directly. Uncle Karl had proposed, but Major Minten had disposed, arranging for Hans to send the letters to Britain through Sweden, via the diplomatic pouch. And to think how upset Kramer had been when he'd found someone else had beat him to it. Too bad, Kramer. Hans gave a little laugh but then squirmed uncomfortably, remembering how obsequious he'd sounded, thanking Minten, then saying,

"There is a girl, Herr Major..."

Minten's eyebrows had flown up.

"I... ah... we were... well..."

Minten had laughed obscenely. "True confessions time, Richter?"

Hans hadn't had to dissemble his discomfiture. "I haven't seen her in several , and of , I haven't heard from her since Poland. I'd just like to write to her and let her know I'm still..." He had paused. "And if she does write back" – he had made himself sound so eager – "I might be able to get a better picture of what's going on in England with the general public than I can get from the papers."

"And in the meantime make sure there's a warm bed waiting when we get to England?" Minten was positively leering at him.

"Uhm, something like that, sir," he'd mumbled.

Minten had to love that. Apparently it was something he understood. Besides, it didn't hurt to have the nephew of a general on the General Staff owing him a favor. Munificence had oozed out of every pore. "Why not, Richter? Why not?" He had leered again. "Consider it a reward for work well done. But the letters to her should go out at the same time as those to your mother, so that it's no extra trouble. It is a bit of trouble, you know, tending to those letters," he had huffed, which had made Hans smile. He'd bet a month's pay that was something that Minten would never take any bother about himself.

"Certainly, sir," he'd agreed hastily. But Minten was not deterred. He had gone on blandly to say that the envelope flaps were to be left unsealed, so censorship was implicit. Minten's munificence only went so far. He wasn't about to leave his tail flapping in the breeze, not even for Karl von der Greif's nephew.

It should be all right. God knows, the text of the letters to 'Darling Julia' should be enough to distract even the most hard-bitten censor. How the hell had he learned to write such passionate love letters when he'd never written a real love letter to anyone? But that sort of letter gave plenty of scope for adjectives he needed if he were to play the 'dictionary game' with Michael.

Too bad they took so much time to code to say nothing of decoding the replies. The English adjectives had to be translated into German, and from time to time he'd translate one incorrectly and the message would make no sense until he'd found the proper meaning. That was the hell of using a German-French dictionary and writing in English. But it was their last resort and thank God they had it. At least no one should suspect the book. It certainly was a reasonable one to have, especially given recent events. He sighed. The letters took time to compose, as well, too much time, especially while he was wearing this damn cast. The sheer logistics of writing it out and destroying the working papers had been incredible.

And signing the letters had been a problem as well. He couldn't very well sign them 'Siegfried' as he had always done before, since the powers-that-be were monitoring the letters and knew all too well who was writing them. But he couldn't just sign his own name either since Michael had been most emphatic that Julia not know who he was. He had settled for Shaszi – sweetheart – feeling for sure that from what he had to say, and with the emphasis on the initial, Julia would know he had written it and give it to Michael. Then he smiled, wishing that he could see the expression on Michael's face when the letter came and he realized where 'Siegfried' was and what he was doing.

Enough of this gloating. It wasn't getting his work done and he was behind as it was. He picked up the top folder from the pile.

\*     \*     \*

Michael leaned back and stretched. The boy had done it! By God, John had done it! It boggled the mind. Not only that he'd still want to after everything that had happened, but that he'd gotten himself where he was. Of course he must have had help from his Uncle Karl, but John was a boy who made his opportunities and made the most of them when he got them.

How excited Anne had been when she'd called him – had it been just this morning? – to tell him that she had a letter from John and how the excitement in her voice vanished into irritation at John's mentioning how he'd used the dictionary that Michael had given him in France. "I wish he hadn't said that," Anne had said while Michael's heart had risen into his throat, wondering if it were possible...

And then, not an hour later, an elated Miss Trimby had rushed in with a letter from 'Siegfried'. It seemed that Julia Henderson had gone home during her lunch hour, had found the letter along with the rest of the morning post, and knew it had to be from Siegfried, though, "She said, sir, that it had a Swedish postmark, that he had signed it differently and the writing wasn't quite the same." She had watched closely as he had opened the letter, not bothering to hide her excitement and agitation. "It is from Siegfried, isn't it?"

Michael had surprised her by laughing as he went through the sham of checking the letter, saying yes, yes it was and would she thank Miss Henderson and leave him to it?

Remarkably enough, she had snapped to attention and saluted smartly, saying "Yes, sir!" But the effect had been spoiled by a broad grin as she went out and shut the door. It was that sort of day.

Incredible. That was the only word. He looked down at the jumble of papers on his desk, the only tidy sheet being the one on top onto which he had copied out the message.

```
In Abwehr. Planning invasion called Sea Lion.
Mid-August soonest. Smash RAF first. Army and
navy arguing broad versus narrow front. Broadest
Ramsgate to Lyme Bay. Barges in French channel
```

```
ports. German river commerce disrupted.
```

Michael hadn't known about the disruption of German river commerce. They had all assumed that the barges were coming from the conquered countries alone. If the Germans were willing to use their own, then they had to be very serious, indeed. Were seven weeks enough to get it off the ground? Yes, he decided that it could be, given Teutonic efficiency and resolve.

But the RAF had to be smashed first. That meant a big air offensive. He picked up a pencil and began tapping it on the desk. The RAF. My kingdom for those squadrons of Hurricanes and even more their pilots that were thrown away so uselessly in the battle for France. The planes could be replaced, but the pilots...

He shook his head as he opened the bottom left drawer and took out the scrambled phone that would eventually connect him with the prime minister, wherever he was. He snorted and gave a little laugh. No telling where Winston was or what he might be up to. These days he seemed to be everywhere and into everything, including weapons development. Some of the 'scientific' notions he had on that score... He was shaking his head bemused, as he put through the call.

It was ten minutes before it was returned, and he heard the familiar nasal tones. "Yes, Michael?"

"I've just heard from that special source of mine."

"So! A veritable phoenix arising from the ashes. By God, that's good news!"

"It is, especially since he's fine and well placed."

"Better and better. What does he say?"

"Nothing is due immediately."

"As we know."

"Yes. He confirms everything, but there are additions."

"Ah." There was a pause. "Anything unexpected?"

"We can look for a massive air offensive and everything will depend on the outcome."

"Hmmm. I see. Bring the text around in the morning, will you?"

"Of course." As much of it as was safe to.

"Usual place. 9 am."

"I'll be there."

"Anything else?"

"Not for the moment."

"Goodnight, then, and thank you."

"You're more than welcome. I'm just glad to be able to bring you some positive news for a change."

There was a low chuckle. "It is a rare commodity these days."

*       *       *

Hans stared at the photograph that had fluttered out of the letter and was lying on the table beside him. He had asked for a picture of Julia to assuage Minten's prurient curiosity, and, he had to confess, his own. But this... No wonder Michael had chosen her. She was unbelievable in that bathing suit.

```
Dearest Hansi,
```

Thank God. No code or it would have been 'Darling Hansi'. This was just a letter from Michael in response to his own.

```
It has been so long since I've heard from you and
with all the war news, I was desperately worried.
Your letter was a godsend.
```

He smiled.

```
But you didn't mention your wound! I had to hear
about it from Annabelle.
```

Annabelle? Who the hell is Annabelle? Or was that to account for how she'd found out about it, since he hadn't mentioned it in the letter?

That was terrible news but I console myself with
the thought that it could have been much worse.
I have told no one about your letter, mein Schatz

So his signature had been appreciated and was being reinforced.

You know how stubborn Father is. And he's so
boringly anti-German. Thank heaven he's forgotten
that we even know each other. And since he is so
adamant on the subject of Germany and the Germans,
I don't dare let anyone know that I even know
anything about you beyond the fact that you're
probably James Richter's brother.

So he was covered, even if someone from this end went around to check up on his correspondence with her, even if they went so far as to ask her about him. He'd have to be sure to leave this letter where it could be found, if someone cared to read it.

And of course, I'd have to know about that, since
James is seeing my roommate, Annabelle Trimby,
whenever he's in town. I think it's serious.

Well, well, well. So that was 'Annabelle'. Michael's secretary. James and the exquisite Miss Trimby. Good luck, old James! Amazing that someone hadn't carted her off long before now. Or 'Darling Julia' either, for that matter. He took another long look at the picture.

Even she doesn't know that I know you, so I'm
especially glad that you signed the letter as you
did. I dare not let even her know about you now,
and she is really curious about my Swedish mystery
man!

Warning noted. He'd been wise not to mention his wound, especially the sort it was. If Annabelle really had mentioned it to

her, Julia might have put two and two together. He'd have to be
doubly cautious in the future.

```
Annabelle sees your mother occasionally and she's
fine. She's been seeing a great deal of Captain
Compton. (Your mother, not Annabelle!) It must be
odd to think of your mother 'keeping company'. How
would you feel if it were serious?
```

Hans sat back and looked out the window toward the canal that
ran along the other side of the street. There was a barge going by,
wash hanging on a line strung from the roof of the cabin to the
bow. They weren't such a frequent sight these days with so many
having been hauled off to the French channel ports for conversion
into landing craft.

How did he feel about it? He looked down at the letter from his
mother, which lay open on the table beside him. She sounded so
happy when she'd said she and Michael were in love. Happy and
a bit shy. Odd to have Mother sounding shy. Even odder to think
about Mother being married to someone besides Father. Even if it
was Michael. There had never been anyone but Father for her but
he'd been gone now for four years, and four years was a long time.
No one knew that better than he did. And Michael would make her
a good husband, if it really did come to that. God knows, he'd loved
her long enough.

He smiled. And here was Michael in this letter... Asking for
his blessing? If that was it – and it had to be – hadn't he given
his blessing four years before? Or did Michael think that after
everything that had happened...

The hell of it was that he couldn't comment on it in the clear
because it would tell Julia who he was. But to tell him in code. Hans
found the thought amusing.

The rest of 'Darling Julia's' letter was chit-chat about London
and what was going on, even a few details about what the war was
doing to the city, but there was nothing of substance until the last
paragraph.

I hope this picture makes up for the one you lost.
It was taken last summer in Brighton, and I hope
that it reminds you of that gorgeous weekend we had
there before you left, what seems like centuries
ago. This insane war keeping us apart makes me
hate it even the more. Pray God it's over soon and
you can come back to me.
My Love,
Julia

Pray God it's over soon and you can come back to me. Finish this up, boy, and get the hell home? Was that what Michael was saying, saying he'd done enough? What could be enough until this war was over? To go home... He ached for home. Just to see it...

But there was no sense even thinking about it. Even if he wanted to go, it was impossible as long as he was carrying this plaster cast around. And there was still too much that needed doing anyway. Germany had to move against England by the end of September or they'd have to wait until spring. After September, the weather in the Channel would be too chancy to make invasion feasible. And by spring – oh, God, please make them have to put it off until spring – Britain should be ready for them.

The September deadline meant that the agents would have to leave before too long, and if he worked it right, he ought to be able to find out where they'd land. Or – there was a broad smile – if he was even more clever, he might even be asked where they ought to land. He knew the southeast coast better than anyone, didn't he? Insane to land them there, but there was no choice since Abwehr needed information on beach and coastal defenses, possible landing sites for gliders, weather, etc., etc.

But how Abwehr thought the agents could get that sort of information and then send it back, he couldn't imagine. That whole area of England was so closely watched, and not only by the military. The population as a whole... Passes were needed just to be there. Not that that was a problem. Papers were only made to be forged these days. By both sides. But strangers in that area would notice. He'd said all that and more, more than once, but had been told, most politely, to butt out, that special preparations were being made to work around those problems. What those preparations could possibly be, he couldn't imagine. Probably just a lot of talk.

He stretched and then looked at his watch. Time to get ready for supper. Bergmann should be done cleaning the carburetor by now, better be done or there'd be no time to change. Damn nuisance to have to wait for someone to help you do almost every little thing.

Not that Bergmann complained. He hadn't, not once. In fact, he'd made it as painless as possible and been damn good company in the bargain. What he would have done without him all these weeks, Hans didn't like to think. Especially at dinner with Kramer glowering at him from the end of the table. He'd hoped to leave Kramer when he'd left Dunkirk, but no such luck. Kramer was Minten's assistant and on the faculty of the School House where they both lived. Lovely. At least there were more people here to dilute the effect. He didn't know which was worse, Kramer's veiled sarcasm and spite in Dunkirk or the politeness he oozed here. If only he knew what it was all about. Since Kramer's hostility had been apparent almost from moment one, it had to be something long ago, from Prussia. But what? He could barely even remember seeing him in Prussia, for God's sake.

And with Kramer breathing down the back of his neck, if he'd had anyone but Bergmann...

The question was, of course, he thought gloomily, how long he could keep Bergmann. Once this cast was off, he wouldn't need a nursemaid any more. But he would still need someone, someone bright who could help him with the work he had to do. God knows Bergmann was bright enough and more than capable, and he was learning the English he'd need for the job fast. Had been since the interrogations had started, helped first by a dog-eared German-English dictionary he'd picked up somewhere, and now the School House dinners where English was the required language. But would he be willing to do it? If he weren't, it would be difficult to resist whomever Minten wanted to foist on him and to have a man of Minten's constantly peering over his shoulder...

There was a discrete tap on the door.

"Come!"

"It should run alright now," said Bergmann as he closed the door after himself. "Damn thing was really clogged up. I'm surprised it ran at all. Ready to get ready?" He grinned.

And damn it, I'd miss him.

Twenty minutes later they joined the others in the large drawing room on the ground floor. It was an elegant room, marred only by several large faded rectangles on the walls that weren't quite covered by framed reproductions of famous paintings.

When he'd first noticed them, Hans had wondered whether the Jewish owner had gotten his paintings away when he left the country, along with the silver service that must have graced the massive sideboard in the dining room, or whether everything had been 'appropriated' with the house. Similar rectangles in the dining form were more than covered by huge area maps of the British Isles. That was the British school room where Hans often held forth, the students gathered around the long table. Only at dinner was some of the former elegance visible.

"Richter. Sergeant Bergmann. It's good to see you both under more relaxed circumstances."

"To what do we owe the unexpected pleasure of your company, Herr Major?"

Dieter had given Major Minten a quiet greeting and then moved off to join the group by the fireplace.

"Just checking on progress."

"I didn't think you spoke English."

"I don't, but I haven't seen this group in a while and I wanted to make sure they're really ready to go." He looked at Hans sharply.

"They are ready, aren't they?"

Hans shrugged. "About as ready as they'll ever be."

"Good. Good." He rubbed his pudgy hands together nervously and looked around. "High time. The British are proving stubborn and short-sighted. The Fuehrer felt that our common Saxon heritage would draw us together as an elite corps, Germany with her own European hegemony and Britain with her overseas empire. In tandem we would be unbeatable. But sadly they didn't see it that way, so we must get our people in place. Britain will have to be taken by storm.

"Their covers are set, at last, and they'll be leaving for Strasbourg in two day to get steeped in their backgrounds." This gave Minten considerable satisfaction. Kramer had tried to pull an end run on that one, to claim that particular idea as his own with Kruger. Too late, you bastard. I already had the papers drawn and on their way to Berlin. But you didn't know that, did you. He looked around and saw Kramer laughing with the two young radio men in the corner by the fireplace. You're a valuable man, Kramer. Don't want to lose you. But you're getting far too full of yourself. Overreaching.

"How will they get there?"

"Pardon?" He looked around, momentarily confused.

"How will they get there?" Hans repeated with a patience he didn't feel.

"To Strasbourg?"

"No." It was all he could do not to laugh. "To England."

"Oh," Minten huffed, "that's still being arranged. But it will have to appear that they've been there for three months. The papers. Have they been reading the newspapers?"

"Of course, Herr Major."

There was a voice in the doorway. Minten turned. "Ah, dinner is served." He rubbed his hands together in anticipation. The conversation was clearly over.

Hans moved to his customary place, half way down the table, his back to the sideboard along the kitchen wall, with Dieter at his right to give help if needed. From that position, Hans could talk to everyone at the long table during their 'English' dinners. Tonight, out of deference to the major, German would be spoken.

True to form, Minten had taken the seat at the head of the table and Kramer, who had just rushed in, sat at the foot. It was going to be an evening. The major adored pontificating, especially before an audience that was sure not to interrupt.

The plates were served at once and Minten dug in, his girth accentuating a formidable trencherman's lack of manners. He talked as he ate, globules of gravy spraying from his mouth and hanging momentarily in the air before falling back onto his plate, or the table, or anything else within range. He punctuated his monologue with pauses to wash down his meal with tankards of British ale.

"Isn't that so, Richter?"

"I'm sorry, Herr Major?"

A frown flitted across Minten's face. "The English are stubborn."

"I think 'tenacious' might be a better word."

"You could say that I suppose." He was clearly annoyed now. "But tenacity implies staying power. They showed none of that in France. The Great War bled them white. They're soft." The last word was a sneer.

Hans took a deep breath. Careful. Careful. "I think it's always dangerous to underestimate an enemy, no matter how weak he seems to be."

The major was seething. Richter had never been brought properly into line, either. In fact, if he weren't so damn good at his job, connections or no... "We're not about to underestimate the British and this group is living proof." He glared at Hans, daring him not to confirm that.

"It is indeed," he said, lying through his teeth. If this was the best Abwehr could do... And Minten's expression told him that he knew it wasn't. He had been stuck with this group. They'd been chosen before he came and so he was trying to make the best of them. But how could he? How could anyone?

Hans' glance swept the table. Two jaded roues, one an alcoholic, a recently ex-call girl, a homely blue-stocking linguist and two bright boys – well, more than boys but only slightly more – who were the radio experts. They would scarcely set the world on fire. But then, he thought grimly, Hitler had already done that.

Mollified, Minten had continued his monologue with the apparently undivided attention of all. It wasn't until Heidi, the ex-call girl, caught Hans' eye and gave a surreptitious wink that he realized that attention was divided in one quarter at least. He hid his responding smile behind his ale glass which was raised in a faint mock toast. She smiled her own reply before turning back to the head of the table.

Lieutenant Kramer had seen the by-play and was not amused. He had tested the waters with Heidi and found them icy. And what could she possibly see in Richter, anyway? He certainly couldn't do her any sort of good while he was wearing that cast, and he probably couldn't do her the sort of good she was used to even when he wasn't, the insufferable prig.

And that Bergmann of his. Damon and Pythias. Too bad there was nothing there, but there wasn't. Either that or they were remarkably discrete. Kugelmann was fairly panting after Bergmann but had apparently gotten nowhere. Kramer had even seen him skulking around the gym, watching one of Bergmann's frequent workouts when Kugelmann had better things to do.

But he had enough on Kugelmann without Bergmann. And Minten, too, for that matter. The question was, as always, when and how to use it to the best advantage. To think that Minten had asked him to help quash that mess he'd gotten himself into with that young boy and girl. Kramer smiled to himself. He had helped all right, most willingly, and as a result, had been made Minten's assistant.

The thought amused him. Minten had not only given him the springboard but put him into the perfect position to take Minten's own job, and the poor fool didn't even know that was what he'd done. Disgusting, those pictures. Would the man stop at nothing? They were children. And Kugelmann had compounded the error by picking the particular children he had. Not the prostitute's daughter. She was probably destined to follow in her mother's footsteps anyway. And, besides, who would take the word of a whore against that of a major? But the boy... Now the boy was another matter.

Still, to give Kugelmann his due, how was he to know that

the brothel bouncer had once been a policeman who still had connections with the department and who certainly was not above a little blackmail? A secure, well-paying respectable job, or he would prosecute on the boy's behalf. It was the father who had arranged to have those pictures taken. He'd gotten the job and supposedly Minten had got both the pictures and the negatives. Minten had gotten the pictures and the negatives, or rather he, Walther Kramer, had been the one to get them for Minten, making a little stop on the way back to have two extra sets of prints made.

Yes, he had Minten right where he wanted him, even if the good major didn't know it. Kramer smirked. It was just a question of waiting until he could be sure that when Minten fell, he would be in a position to step right into the job. And too, by then he just might be able to bring Richter crashing down in the bargain. It would be sheer pleasure to see that sanctimonious goody-goody humiliated.

But finding the chink in Richter's armor would take time. Kramer had never seen such a spotless record and in his nearly two years with Abwehr, he had seen plenty of records. In fact, it was almost too spotless, as if Richter were going out of his way to keep his nose clean, especially since he'd been in Hamburg. Cathedrals, museums, drives in the country and not even that since the agents-in-training had come. No one was that good without a reason. He had to be hiding something, unless he was biding his time until he got his cast off. But Kramer wasn't about to wait for that. If he couldn't find the chink in Richter's armor, he'd make one, and that attractive niece of Kapitan-zur-See Schroeder's should be the perfect way to do it. The Kapitan had been less than anxious to have his niece help, but he couldn't very well afford to refuse. It was amazing what one could find out from records if one could put two and two together and then go out there and find proof of four. And there was a very large four in Schroeder's record.

But Richter's record was quite another matter. The only thing even faintly resembling a blot on his copy page was that Lord Haw-Haw business. Richter had been a fool to refuse to make that propaganda broadcast to England. His precious Uncle Karl had run interference for him and it had worked. Richter hadn't wanted to make life any more difficult for his mother. Shit. That fool woman should have left England long ago. Motherhood. The perfect Aryan excuse. The Fuehrer had elevated motherhood to the level of sainthood. What a farce.

His own mother was on her fifth husband. She had chosen well, Mother had. Her husbands had made her a very wealthy woman. But it had taken hard work. She had spent her son's childhood catching, using up, and discarding, in a variety of ways, wealthy husbands. Three, including his father, had died, Number Four quite conveniently about eight years ago when she was already on 'friendly terms' with Number Five. And with all that, she was only forty-five. A son had been an inconvenience and so there had been a succession of governesses. They had been a challenge. Especially the last one. Her departure had been most spectacular. But then, it had been time for him to go off to school anyway.

His mother had been glad to get rid of him that summer he had spent with Uwe and Birgid. Number Three husband had died and Number Four was in the process of being firmly hooked. He wondered how many of them that summer knew she wasn't really ill after the death of the 'dear departed'. It has been humiliating. Number Four was still married at the time and was going through a divorce. It had created a major scandal.

Had they known? Undoubtedly... That had to be the reason they ignored him. It was as if he wasn't even there. Uwe hadn't been so bad, but Uwe was a nothing.

And there had been the climax of that hateful summer, the day before he left for home when Richter, his brother James and Georg Brandt had sat high and mighty on their horses, laughing down at him as he sat in that mud puddle where his horse had thrown him. That day he had sworn that no one would ever laugh at him again, and they hadn't. And he'd sworn, too, that one day he'd bring the three of them down into a puddle of their own while he stood over them laughing. Georg's father had taken care of Georg for him. But the Richters... He'd thought that was hopeless, had almost forgotten until Richter's name had cropped up in that message from Admiral Canaris to Major Minten. And Richter hadn't changed. Not at all. Still the golden boy, now with a Ritterkreuz and impeccable connections.

He considered that. Richter had connections in England, didn't he. A lot of them. And there was the matter of the leak. Hauptmann Kruger – ambitious bastard – assistant to the head of Abwehr Security had been in yesterday to see about security arrangements for Sea Lion planning at this end and with the added brief of checking up on the agents-in-training. Kramer covered his snort with an abortive cough which caused a brief pause in Minten's monologue. He smiled an apology and the major picked up where he'd left off. Unmitigated pompous ass.

Kruger had brought up the leak as the very last point on the agenda, after Kugelmann had been sent from the room. He had wanted nothing in writing and nothing was to be repeated, to anyone, for any reason. They would appreciate his caution, he said, because it concerned a leak at a very high level, very high indeed since it concerned Sea Lion. "And since the planning for Sea Lion involves Abwehr both here and in Berlin as well as the OKW, the OKH, and the OKM, there's no telling where it comes from." Kruger had shaken his head at that. "But it is thought that this leak has to be related to British jubilation over the resurrection of a long lost agent.

"We thought we had rounded up every one of those bastards until a few days ago," Kruger had said, "but someone escaped the net and is telling them a great deal, and whoever it is, he's being protected. Not even his code name is known."

They were to keep their eyes open and mouths shut. Kramer had almost laughed at that. Minten with his mouth shut?

"So the British have their own leak," the fool had said. All Minten saw was the good side. It didn't even occur to him that he should have been running this 'leak' from London. If he had been in charge of the Hamburg station instead of Minten, he never would have put up with it.

But if there was a leak to London... Yes, the leak might be the way. With all Richter's British connections, it ought to be possible to make it look as if he were tied to it, at least tangentially. And since Richter was under Minten's control, if Richter were brought down into the mud, some of it was bound to splash off onto Minten. But with 'dear Uncle Karl' and Admiral Canaris being as thick as thieves, he'd have to move carefully. Kapitan Schoeder was as good a starting point as any.

"Is that clear?"

My God, was that fatuous fool finally done? Kramer stretched his back unobtrusively and checked his watch under the table. Minten had been at it for over an hour. A relief to have it done and, from the rate at which everyone was leaving the dining room, he wasn't the only one who was relieved.

*       *       *

"Hauptmann Johann Richter here to see Kapitan-zur-See Schroeder, as requested"

"Certainly, Herr Hauptmann." Her smile was professional. "Ten o'clock. You're right on time."

"Isn't everyone?" She hadn't seemed all that attractive when he'd first come in, but, professional or no, that smile was something.

"No. And usually the higher the rank, the later they are."

"That's what you get for doing business with a lowly Hauptmann, especially one who's the man in the iron cast. And I'm at the mercy of a prompt driver. He's only a sergeant."

She was smiling again, a real one this time. "And just how did you get your 'iron cast'?"

"France."

"The Ritterkreuz, too?"

"No. Poland."

"Real warriors are another rarity in this office. The most impressive thing most of them fire is a secretary here and there."

"My, my, aren't we the cynic this morning."

"Yes, I'm afraid we are." She paused. "There was a particularly difficult man in here earlier and I'm afraid he set the tone."

"Sit down, please, and I'll see if my uncle's ready to see you." She rose and started toward the door into the inner office.

"That explains it," he said.

She turned, her hand still on the knob. "Explains what?"

"You aren't like any secretary I've ever met, especially here."

She laughed away her confusion as she took her hand off the knob and tapped on the door.

Not only a delightful smile, he thought appreciatively, but the rear view wasn't bad either.

"Come!"

She went in, closing the door softly after herself. "Hauptmann Richter is here."

The Kapitan was a tall, distinguished-looking man, befitting the room, which was large and looked more like the library of a country manor house than the office it was. He was standing by the window looking out. It was a moment before he turned and spoke. "Promptness is a virtue."

"It isn't the only virtue he has."

"Oh?"

"A sense of humor."

"That would appeal to you, I know."

"So many people have lost theirs."

"If they ever had one in the first place." He hated having to involve her in this, knew that she didn't like it any better than he did.

"That should make it easier for you."

"In one way, but far harder in another."

"Why harder?"

She hesitated, trying to find the right words to explain it, thinking as she did that he sounded so tired, and that there were deep-etched lines in his face that hadn't been there a few days before.

He hadn't been the same since that Lieutenant Kramer had been in yesterday. Odious man, Kramer. But what could he have said to Uncle Friedrich to upset him so? Uncle had cancelled his last appointment for the day and had sat there, staring out the window, for over an hour.

When she had gone in to say good-night to him, he had been positively abrupt with her. "A Hauptmann Richter will be here within the week. I want you to get him to take you out to dinner."

"Is that all?" Her voice had been heavy with sarcasm, but the agony in his face had made her sorry at once. "I'm sorry, Uncle. What's wrong?"

"I don't like this either, Annaliese, but I have no choice."

"It's important?"

"Very."

"Then I'll try."

"Annaliese!"

She started. His voice had penetrated her thoughts and brought her back to the present. "I'm sorry. I just wish I knew what was going on."

"And I wish I could tell you, but I can't. You said there were ways that his sense of humor made things harder. Why?"

"Because I think I would be very pleased to have dinner with him and having to wangle it for reasons I can't understand spoils that.

"And he's a warrior soldier, not a paper pusher. Ritterkreuz in Poland. Cast in France."

"I knew about the Ritterkreuz."

"Then why all the secrecy? He's not a spy."

"Maybe not originally, but he's working for Abwehr now and there are certain things they want checked out."

"I still don't understand what my having dinner with him will tell them."

"England, Annaliese. You lived there for a year. You speak the language. It would be a natural thing for you to talk about with him. I need to know what he says and how he says it. It's your impression of him that counts. You have a good sense for people and know how to listen."

"But what if he doesn't ask me?"

"Perhaps we can have him over for dinner. Or I'll arrange to have several conferences with him. We'll work out something. But it has to be soon."

"All right." She sighed. "I'll see what I can do."

"You can do plenty." There was the barest trace of a smile. "I've seen you operate, remember? And sweeping young men off the doorstep for the past few years is an exercise that has given me great faith in your ability to get what you go after in that line."

"But it's always been for me before. It's never been important to anyone else."

"It is important, as I said. But don't worry. Everything will work itself out." He pulled her to him in a rare gesture of affection, wishing that he really felt that everything would indeed work itself out. Lieutenant Kramer was a devious, power-hungry bastard and it wasn't likely that this would be the end of it.

Then he remembered holding her just this way on that terrible night when he had had to tell her that her mother – his sister – and father had been killed in a train wreck in Bavaria, reassuring her, telling her it would be all right, that he and Aunt Karin would take care of her, that they had only two boys and had always wanted a little girl as well. And she had become their little girl in fact if not in name.

He released her abruptly and almost pushed her toward the door. "Send him in."

She nodded bleakly.

"And smile that rapturous smile of yours. You're not exactly going to the guillotine."

She managed a hideously fake smile, wrinkling her nose at him at the same time. He couldn't help laughing and so she was really smiling as she came into the outer office.

Hans was watching her, thinking that Bergmann was right. He was in a rut. Only one dinner out with Uncle Karl, and one night at

the theater since he got here. Other than cathedrals and museums...
It wasn't enough. And when she was smiling, he knew just how
much it wasn't enough.

"You may go in now, Herr Hauptmann."

He came to his feet in a movement that was at once both
awkward and, under the circumstances, graceful.

"You did that well," she said.

"Practice."

"Long practice?"

"Six and a half weeks. I hope tomorrow will be the end of it."

"I hope so, too. That can't be easy, especially since it has been
so hot."

He was beside her, looking down at her, realizing for the first
time how small she was, small and fine-boned. That decided the
issue. "Why not help me either celebrate my release or drown my
sorrows at the prospect of two more weeks in captivity? Tomorrow
night?"

There was a sharp intake of breath before she replied. "We
haven't been introduced." A rather odd smile took the sting out of
her words.

"I'll ask Kapitan Schroeder to do the honors. If he will, will he
do?"

She looked at him speculatively. "He won't 'do' anything if you
don't get in there."

He was smiling as he walked into the office and across the soft
pile of the padded oriental rug. "Herr Kapitan, Hauptmann Johann
Richter here as requested."

"Sit down, Hauptmann Richter. Do you need a special chair?"
My god that really was a monstrosity of a cast. At least she wouldn't
have to worry about fighting him off.

"No, thank you, Herr Kapitan. This will do nicely." He lowered
himself into a beautifully upholstered wing chair by the fireplace.

Kapitan Schroeder settled himself into the companion chair
opposite, saying, "I'm sorry I kept you waiting, but I had some
instructions for my secretary."

"And your niece, I believe."

"Ah, so she told you that. She doesn't often mention it to anyone here."

"Shall I take that as a compliment?"

"I would say so."

"It's hard to tell?"

The Kapitan shrugged. "She's her mother's daughter in addition to being a superb secretary."

"You wanted to see me?"

"Yes. I've been told that you know something of the south and east coasts of England."

"Parts of them."

"We have naval charts of the coast, of course, as well as some excellent recent maps of terrain and defenses, and so I have my own ideas of where the agents you've been training should be landed. But more than naval convenience has to be considered. That's where you come in." It was a farce, simply an excuse to get him into the office to meet Annaliese. The two landing sites had been chosen long ago. But he had to play it out and he did, for nearly forty minutes.

Finally he sat back from the map he'd laid out on the coffee table between them, watching as Hans made a few final notes to leave with him. Richter seemed a good sort, bright and apparently apolitical. What was Kramer fishing for? Whatever it was, he just hoped that Richter would be able to take care of himself when the time came.

Hans looked up at last. "There's just one other thing I need to ask."

"Yes?" The tone was polite, nothing more.

How would he jump? Schroder wasn't the easiest man in the world to talk to. "Would you mind introducing me to your niece?"

A look of amusement crossed the kapitan's face. "Observing the formalities?"

"At the lady's request."

Schroeder chuckled. "I thought the modern generation was beyond all that, especially my niece."

"Apparently not."

"What do you have in mind?" It was the uncle-protector speaking now.

"Just dinner and, I hope, a celebration."

"A celebration?"

"You might call it my coming out party. I hope to be getting this cast off tomorrow morning."

Annaliese was right. Richter did have a sense of humor. But if that was what he wanted to celebrate, there wouldn't be his cast to protect her. "And if it doesn't come off in the morning?"

"Two more weeks."

"God forbid."

"I hope He does."

"That would seem well worth celebrating. I'll be glad to introduce you, but I warn you, the lady makes her own choices. I can give you no guarantees."

"None asked for."

The Kapitan was smiling in spite of himself. "And no quarter given?"

Hans smiled back. "No quarter given."

Damn. Damn. Damn. May Kramer's soul be consigned to the nether reaches of hell. "Very well then." He opened the door and allowed Hans to precede him into the outer office.

Then the Kapitan came fully erect, clicked his heels and made a formal bow towards his niece who was standing by the filing cabinet. "Fräulein Annaliese Scheuermann, may I have the honor of presenting Hauptmann Johann Richter?"

She bobbed a curtsy, saying, "Certainly, Herr Kapitan," before putting out a regal hand that Hans took with great solemnity. "Herr Hauptmann Richter, I am pleased to meet you."

"Are you indeed?"

She flushed and then laughed at herself. "That remains to be seen."

"You see what I mean, Richter?"

"I certainly do, Herr Kapitan. Thank you."

"And just what is all this about?"

Hans turned back to her as the Kapitan disappeared into his office and shut the door. "He told me that he would make the introduction but that 'the lady makes her own choices'."

"Whether to celebrate or console?"

"I'm delighted if those are the only two choices open to you."

"It would seem that they are, Herr Hauptmann." And they were. And why, oh why did that have to be the case with the first really interesting man she'd met in months?

"Shall I pick you up at 7:30?"

She nodded, a smile growing slowly but then fading as she leaned over her desk and wrote her address on a piece of paper.

He watched her, bemused, wondering if she knew the power of the wattage of her smile. She had to. My God, she was incandescent.

She handed him the paper, and they shook hands formally – for once Hans blessed the German custom demanding that – and he left.

Her eyes followed him out the door and she stood looking after him for a long time before walking back into her uncle's office. He was putting away maps. "Tomorrow night," she said. "I didn't even have to try."

"That doesn't make it any easier, does it."

"No. Damn the war, anyway." She turned away to hide the tears in her eyes. It was all so maddening. She walked back to her desk without another word.

*     *     *

"Bergmann." Hans was settling himself into the front seat of the Kuebel at the end of the day.

"Sir?" Dieter got into the driver's seat.

"I have decided to take your advice."

"Which of my invariably superb advice is that?"

"To get out more."

"Who is she?"

Hans gave a little laugh. "How did you know it was a she?"

"Nothing else could get you out."

"Kapitan-zur-See Schoeder's secretary and niece."

"Two at once! My, we are broad-minded."

"Hehe. No, they are one and the same."

Bergmann smiled. "Indeed. And I applaud your taste."

"You know her?"

"I've seen her. Messenger duties. Rumor has it that the lady is very selective indeed. Eyebrows will be raised."

"She's simply been waiting for my elegant self to appear."

"Apparently." The tone was dry. "But why now? She's been there all the time."

"I hadn't seen her before, and she's definitely the first woman I've seen here who's worth bothering about. Or maybe it's just that I'm finally willing to get off my duff, and she was the first reasonable candidate I saw. It was impulse, really. I hope we'll be celebrating getting rid of this damn load I'm carrying around."

"Which load?"

Hans snorted. "I wouldn't touch that one with a ten foot pole."

Dieter grinned. "But I bet you'd be willing to touch her with a ten foot pole."

"That remains to be seen."

"Where are you taking her?"

"You tell me. As you have frequently pointed out, I haven't been much of any place worth going to in this town."

"Dinner?"

"Yes."

"Dancing?"

"That depends on whether or not I'm still lugging this cast around. But even if I'm not, I doubt it. Damn arm will probably be in a sling."

"I'll check it out for you. But why not that place your Uncle Karl took you to?"

Hans face cleared. "Just the place. Good. Good. I'll make a reservation."

"Am I to chaperone?

"Her or me?"

"Do you need a chaperone?"

"I'm irresistible. I've always had trouble fighting women off."

"You then." Dieter laughed. "If the lady works for the military, she's had to learn to take care of herself. And from all reports, she does it very well."

"Better and better."

"I'd say so."

"I guess I ought to ask you to drive us, if you don't mind. Even if I don't have this cast on... I'm still going to need a nursemaid for a while."

Dieter stared straight ahead, trying to concentrate on the road. They had never discussed what would happen when the cast came off. He didn't like to think about it, about going back. To what? He had to ask. "Then what?"

"What do you mean?"

There was a sharpness to the question that gave Dieter pause. But it was too late to go back. "After the cast is off, you're not going to need me for long. I'm wondering what I'm likely to be doing then."

"What would you like to do?"

That tone was still there. He took a deep breath. "Frankly, I'd just as soon stay here."

Hans all but sighed with relief. "I'm glad to hear that because if you're willing to stay..." He hesitated. "If I'm assigned to Abwehr permanently, and it looks as if I'm going to be, I'm going to need help."

Hans heard a low chuckle before Dieter replied. "You mean you want me to be your Kugelmann?"

"Something like that, only I wish you hadn't made that particular comparison."

"No interest in juveniles?"

Hans snorted in disgust. "Don't tell me they're into that."

"That's what I hear. There was some sort of flap about it before we got here, but it all died down. The lid was put on tight."

"Is nothing beneath Minten?"

"Nothing but his own refuse."

"Sounds as if he's up to his elbows in it."

"If not his neck."

"Think about it, will you, and let me know?"

"About Minten's refuse?"

Hans shook his head, laughing. "That's not worth even one second of thought. No. About the job. You could have a tank, you know."

"I'd wish you'd stop talking about that. I told you..." He drew a long breath. "I don't want one. I've never wanted one, and I won't ever want one. So I don't need to think about it."

"Oh?"

"I'll stay. I may never get another chance to be a secretary of sorts. It should be a novel experience."

Hans was grinning his delight. "But no dictation on my lap, I warn you."

"No chasing me around the desk?"

"I'll try to contain myself."

"And I'll try not to overwhelm you with my beauty."

Hans had a sudden ludicrous vision of himself, cast and all, chasing a solemn and sinister-looking Bergmann round and round a huge desk, wondering what on earth he was going to do with him if he caught him. He started laughing, hard.

Dieter could do nothing but laugh with him, not even knowing why. His remark hadn't been that funny.

# Chapter VIII

"Well, Richter, you're looking pleased with yourself this morning."

"Kramer." Hans tried to say it pleasantly as Dieter pulled out his chair for him and then pushed him up to the table. They had it down to a science now. "I'm not sure that I'm really pleased. Half pleased, perhaps. I'll know more about the other half later this morning."

"What's the pleased half?"

"That our students are on their way to Strasbourg, and we'll be having some evenings off. It'll be good to have some time to relax."

Kramer looked at him with a peculiar intensity. "And will you be out relaxing this evening?"

"Hopefully."

He concentrated on stirring a lump of sugar into his coffee. "Who's the lucky lady?"

Why did he think that there would be a woman? "Fräulein Scheuermann."

"Oh yes." Kramer nodded, satisfied, and Hans wondered why. "Isn't she Kapitan Schroder's secretary?"

This time it was Hans who nodded as he sipped the coffee the kitchen girl had set before him.

"And the other half that you're not sure about?"

"I hope to get this cast off this morning."

"I'm sure you'll be glad to get rid of it. I know it's been difficult for you."

Why the hell was Kramer being so cordial? Usually he was anything but. Hans managed to nod again as he started on a piece of roll. Then, after a moment, "And you, Kramer, you're looking pleased with life yourself."

Kramer was more than pleased with life. He was smug, even more than he would have been otherwise because of the news that Fräulein Scheuermann had indeed succeeded in getting her hooks into Richter, as ordered. Everything was going his way. He

159

knew the signs. He thought of such times as 'magic times', the times when everything he touched turned to pure gold. Everything would continue to go his way, just as he wanted it to, and for quite some time. And that was something to be pleased about. But unfortunately, that wasn't anything he could explain to Richter. Fortunately, there was a convenient and far more prosaic reason to give. "It's my birthday."

"Many happy returns of the day."

Dieter muttered an echo.

"Thank you." He paused and held his left arm out across the table. "I opened it just before breakfast." Kramer pulled his arm back and proudly fingered the watch on his wrist. "Bernhard von Hesselrint, the Ruhr industrialist." He couldn't resist letting Richter know that he had connections of his own.

Hans gave a sharp nod and a perfunctory, "Handsome."

"It is," agreed Dieter, without much enthusiasm.

"Thank you. I think so, too." And then the thought hit him. If Richter had so damn many connections through his uncle... What other connections could Richter have, ones he didn't know about? His Uncle Karl was bad enough. Karl von der Greif seemed to know everyone. But to also have unexpected reinforcements arriving from an unforeseen quarter would never do. And he had just given himself the perfect opening to ask. "Tell me, Richter, is General von der Greif your godfather as well as your uncle?"

Hans just managed to make himself answer easily, "No, he's not. Why do you ask?"

"I was just curious. He seems to take such a great interest in you."

Hans didn't like Kramer's unctuous tone or the direction this conversation was taking and so there was the briefest of pauses before he replied, "He and my father were good friends, even before he married my aunt."

Kramer wondered if he'd hit a nerve. But what sort of a nerve could he possibly have hit with such an innocuous question? He pursued it.

"Then who is your godfather?"

Hans took his time sipping his coffee, wary now. What the hell business of Kramer's was it anyway? Easy. Easy. No sense in making an issue out of it, or he'd be more curious than he already was. Michael himself had said, "Tell the truth about anything that can be checked. Shave the lies fine. Lie only as much as absolutely necessary and no more, for if you hide the obvious and are caught out, they'll have reason to wonder what you could be hiding that isn't so obvious." So Hans told the truth. "I was baptized in our home church in London. My godfather is British, an old family friend. No one you'd know."

"British?"

"Yes." Hans signaled the kitchen girl to bring more coffee, hope that would prove enough of a distraction to get Kramer off the subject.

But Kramer wasn't to be put off. He sat there stirring his coffee, his face screwed up in pretended concentration. "Weren't you born in Berlin during the last war?"

Hans nodded curtly. "That's right."

The kitchen girl was pouring more coffee.

"Why weren't you baptized there?"

"It was too chaotic in Berlin during the war and since my father had to be gone a great deal of the time, it was scarcely a priority when he could be home, especially since none of his family lived there. After the war, when things calmed down, I was already four so they decided to wait until we moved back to London so that both my godparents could be there."

"I see. Sensible since one of the enemy could scarcely have been registered by proxy, not in Berlin during the war." And his godfather was one of the enemy again. Interesting. Had Richter deliberately avoided giving his name? He'd better not press it. Might make him suspicious. But it bore looking into along with this woman he was writing, Julia Henderson. And where was he baptized? In his home church. His file said Protestant. Anglican? It should be easy enough to check out even if his mother had moved.

"Somehow I've never thought of him as the enemy."

Kramer's eyes were glittering. "I'm sure that you haven't."

Dieter was sitting back in his chair, watching and listening carefully. What was Kramer after? What could Richter's godfather possibly have to do with anything, British or not? But there was no doubt in his mind that the Hauptmann was uncomfortable about it. Still, who wouldn't be uncomfortable these days with a British godfather and a brother in the Royal Navy?

Finally, the conversation veered into other directions and after about ten minutes, Kramer got up to go to headquarters, leaving only Hans and Dieter at the table. They were in no hurry to follow him out.

Dieter's voice was quiet as he asked, "What's going on?"

"I wish I knew. Something must have happened that summer in Prussia but what could it be?"

Dieter shook his head. They had been over this ground before. "You never know with him. All I do know is that I don't trust him, especially when he's affable. I'd watch out if I were you."

Kramer moved rapidly up the steps, ignoring the greeting of the guard as he passed through the entryway and started down the steps, heading for the Code Room. That little prick Dunkel would code the message for him, see that it was sent out and keep his mouth shut in the bargain. Thank God Minten and Kugelmann were in Strasbourg with the agents. Wouldn't do for either of them to walk in during the proceedings.

The message would go out today. Twenty-four to forty-eight hours for Horst to check it out and up to a week for the letter to get back. To him directly. Code name Felix. Minten wouldn't need to know anything about it that way.

Too bad Horst couldn't radio back. Letters took too much time. But Horst never radioed himself. It was too dangerous. There was too much chance of his being compromised if the radio could be moved frequently, and Horst had to stay where he was. Oh, there was a radio man he contacted by way of a dead drop, but only in cases of extreme emergency, and this was scarcely that. Seven to ten days. Too long, but it would have to do.

The church ought to be near Richter's home. If it wasn't that one, if she'd moved... Horst would take care of it.

Kramer burst into the Code Room. "Where's Dunkel?"

"Here, sir." The face that turned to him was full of fear.

*     *     *

"Tunic off, Herr Hauptmann."

Hans was standing in a small orthopedic examining room. "Unfortunately I need some assistance, nurse." And it was unfortunate. She was an ancient, skinny, and very sour-looking woman. Prune face.

"Certainly, Herr Hauptmann." She was the model of efficiency and before Hans knew what had happened, his tunic and undershirt were off and she was helping him step onto a stool and turn to sit on the examining table.

"Doctor will be in presently." She made it sound like the second coming.

Nothing to look at but her as she turned to put the x-rays into the light boxes on the wall. Was she going to stay? He hoped not. She neither moved nor spoke. No magazines in here. He should have brought one in with him. But with the cast and sitting on this table to boot, a magazine would have been too hard to handle. Damn cast. Damn table. He leaned back against the wall and yawned, wishing that Bergmann were here, that he hadn't had to play messenger.

There was a tap on the door. The nurse reached for the handle and pulled it open, all but bowing as the doctor came in, a ferocious frown on his face. He and Hans stared at each other until Hans could stand it no longer and let out a whoop of delight. "Georg! How the hell did you get here?"

The nurse was looking from one of them to the other in disbelief, obviously scandalized at such irregular proceedings within her domain, especially since 'Doctor' was grinning from ear to ear.

"I'd ask you the same question, Hans, except that I'm intimately acquainted with the snipers' bullet that brought you to this pretty pass." He turned. "Nurse, you may return to the front desk. I'll call if I need you. This one I can manage myself, thank you."

"As you wish, Herr Doctor." Every fiber of her being denoted extreme disapproval at what she considered most unprofessional goings-on.

She marched out, shutting the door with deliberate quiet.

Georg looked after her, shaking his head. "Ah, the lovely Nurse Schlagel. She does brighten the day."

"And the way she whipped my tunic and undershirt off... The practiced hand." Hans rolled his eyes. "She could have had me au natural in five seconds. Amazing. Watch her."

"I shall. I just wish she were worth watching."

They grinned at each other.

"When did you get to Hamburg?"

"Yesterday. I wasn't due to start here until tomorrow but when I came in to look things over and saw your name on the list for today, I couldn't resist checking out my handiwork."

"But what are you doing in Hamburg, my fine plastered friend? I last saw you on your way to Dunkirk. This is an odd place for convalescent leave."

"Ah, no convalescent leave for this poor broken body. It was once more unto the breach, dear friend, with no less than Major Minten again leading the way."

"My God," Georg groaned. "He'd be enough to fill any breach all by himself. What does he need you for?"

"Secrecy, my dear Georg." His voice was light, easy, but his face was grim. "Our fair major is the new chief of the Abwehr station in Hamburg. I am virtually in-dis-pen-sible to him, it seems."

"More the bad luck for you."

"And there's more bad luck than that. His assistant is someone who knows you and loves me not at all, one Lieutenant Walther Kramer."

"God. Is that bastard here? If he 'loves you not at all', then you're in good company. He loves me not at all, either."

"Why?"

"I don't know. I wish I did. Maybe something to do with my father, but it started before then. In fact, when he heard that Birgid and I were to marry, he hopped on his little high horse and galloped to her side to 'save her', telling her that marrying me 'wasn't politic'. It wasn't, to say the least, but bless my blushing bride, she shipped him off post haste with a burr in his ear. He hasn't spoken to either of us since. Thank God." Georg grinned but it soon faded. "I'd watch out for him if I were you. He's bad news. Out for number one. Just like his mother. And he wouldn't hesitate to stab you in the back if it meant another rung up the ladder."

"Ah, relatives... I have a cousin here in Hamburg. Went to see him one day. I can't imagine what got into me except that I knew his mother would be hurt if I didn't. We sold out the family office here to him a couple of years ago. Think we could give Gunter and Kramer to each other?"

"Do they deserve each other?"

"Definitely."

"We can try, except that the less I see of Walther Kramer, the happier I'll be."

"Amen."

"Enough of this unpleasantness." Georg turned to the x-ray boxes and studied the 'before' and 'after' very carefully. "Good. Very good. I am an excellent surgeon, indeed. And," he looked at Hans gleefully, "I think, my friend, that we can get you out of this ludicrous contraption."

"By God!"

"No. By me. God will have very little to do with the process, I'm afraid. He's already tended to His part. Now I shall tend to mine. And my language shall be foul in the extreme. It's a miserable job.

"And," he added, "I'm afraid that you're not home free. You'll need a sling for at least two weeks as well as a graded exercise program for longer than that, with Father Georg frowning over your shoulder the whole time to make sure that you're being a good boy and not overdoing it, as you are far too wont to do."

"I shall be good, Father, very good indeed. Anything to get this damn thing off. A bath. I shall sit up to my neck in water. I shall use the loo unattended. I shall pull up my own pants. I shall cut my own meat. All those blissful details of life one takes so for granted."

"Look. Don't get too frisky too fast. That's all I ask. If it's only uncomfortable, okay, but if it really hurts, you've gone too far."

"Agreed, oh wise purveyor of the healing arts. Anything. An-y-thing. Just get this damn thing off!"

"Your wish is my command." And with that, Georg opened the door to usher Hans out.

*    *    *

The next morning Annaliese was smiling as she got off at the tram stop nearest the Military District Headquarters Building. It had been a real celebration after all. How right she'd been when she'd given in to impulse and bought that terribly expensive red dress almost two years ago. There weren't clothes like that to be found anywhere now. The expression on his face when she'd come down the stairs had made it worth every penny. And how handsome he'd looked without that monstrosity of a cast. No. Handsome wasn't the right word. He wasn't handsome, really. Just... such a good face. And he was compact, well-knit, just the right size. 5'9"?

Anyway, the top of her head barely grazed his chin when they were dancing, even though she was wearing her highest heels. They had delighted him. He had laughed, saying they were charming and absurd with all those straps, and he didn't understand how she could walk in them, let alone dance. But she had. And oh, how they'd danced. She gave a shiver of pleasure, remembering how close he had held her, his left arm temporarily out of the sling, his left hand holding her right hand to his chest so intimately, telling her, "I'm afraid you can't back away or you'll pull on this newly liberated wing of mine." She hadn't wanted to, anyway.

When she had laughed up at him, the expression on his face... as if he wanted to kiss her. Ridiculous. She was behaving like a silly school girl. He hadn't kissed her, not then and not later. Oh, how she wished he had. For once, she thought ruefully, she wished a man weren't such a gentleman. Maybe next time. She smiled. And there was to be a next time. Saturday night. Two nights from now. There hadn't been anyone. Not for a long time. And not even Ernst had had that sort of effect on her the first time they'd met. Poor dear Ernst. Her heart twisted. She had loved him and now he was dead. In Poland. Ten months ago. Ernst had been such fun. But there had never been the excitement, the tension with Ernst that she'd felt last night.

In an odd way she'd met Hans because of Ernst. If she hadn't spent that year in England... If she hadn't... It had been hard, hell really, to remember what she had to do for Uncle Friedrich. It had made her feel so cheap. And it had come close to spoiling things, having to quiz him about his life and what he thought so she could report on what he said, especially since those were the sorts of things she would have wanted to know just for herself. Damn you, Aunt Karin, she thought, for not letting me marry Ernst, for thinking him so 'unsuitable' that you had me shipped off to England for a year as au pair for the family of a British naval captain who was an old friend of Uncle Friedrich's. Supposedly it had been to improve the English she had been studying at university, but really it was to make her forget Ernst. It hadn't worked, but by the time she got back, Ernst had been called up and one delay had followed another and then Poland...

But now was now, she reminded herself firmly, and she had to get to the office. No sense standing here in the middle of the sidewalk day-dreaming.

She started walking briskly toward the Military District Head-quarters building down the street but slowed again as she thought about how she and Hans had talked and talked, such easy, fascinating talk. What a life he'd led. An American mother. A German father. Summers in Prussia and the United States. Travel. All of it. But the shock of hearing that he had a brother in the Royal Navy... Was that why he was being checked out? Even so, his views were unremarkable except for saying that the British would fight to the death and so it would be a terrible blood-bath if there was an invasion. How had he put it? "They have sat safe behind their Channel moat since 1066 and Germany will cross it at her peril."

And he'd been discrete about his work. He had to be in on the planning for Sea Lion – with his background they'd have to want him for that – but he'd given nothing away, deftly changing the subject when she'd skirted it. Even what he said about the possibility of an invasion had been general and in response to an 'if we invade' question.

She nodded absently to the guards as she crossed the reception area and went up the stairs.

He was such a good sort and his relationship with his driver, Sergeant Bergmann, was most unusual. He had introduced her to him formally. Well, not so formally. She smiled, remembering how he had referred to the sergeant as 'my nursemaid.' She had laughed at that, wondering how a man who looked so much 'the tough' could ever be a nursemaid, but then Bergmann had smiled at her laughter and that smile had transformed him, hiding the long scar on his cheek, turning him into a happy-looking boy. Boy indeed. They had to be about the same age.

Whatever, he was scarcely the anonymous driver who faded into the background. She couldn't imagine Sergeant Bergmann fading into the background anywhere. And he and Hauptmann Richter were friends. That was obvious. But it had made no sense until the Hauptmann... Damn German formality. How soon would she dare call him Hans? Hans Richter. She rolled the name off her tongue. Lovely. She laughed. Silly school girl. But officers and their drivers were rarely friends, and it had made no sense until he said that Bergmann had been his tank driver through Poland and France. Then everything had made sense, including the sergeant's Iron Cross First Class. Kuebel drivers never had an Iron Cross First Class, let alone 'nursemaids'.

She checked her watch as she walked through the office door. Damn. Five minutes late and the door to Uncle Friedrich's office was open. Unusual. She shoved her purse into the bottom drawer of her desk.

"Annaliese?"

"Yes, Uncle. I'll be in in a minute."

"Now, please."

She froze. What was wrong? There was something in his voice that she didn't like. He knew that she always came into his office first thing. Then she was patting her hair into place and rushing through the doorway, only to stop dead in her tracks.

Lieutenant Kramer was lounging in the wing chair by the fireplace, eyeing her speculatively. A snake. That's what he reminded her of. Those damnable glittering eyes. "I'm sorry. I didn't know anyone was with you."

Kramer didn't bother to rise.

"I'm sorry, my dear. Lieutenant Kramer is most anxious to ask you some questions about your... ah... excursion last night."

So Lieutenant Kramer really was behind it after all, just as she'd thought. She turned and shut the door after herself.

"Did you have a pleasant evening, Fräulein?" he asked in a lazy drawl.

She wanted to smash that smug face into oblivion but instead managed a cool, "Very, thank you, Herr Lieutenant."

His smile was positively lewd. "I'm sure that cast didn't help."

Keep the tone level. Keep calm. Don't show your anger. Sweetness. That was what was needed. She almost managed but not quite. "Then you haven't seen him since yesterday morning. The cast is gone."

"I'd forgotten. He said it might be."

So he knew Hans or at least saw him occasionally to speak to.

Kramer went on. "Then I'm sure it was a more interesting evening that you otherwise would have anticipated."

She caught her uncle's eye. His jaw was working. "It was a pleasant evening."

"Productive?"

"What do you mean?"

Kramer thrust himself forward in the chair and snapped, "You know damn well what I mean. What did he have to say about England?"

"Not very much. It was hard to keep him on the subject."

"Tell her to be more forthcoming, Herr Kapitan."

"Answer his questions, Annaliese," came the weary voice. He wasn't looking at her.

"I thought I had. I'm sorry." She wasn't sorry in the least.

He asked again. "What did he say about England?"

"That he was raised there, that his mother still lives there and that his brother is in the Royal Navy." She heard the sharp intake of her uncle's breath. Kramer must not have told him that, if he knew.

"What else?" He was abrupt.

"That he fought British troops in France."

"Did he say anything about interrogating British prisoners in Dunkirk?"

That surprised her. "No. He didn't mention it."

"I'm not surprised."

"Why?"

"Oh, there was a nasty incident. That man of his, Bergmann, broke a prisoner's neck during a session."

She looked away. He was trying to imply that Hans and Sergeant Bergmann had used physical violence in interrogating prisoners and that the sergeant had gone too far. His sinister face rose before her unbidden and then his smile. That wasn't the smile of a torturer-murderer. But why would Kramer say it if it weren't true, at least partially? The lieutenant may have been a lot of things but he didn't strike her as being a fool and that sort of thing would be easy to check out. "How? Why?"

"Ask Richter about it sometime and see what he says."

"And how am I going to do that since all I'm supposed to know about him is what he tells me?"

Kramer flushed. She had him there. His reply was scathing. "I'll leave that to you. Will he ask you out again?"

Her heart fell. "I think so." Somehow she couldn't bear to tell Kramer that he already had.

"Make it a certainty."

She shook her head. "If I push too hard, he'll run in the opposite direction. He's not the sort who appreciates an aggressive woman."

"He would if she made it worth his while." Kramer was sneering at her.

She worked to control her rage. "I won't sell myself. Not for you, not for anyone."

"Oh, yes you will. If it's necessary, that's precisely what you'll do."

Her fists were clenched and she was fighting back tears. Why, oh why did she have to cry when she got angry? It only gave him the advantage. If only she could claw the damn smirk off his face. Instead she took a deep breath.

But it was Uncle Friedrich who spoke, his voice a study in cold fury. "No she won't, Kramer. I won't have my niece prostituting herself. There I draw the line."

Kramer rose, leaning toward the Kapitan, the very picture of menace. "You can't afford to draw any lines. Cross me and you know where that will lead you and your whole family, including this precious niece of yours. She'd be the crown jewel of any SS bordello. At least there she wouldn't be selling herself, as she put it, she'd be giving herself, and joyously, for the Fatherland."

Annaliese's heart seemed to stop.

There was a crash as her uncle's chair fell over. He was on his feet. She looked at him, imploringly. Get violent and Kramer would only tighten the vise. Their eyes met and held; what he saw in her face took the madness from his. He leaned back against the wall.

Kramer looked on with satisfaction. "I'm glad you've decided to be sensible. Fräulein, make sure he asks you out again. You'll have a list of specifics that I want you to ask him about, including his godfather."

"What are you after? He seems a fine man."

"'Seems' is the operative word. Remember Dunkirk? But what I want is none of your concern. All you should be concerned with is doing what I ask."

With that, Kramer stalked out, not even waiting for a reply.

Annaliese shut the office door after him and turned to look at her uncle who was staring out the window again, the picture of dejection.

It was an effort to control her voice, to keep it from shaking. "Uncle, I'm afraid you're going to have to tell me what this is all about. If I'm facing an SS bordello, I deserve to know why."

He didn't look around. "He said that just to scare you. He hasn't that kind of power."

"What kind of power does he have? I've never seen you like this." Tears came back to her eyes.

Finally he did turn and came over to her, putting his arms around her, holding her gently and rocking her from side to side.

Her voice was muffled by her tears and his uniform jacket. "I'm sorry. I'm so sorry. He frightens me. This has to be hell for you."

"You're right about two things. It is hell and it's time you knew. How he found out, I can't imagine. I thought I had taken care of everything." He heaved a great shuddering sigh. "You remember when you first came to us and your aunt fell desperately ill?"

"Of course. How could I forget? I was terrified I was going to lose her, too."

"So was I. That's what's causing the problem now."

"What on earth kind of problem could that be causing you after all these years?"

He went on as if he hadn't heard her. "I was in charge of the Welfare Fund for Sailors at the time and we were desperate for money. Everyone was. Inflation... The operation wasn't that expensive – and the Kriegsmarine paid for it – but she required a long convalescence and some specialized treatment that they wouldn't pay for and which cost a great deal."

She dreaded what she knew was coming. "There was my stock. Why didn't you sell my stock? I would have given it to you."

"I know. But you were a child and it was all you had. Besides, inflation was eating up money, and it was barely worth the paper it was printed on." He let her go and turned away. "I needed a lot of money and the bank wouldn't loan it to me, so I took it from the only available place, the Welfare Fund. I got it by making payments to non-existent war-disabled sailors. Just enough each month. And when things got better, I paid it all back, every penny. But Lieutenant Kramer has conveniently ignored that and besides, there's no way to prove it. I was too clever by half."

He turned back to her again. "Can you imagine what he could do with that? Robbing the war wounded, the very men who were my responsibility?"

She just looked at him, but he was staring out the window again. It was all so sad. She couldn't imagine him doing that. He had to have been desperate.

"I'd be ruined. So would the boys. That's the problem. I did it. I should be the one to pay the price, not them, not Karin, and certainly not you."

"Does he have proof on paper?"

"Yes."

"You've seen it?"

"Yes."

"Where does he keep it?"

"I wish I knew."

"I love you, Uncle Friedrich."

His eyes filled with tears. She hadn't told him that in years. "I love you better than life itself, Annaliese."

"I'll do all I can."

"I'd give anything if you didn't have to."

"At least Aunt Karin is alive and well."

"It's the only thing in this terrible mess that I have to be thankful for. That, my dear, and you."

She didn't reply but her face softened as they looked at each other until she finally turned and went to her desk. The phone was ringing.

\*      \*      \*

Three days later, a nondescript man in the London business uniform – a pin-striped suit and bowler hat – climbed the steps of St. Peter's church on Eaton Square and pulled open the door. The vicar was up by the altar talking with a woman who was cleaning the floor.

The man walked up the aisle to the handsome wrought iron gate that separated the choir stalls and the altar from the rest of the church. He stood admiring the gilded angels that topped the open work divider until finally the vicar turned and walked toward him.

"May I help you?"

"I hope so. I'm doing some research into our family history. There's been some confusion about an inheritance and I would like to clear up some points. Your baptismal records may help."

"Certainly, but perhaps I can give you the information myself?"

"1915 through 1924?"

The vicar laughed. "That was before my time, I'm afraid. But if you'll come with me..." He turned to lead the way.

"I'll be glad to make a contribution."

"That's not necessary," he said back over his shoulder as he pushed open a door that led to a hallway behind the choir stalls.

"But I insist."

"Then I accept, gratefully." He opened the door to a room that could only be the vestry. There were large carved wardrobes, handsome pieces, on one side wall, windows high on the wall at the end and a round oak table with four chairs around it in the middle.

"Now, if you don't mind waiting here, I'll have to get the volumes concerned for you."

"They're bound to be heavy," the man said doubtfully. "Perhaps I should help?" The vicar was a small man who looked rather frail.

"That's not necessary," he said drily. "The verger's over eighty and he manages them very nicely." With that he was gone, leaving the man standing in the middle of the room, feeling foolish.

The volume was large and very heavy, but it was the only one. The vicar set it down in the middle of the table and stepped back, dusting his hands off against each other though the volume looked clean and the heavy leather cover binding well cared for. "Do you need any help with it Mr...." The vicar's voice trailed off as he realized the man hadn't mentioned his name.

"Smith. Harold Smith. And you're Vicar Rogers?"

"Yes. Yes. Do you need any help?"

"No. Thank you. And this may take some time."

"Take your time, by all means." Why did this man make him so uneasy? He certainly looked innocuous enough. "When you're through just come into the church. Usually the verger does this, as I said, but he's on holiday this week. So..." He gave a nervous laugh. "Never mind. I'm sure you're not interested in our... domestic arrangements. Just... Let me know when you're finished. I'll be in the church."

"Thank you."

The vicar noted Mr. Smith's odd smile again as he turned to go out of the door, but by the time he was three steps down the hall, he'd forgotten about it. The inspiration for Sunday's sermon had suddenly arrived.

Mr. Smith riffled through the pages to January 1919. With the chaos after the war, it was doubtful that they would have arrived in London by then but it was the safest place to start. He traced quickly down each page with his right forefinger and finally there was April 17, 1920. The boy's fourth birthday. A long time to wait for a baptism. But that was the name. John Michael Richter, son of Anne and Gerhard Richter. He scribbled some cryptic notes on a piece of paper so that there would be no mistake.

Godfather. He stopped, pen in mid air. Interesting. Very interesting indeed. And to think he thought that he was being sent on a fool's errand. Whoever wanted to know about this might well be onto something.

He leaned forward and copied the rest of the information with scrupulous care. Godfather, Capt. Michael Paul Cosgrove Compton, DSC, RN. Thank heaven he wrote a legible hand. Godmother, Sarah Miles Parrish. The man smiled, a real smile this time, as he shut the volume and rose.

When he came out into the hall, he was surprised to see the vicar hovering the keys in hand. "Have I kept you waiting to lock up?"

"No. No." He gave a dismissive gesture but Mr. Smith knew he had all the same and put his hand into his pocket.

The vicar looked in surprise at the note that was being handed to him. It was five pounds. "That's more than generous, Mr. Smith." He slipped it into his side jacket pocket keeping his hand over it as if he were afraid it would get away.

"You've been a great help."

"I'll put it in my discretionary fund. This will be a great help since I seem to have more discretion than funds these days." He beamed, pleased with his little joke.

That odd smile appeared again. "Glad that I could help you in return. Good day."

Mr. Smith was whistling as he walked out into the sunshine.

# Chapter IX

Lieutenant Kramer leaned back in his chair and focused on an unseen spot on the ceiling. Horst's decoded reply lay on top of a welter of papers that covered his desk. Kramer liked to look busy, even when he wasn't.

Slowly he sat up and read it again, then rose and began pacing in the small space available. Richter's godfather was Captain Michael Compton, RN (Ret), a high-ranking intelligence officer, possibly a section chief in MI6. This Captain Compton's cover must be very good, indeed, if even Horst wasn't sure what position he held.

The implications were mind-boggling. Intelligence. Intelligence. Intelligence. The word repeated itself over and over with each step, then he stopped. Could Richter really be the leak? That would be too good to be true. What a coup that would be! But if he were, how was he getting the information to London? The whole British spy network had been rounded up. And even if someone had survived, when and where could Richter be contacting him, since he never went anywhere or talked with anyone who was in the slightest out of the ordinary? The only people he wrote to were those relatives in the United States, his mother, and Julia Henderson. Julia Henderson.

He leapt at the paper and read it again. Julia Henderson was secretary to Admiral Thomas Markham, Third Sea Lord, Admiralty. And Compton was a retired naval captain. A connection there? That would be rich. Richter's precious Uncle Karl had arranged for the correspondence with his mother, for God's sake, through Admiral Canaris and Major Minten. And Minten had okayed the correspondence with Miss Henderson himself, probably without asking anyone. If that were it, thank God he hadn't been involved.

And then Kramer was laughing, laughing so hard that he collapsed into his chair just as Minten threw open the door, nearly taking it off the hinges.

"What the hell do you think you're doing, Kramer?"

He didn't bother to rise. In fact, his only condescension to the major's rank was to reduce his laughter to an insolent smirk.

"My job, Herr Major."

At that Minten's anger escalated to an apoplectic rage. He stormed around the desk and grabbed the lieutenant by the lapels, hauling him to his feet. This only made matters worse, since Kramer was half a head taller than he. So he let go, and Kramer fell back into his chair.

The lieutenant brushed his lapels into place, apparently unconcerned, before looking up.

"I can see that you're upset about something."

Minten leaned on the desk on his fists, his voice full of menace as he struggled to control himself.

"Upset isn't the word for it, you insolent bastard. This time you've gone too far."

"In what way?"

"Trying to run our man in London."

Kramer's face darkened. How he found out? Dunkel? If Dunkel had talked, then Minten knew everything, and that wouldn't do. Caution. He had to be sure. And so Kramer was properly apologetic.

"I am sorry, sir. It won't happen again."

Minten stood erect, a satisfied leer appearing on his face. "See that it doesn't. I want all of the details, and I want them now."

Kramer's heart lifted. So he didn't know!

"Just a routine check on the woman Richter is writing."

"I was going to do that as soon as I got back." The major was literally huffing and puffing in his irritation. It hadn't even occurred to him, and he realized that it should have.

"I'm sure that's the case, Herr Major, but it worried me suddenly, and since you were in Strasbourg, I thought it shouldn't wait. Better sooner than later. After all, it's the only direct contact anyone has had with England that is outside normal Abwehr channels. And with that leak... I was sure it would be nothing, but I was anxious not to leave you open to criticism if anything came up about it later."

Minten wasn't to be so easily taken in. "Then why didn't you have the reply sent to me?"

Kramer put on a look of ingenuous consternation. "I should have thought of that, Sir. I'm really sorry."

"Sorry, my ass. You've been taking far too much on yourself lately. Overreaching. You're after something. Trying to make me look the fool. You'll not make me look the fool, not over this or over anything else." Minten's eyes were mere slits in a red and very angry face.

It was then that Kramer's irritation got the better of his discretion. "I don't need to make you look the fool, Minten. You are the fool."

The major leaned back onto the desk, every curve of his rotund body a quiver, his voice harsh.

"Now you've really done it. When I'm through with you, you'll be lucky if you're collecting garbage on the Hamburg waterfront."

Instead of replying, Kramer reached into the bottom right-hand desk drawer, took out a thick gray envelope, and threw it carelessly onto the desktop between Minten's fists. "You'd better look at this file first, Herr Major." His gaze met Minten's steadily.

It was Minten who looked away first. There was something about the way Kramer was behaving, about his unconcern, that made him terribly afraid. He stood up without touching the envelope.

"You'd better do as I say. It just might make you change your mind." Kramer's smile wasn't pleasant to see.

Slowly the major reached out and took the envelope, opening it carefully to hide the shaking of his hands. A stack of pictures. He blanched as he took them out. The top one was enough. There was no need to look through the rest.

"Where did you get these?" His voice was a hoarse whisper. "I destroyed them with the negatives, myself."

"Not soon enough, apparently."

Minten started to put the envelope into his pocket.

"By all means, consider those a gift, Herr Major. There are more where they came from."

Minten just stared at him before a wintry smile appeared. "Blackmail."

Kramer spoke in a voice of sweet reason, which was all the more aggravating. "In a way. Just leave me alone. Let me do as I wish without any questions and you'll be alright." For the time being, anyway.

"What are you after?"

"I'll tell you when I'm ready and not before."

Minten flushed. "Just don't take too long." He was controlling himself with an effort.

"Threats, Herr Major?" Kramer was a study in condescension. "You're in no position to threaten me about anything." Or you won't be, you fat fool. Too bad Dunkel knew what was in those messages. Dunkel would have to go. A shame. He could have been useful again. At least it should be simple enough to arrange. Even on such short notice.

Minten had been glaring at him, speechless for once. Now he turned to leave.

"And Herr Major," -- Minten looked back -- "I know you'll be praying nightly for my health. I have deposited a set with someone I have good reason to trust. And trust is such a rare commodity these days, isn't it?" Kramer gave a sardonic smile as he went on. "That person has instructions, should anything happen to me, to hand-deliver his set --in a sealed envelope, of course -- to the Fuehrer himself. And he is in a position to do just that.

"Somehow, I don't think the Fuehrer would be very happy with you. You know how he values children, especially Aryan children."

Kramer's eyes seemed to be boring right through him as he stood there, sweating, but Minten managed to pull himself together enough to say, "Your round, Kramer."

"No. The winner and new champion."

Minten turned his back on the sneering face and went into his own office without realizing that he had until he was there. He shut the door, sank back into his chair, and reached into the lower right desk drawer with practiced ease, fondling the brandy bottle before pulling it out. He didn't bother with a glass.

What the hell could he do? Kramer had him by the balls. But there had to be something. He'd been in tight places before, and he'd always gotten out. This was the worst, by far. He was sunk in gloom.

But finally his brain began ticking over again, in slow-motion at first, then faster and faster. Why had Kramer really written to London? The girl was only part of it; she had to be just a screen, because Kramer had used his ace in the hole - those pictures - to keep him from going after the rest. What the hell could it be?

Then suddenly he was galvanized. The Code Room. He sat up, thrust the bottle back into the drawer and slammed it shut. By God, there was something he could do! Kramer didn't know the right codes and didn't know squat about coding or decoding anything. Someone had to have done it for him, and since he hadn't gotten a copy of the message, Kramer had it done quietly. Whoever did it for him was the only person in Hamburg besides Kramer himself who knew what Kramer was after. And if he were ever to have the upper hand with Kramer again, he had to know, as well. The Code Room was the place to start.

Thank God the head of the mailroom had twitted him about a letter going straight through to Felix – Kramer's codename – since nothing ever had before. Minten had had to fake having given his permission. "Have to let these young ones try their wings sometime," he had said, and how it had galled him to say it. But by heaven, he'd clip those wings, and when he was through, Kramer would never fly again.

He stopped, his hand on the door. But he had to move slowly, carefully. Those pictures... He pulled the envelope from his pocket and began looking at them, really looking at them, one after another, and for a moment he forgot the cost, forgot everything as his heart started pounding and the stirrings began, stirrings his wife could no longer cause.

Dorothea. Fat, stupid cow. A veritable breeding machine. She disgusted him now. Was she aware of that? Probably. She had certainly seemed happy enough to stay down in the Harz Mountain District where she had been raised and where her precious mother still lived. They had agreed that life there was 'more stable for the children'. Yes, she had seemed content to stay there and let him go. And perhaps a shade relieved? It didn't matter anymore. He was glad to be rid of her. At least she was a good mother. He had to say that much for her.

He sighed as he put the pictures back in the envelope. They had to be destroyed. Couldn't leave them for anyone else to find. There simply wasn't a place that was safe enough anymore. Pity.

Get the information in those messages. His hand tightened around the doorknob and he turned it. That was his first priority. Then he'd figure a way out of this, just as he had figured a way out of everything else.

*       *       *

Dunkel sighed and walked down the street towards the tram stop. His day off. Damn that Lieutenant Kramer, anyway; if only he had the nerve... But he didn't, did he? His mouth twisted in bitter anger. Who the hell did have the nerve to do anything beyond what he was supposed to do these days? Step out of line, even a little, and there was no end to the problems it could cause. Kramer had shown him that, hadn't he? Now what could he want? He'd coded the bloody message and decoded the reply, hadn't he? Without a peep. Who the hell cared about somebody's bloody godfather, anyway? Even if he was in British intelligence. Whoever saw his godfather? All Dunkel had ever had from his godfather was the silver baby spoon and pusher set that had been given to him on his christening day.

"I need you for something special, Dunkel," Kramer had snapped into the phone. "Something very special. And I want you to come in right now."

"But it's my day off!"

"Day off be damned. If I need you, you'll come, and right now."

People had been walking by him in the hallway, so he couldn't argue, wouldn't have anyway, he thought angrily. Damn Kramer and damn the tram stop for being five blocks away.

He was so lost in thought that he didn't hear the roar of the engine as he stepped out into the street. There was a shout and he looked around. The horrified face of an old woman, mouth agape, was the last thing he saw as the car slammed into him and half dragged his body around the corner before it finally slipped off and under the right front tire. The driver had to wrestle with the wheel, barely managing to keep control of the car, and almost sideswiping a small oncoming truck before straightening out and speeding away.

*   *   *

Kramer threw down the pencil. Damn. This coding business... It wasn't all that difficult, but it took so much time. Too bad it wasn't safe to use anyone else in the Code Room, but while one accident -- providing Schwebel succeeded -- would seem to be just that, two would raise suspicions. He'd have to keep everyone else out of it from now on and figure out the coding and decoding himself. At least Minten didn't know he could do it. He hadn't let him in on that little secret because he hadn't wanted to get stuck doing it. And thank God!

If only that ass of a major had waited until everything was finished before interfering. How much brandy was left in the bottle he kept in that desk drawer? Not much, he was willing to bet. He'd be doing Abwehr a favor just by pushing the drunken sot out. But the timing had to be right. If he could just plug the leak or even seem to have done so, then the timing could be right, no matter what else was going on.

The more he thought about it, the more he was certain that it had to be Richter, and that this woman, Julia Henderson, was the key. She was the only odd note in Richter's otherwise impeccable life. And she was odd, period. Richter couldn't have laid eyes on her in the last year and a half, and before that only if she'd come to Germany, which, given her father's attitude, was unlikely in the extreme. It was a very peculiar way to conduct what was, on paper at least, a hot romance.

Yes, indeed, the whole thing deserved to be looked into very carefully. And with his godfather being...

The phone at his elbow rang. He picked it up, growling, "Yes?"

There was a brief pause, then "Oh, yes. Schwebel."

"Good. Good." He rubbed the back of his neck nervously. "Things will be taken care of as they always are." Then he hung up and let out a long breath he hadn't realized he'd been holding. That was that. Dunkel would cause no more problems. A thorough-going professional, our Schwebel. It wasn't the first time Kramer's Gestapo connections had proved helpful. He'd even seen that Dunkel's room was taken care of. Now if he could just figure out...

And then he was leaning back in the chair, lifting his arms in exultation. Why hadn't he thought of it sooner? Things were moving almost too fast. Still, he should've thought of it an hour ago, if not yesterday. The test. It was a perfect test. He reached for the phone.

"Kapitan-zur-See Schroeder's office." He even added 'please' as an afterthought. Things were indeed going his way. Suddenly, he was sure what the results would be. Richter was it! He had to be. Too many pieces fit for him not to be, especially when you considered the timing of the resurrection of this Lazarus of the British. And he would fall into the trap. It couldn't go any other way. The stars were right this month. He had pooh-poohed Madame Chagall when she'd insisted they were the other night, but maybe there was something in this astrology business after all.

The phone was still ringing. Where was that bitch?

Just then there was a click and he heard her voice saying, "Kapitan-zur-See Schroeder's office."

"You certainly waited long enough to answer."

"Who's calling, please?" The acid in her voice should have dissolved the phone line.

She knows damn well who it is. "Kramer. Tell the Kapitan I'll be up in ten minutes."

"I'm sorry, Herr Lieutenant," the voice was brisk, business-like, but there was a hint of pleasure as she went on, "but the Kapitan is out and he won't be back for about an hour, and he has a luncheon meeting at one."

The same one Minten would be attending. Kramer hadn't been asked, which had been a source of considerable irritation to him. But now he saw that it was just as well. The stars again. He would have time to get the letter without any interference from either Minten or Kugelmann.

"Are you still there, Herr Lieutenant?"

"Yes, I'm still here." He checked his watch. 1030. Was that all the later it was? So much had happened this morning that it should've been noon, at least. "I'll be there at 1140."

"I hope he'll be back by then."

"I hope so, too, for his sake. I hate to be kept waiting."

He slammed down the phone, his expansive mood gone suddenly. He had wanted to see Schroeder now. Things were breaking fast. There had to be time for Schroeder to get Richter in today. If it were Richter who was handing out the information – and it had to be – the agents were leaving for England in six or seven days, depending on the weather. Richter would want to get the information about the landing sites to London as soon as possible. Landing site. Let him think that they were all landing together. Give him just one of the sites. Give him the blonde whore. Kramer's smile was nasty. That would teach her to refuse him. She wouldn't refuse him or anyone else ever again. The British hanged spies. That thought gave him a great deal of pleasure, those long legs jerking, then limp, dangling. If he couldn't get that sort of reaction out of her one way, he would another.

And if Richter wasn't passing information, well then, her stars were right.

Horst would have to be somewhere nearby to see how they were captured, if they were. But even he couldn't know it was a set up. He'd have to think he was there simply to see them safely on their way. If Horst knew what was really happening, he'd scream to high heaven and that would never do. When Horst screamed the powers-that-be listened. And if Horst were compromised... But Horst hadn't survived this long by taking unnecessary chances. He'd keep watch briefly until it was safe to do otherwise. If the group were caught in the ordinary course of events, that was one thing. But if the Englanders were there, ready and waiting, that would be quite another.

Was Richter brazen enough to use a direct correspondence through channels provided by Abwehr, for God's sake? Could he think there was safety in the obvious, a la Edgar Allen Poe? Or was he just that sure of himself? If he was, so much the better. That sort of arrogant confidence was the pride that goeth before a fall, especially in the spy business. Codes could be broken and by the Code Room. It was the only way. Breaking codes required experts, and he was scarcely that, though he knew far more about codes than Minten gave him credit for.

And since Richter hadn't signed his name to the letters, no one there would know who'd written them. Schatzi. Stupid. And if the breaker were told that it was top-secret, not to be mentioned to anyone... He usually handled Minten's business to the Code Room himself, and they reported to him directly. But even if Minten did find out what he was doing, he wouldn't dare raise a fuss. Wouldn't, in any event, since this would be viewed as part of a normal security check. No, no one would question anything more than Dunkel had questioned him on the phone.

But he had to take care of the pictures. That 'pictures to the Fuehrer' business had been a bluff, and he'd have to make the bluff real. Fast. He should've thought of it sooner. Just so long as Minten thought he already had.

*       *       *

Kapitan-zur-See Schroeder waited a discreet fifteen minutes after Kramer left his office before asking Annaliese to get Hauptmann Richter to "come up, please, at his earliest convenience," but she wasn't fooled.

"Hans? This is Annaliese."

"Yes?" She could hear him smile through the phone. She hated it, hated everything.

"Uncle Friedrich would like to see you as soon as it's convenient."

There was a pause and she heard the shuffling of papers. "It had better be right now then. I'll be tied up most of the afternoon."

"Just a moment."

She pressed the button on the intercom: "Hauptmann Richter says that he can come now. I think you have time, just before the luncheon meeting. He's tied up this afternoon."

"I'll see him now, then."

She picked up the phone. "Now will be fine."

"I'll be up in a minute."

He sat there looking at the phone, puzzled. She was maddening, blowing warm and cold in turns, seeming without rhyme or reason. She had put on her 'business voice' just now. With her 'business hair' - the braids she wore over the top of her head when she was in the office were far too severe. When her hair was down, it hung in soft waves on her shoulders...

He sighed. Why did he persist? Because when her hair was down and she was blowing warm... He smiled, remembering. Her sense of humor. He was grinning broadly. She refused to be daunted by the bureaucracy through which she had to thread her way every day. He had run into her in the file room after their first dinner together, and she had been laying into a woman aptly nicknamed 'The Dragon', who turned out to have been her predecessor. No wonder Schroeder had wanted to get rid of her.

Annaliese's account of those proceedings the next time they were together had reduced him to helpless laughter, much to the irritation of the people sitting around them. They had received some exceedingly baleful stares, which had only made them laugh all the harder. And when she started on Minten, it was almost as if she had jowls to flap. He was still chuckling as he climbed the stairs.

But she had on a 'business look' to go with her 'business voice' and 'business hair'. "Hauptmann Richter here as requested," he said, snapping himself to attention.

At that her face softened, and he knew all over again why he persisted. "Far better, Fräulein. For a minute you reminded me of the Dragon."

"Was I really that bad?"

"Yes, indeed."

"It's been one of 'those mornings'."

"Shall we balance it off with one of 'those evenings'?"

"If you would ask me tomorrow, I'd say yes. But I can't this evening."

"I've been replaced in your affections." He put on a look of profound sorrow.

"Very definitely." Her smile belied her words.

His eyebrows flew up in mock horror.

She went on, laughing at his expression. "By a four-year-old boy. Rather, one who is four today. Gustav's elder son. There's a family dinner."

"Then I'll ask again tomorrow."

"And I'll accept tomorrow. But you'd better get on in there. You're here on business, remember?"

"You make remembering that very difficult."

"I'm glad." She flashed a smile as she bent to the intercom. "Hauptmann Richter is here."

"Send him right in."

He gave her a small wave as he went through the door, closing it behind himself. She stared at the paneling where the image of him seemed to linger. She really didn't have to go to Reinhardt's party. She had told him only that she would try to be there. Uncle Friedrich could take his present to him, and that was the main thing.

Still, she hadn't been home for dinner in two weeks, and it was a special occasion. Home. It was still home in a way that the apartment could never be. And she just couldn't bear the thought of having to 'report', having to see Lieutenant Kramer two days in a row. He made her feel dirty. She was a sneak, a sort of spy for a man she couldn't stand against a man she could stand very well, indeed.

Annaliese turned back to her typewriter, but her hands stayed in her lap. What could she do? She had the sinking feeling that she was going to have to make a decision and soon. She couldn't go on this way. Either she'd have to stop seeing him or... She was surprised to discover that she couldn't bear the thought of not seeing him again. Ridiculous. They had been out together only three times. After three evenings together, why should the idea of not seeing him again upset her so much?

He was so decent, so much fun. And he wasn't a grabber. My God, she hated men with roving hands. And he wasn't Kriegsmarine, so there was no fear of his trying to climb the career ladder through her uncle's connections. Hans was the only sane thing she had found in the last year, since Ernst had died in Poland.

But he was so different from Ernst. Formidable. That was the word. And Ernst had never been that. Hans gave her the feeling that there was something going on below the surface, something guarded that she might never be able to touch. She couldn't begin to read his thoughts, and she had known every thought Ernst ever had. Was that part of Hans' fascination? That certain air of mystery, of a puzzle to be solved?

If she wanted to continue seeing him, the time would come when she would have to tell him about Lieutenant Kramer. If it were her past, her secret, she would've told him at once. But it was Uncle Friedrich's past, Uncle Friedrich's secret, Uncle Friedrich's life. And if she told Hans what she was doing for Lieutenant Kramer without telling him why she was having to do it, he'd despise her. He might anyway. She had reported on him, on their personal conversations. Oh, God, was there no way out?

She began hitting the keys of the typewriter, making herself concentrate on typing the report and finally managed to forget everything else until Hans came out twenty minutes later.

His eyes caressed her face and she felt utterly helpless.

"I'll call you in the morning."

She could only nod.

"And a happy birthday to whomever. Tell him I'm jealous." He was puzzled by the look of sadness on her face.

"He'll be pleased to have a temporarily disabled war hero jealous of him."

"Wait until tomorrow and I'll show you how disabled I am ." The sadness was fading from her face.

"A promise?"

"No. A warning." He gave her an exaggerated leer and that did it. She smiled.

"Goodness! I'll have to be careful."

"Goodness has nothing to do with it." He tried to imitate the Mae West stance but missed, and they were both laughing as he went out the door. His laughter stopped before he was even halfway down the stairs. It was just as well that she was tied up this evening. Need to get word to 'Darling Julia' as soon as possible, and even if he did it tonight, there was no guarantee it would get there in time. And he'd have to write to mother, as well. That was the understanding. He smiled briefly, thinking how surprised his mother would be to hear from him again so soon.

*       *       *

It was a beautiful evening, a good evening just to be alive, thought Hans, as he and Dieter walked into a sidewalk café down by the harbor. It was supposed to offer 'real home cooking.' The phrase had always amused him. Some of the homes where he'd eaten would be no advertisement for any café. But anything to stay out of Kramer's way now that there wasn't the diluting effect of the agents-in-training at the School House. And they ought to be able to eat fairly quickly here. With those letters to be written, anything even resembling leisure was impossible.

As they started to sit down, Hans saw a rotund figure back in the corner, sitting at a table slightly apart from the rest.

His voice was low, urgent. "Minten. Let's get out of here."

They both turned, but it was too late. A commanding roar came across the open space. "Richter!"

"He's drunk," Dieter whispered from between clenched teeth.

Hans nodded as he waved and called, "Sir!", hoping against hope that it would be enough. It wasn't.

Minten's peremptory "Come here!" was accompanied by an erratic but imperious wave.

Dieter rolled his eyes. "I'll wait inside."

"See if you can find Kugelmann and get me out of this."

Dieter nodded and disappeared to the doorway into the café as Hans threaded his way between the tables amid the stares of the now-curious diners.

Minten pulled out the chair on his right, tipping it over in the process. Hans caught it awkwardly with his good hand as more stares came their way.

"Sit down, Richter."

My God, the man was blind drunk. How the hell was he going to get away? In this state, Minten could keep him here for hours.

"I said, sit down!" The major was angry.

"Certainly, Sir. I was just looking for a waiter."

"Of course." Minten subsided, mollified. "I could use some more myself."

Miraculously, a waiter materialized at Hans' elbow. "Light beer for me. Coffee for you, Herr Major?"

"No coffee!" Minten roared. "A double. You know what I want, man!"

The waiter knew all too well. "Anything else, Sirs? Some supper?" He asked tentatively, hoping against hope that the major would eat something, instead. He had been through this before. At least, he thought philosophically, the major had always paid the damages promptly.

"Wurst and sauerkraut," said Hans in surrender, realizing that there would be no peaceful dinner with Bergmann this evening.

The waiter's eyes lit up, for Minten was saying, "Change that. Sauerbraten and potato dumplings. And beer. No, wait. Ice coffee."

Hans shuddered. Sweet ice coffee with all that whipped cream on top of sauerbraten and potato dumplings? To each his own. Minten must have the digestion of a horse.

The waiter scuttled off before the major could change his mind again, mentally noting that he would have to see that the Hauptmann got good service.

Minten leaned back, a sly look making slits of his already piggy eyes. His monocle was hanging by its cord, resting on the shelf made by his stomach. Hans looked toward the harbor to hide his smile. Minten was wearing a corset.

"Tell me, Richter."

"Yes, Sir?"

"What's Kramer up to?"

Odd, thought Hans. At that moment, Minten had sounded stone cold sober. "I'm afraid that I don't know what you mean."

"Why don't you know?" His voice was whining, irritated. "You should know. You've known each other since you were children."

"In a way we have but never will, certainly. I hadn't seen him in years before Dunkirk."

"Then what's he after?"

Hans suppressed a groan. The major hadn't heard a word he said. They could go on like this all night. He had to say something.

"What we're all after? Great Britain?" That couldn't possibly be what Minten had in mind, but at least it might serve to get him off this nonsense onto something comprehensible.

Minten was choking down a laugh along with the rest of his schnapps. "He may be, at that. That may be it exactly." And then he was laughing uproariously, slamming down his glass with such force that the table tilted dangerously. Only Hans' quick action kept it from falling over, but he couldn't save the glass, which smashed on the pavement.

The waiter rushed over, but the major waved him off, oblivious to the now-hostile stares of the other diners.

"How did you guess, Richter? I could see that it was just a guess." He seemed delighted by Hans's perspicacity.

"Guess what, Herr Major?"

"That he's after Great Britain and my job, in the bargain."

He was making no sense at all, except about the job. Minten could very well be right about that. Was that why he was hitting the bottle? Was he afraid of losing his job to Kramer? "But, Sir..."

"Don't bother to try to defend that bastard. I took a viper to my bosom and now he's about to bite me."

Minten's face had become the picture of misery, and it was all Hans could do not to laugh. What else could he expect if he took a viper to his bosom? And was the viper's home on that prominent stomach shelf? The mental picture was too much for him. He covered his laughter with a fit of coughing.

Fortunately, Minten was too sunk in self-pity to notice. "I trusted him, Richter," he whined again. "Made him my assistant, for God sake. And look how he repays me. Just look!"

Hans could see nothing, of course, but was momentarily saved from more of the same by the timely arrival of the waiter with his beer and Minten's ice coffee.

"You haven't asked how he's repaying me."

"How is he repaying you?" Hans asked wearily.

Minten looked at him out of the corner of his eye, studying him for a moment before saying, "I'm not going to tell you. I'm not going to fall into that trap. He knows and I know. That's one person too many. I don't trust you, Richter, or at least not that much. Don't trust anyone, ever. It doesn't pay these days." He sank into a morose silence.

Hans had the feeling he stumbled into the Mad Hatter's tea party. The major had asked him to ask, then refused to answer. The whole thing was ridiculous.

Then Minten was leaning across the table, his voice low, con-fiding. "It is England, Richter." He looked around to see if anyone was listening. Apparently satisfied, he turned back. His breath was an abomination. "He used my absence in Strasbourg to invade England all by himself." Minten was so pleased with this obscure bit of humor that he was tipping back in his chair, guffawing with pleasure. Only the fact that Hans reached over and grabbed him saved him from falling over backward.

"Don't touch me!" He tore himself away as his chair came up right. "I don't like people touching me!"

Hans looked around frantically, trying to find Kugelmann, Dieter, anyone, saying absently, "My apologies, sir."

The waiter rushed out with their dinner plates. Hans began eating at once, hoping he could find an excuse to leave as soon as he was through, and hoping, too, that Bergmann was tending to his own supper. They had to get out of here. He had work to do, though he could scarcely tell Minten that.

The major leaned across the table again, dragging the cord of his monocle across his dinner plate. "He's trying to take over the very best man we have in England for his own purposes. He sent a message while I was gone. He knew he'd never get away with sending anything while I was here. And the reply came late yesterday afternoon."

Hans was interested at last, vitally interested.

"I radio. Not Kramer." Minten was sitting upright, angry now, a streak of grease where his monocle cord had touched his jacket. His face was fiery red. "But I can't stop him. Not yet. That's the hell of it. I have to let him continue looking into whatever it is. But at least I should find out in the morning. I'm sure it was Dunkel. The only one left. His day off. I'll have him in my office first thing in the morning."

"Who's Dunkel?" And what the hell was Kramer up to, and why did he suddenly remember Kramer asking about his godfather? Hans was filled with foreboding.

"Code Room. Dunkel's in the Code Room. He has to be the

one who did it for Kramer. Day off. Went home, then out again. Kugelmann is trying to find him."

At least that explained where Kugelmann was. "But I don't understand. Kramer's your assistant. If he's doing something... Just order him to stop."

"He isn't taking orders from anyone right now, not as far as I can see. But he's gone too far this time. Too far. I'll just play out the rope until he has enough to hang himself." Minten's smile was an obscenity, but he was sweating profusely. The heat? The schnapps? No. Kramer was holding something over his head –- that had to be it –- and there had been some rumors... And Minten couldn't act because of it.

Minten still hadn't touched his food, and Hans wondered if he ever would. "He wants to plug that damn leak himself, get the credit, make me look like a fool, and take my job."

"What leak?" It was an effort for Hans to keep his voice relaxed, matter-of-fact, an effort to swallow the food he was putting into his mouth.

Minten's lip curled into a parody of a knowing smile. "You're not supposed to know that there's a leak to London. You're not supposed to know there's a leak to anywhere, let alone there. Berlin said that only Kramer and I were to know. I don't know whether the information is coming from Berlin or from here, but it's one of the two. No one is sure. But no one must know. You must not know because you could be the leak, Richter!" Minten roared with laughter at this great joke. He jabbed at Hans with a stubby forefinger. "You could well be!" It set him off again.

Hans forced a grin then concentrated on his dinner, his mind racing. The letter. My God. He had to write the letter, but it would be the last, for the time being, at least. If Kramer wanted to plug the leak and was writing London and if Minten didn't know why... That breakfast table question about his godfather came back like a bad dream.

"Don't you see how funny it is, Richter? You with an uncle on the general staff. You who know almost every important command officer in the Wehrmacht. You, whose appointment came through Admiral Canaris himself. That would be priceless. Oh my, oh my." He started laughing again. "The shit would really hit the fan if you were." And then he was off laughing so hard that there were tears streaming down his face. He dabbed at them ineffectively with his napkin.

"Somehow, the humor of it escapes me." Hans' tone was irritated as he cut into his last wurst, trying to keep his hands from shaking.

"Of course, it does. Of course, it does." Minten had stopped laughing abruptly and his voice took on a hard edge. "Because it's anything but humorous." He burped without noticing. "There's nothing funny about it at all."

And that was true. It was serious, deadly serious, and he needed all the help he could get, including Richter's, because Richter could bring those formal connections to bear for him if he wanted to. The thought served to sober Minten momentarily.

"The thing that really puzzles me is that we smashed their spy network, squashed them all like bugs. I don't see how we could have missed anyone. I was there! But we've learned all about it, all about the rejoicing on the Thames when that man rose like a phoenix from the ashes. It's unbelievable. How could he have escaped? We played out the string to the very end. They talked. Oh how they talked." Minten sank into a drunken reverie, remembering how they had talked, how they had been made to talk. He brought himself back with an effort. "So where did this one come from," -- a pause -- "unless he operates alone?" Minten lifted his glass and drained the dregs.

Thankfully, before Hans had to say anything, Minten turned confidential again, leaning on the table as he shoved his congealing meal into his mouth at last, spraying fragments of potato dumplings as he talked.

"I think it has to be from Berlin, but I'm leaving no stone unturned here. Kramer's not going to steal my thunder. If the leak is here, I'll beat Kramer to it. I'll teach that great farting asshole to cross me." He pounded his fist on the table, rattling everything on it, his face livid. "I'll teach him. He has no idea what he's let himself in for." Minten went back to his supper, momentarily content.

Hans was unconvinced.

*     *     *

The major's heart was pounding, his stomach churning, his mood vicious. Kugelmann had told him that Dunkel was due in at 0800 and that Fenstermacher would send him up from the Code Room at once. It was already quarter past. Where was he?

It had to be Dunkel. Dunkel was off yesterday; he hadn't shown up in his room last night. A girl? And it was just as well. He would have been too ... tired to see Dunkel last night, even if he could have been found.

He sighed. Last night. Stupid to tell Richter about the leak. Very risky. So why had he done it? He grimaced. Drunken thoughts of testing Richter. Or was that a rationalization? Hard to say, but he had watched Richter closely, and there had been no indication of anything at all when he'd heard. So either Richter really was as innocent as a newborn babe –– he snorted –– or he was the best damn actor on the block, and he seriously doubted that.

Not that there was any danger of Richter telling anyone. He wasn't the sort who blabbed. And surprisingly enough, he wasn't even the sort who would use it to his advantage, whatever sort of advantage could be gained from that particular piece of information, which was none as far as he could see. But no one was to know. Berlin had been most explicit, and if it did get out that he had told Richter... He shivered.

Where the hell was Dunkel? "Kugelmann!" Minten bellowed, then held his head in agony.

The door opened.

"Kugelmann, where the hell is Dunkel?" God, his head was splitting.

"I was just coming in, Herr Major. He's not here and it's bad news."

"I'll have his hide."

"Someone has beaten you to it. That's the reason I couldn't find him last night. He's dead."

Minten's jaw dropped. "How?"

"Hit-and-run."

Minten blanched, his head forgotten for the moment.

Kugelmann nodded, agreeing with the major's unspoken thought. "Convenient."

"Very."

There was a long moment of silence until finally Minten reached into his bottom right desk drawer and pulled out the bottle of brandy and two glasses. Neither man had any doubts about whom Dunkel's death convenienced.

# Chapter X

Annabelle couldn't believe what she was seeing. She had heard the thud and burst through the door to find Captain Compton storming around his office in a fit of rage, his language graphic and totally unprintable. She had never seen him like this. Angry yes, but never like this. And what a mess. The safe was open and there were papers and files flowing out of it onto the bookshelf. The books that usually stood on the shelf, hiding the safe door, were in a heap on the floor, some with pages open and riffling in the breeze coming in through the open window.

The books. That had to have been the reason for the thud. Her heart had stopped. She'd been afraid he'd tripped and fallen. But obviously he was fine, at least physically, and there was nothing but the books to account for the sound.

She listened carefully to what he was saying, trying to understand, wincing occasionally at his language as he continued to rage and pace, oblivious to the fact that she was there. He was angry at himself but that was all she could tell. What could have put him in such a state? The only thing that had happened that was out of the ordinary was the arrival of a letter from Siegfried and a letter from Siegfried always put him in a very good mood.

Finally, he saw her standing there, gaping. "Damn it, woman, close your mouth and then shut the door."

She flossed as she moved to comply. "Captain..."

An impatient gesture cut her off as he flopped into the nearest chair, apparently spent for the moment.

She stood there watching him, terribly concerned. He was leaning forward in the chair now, forearms on his knees, looking at the floor. What did it remind her of? Boxing. Someone or other had taken her to a boxing match. It had been almost as grueling for her as for the men in the ring who had managed to slog themselves into a state of utter exhaustion. The loser had awaited the decision of the judges while sitting on a stool in his corner in just such a fashion. She had an almost overwhelming urge to hug him until whatever it was, could be worked out. There was the ghost of a smile as she thought of the consternation that would cause.

The poor man was under a tremendous strain. Total destruction of their network in Germany, except for Siegfried, and the worry, amounting to terror in some circles, about the prospect of a German invasion and on and on.

Her thoughts were interrupted by his great shuddering sigh, and she saw that he was looking at her with an utterly woebegone expression.

"I'm terribly sorry, Miss Trimby. There is no excuse for my talking to you like that."

"Captain Compton," she kept her tone brisk and matter-of-fact, "there must be every excuse or at least every reason for it. It was so totally unlike you..." Then she gave up and gestured helplessly. "Please. Next to what's been going on... What must be bothering you... It just doesn't matter."

He gave a weary smile and heaved himself out of the chair. "Thank you, my dear. I should have expected you to say something like that. You always seem to say the best possible thing, whatever the circumstances."

"Thank you," was all she could think of to say as she moved towards the heap of books and started to pick them up.

"Leave those, please. I'll tend to them later."

"That's all right. It's done." And then she was standing waiting as he shuffled through some papers on his desk.

"I want you to get Miss Henderson over here as soon as possible," he said absently. "If she's busy, I'll square it with Admiral Markham."

"Is there anything else?"

He was staring at the open door of his safe. "Not for now. Just let me know when Miss Henderson will arrive."

He didn't seem to hear her "Yes, sir," for he was already at the safe, taking out the rest of the papers in the files.

Michael sorted through the papers, put them back in order and tapped the edges until they were in a neat stack. And he did the same for the folders, put the papers on top and carefully placed the whole thing in the safe. Only then did he look over at his desk. Just one file was lying there now, like a buff-colored reproach. It took considerable effort for him to walk over and pick it up. His hands shook as he opened it and studied the top sheet again. He was still studying it as he sank into the upholstered chair on the other side of his desk, one of several usually reserved for visitors.

He looked up in pain. The chair. He had a sudden mental picture of John sitting in that same chair almost four years before. He virtually shot himself out of it and into another by the low table near the porcelain that stood in the corner.

John's last message was a bombshell. The plaintext alone was cause enough for alarm. He read the last two paragraphs again.

```
You know, darling, that I can never forget you,
never stop loving you, but things have changed. My
life is very different now. I have found someone
here who is becoming very important to me. I
haven't told her about you. I may never tell her.
You're enough to strike fear into the heart of the
most secure woman, and I don't want you to frighten
this one off. It's never mattered before.
And so, darling Julia, you won't be hearing from
me again, that is unless the situation changes
radically. Know that you always have a special
place in my heart.
I shall always think of you with love.
S
```

And he looked again at the scribbling on the two sheets of the translation underneath the letter.

```
Filial blessings.
```

That had made him smile when he first read it. First things first, John? But now the smile was bitter. Under the circumstances, filial blessings were something beyond generosity. He made himself read on.

```
Leak to London known. Personal enemy checking on
my godfather. Checked church.
```

He ran his hand across the top of his head and sighed. If you were the cause of John being caught out... He didn't think he could live with that. He wasn't naïve enough to think that his cover was perfect, but he hadn't even thought about the danger of that connection. It was such a natural thing. The boy shouldn't have taken the risk. He should've laid low and come home as soon as possible.

Michael gave a sardonic little smile. John had always taken risks. Why should he behave any differently now? And why did it suddenly seem so much worse? Because for the first time he seemed close to being caught, of course. And where before there had been whole networks of spies to absorb the blame, now there were none. And there were no longer the free Low Countries of France to run to, if he needed to run. Germany was all over the continent. And he had sent John into that. Sent him there. God.

He rose, went back to his desk, and began to copy out the section of the message that would be used.

```
6 spies land between 12th-15th. Dungeness promon-
tory. Little Stone. Trawler.
```

Funny that they should put down that many on one spot, especially on the southeast coast. True, they needed masses of intelligence from that area for the invasion, but to land six agents in the same spot, and one where civilian movements were so strictly regulated? It didn't make any sense.

Unless it was a trap. If someone was checking to see if John was the leak, and if they were checking on who his godfather was, for God sake... No. Abwehr had never been noted for its great and good sense in dealing with its agents but not even Abwehr would throw away six agents just to check out a leak. Not when timing was getting so short. They'd tried to send in a whole basketful of agents along with the refugees streaming in from France and the Low Countries, but it had been pathetically easy to weed them out. Too hastily trained. Weak covers. But even more the supplies they carried had been a dead giveaway. Idiotic. Most of it was the simplest sort of stuff which could have been bought in any chemist's shop.

And they didn't seem to be doing any better with this lot. Six foreigners suddenly showing up in any seacoast area, let alone on the southeast coast... Or were they that confident of their landing site? How could they be? Someone to meet them? A safe house arranged for? By the man in London? They'd known there was still someone. All the rest had been caught and turned by the Twenty Committee, including their radio men.

This man had escaped so far. How to catch him? It would have been relatively simple if he'd done his own transmitting, but he didn't. And he was very careful about how he contacted the radioman. Always a brief call from a public call box telling him where to pick up the latest packet. The Twenty Committee had followed that part of the charade carefully, trying to get at least a line on him, but the trouble was he rarely used the same drop twice in six months, and the messages were passed at such irregular intervals, anyway, that it was hopeless to try to keep a watch anywhere. And they had to let the messages go through for fear he'd know something was up and go to ground. At least no earth-shattering secrets had been involved as yet but of course there was the problem that he might be sending vital information out some other way, especially maps. Probably through the mail. Through Sweden? Same postal drop John used? Doubtful. They wouldn't want to risk compromising it that way. But still, it would have to be checked out.

First things first, though. Today was the tenth, so there was very little time for MI5 to deal with it in a way that wouldn't compromise John. They certainly couldn't be picked up on the beach, unless they happen to run into one of the normal patrols, and any increase in the number of patrols would be noticed. They'd have to be trailed and picked up elsewhere, hopefully with their London connection if he was fool enough to appear. Or they'd have to be picked up at sea. They couldn't increase the number of ships patrolling that area, either. That would be noticed, as well. It meant having one ship in the right place at the right time.

He pressed the intercom button and heard the faint sound of the buzzer through the door.

"Yes, sir?"

"Ring up Colonel Harries and tell him it's imperative that I see him. Wait. Any word on when Miss Henderson can be here?"

"I had just finished talking to her when you buzzed. She'll be here within the next ten minutes."

"Good. And ask for an appointment with Colonel Harries any time after" – he looked at his watch – "three. Stress that it's urgent."

"Right away, Captain."

He settled back in and finished his copying.

```
Invasion  plans  unsettled.  Army-Navy  bickering.
Early  September  soonest.  River  commerce  suffers.
Training  accident.  Fires.  Many  wounded.
```

Michael nodded. That ought to setback their schedule. He had heard about that operation, the sea aflame around the training barges. The Free French had made a good start. He'd been afraid that they had exaggerated their success but apparently not.

And then there was the last sentence. He didn't copy it.

```
Must  go  to  ground.
```

Bloody right. And stay there. He resisted the urge to throw something. It had been that sentence that had caused the previous explosion. Now it just made him feel sick.

John had to get out of that cast and come home. He couldn't stay there. Not any longer. Not with a personal enemy who was checking on him. But how to get him out? It would have been easy from Dunkirk. Any small boat on a calm night would have done it. But from Hamburg... Hamburg was a different matter altogether.

There was a tap on the door. He shoved the papers into the folder and slipped it into the middle drawer of his desk before calling, "Come!"

"She told me to knock and come right in. You wanted to see me, sir?"

Michael stood and walked around his desk toward her. "Yes, Miss Henderson. It was good of you to come so quickly. Please, sit down."

"Thank you." She settled herself into the chair by the low table where Michael had been sitting earlier and crossed her legs to good effect. He couldn't help but think that she, all by herself, could make girl-watching into a science. Incredible, especially since she had brains and sense to go with her good looks.

"I had just come back from lunch when your call came in and the Admiral's at a meeting so it was a convenient time to get away."

He sat down across from her. "Still, I appreciate it. Something urgent has come up. I know you're used to dealing with highly confidential matters. And I know, too, that you and Miss Trimby are not given to indiscretions, even with each other."

He paused so that she could say, "We don't discuss office business. That's always been understood. Once you tell even one person, it's far easier to tell another."

"Precisely." He was pleased. Not many people appreciated that point. "I don't want to seem to be questioning that, but I just want to make sure for my own peace of mind. What have either of you had to say to the other about Siegfried?"

She thought for a moment before she replied. "The only time we mention him is when a letter comes. She knows that, of course. And I told her once that I'd like to meet the man who could write the sort of love letters he writes." She smiled. "They are rather remarkable, at least in my experience."

For a moment he was amused, thinking that she ought to be in a position to know. She must've had many, many love letters in her time, even as young as she was. "Anything else?"

"Just that no one knows who he is or anything about him, except you."

A frown flickered across his face. He didn't like even that being discussed. "Are you sure there's nothing else?"

"No. We both know how dangerous even our speculations could be for him."

"Good. I'm glad you understand that. I wanted to make sure you did because now there are even more compelling reasons for being careful."

He took a deep breath not wanting to go on but there was no choice. She was watching him, waiting. Marvelous to have a woman who didn't ask a million questions. Like Anne. He pushed the thought of Anne aside. "Has anyone ever approached you about whom you write? Asked you about something or someone you didn't understand?"

Her eyes widened. "Yes. Just this noon."

He stiffened, then leaned forward, his eyes cold. "Tell me."

"At lunch. Just now." She paused, startled by the abrupt change in him. "Are you all right, sir?"

"Yes. Tell me what happened."

"It was odd. I'm sure he was only confused because of Annabelle and James."

Michael sat absolutely still. Oh, God. Control yourself. Let her tell it. If you press her, you only upset her and she'll never get it all out. "Never mind. Just tell me."

She could feel the tension in the air. It had to be fearfully important for him to be so upset, for him to be so... She couldn't put her finger on what he was. She just knew that it had to be crucial.

"I was having lunch at a pub across the street – they serve marvelous ham salad buns." Michael's face darkened to near apoplexy. She rushed on. "I was alone at one of the tables and a man I'm sure I've never seen before came up and greeted me like a long lost friend. 'Miss Henderson, it's so nice to see you after all this time.' I had a mouthful of ham salad bun at the time and there was nothing I could do. He had a pint glass in his hand and since there were no other seats, he sat down.

"And then he asked me... He wanted to know how John Richter was where he was and what he was doing. Was I still hearing from him? The whole thing struck me as very odd indeed.

"I told him that he must've confused me with someone else. That I didn't know anyone named John Richter. By the way, isn't that James' brother, the one in the German army?"

Michael nodded.

"Why would anyone think that I'd be hearing from him?"

He shrugged. "You're probably right. He has you mixed up with Annabelle and James. Tell me the rest. I want to make sure."

She was staring at him, her eyes enormous, her brain racing. Captain Compton was in a very strange mood over this. And that man had seemed so positive about it, saying that he had met her on the beach at Brighton with John Richter about four years ago. And Annabelle hadn't known James four years ago. She had met him only in June. There was that picture. My God. Captain Compton had asked her for a picture, preferably one in a bathing suit. She had laughed about it at the time. But the picture she had given him had been taken on a beach that was obviously Brighton.

"Go on, Ms. Henderson." Michael's voice was gentle, coaxing.

Suddenly there were tears in her eyes. "Oh, my God." It was a whisper.

Michael rose and turned away walking to the window. She knew. He should have known she would figure it out. With a mind like hers... He'd made sure of that mind four years ago when he'd first asked her to do this. And if she hadn't figured it out, he would have had to tell her. She had to know, for her own protection and for John's. He should have told her when their correspondence had become known in official German circles, when John had sent the first letter through Sweden. But he had held onto the last shreds of secrecy even then. John had been safe so long as only he knew. His sole knowledge was a kind of talisman. At least he had the sense to cover John, to say in the last 'Julia' letter that she'd have to deny knowing him. But to have her, or anyone, know...

He heaved a long shuddering sigh and turned back to her. Tears were streaming down her cheeks unchecked. He offered his pocket handkerchief, but she waved it aside and dug into her purse, bringing out a tiny square edged in lace. Fat lot of good that would do her. He kept his own and waited.

"I'm so sorry, Captain Compton. It's a silly reaction. Infuriating really. I should have realized..."

"Realize what, Miss Henderson?" He braced himself for the words he knew were to come.

"He's Siegfried, isn't he."

Michael released his breath, realizing only then that he'd been holding it. "Yes, I'm afraid he is. He's also my godson."

She looked down at the handkerchief she was twisting between her hands. "No wonder you've taken such care to keep everything to yourself."

"I would have in any event, but you're right. I've gone beyond normal caution with this. I don't like your knowing. I don't like it at all. As you said yourself, once you've said it to someone, it's far easier to say it to someone else. That cannot be done under any circumstances, whatsoever."

"I understand." Her voice was low, firm, under control.

"You've been reading his letters, of course."

"Yes."

"And now you're going to read the replies I wrote. If this man comes again, you have to be prepared. You'll have to be in a position to use your own judgment in dealing with him. You were operating in the dark today, and perhaps it was just as well. You are able to be quite natural about denying knowing... him. Did you get angry about it?"

"Yes. He kept insisting until I got very angry indeed."

"That works for us this time. It was natural anger and so all the more convincing. But the next time, if there is a next time, you'll have to be ready for him. What he said to you tells me that they're reading his mail."

"The picture..."

His smile was bleak. "Is that what gave it away?"

She nodded and looked down.

"It was quite a picture. I'm not surprised that someone over there took notice."

She gave a wisp of a smile.

"Anyway, they're reading his mail which means they shouldn't be surprised that you denied knowing him. 'You' wrote on 'your' last letter that 'you' would have to deny knowing him because your father is so violently – 'boringly' is the word I used, I think – anti-German."

"He is violent on the subject. He always has been. He was gassed during the last war. But what if I hadn't been contacted? Would you still have told me?"

"Who he was? Yes. It's time you knew. And I would've warned you someone might contact you and that you should be careful not to arouse his suspicions. Just look him over carefully and come to me right away."

"Does that mean they're suspicious of... him?"

"Not necessarily. He's been allowed to write to you but the correspondence is certainly outside normal channels. So this may be routine, just to check on your bona fides." He wished he believed that it was just routine, but he didn't. "Still, since this man is their man, I need to know everything you can tell me about him."

"He was five foot ten, six foot at the most and stocky. Probably mid-forties. Wearing the typical London business uniform. A bowler, dark pinstripe suit but with an old-fashioned wing collar. It did strike me," she rushed on eagerly, "that he was trying to look like Neville Chamberlain. The wing collar. The umbrella. Everything. But his face was round and he wore gold rimmed glasses. There was one other odd thing about him. His smile. It took me a moment to realize that that was what it was. His mouth opened and turned up but the rest of his face was... Uninvolved. It's hard to explain." She shivered. "I've never seen anything quite like it."

"Anything else?"

She screwed her eyes shut and concentrated. He waited. After a few moments she looked up. "He had an antique Prince Albert watch chain with a beautifully worked gold fob hanging from it. No wedding ring but a large gold ring on his right ring finger with some sort of crest on it. There was a small mole on his cheek, really along the jaw line just below his right ear. Large space between his two front teeth."

Michael had grabbed a pencil and was scribbling furiously.

"Light eyes. Hazel, I think. Brown hair thinning on the top and streaked with gray."

"Walk?"

"I didn't see him walk. I didn't notice him until he was standing beside me and then I left him. He didn't leave me."

"Accent?"

She shrugged.

"Anything more?"

"No, that's it, I'm afraid."

Michael put down his pen and smiled. "That's quite a lot. Remarkable really. Can you do that for everyone you meet?"

She gave a little laugh, self-conscious suddenly. "No. Not really. Just with some people. But I do have a visual memory. He must've made an impression on me because it was all so peculiar."

"Thank heaven he did. I wish more people could do it. My life would be so much easier." He hesitated. "Did you get his name?"

"Williams. Harold Williams."

Michael made a note. "Probably not his real name but still... You're sure that you've never seen him before?"

"Positive."

"And you would remember if you saw him again?"

"I could never forget that smile. And yes, because I've made the effort now because it's important. I know I would."

He scribbled some numbers on the bottom of the next page of the notepad and tore it off. "My phone number is here and the special message center that can reach me anywhere. Call me the moment you see him again, even if it's just on the street. We'd like to find out who he is if we can, where he goes, and above all, whom he sees."

She nodded and studied the numbers as Michael reached into his bottom right-hand desk drawer, behind the scramble phone, and pulled out a small framed picture. Then he went to the safe and got out the folder which held all the copies of 'Darling Julia's' replies. He handed those to her without comment.

In exchange she handed him the paper with the phone numbers on it.

"You're sure you know them?"

"Yes. I already knew the one for this office."

Michael nodded and absently returned to his desk where he started trying to organize the keywords for what would probably be 'Darling Julia's' last letter to Siegfried. But it was hard to concentrate. He put down the pencil and sat back. There could be no full reply until he had checked out St. Peter's, and he'd have to do that himself, without Anne knowing. But this letter... He had to get to work on this letter. It needed to go out soonest. He picked up his pencil and tried again.

Julia studied the picture. Good face. Solemn. Young. But then it had probably been taken before he left for Germany. Four years ago? He certainly didn't look like James. Much finer drawn. Smaller? Probably. She had never seen Mrs. Richter, but from Annabelle's description of her, John must look more like her and James more like their father. And wasn't it Mrs. Richter...? Oh, God. Poor Captain Compton. This whole business had to be hell for him.

She put the picture down on the table carefully and picked up the letters, glad that the captain seemed to be working at something so she could take her time. After a moment she was smiling here and nodding there. It wasn't the way she wrote herself, but it was good. Relaxed, easy. And the letters reinforced the picture she had given him. No wonder this Mister Williams felt safe in insisting that Brighton was where he had met her with John Richter. And no wonder Captain Compton felt sure that the letters were being read.

She looked up, finally. "Will you mention Mister Williams in the reply?"

"Definitely. And I can do it in clear, thank heaven. That will let John know they're checking on him and will cover what you had to say to the man, as well. In this case it's a help that they're reading his correspondence. Are you through already?"

"Yes. They're rather marvelous. It's hard to believe that a man wrote them."

He smiled. "Thank you. That was the most difficult part. Do you have any questions?"

"Not really. But if I think of any, I won't hesitate to ask."

He rose. "I don't have to remind you..." He didn't finish, fearing that she would feel she wasn't trusted. She wasn't. He didn't trust anyone. Not about this. But since he'd been forced to trust her, there was no sense letting her know how he felt.

Julia was standing now, purse in hand, smoothing down her skirt. She looked up. There had been anguish in his voice. "Mister Williams reminded me, sir. He reminded me in a way I could never forget. And I won't forget with Annabelle, especially Annabelle. James..."

Michael nodded.

She smiled. "Besides, you can't get marvelous love letters from a mystery man for over three years without forming some kind of attachment to him. John Richter doesn't belong to me, but in an odd sort of way Siegfried does. I will take care for him."

Michael searched her face. 'I will take care for him.' An unusual way to put it. And then his face softened as he felt a surge of relief.

"Yes, I believe you will." And he did. "Thank you."

Their handshake was almost a formal ceremony.

He saw her out through Annabelle's office. Julia gave her a little wave as she left but she said nothing. Annabelle looked after her, sensing that something important had happened. It wasn't like Julia not to say anything. She looked so serious. But Annabelle knew she'd never be able to ask about it.

Then she felt Captain Compton's eyes on her and she looked up, startled. "Sir?"

"My appointment with Colonel Harries?"

"He regrets not being able to see you before 6:30, but he's free any time after that."

"Please call him back and tell him 6:30 will be fine. Then get Mrs. Richter for me, if you will."

He didn't hear her, "Of course, sir," since he was already back in his office, closing the door. He gathered up the folder from the table and put it into the safe and was just putting John's picture back into the drawer when the intercom buzzed. "Mrs. Richter is on the line, sir, and your appointment has been confirmed for 6:30."

"Thank you, Miss Trimby." He picked up the phone. "Darling?"

"Michael! I'm so glad you rang. I've had another letter from John!"

"How is he?" It was hard to sound enthusiastic but he managed.

"Very well. The cast is off and his arm's coming along. And can you believe that Georg Brandt has been assigned to Hamburg and is taking care of him again?"

"That's reassuring, I know. May I read it when I come?"

"Of course. When are you coming?"

"4:30, give or take a little, if that's all right."

"It's more than all right. I'll give you tea."

"Sounds marvelous. I'll see you then."

"When you said, 'give or take a little'..." Her voice trailed off.

"Yes?" He smiled, forgetting everything but his delight at hearing what he knew she was going to say.

"Make it sooner if you can." She sounded wistful. "I haven't seen you in ages."

He'd been away for three days and now that he heard her voice, three days did seem like ages. "I'll be there as soon as I can."

She gave a little laugh. "That will have to do, I guess. But it can't be soon enough. Bye, Michael."

He was still smiling as he hung up the phone but his smile disappeared as he picked up the receiver again and gave the operator the number for Saint Peter's rectory himself. He was put right through to the vicar after telling the secretary that his name was Howard Anderson.

*     *     *

It was after 4:00 when Michael left Vicar Rogers in the park across from the Grosvenor Victoria Hotel where they had met because he hadn't wanted to risk having Anne see him going into the church. Max, the driver he had finally consented to have as his own, had been dismissed with orders to pick him up at Anne's at 6:10. Amazing how much simpler Max had made his life already.

But right now he didn't want to be driven anywhere. He was angry and depressed. He wanted to walk, and he wanted Anne. And so he didn't wait until the vicar had ambled out the other end of the park before heading up to Buckingham Palace Road toward Eccleston Street.

Michael had told the vicar who he was, of course, since he knew he'd been recognized. And he had couched his questions in hush-hush Foreign Office terms, saying he was after someone who had been using information from baptismal records to obtain birth certificates of children who had died at a tender age so that passports could be secured in those names. It was pretty thin and he wondered idly if the vicar believed him. It didn't matter. The vicar couldn't possibly know what it was all about. Besides, a vicar was used to mysteries and keeping secrets.

A strange man had been in. Harold Smith. Same first name, same description, same odd smile. Harold whoever-he-was would do well to get rid of that unusual gold fob, to say nothing of changing his name. He had said that it was a matter of an inheritance. The years 1915 to 1924. And John was baptized when? 1920? Old for a baptism. He shook his head to clear the mental picture of a small solemn boy in short pads, knee socks, and Eton jacket.

It had to be the same man.

He turned up Eccleston Street.

Perhaps it was the school that undid him, the undistinguished-looking red brick St. Peter's school where both James and John had gone to prepare for public school. He stopped and looked at the building, remembering going into some sort of pageant there with Anne and Gerhard. John had played an angel. Incredible casting.

But then he was angry, very angry and he was walking quickly, trying to put the school behind him. Anne and John. John and Anne. And Gerhard. Gerhard's son, too. The names repeated themselves over and over with each step until he was swearing under his breath, replacing the names burning his brain with every vile word that he had ever heard, adding a few combinations that had never occurred to him before.

Finally, he stopped and looked around. He had gone too far. He turned and walked back down Belgrave Place towards Eaton Square, thinking that he couldn't be in this mood when he saw Anne. And why was he seeing her? Why today? He had far too much to do to take the time. Oh God, he just wanted to see her, needed to see her, today more than ever. Ironic. He needed to see her because he loved her, because he needed her to wash away, for a little time, at least, his agony about John. But she was a living reminder, living reproach for what he'd done to his godson, her son. He was damned if he did, damned if he didn't. It was abominable. Even more than abominable because he had John's blessing.

Then his feet were pounding harder and harder until he was in front of the house, bounding up the steps and through the door without even ringing the bell. He hesitated in the hall, then, hearing the piano, burst into the music room.

She started when she saw him and stopped playing abruptly, her hand still on the keys. "Darling!" Her smile was dazzling. She rose. "I didn't hear you come in."

"I'm afraid I just walked in."

Her smile faded. She had turned towards him but stopped, a little afraid of what she saw his face.

Michael looked at her standing there, love and concern written all over her, along with something else he couldn't quite place. He was angry and he ached for her, for himself, for her son.

Finally heard her say, "What is it, Michael?" She had moved.

He couldn't stand it. He wasn't aware that he'd moved but suddenly he found himself holding her to him ferociously, found himself saying, "Marry me, Anne." And then he was trembling. What had he done? And why? Why today of all days? He buried his face in her hair.

She couldn't have moved if she'd tried, but she didn't try, content to stay in his arms and let the fierce joy at his words rush over her in waves, needing time to believe that he had really said it at last. And she felt his trembling. He had been afraid? Surely he knew that she loved him, that there could only be one possible answer.

She started to pull back to look up at him but his hand at the back of her head prevented that. His face was still in her hair. So she said it without seeing him. "Yes, Michael."

It was almost a flinch and it made him release her enough so that she was able to look up at last. "Yes! Yes! Yes!" She still couldn't see his face.

He was staring at the wall, his jaw tightening in a fit of agony. He couldn't possibly marry her. He couldn't do that to her, not with John hanging over them like the sword of Damocles. He had opened his mouth to tell her when he looked down and saw her face, that wonderful, enchanting face looking up at him. Who could resist that face? Who could resist her? Who would want to? How could he not marry her? How could he bear that? He groaned as he pulled her to him again, kissing her until they were both breathless.

And then his laughter started. What a fool he was. What a stupid, arrogant fool. He had created hell in heaven. Well, so be it. He couldn't spoil it for her. Not now. Not ever if he could help it. Oh God, don't let me ruin everything. She would be his now and he'd damn well keep her as long as she'd stay. His heart stopped with his laughter and he let her go. When she knew... But the sight of her standing there pushed it all away. She was irresistible, worth everything.

"Oh, Michael." She shook her head fondly. "You're impossible. Honestly, what a proposal. You come storming in here, looking like a thunder-cloud, grab me and hold me until I nearly suffocate, in effect tell me to marry you and when I say yes, you kiss me ferociously and then you laugh yourself silly. That's scarcely the stuff dreams are made of."

He just looked at her. I won't spoil it. I'll do this right, by God. And then his eyes were sparkling. "Come here."

She came.

"Sit there." He pointed to a chair.

She sat.

And then he was down on one knee, her right hand lost between both of his, a properly pleading expression on his face.

"Your eyes," she said.

"What about my eyes?"

"You're trying not to laugh. It shows."

"Indeed. Sorry." He looked away for a moment working on his expression, then turned back. "Better?"

"Definitely."

"Now be quiet. You're distracting me."

"Yes, Michael." She managed to look as meek as Moses. It was all he could do to not laugh again.

"That's better." He paused and took a deep breath. "I, Michael Compton, being of sound mind and body..."

"Are you writing your will?"

"Hush. Where was I? Reasonably sound mind and body."

"It was totally sound before."

"Yes, but you're driving me out of it."

"Mind or body?"

"Both. Now hush, will you? This has to be done properly."

"Sorry." She wasn't in the least. She was enjoying herself enormously.

"And adequate financial means." He looked up at her expecting an interruption but she didn't say a word. "Do formally request your hand in marriage, Anne Richter." He grinned. "Your hand and all the rest that goes with it."

"And I, Anne Richter, being totally out of my mind and exceedingly restless in the rest of me at the moment, do most graciously accept your proposal. You may now kiss the bride."

"Only after you help me up," he complained. "You've kept me down here too long. This floor is hard."

She stood and gave him a hand, which he really didn't need. Then they were both laughing, delighted with each other. It was a moment before he began to dutifully kiss the bride. After a moment it was anything but dutiful.

Her eyes were shiny when she was able to look at him again. "You do have an incredible facility for making me utterly happy."

He held her to him praying fervently that it would stay that way.

She pulled back again. "When?"

His face was grim as he replied. "As soon as something very difficult is resolved."

She traced the line of his jaw with her finger, puzzled by his sudden change of mood. "When will that be?"

"Sometime in September." The Germans would either have come by then or they wouldn't be coming until spring, if then. And John would either be safe again, temporarily at least, or... He couldn't bear to think about the alternative.

Her look was woebegone. "So long?"

"I'm afraid so, darling." He kissed her gently. "There's nothing else for it." Maybe he could tell her by then. Dammit, boy, your cast is off. Get out of there. Come home! Then he could tell her. John would be safe. But if the worst happened... His jaw tightened. If the worst happened, he would be free to tell her because it wouldn't matter anymore. Nothing would matter. She would never forgive him. He crushed her to him. "Let me love you, Anne."

"Now?!"

"Right now."

"But Hannah..." Then she grinned up at him. "I'll send her to Harrod's. She loves to go to Harrod's. And there's just time."

He looked at his watch and his expression was rueful as he said, "I only have a little over an hour." He had forgotten about Hannah.

Anne gave a little laugh. "That's enough time."

"Do you think she'll guess?"

"Are you trying to get out of it now?"

He smiled his reply, shaking his head emphatically.

"I'll simply tell her why."

"You'll tell her?" He looked horrified.

She really laughed at that. "About getting married, for heaven's sake. The things from Harrod's will be for a celebration, later tonight. We can celebrate later tonight, can't we?"

He laughed back at her. "Of course. Or I should say I hope so. If I'm up to it. If I can come back. But she'll guess."

"Perhaps. But right now I don't care."

"And right now, neither do I."

She disappeared out through the door as he looked after her, hating to have to leave her even for so short a time, for so good a reason. His happiness left with her and all the doubts and fears came rushing back, nearly engulfing him. But at last she was back, they were upstairs, and she was in his arms, kissing away everything but his awareness of her.

# Chapter XI

Odd patrol area, thought James, and then he shrugged. The boundaries were changed at irregular intervals to keep Jerry from sneaking E-boats in along the dividing lines, and because they were, that had to result in one area or another being smaller from time to time. This had to be one of those times.

The Old Man was lounging on the bridge, apparently enjoying the night air – he didn't do that very often these days – and looking like a new man. They had all been able to catch up on lost sleep in Pompey – how the hell had the Royal Navy come to christen Portsmouth 'Pompey?' – during the thirty-six hours it had taken to repair the condenser. There hadn't even been an air raid. And tonight should be quiet for once, since no convoy was due through. They had just brought one out with them. It had been picked up east of Dungeness by a corvette and a minesweeper that would take them as far as Ramsgate, leaving *Vectis* to patrol either side of the Dungeness promontory. No ship was wasted. There was no such thing as a free trip these days.

"James." Lieutenant Commander Fredericks deliberately kept his voice casual. "Let's stooge around here for a bit. Vary things enough to keep Jerry on his toes."

The captain looked around. The promontory was just visible through the darkness off the port beam and they had to stay east of it in a maddeningly small area for the next hour and a half. The whole patrol area was small, God knows, but to have to stooge around in such a small section of it...

Had it been just yesterday in that small dockyard office? Time sense was warped these days. It was an effort to keep track. He had thought he was there to discuss some rather pressing supply problems until the supply officer had retired to some unspecified place, leaving him alone with a naval officer, a captain he had never seen before.

"Lieutenant Commander Fredericks, I have a rather peculiar assignment for you. But it must be carried out in absolute secrecy and within the framework of a formal patrol. Only you must know, and I cannot stress the importance of that enough. Do you understand?"

"Of course." Pompous ass. What could be more clear?

"Starting tomorrow night for the following three nights you are to patrol off the Dungeness promontory. The patrol area will vary slightly from night to night. Tomorrow night, for instance, the area will be from just east of the promontory across Rye Bay to the west. The next night perhaps from west of Dungeness east up to the Hythe. But you will be out in that general area for the next three or four nights no matter what happens in the area will always include the Dungeness promontory, especially the area off Littlestone. Everything must appear to be perfectly normal. It wouldn't do to arouse any suspicions, including those of the officers and the crew.

"Tomorrow night you must stay to the east side of the promontory, no further than four miles off, two miles by the tip, between 0230 and 0400. But if the sea state is more than 2 or 3, the rules don't apply. They won't be coming."

"Who is this mysterious 'they'?"

"We have information that a group of six spies will be landing on the east side of the promontory just north of Littlestone during one of the four following nights, starting tomorrow night, whenever the conditions are right. A trawler will bring them in as close to shore as possible, then they'll row the rest of the way. We'd like to catch them in the channel, if we can, so it takes a fast ship. But we have no illusions. It would be very easy for them to slip by. Trouble is that we don't dare increase the number of ships on patrol or the number of land patrols either, for that matter, for fear of compromising our source. Do you understand?"

"Yes, indeed. You want me to find the needle before it gets into the haystack on a dark night without an electric torch. You know roughly when they'll be arriving and where, and you want me to intercept them before they get loose on land without letting my crew suspect that anything unusual is going on because if we are too obvious about it, you'll kill off your source, maybe literally, and you wouldn't know if or when any more were coming. Good luck to us all."

The captain smiled appreciatively, which made Fredericks realize that he might not be such a pompous ass, after all. "Good. I thought you'd get the picture." Then he was business-like again. "You'll have to do this job every night since, for obvious reasons, we don't want to have to tell any more people than absolutely necessary and because it's logical for you to be there tomorrow night. You're on your way back to Dover. And you'll have to be the first in that area for the next four nights, even if they're caught the first night, because it has to seem that they've been caught purely by chance."

He began collecting his things. "You'll have the proper written orders, of course, but only the usual sort for the general area and the time of your patrol. Are there any questions?"

"No," said Fredericks. "It's clear enough. I'll do my best." A needle. Apt analogy. One ship in an area that size... If only they had radar. Then it would have been simple.

The captain had his briefcase in his left hand. He thrust out his right. "Good luck."

He took the proffered hand. "Thank you, sir."

"I'll send Christopher back in. I imagine, unless things have changed dramatically in the last year, that you really do have some supply problems to discuss with him."

Sensible man. "Indeed, I do. Thank you."

So here they were, just east of the Dungeness promontory, moving towards Littlestone at 0300 and his heart was pounding. He wasn't cut out for this cloak and dagger stuff, skulking around, hiding the real mission from the crew. God help them if they did have to stooge around here for the next three nights. It would be obvious to everyone that something was up. And he certainly couldn't be on the bridge every night.

It was a beautiful night. Sensible night for them to come, actually. No moon. No clouds either, thank God. Made for maximum visibility on a dark night. He'd made a point to 'nap' in the afternoon and, to his surprise, he had actually managed to get some sleep. So he hoped it wasn't illogical for him to be on the bridge. In the North Atlantic he had been fairly often but rarely on channel patrols unless something was going on. There was too much to be done in the harbor during the day and he had to be up too much of too many nights for a 'social hour' during the middle watch to be reasonable.

In fact he didn't know how much longer he could stay out here tonight. All the watch officers were more than competent, thank God, and he didn't want to seem to be implying anything else by his presence when it wasn't necessary. At least Number One wasn't the officer of the watch. Oh, Number One was capable enough. That wasn't the problem. Every detail was tended to punctiliously, and no fault could be found except the biggest one of all. The man was an unmitigated ass.

Damn waiting, anyway.

"Sir."

Fredericks was startled by hearing a voice so close to his ear. Rigby. The boy must walk on cat's feet. Good. A mug of cocoa. Something to do. An excuse to stay for a while longer. "Thank you Rigby."

He saw the faint gleam of white teeth through the darkness and heard his "You're welcome, sir." Nice boy, Rigby. He was coming along well. Good signalman.

He had just taken his first sip and was relishing the warmth going down his throat when he heard, "Object. Green 2-oh."

Already?! By God! He worked hard to keep the excitement out of his voice. "Close it, James. Whoever he is he shouldn't be here."

Frederick raised his binoculars with his left hand, oblivious to the fact that he still had a cup of cocoa in his right.

There it was. Closer than he thought and heading towards the coast. The trawler – it had to be a trawler – would cross *Vectis'* starboard bow no more than 1000 yards out unless there was an abrupt change in course.

It was an effort not to leap onto the compass platform in response to James' "Action stations, sir?" Fredericks cursed. He should've thought of it himself and at once.

"Yes. I'll take it." He stepped onto the compass platform as James stepped off and reached for the alarm button, shouting "Challenge. Starboard ten. 200 revolutions." Closing fast. Don't give them time. It had to be the trawler. No one else would be out here alone, especially at this hour. Make sure. Make sure.

He released the alarm button, concentrating so hard on the faint bow wave of the trawler that he was unaware of the pounding of his feet as the rest of the signal and ASDIC contingent arrived. Nor was he aware that Rigby had grabbed the mug from his hand, spilling cocoa all over himself in the process. Rigby swore as he put his mug and the captain's into the corner of the desk. Cocoa was murder to get out of a uniform. This had better not be a false alarm.

"No reply, sir."

Fools. They should have given some sort of reply. It might have given them ... Ten seconds. His smile was grim, unseen in the darkness.

Blind them with the 24-inch searchlight on the tower aft. Better than a star shell at close range, and it would attract far less attention generally. Didn't want the trawler reinforced, if he could help it.

Closing. Close enough for the light and the angle was right... NOW! "Searchlights! Guns, fire as you bear."

The trawler's bow gun was spitting at them, getting in the first shot. Damn.

A finger of brilliant light was stabbing through the nights, weaving slightly and then holding onto the trawler's fo'c'scle, even as *Vectis*' guns began firing. Salvo followed salvo from all four guns in a series of deafening cracks. Good. Good.

Nowhere to run, you bastard, Fredericks thought with fierce joy. We've got you between Scylla and Charybdis, between *Vectis* and the coast. And you'll have to run our gauntlet.

The trawler was turning slowly to port now, trying to cross *Vectis'* stern so that only the X and Y guns could bear while she made for open sea. Can't have that.

He bent to the voice pipe. "Hard a-port."

Shell splashes straddled the trawler – Good! Good! – And their gunnery had been atrocious so far. But then night gunnery was always a chancy business. Good again. Spray from that last shell was flying over the trawler's stern. Drill after drill was paying off. And experience. *Vectis* had had plenty of experience lately.

Keep your mind and your business. Stop admiring... He spoke into the voice pipe and then the ship was healing sharply, turning, just as a geyser interrupted where the stern should have been. Trawler getting their range now? – Surprising, considering the glare from *Vectis'* searchlight – or had they just been lucky with that one? Now if they'd been up against an E- boat... He shuddered. So close in, with an E-boat maneuverability and speed and torpedoes...

Another straddled. Colin was doing well. At least he could see above the smoke. The reason the gun control tower was so high, along with the longer line of sight. The air stank of cordite and there was a metallic taste in his mouth.

"Midships." He watched. "Meet her. Steady on 1-8-5." The trawler hadn't a prayer of out running *Vectis* but there was good fire from her now, he admitted grudgingly, and rapid. They weren't lacking in courage, and with the captain handling her as well as he was... Who knows. If they got in a lucky shot...

BOOM! A tremendous explosion lifted the stern of the trawler out of the sea. It slammed down and disappeared into the wave its fall created. Amazingly she rose again, the whole ship shuttering, shaking off the water in a white foam.

Another hit. The stern again. And then there was pandemonium as flames began leaping from the trawler's deck. The stern was settling rapidly, and figures were leaping into the sea, black stick figure silhouetted against the orange of the flames. For once they were German stick figures, Fredericks thought with satisfaction. Too often, on channel convoys, they had been British. It was good to be getting back some of their own.

Amazing. The trawler's bow gun was still firing. A geyser rose just off *Vectis'* starboard bow. Another one of those could be trouble.

And then another explosion rent the night. "God." It escaped from Fredericks as a sigh. Awesome. The magazine. It had to have been the magazine.

"Cease-fire! Searchlight off!"

The quiet was a relief. And then the flames were gone. Everything was gone as the Channel and the night swallowed the trawler whole.

"Port Twenty." They began to circle so they could drift downward toward the wreck on the wind.

"Away seaboat. Rig nets. Slow ahead together." The orders came rapidfire, one after the other. There was a pause before he started again.

"Midships." He watched the gyro-compass carefully. "Meet her. Steady on 1-2-Oh.'"

"Lower to the waterline." The watch began lowering the whaler. Fredericks winced as he heard the blocks of the falls squealing. Needed grease. That would have to be taken care of.

"Stop engines."

The ship began to slow. "Slip!"

The whaler hit the water and eased away from the side with the aid of the boat, even before the ship came dead in the water. The whaler was off towards the sound of the cries that could be heard from one group as the ship began to drift on the breeze toward another. The smaller searchlight on the bridge picked up a few bobbing heads as the ship closed in on them with seemingly infinite patience and caution.

Finally, the survivors were scrambling up the nets and being hauled aboard none too gently to stand, dripping, on the deck. James looked closely as there was a hubbub and a clustering at the rail. What the hell...? Good grief, it was a woman! He was transfixed. What on earth was a woman, especially a woman in a skirt, doing on an armed German trawler just off the British coast in the middle of the night? And why was the trawler here anyway? Unless... "Spies?"

Frederick shrugged. "It would certainly explain why they are here. Nothing else does. Even if the Germans are foolish enough to send a single trawler off after our convoy suddenly, they wouldn't send one on a fool's errand. Their information about our convoys seems infallible. And trawlers don't lay mines."

"But on the southeast coast? I thought that the southeast coast was sewn up tight, movement restricted and so on."

"Can anything that long be sewn up tight?"

James' answer came slowly. "I guess not." The thought wasn't consoling.

After what seemed like an eternity, but was, in reality, only ten additional minutes, the whaler returned and five more survivors climbed the nets, including one man in the remains of a business suit.

While the whaler was being hauled up and the ship gotten underway, the prisoners were sorted out. The enemy officers and the man in the business suit were sent to the wardroom, the enlisted men to the crew's quarters forward, and the woman to the captain's harbor cabin, all under guard and all the guards ordered to permit no conversation whatsoever between the prisoners and the crew. Stillson was seeing to it all with his usual irritating efficiency.

It was an hour into the morning watch before they were able to secure from action stations. Colin's turn, thought James gratefully, as he made his way aft along the iron deck and down the ladder to the cabin flat. Murphy was standing guard at the door to the captain's harbor cabin, arms folded across his massive chest, holstered sidearm belt around his waist. James gave him an exaggerated wink and won a grin in reply.

He took off his jacket and flopped onto his bunk before he bothered to kick off his shoes. The ship was already buzzing with the talk of spies and 'Mata Hari'. Either that woman was really beautiful or rumor had made her so, given the 'romance' of the situation. She was damn lucky to have been caught at sea. Because she had been on a German ship at the time, she couldn't be considered a spy though that was what she had to be. And spies were hanged. James shuddered, then settled back and closed his eyes. He was asleep almost at once.

\*      \*      \*

Harold Cummins, traveler in ladies' lingerie, had seen most of the action from the vantage point at the top of the lighthouse on the promontory. He had been coming this way on and off for several years. In fact, he had probably sold the keeper's wife everything she had on except her dress and shoes. They were always glad to see 'old Harold' and tonight had been no exception. It had been several months and 'old Harold' had brought a bottle of now scarce scotch with him.

They were lucky to still be here, they told him. The light was rarely used and then only on the direct orders of the Admiralty, when a convoy was coming through. There had been talk of having it manned by the military, but Fred had managed to convince the powers-that-be that not only would he and the other keeper know how to care for the light better than anyone else, but they'd all be willing to serve as Coast Guards, as well. "A real tiger, Fred was," Eunice had said. "There was no arguing him down." And so they had stayed.

It had been a godsend for 'old Harold'. That peculiar smile flashed in the darkness. They were a gold mine of information and they never suspected the thing. But then, no one did. Who on earth would think a traveler in the ladies' scanties would be anything but what he said he was? And because he'd been a traveler for years, he had no trouble getting the necessary permits to travel all over the restricted zone that closed off the coast.

He hoped they would come tonight. The weather looked promising enough and God knows, he didn't want to stay on. One night 'enjoying' Fred and Eunice was about all he could stand at one time. If the car he left in the Littlestone car park was gone in the morning, they'd have come. If not, he'd have to stay. Thank God for the scotch. It had paved the way for him to stay for a week if necessary. Fred had all but fallen on his neck when he'd handed over the bottle. But he'd drunk too much of it himself, to fortify himself against an evening of Eunice's chatter, and then with an excellent dinner on top of that, all fresh from their garden and from the chicken run... Gradually his eyes closed and after a few moments the sounds of gentle snores filled the tiny spare room.

"Harold!" There were violent bangs on the door. "Harold, wake up!"

His eyes seem to be stuck together, but he managed a grunt that must've been audible, because Fred said, "Good. Glad you're up. Eunice was watching. Bit of a dustup out there. Come on up top." And then there was a thudding as Fred pounded out the door, towards the lighthouse.

Harold threw on his robe and slippers before walking across to the lighthouse and pulling himself up the spiral staircase, huffing and puffing, cursing his age, the heavy dinner, and all that scotch. To them he was simply a reasonably prosperous bachelor who appreciated home cooking and a bed for a night or two, especially when he could still collect his per diem. He had to keep up the image.

A string of light in the distance and the sound of gunfire greeted him as he stepped out into the narrow cat walk around the top of the tower. Fred thrust the binoculars into his hand as an explosion boomed through the night.

"Two miles off, at most," came Fred's excited voice. "The bigger ship's got to be one of ours. A destroyer."

Harold adjusted the binoculars. There they were. He bit back a curse. Caught fair and square. He'd have to find out something about Channel patrols from these people. Since they were Coast Guards, they ought to know. There seemed to be only two ships. The smaller one was probably a trawler, and the only German trawler expected in these waters was the one landing the agents. Damn. Blind luck? Somehow he managed to sound enthusiastic as he said "Done for! Jerry's done for!"

Fred whooped. "'Bout time Jerry got back some of his own! Let me look!"

Harold handed in the binoculars and stood there watching in silence, hands in the pockets of his robe, shivering slightly in the breeze. Eunice was looking steadily through a spyglass, as she had been since he'd arrived at the top.

The final explosions brought a delighted shout from her followed by a moment of silence as the flames disappeared. He'd seen enough. "Looks as if the show is over. I'm chilly. Back to bed." But he didn't move as the thought occurred to him that he'd have to pick up the car first thing in the morning. People didn't leave unattended cars around for long, especially these days.

Fred still had the binoculars at his eyes, even though everything was in darkness. He lowered them with a sigh. "They'll be picking up the survivors now."

Harold had started for the stairs, but he stopped and turned back. "Where will they take them?"

"Depends. Dover probably. Those patrols are really paying off."

"Do they always have a ship patrolling around here?" He was grateful for a natural opening to ask.

"I'd say they do, most nights. Of course they don't tell us, but sometimes, when the moon is out and conditions are right, we can see them. And the convoys come by, too. This can be a very busy corner. E-boats some nights. Now that's a show."

"You two can stand here nattering all night if you want to, but my turn is up and I'm going to bed." Eunice started down the stairs. Fred and Harold followed her down, taking their time as they went round and round on the inside of the wall. Harold gave a harsh chuckle.

"Spectacular entertainment."

Fred turned back and smiled up through the darkness. "Thought you might like to see it."

"Cuppa, Harold?" Eunice's voice came up from below.

"I thought you were going to bed, Eunice." Fred sounded irritated.

"Let's have a short one, Fred," said Harold. He wasn't ready for sleep, not yet.

It wasn't a happy celebration. Perhaps it was an anti-climax. Or maybe they were just too tired. But Fred was glad that the drinks Harold poured really were short. Harold had certainly put them down before dinner and good scotch was too rare a commodity in Fred's life these days for him to be content to see it poured out at one go. He wanted this bottle to last a long time.

After just the one short one, Harold had smiled that weird smile of his and disappeared into his room. Fred turned out the lights and opened the blackout curtains in the bedroom to let in some air. That was the trouble with blackout curtains. Got stuffy if you wanted to leave the lights on. Those smiles of Harold's gave Fred the creeps. He didn't smile that way very often anymore, thank God, because he did have another smile, what Eunice called his 'real smile'. And he was good company. Not many people were as good company as Harold.

Fred pulled up the covers and yawned as his wife turned on her side, away from him, grunting a bit as she settled herself. Jeffers' shift. He was out there somewhere in the night. Jeffers could have stayed in the tower, but he hated heights. He'd never make a lighthouse keeper. It was the last thought Fred had until morning.

*     *     *

"What's wrong?" Richter looked as if he'd been put through a ringer. He had swung into the passenger seat of the Kuebel, slammed the door shut and then slumped down into the seat, leaning his head back against the top of it without saying a word. Dieter waited, watching him. Must've been one hell of a day.

"Let's go back to the house." Even his voice was weary.

"What about dinner with Hauptmann Brandt?"

"I called him and put him back an hour. I need time for a good stiff drink, a hot bath, and twenty minutes in the sack for I can go anywhere."

Dieter repeated his initial question. "What's wrong?"

"Captured. All of them."

"The agents?"

He nodded.

Bergmann gave a low whistle.

"Three taken from the trawler before they had a chance to land. Caught by a patrolling destroyer. Trawler sunk. The other three..." Hans snorted. "Damn idiot got thirsty. Thirsty! Such a waste. For want of a drink, three lives were lost. They'll be hanged. Hanged!" Dieter watched him, saying nothing. What could he say? Hanged. Jesus. Which three? All six? Not the time to ask. Later. He turned the key in the ignition and the engine roared to life.

"I don't understand it." Hans was having to speak louder now, over the sound of the engine. "Kapitan Schroeder told me that they were all going over to one beach, the one the trawler was heading for. If they had then none of them would hang. They'd all go to the POW camps but they'd be alive." Actually it made more sense to send them to separate beaches. More of a chance for at least one of the groups to get through. "I should've told them, but it never occurred to me! Besides, the hours might be different now."

"Tell them what? What hours?"

"The opening and closing hours of pubs. The laws are strict. Still, the fool could have used common sense. Anyone ordering a drink at nine in the morning is bound to be noticed, and the last thing they needed was to be noticed. The pub keeper must've been getting organized for the day when he walked in, thinking the place was open for business.

"They'd put in at the wrong beach and didn't know where they were. All the town and directional signs have been taken down to confuse spies that land and, presumably us, if we invade."

Dieter noticed the 'if' but said nothing.

Hans went on. "So he had to have been trying to find out where they were. But in a pub? The most incredible part of all... I still can't believe it. They told him that the pub didn't open until ten, that he should come back then and the fool did! The police were waiting for him."

Dieter just shook his head. What could anyone say to that?

Hans sat up straight. If he hadn't been so tired, he would've seen it sooner. Two landing sites and two trawlers. It had to have been planned that way all along. That one landing site business had never made sense. But Schroeder had told him in no uncertain terms that there was to be only one landing site, that it had been narrowed down to three and that was what he needed Hans' advice about. By the time he left for the office, he knew which one it would be. A test or a trap. For him. It had to be one or the other.

But why Schroeder? What did he have to do with anything? Or was it because it was so unlikely that he'd be involved that he had been used? A screen? And how... And for God's sake, why would he be involved? All Schroeder did... He was the naval liaison officer for both the Hamburg Military District HQ and the Abwehr station in the same building. Unusual to have a full captain doing that, but since the Navy was the weakest branch, they tended to put their bigger guns where they do the most good, where, like Schroeder, they'd outrank almost everyone they dealt with.

But the trap had been Schroeder's. Spy missions to Britain were only a very small part of what he did and even then he was involved only in the naval – the delivery – aspects. Someone had to have put him up to it. But who? Not Minten. He had that remarkable talk with Minten after he had seen Kapitan Schroeder and Minten would never have talked as he had, drunk or not, if he were testing whether or not he was the leak.

So it wasn't Minten; there was only one other possibility and that was Kramer. But if Kramer were behind it, how had he managed to involve Schroeder? What he'd been told was classified information, top-secret stuff, and a man like Schroeder would never give out that sort of information to someone who had no 'need to know' without written orders from a superior officer. And since Kramer was only a lieutenant... And they weren't friends.

Hans shuddered at the thought. They barely spoke at meetings. And Schroeder wouldn't have done it for political reasons. He stayed above all that, well clear of the periodic jockeying for position that went on in any military HQ – or unit, for that matter – this one included. It didn't make sense. None of it did. Unless Kramer had something on Schroeder just as he had to have on Minten. His heart fell. There was one way to find out. Annaliese. She would know. And even if she didn't, she would know if Kramer and Schroeder saw each other, at least if they did in Schroeder's office. He hated involving her in even so small a way, but there was no choice. He had to know. The question was how to do it without making her suspicious.

Was she herself involved? God. He was becoming positively paranoid in his old age. He had asked her out, after all. And if she were keeping an eye on him, she would scarcely have turned him down to go to her nephew's birthday party. No. Not a nephew. Some sort of cousin. Never mind. Jesus. It was time he got out of this business. Next he'd be suspecting Bergmann.

Don't trust anyone. Michael's words popped unbidden into his brain. All right, he'd be careful, even with her, especially with her and especially when he asked her about Kramer, because if Kramer were involved, especially if he really had been willing to jeopardize a vital mission to spring this little trap of his – would even Kramer go that far? – then the stakes were high.

He shivered. If Kramer really had done that, he'd muffed it. Michael had handled things well. A capture at sea by the only patrol vessel in the area. That's what Horst's message had said. He'd been down there to keep an eye on things and to leave a car. Minten certainly hadn't looked too happy when he heard about that. Had he known and if he hadn't, didn't that point the finger at Kramer all the more? And if Kramer were willing to risk Horst in the bargain... My God.

And Dunkel. How could he have forgotten about Dunkel? He

never even heard of Dunkel before Minten had mentioned him. Minten had said that Dunkel had all the answers and that he'd get them out of him in the morning. Morning had come in there had been no answers to anything because Dunkel was dead. Hit-and-run. An accident? Whatever it had been, Dunkel's death certainly was convenient for some.

"... hanged, as well?"

"What did you say?" Hans asked. "I'm sorry. I was thinking about something else."

"I asked if you were sure the others wouldn't be hanged as well."

"They were still on a German ship in the Channel. The British are exceedingly civilized about such things. They'll be interned."

"Thank God for that."

Hans nodded. Thank God, indeed. But the others... Why the hell did they take on that lush? You'd think they'd have picked the best Germany has to offer and instead they chose a lush of an aging playboy. I said something about it the first week they were here but was told that the choice had been made, thank you, and that I should keep my opinions to myself.

What to do? They'd have to send in another group at once. That was certain. But time was so short that they couldn't afford the six weeks of training this last lot had – fat lot of good it had done them anyway. More like four weeks, and that was at the outside. They'd have to act fast. Choose a group. Get going.

But by the end of the meeting, Minten hadn't seemed concerned about that, or anything else, for that matter. In fact he'd seemed excited about something. Elated was more the word, actually. Could he possibly have something up his sleeve? If he did, he'd better put it out in a hurry. Time was of the essence.

The Kuebel pulled up in front of the School House. A drink. A hot bath. Sleep. Then dinner with Georg. There was nothing like dinner with Georg to take the edge off a lousy day. He needed a good laugh.

*     *     *

Minten was pacing the floor. For once he couldn't sit still. God sent. The whole damn fiasco was God sent. Triumph from tragedy. It was brilliant. He had said that he would find a way out of that business with Kramer and he had. Oh, he had, in spades. And best of all, Kramer couldn't do anything about it. Not one damn thing. The orders would be coming from Admiral Canaris himself. Emergency orders. Minten gave a vicious little laugh. He couldn't wait to see the expression on Kramer's face.

Everyone had to do his part to pick up the slack, right? Even Kramer. Especially Kramer. Minten started laughing. Kramer would hate every minute of it. Then he was howling with laughter, slumping back into his desk chair, breathless, tears streaming down his face. My God, how he would hate it. It was dangerous and Kramer hated danger with a passion. He was a coward. He'd fight like a rat at first, feinting in first in one direction, then the next. But finally he'd realize that he was cornered. Then he'd turn and slash out at everyone and everything. Let him slash. His claws and his teeth have been pulled.

The pictures-to-the-Fuehrer business was a bluff. He was sure of it. He'd checked. Kramer had no connection with the Fuehrer or anyone even remotely close to him, and no one got to the Fuehrer or got anything to the Fuehrer except to the very inner circle of men around him. Kramer did have connections but they were strictly moneyed, not political. No, unless the pictures got to the Fuehrer, he could contain the situation. No one else would care. Not these days.

Trouble with Kramer was that he was beginning to think he was infallible. To survive in this business, you had to disabuse yourself of that notion and fast. If Kramer hadn't, well so much the better.

Kugelmann had to go to over twenty photographers before he'd found the right one. Kramer had chosen well. "The sign above the door said "passport photos taken", but the bulk of the business was really hard-core pornography. High-quality stuff. Buying was part of the price that Kugelmann had to pay for the information. At those prices, the man was making a fortune. The photographer had remembered the pictures because of their unusual content. In fact he had tried to get Kramer to sell in the negatives. He hadn't thought much of the quality of the pictures, mind you, but the content was worth something. And Kramer had been careful. He had insisted on being in the dark room while the prints were made and put through the dryer so that no additional copies could be made. Two sets. No copies of the negatives. "The lieutenant was in too big of a hurry for that. It would have meant leaving them for several days and he didn't want to do that." Thank God.

He, Minten, had destroyed the only set of negatives along with the original prints. And he had burned one of the two sets that Kramer had made. One set left. Where were they? Minten was willing to bet that they were still in Hamburg. Kramer would want them somewhere where he could keep an eye on them.

But where in Hamburg? His office and his room had been searched and he was being watched, so he couldn't have sent them out of the city. Kugelmann had even checked out the bordello Kramer frequented. What was that whore's name? Sonya? Sonya. Nothing there either. Well, if Kramer's went for the pictures, let alone tried to send them out of Hamburg, he would know. Kramer couldn't get a flea out of Hamburg without his knowing. A safety deposit box? No. As far as that could be checked, there was no safety deposit box. Even if there was one hadn't been found, he would have to go to the bank himself to get them out. And then...

Kramer couldn't send them to Admiral Canaris either. Everything that went to Admiral Canaris had to go through him, unless it was sent by hand, and then the men who were watching him would get them, as well. Besides, after today it wouldn't do him any good anyway.

Canaris had been furious when Minten had called him about the agents. He began sweating, just thinking about it. He was glad to have been at the other end of the phone line. But the admiral had been purring after he heard Minten's plan. "Excellent, Minten. Really excellent. This may be even better. A stroke of genius." High praise indeed, but the admiral was right. It was a stroke of genius.

Kramer would be off his back and so would that bright and all too capable Richter. Richter was a comer, real talent and with his connections...

Still, it was too bad. Richter had a way with raw intelligence data and with agents, as well. He knew how to tell them what they needed to know without boring them to death. Good mind. Congenial. People liked him. That was all too rare in this business and certainly would never be said of Kramer. And yet, with all that, Richter showed no signs of trying to scramble up the Abwehr career ladder. Still, it wasn't wise to take chances. Canaris had his eye on Richter so let Richter take the chances, Richter and Kramer, while he, Minten, was safe in Hamburg. But Richter had to volunteer. Canaris had been most specific on that point. Richter was perfect. There was no one else really. He had to be willing to do it.

A tap on the door interrupted his thoughts. "Come!"

It was Kugelmann. "Are you ready to leave, Herr Major?"

"Yes, my boy, I am."

My boy? My, my, aren't we expansive suddenly? What had happened? He'd thought Minten would be drunk and snarling after having been read out by the admiral. And why the hell did he want to see Hauptmann Richter anyway? Minten had been with him all day for God sake. Well, he'd know soon enough. Minten could stand being mysterious just for so long.

"And Kugelmann, when we're through with our little visit to Hauptmann Richter, if things go the way I think they will, we must celebrate."

Kugelmann suppressed a sigh. Minten's 'celebrations' were a real pain in the ass. He almost giggled. Sometimes the ass was Minten's.

But the major had gone on, oblivious to everything but his own lascivious anticipation. "Something special. Something unusual. I'll leave it in your hands." He paused at the door, his eyes fixing on Kugelmann's. "And I am quite sure that I am leaving the choice in excellent hands."

"Have I ever failed you?" Kugelmann asked wearily.

Minten's smile was wintry. "No, you haven't and I'm sure you don't want to start now."

He turned and sailed out the door.

\*     \*     \*

"What...?" Hans shook the sleep from his brain. He was sitting in his room in the chair by the window, wearing only his underwear. A letter from his mother was in his lap. There was another, from 'Darling Julia', on the table beside him, next to his half-finished drink. The ice cubes were almost melted.

There was another tap at the door, louder this time. He cleared his throat. "Who is it?"

"Heinrich."

"Just a minute." He struggled into his pants. Blast fly buttons anyway. Why couldn't they use zippers?

When he was finally able to open the door, Heinrich spoke quickly keeping his voice low. "Major Minten is downstairs. Sergeant Bergmann said to tell you he was sorry you didn't have more warning, but Corporal Kugelmann forgot to call as he'd promised to do when the major left Headquarters."

Damn. "Tell the major I'll be down in a few minutes."

"He said he'd rather see you up here."

Odd. "All right. Wait two minutes and then go down and ask him to come up. I should be ready by then."

"Very well, sir." He hesitated. "Do you need any help?"

"No. But thank you for asking." Hans smiled. "It's nice to be able to take care of myself again."

Heinrich nodded and turned as Hans shut the door and rushed to the armoire for clean socks. That turd Kugelmann forgot to call. Or maybe it was just too much trouble. Whatever Minten wanted to see him about had to be plenty confidential if he was willing to walk up a long flight of stairs to talk about it behind closed doors. Minten never walked anywhere, let alone up stairs, unless he had to.

And what could he possibly want, anyway, that he couldn't have said almost at any time all day? He sighed. At least he'd had time for a bath, had a drink, the mail, and a bit of a nap.

He pulled on his socks, a smile growing slowly. Mother and Michael were really getting married. It had been a shock to find Michael's note in with his mother's letter in his real hand, not the writing he used for the Julia letters. Officially asking his blessing. And then he was laughing as he pulled on his boots - and going into his prospects at what, fifty-four? How medieval can you get?

And Mother sounded so happy. Hans stood and struggled into his tunic. Damn arm. He paused, brushes in hand. She really had. It was time, Mother, time you are really happy again. God knows, I've given you enough cause for unhappiness. Not that you've complained. Really, you said very little, but the little you've said made me know the cost. But in this letter, there was nothing but Michael and happiness. He gave a little laugh. And so why did he find that upsetting? Thought of Mother being married to someone but Father? Even Michael? It was time.

He used the brushes savagely. 'Darling Julia's' letter had been a bombshell. She knew. And from what the letter said, Michael had told her. Probably had to because of the contact. Routine? Not bloody likely. Abwehr wouldn't risk this Horst of theirs with a face-to-face contact for routine check. Kramer again? Probably, given what Minten had said. Who the hell knew anything for sure anymore.

He threw his dirty clothes into the armoire and slammed the door, then stood, looking around. The room was presentable enough. He sighed. He'd know more when he decoded the letter. No sleep tonight. If someone really had been to the church, then he'd know for sure.

There was a tap on the door.

Hans opened it and came to attention as Minten entered. "Herr Major."

"Hauptmann Richter."

"Sit down, please." Hans gestured toward the chair by the

window. It was the only comfortable one in the room.

Minten settled himself and pointed regally towards the desk chair. "Make yourself comfortable. Surely by now there's no need to stand on such ceremony."

He wants something. Whenever he's this cordial he wants something. Hans sat down, saying, "Thank you, Herr Major. But I thought this was an official visit."

"It is. It is," he hurried to agree. "But even so..." Minten paused. Hans didn't help him. "I'm afraid that the Fatherland needs your services for a rather... ahhh ... delicate assignment."

Uh oh, this was going to be bad. Hans's voice was smooth and easy as he said, "As always, I am at the disposal of the Fatherland." "Good. Good. Minten was rubbing his hands together nervously. "But this is a request, not an order. You are not to agree if you have any reservations about it. Admiral Canaris was most specific on that point."

From Canaris himself...?

"This is something far above and beyond the call of duty. You'd be playing a difficult and dangerous game, and it would mean your neck if you got caught, literally."

Hans stared at him. What the hell could he possibly be talking about?

"But the contribution you could make is beyond calculating. Still, should you refuse, there will be no penalty. You would continue here permanently unless the Wehrmacht had urgent need of your services again." Minten coughed delicately.

Russia? There were rumors afoot about Russia. Is that what Minten was threatening him with if he refused? Probably. He shivered. "I understand." He didn't.

"Good. Good." Minten glanced out the window.

What on earth was he so nervous about?

"You were at the meeting this morning, so you know what happened to the two groups we sent to England."

Of course. Idiot! "Yes. Tragic." What was this?

"And so unnecessary for one group at least. The man should have shown some self-control." Minten snorted with disgust.

That was the pot calling the kettle black.

"We must have at least one other group in place within four weeks."

So what else is new? "It's not much time."

"No. It's not. We had six, almost seven weeks for the last lot and look what happened to them. That idiot Grupner." Minten snorted again. "The others were bad luck. Bad luck and naval stupidity. Next time we'll make sure there's a diversion to draw off the patrol ship. Stupid of Schroeder not to think of it." He gave an exaggerated sigh. "But that's all water under the bridge now."

Hans saw his chance. "Speaking of Kapitan Schroeder, there's something about all of this that puzzles me. He consulted me about possible landing sites two weeks ago, and he gave me the impression that both groups were to land at the same place."

Minten was astonished. The landing sites had been set for weeks. Why would anyone need Richter's advice about that any-way, especially so recently? Most peculiar. And one site? "You must've misunderstood. There are always two sites."

Ah. Then it had been a trap and clearly not one of Minten's making. He couldn't have faked that expression, nor would he have answered as he had. If he'd been part of it, he would've been evasive. Kramer's trap. It had to be. Kramer really had handed him those three agents. Unbelievable. He didn't care how he won. Betraying his own side, for God sake. And Dunkel... But how did Schroeder fit into this? "I'm sure that was it. It's beside the point now."

"Yes. It is. As I said, water under the bridge. We won't make the same mistakes again."

"I'm sure."

"As I also said, we have to have another group in place within four weeks. Our agent in London has contacts all over the southeast coast so he'll have to concentrate his efforts there. There's no time... But it means having someone else in London. One man can't do it all. We need someone who knows London, who has contacts in government circles, someone who could move freely and with confidence."

Hans was watching him closely, thoroughly confused. What could Minten be getting at, and what could he have to do with it unless... No. He couldn't mean that!

"We need you, Richter."

There was no sound in the room. Minten waited anxiously, watching the struggle of emotions on Hans' face. Triumph from tragedy. That phrase had been running through his brain for hours. But it would be only if Richter agreed to go. Then he, Gerd Minten, would have solved everything for everyone, including himself, and within twenty-four hours.

He was sweating as the silence went on. Richter had to agree. He was perfect. Even with his mother and brother... Because of his mother and brother. The perfect cover. There was no question of Richter's loyalty. He had come back to Germany even though he had to have known he'd be called up. And he'd stayed when he could've run. Not only stayed, but served brilliantly, both before and during the war, frequently at unusually sensitive jobs for his rank. And now for Abwehr. Yes, indeed. Richter was perfect. Minten shifted in his chair. Why was Richter looking at him like that?

Hans' mind was in chaos. He couldn't believe it. Home? To go home? Oh, God, he wanted to go home. To see it, touch it, feel it, taste it, hear it, smell it, wallow in it. But... Careful. Don't jump at it. Remember what you are here in Hamburg for. If you were what Minten thought you were it would be a delicate and dangerous assignment. And... "How?" The question burst out of him.

"How what?"

"You talked about my having connections and moving around London freely. How can I do it? Someone would be bound to recognize me sooner or later and that would be that. And my mother..."

Minten was smirking. "That's the beauty of it. Everyone would know you were there, including your mother."

Hans gave him a blank stare, which made Minten burst out

laughing. "You'll simply sail across the Channel in your own little boat and go home."

"Are you out of your mind?"

"Far from it. It's so simple that I don't know why I didn't think of it before. You would be 'defecting', say from Dunkirk. You were stationed there before and with all this invasion talk, there'd be no reason why you wouldn't have been posted back there. You'd be fed up, disillusioned with the Third Reich, and so you sail home to the bosom of Mother England and your family, suitably contrite and bearing a wealth of intelligence that will have their mouths watering. All carefully doctored, of course. You will be anxious to help them in every way, making speeches on the evils of National Socialism and so on. They might even ask you to help analyze intelligence from Germany. And if you got in far enough, you might even be able to zero in on the leak for us." Minten was positively beaming at the prospect. With his connections, Richter would be tied up in red tape for a far shorter time than anyone else they could send.

"Then I'd be going alone."

"No, no. You'd have a radio operator with you."

"Fine. That's just fine. I sail into one of the Kentish ports in a small sailboat, complete with radio and radio operator and announce that I have returned to the bosom of my family. I can see it all now."

Minten's eyes narrowed. Richter was going too far.

"You wouldn't have the radio with you. That would be delivered after you got there. A suitcase radio. It could be left at a luggage place in one of the railway stations."

"Victoria. That's near my home."

"Good. Good. But we can settle all of the details later, if you decide to go." Minten's eyes were gleaming. He had him. He was sure that he had him. Talking about which station.

"I would rather go alone. It would be far safer. No one to compromise me and..."

"There will be a radioman," Minten snapped. "The two groups

must be kept totally separate. It's safer for you as well as them. The operators we have there now are having to send too much as it is and too much output from one location is dangerous. Even though we've limited the length of individual transmissions, they have to move frequently. It's a damn nuisance. Besides, you would be too valuable for us to be willing to risk compromising you in any way. You must be self-contained, must not be exposed to any of our people there.

"Besides, coding and decoding takes a lot of time, more time than you'll have. So he'll help you with that, too."

Hans nodded. It did take a lot of time. Too damn much time. Tonight for instance...

But Minten was droning on "and if he 'defects' with you, it would be natural for you two to see something of each other once you got to London, natural for you to see that he had a place to live and, hopefully, a good job. Good for him and good for us."

"You don't want much, do you."

Minten said, with a ponderous attempt at humor, "Just to win the war."

"We all want to win the war."

"Then you'll do it?" He sounded childishly hopeful.

"Probably."

Minten was beaming again.

"The more I think about it, the more logical it seems. I do have connections in London and with the experience I've had here, analyzing information, I know what sorts of things you'd want."

"And you're very good at it, if I may say so," Minten broke in eagerly.

Hans went on as if the major hadn't said anything. "And I might, just might, be able to carry it off. But this radio operator business worries me. If he goes with me and gets caught, then I get caught. Why can't we go separately?"

"Because he needs to be above suspicion too, has to have a natural relationship with you. Each of you, like Caesar's wife, must be above reproach, pure as the driven snow in your connections.

It's part of what will protect you both."

"When you think about it, what good will a radio operator be? We'll be watched for a long time. He wouldn't dare pick up, let alone operate the radio while we were being watched. By the time we're clear, it will be too late to get information for the invasion."

"You will have a radio operator!" Minten spoke each word separately and with barely veiled rage. He paused, taking a deep breath trying to be calm. "And that's that." He had himself under control. "At the very least, he can handle the coding and decoding. Initially you'll have a system of blind drops and a way to let one of the radiomen know where to pick up the messages so he can send them. When things calm down, when it's safe, then your man can pick up the radio and start transmitting. We see this as a long-range penetration, just in case that proves necessary," he concluded hastily. Then he looked at Hans, hard. "I have faith in you, Richter. You'll work it out."

"Will I have a say in the choice of this radio operator?" Hans didn't like it. There were already three people on his conscience. He didn't want a fourth. But if it were the only way...

Minten stretched luxuriously wishing he had a drink. But Richter hadn't offered him one and at this point it wouldn't be politic to ask. He couldn't wait to see the expression on his face when he learned who it was. "I think we have just the man for you."

"A volunteer, I trust."

"He hasn't yet, but I'm sure he will when he hears that you're going." Minten's smile was sly.

"Who the hell...?" Hans' heart turned to lead. Someone he knew. Someone who would go if you were going.

"You wouldn't like to guess?"

A kittenish Minten was almost more than he could bear. "No."

"Bergmann, of course. The logical choice, wouldn't you say?"

Sound of his heart pounded through his head. Bergmann. Bergmann. Bergmann. Stay calm. "He doesn't know one end of a code or a radio from the other." Not Bergmann. Never Bergmann. His family.

It was too dangerous for him. The radiomen would have to be either turned or deceived, if Michael would permit his staying on the loose. Bergmann wouldn't dare let himself be turned. Not with a second network around, no matter how separate it was. And if he couldn't be turned... Could he maintain that sort of deception with Bergmann?

Minten was puzzled. Richter liked Bergmann. And with Bergmann's background, he wouldn't dare let himself be turned even if they were caught. "That won't be a problem. He's bright, far brighter than either of the last two men we trained for England. They didn't know anything about radios either, before we got a hold of them."

"But his English..."

"His cover can account for that, and if he's with you, that shouldn't be a problem." He was looking at Hans with speculation. "In another moment I'm going to think there's something wrong with Bergmann, some good reason for you not wanting him. Perhaps something in his background?"

Would Bergmann never live that down? The 'sins' of the father... He couldn't permit Bergmann to go but he couldn't object without raising doubts which would get Bergmann into trouble. "There's nothing in his background," he said angrily, "and there's no man I'd trust more than Bergmann. It's just that I don't want to be responsible for anyone else. With the last six agents getting caught so quickly..."

"This will be entirely different."

"I certainly hope so. But given the danger, he had to be a genuine volunteer, and I want to be there when you ask him. If he has even the shadow of a doubt, I don't want him. It would be too dangerous for him and for me. Believe me, I know him. I'll know."

Minten's mouth snapped shut. That way Bergmann could volunteer and Richter could not refuse to have him, could do nothing about it because no pressure could be brought to bear. Bergmann was perfect. He would never dare to defect because of his family. But from what he'd seen, Bergmann would never betray Richter anyway. So convince him, Bergmann, or it will be so much the worse for you and yours. "Of course, Richter." He was losing cordiality again. "We want to make sure you're happy with all the arrangements."

I'll just bet you do, thought Hans. But if it had to be... And the more he thought about it, the more he realized that there was no way out for Bergmann. It wasn't safe for him to refuse or to be refused. And if he had to go, Bergmann might as well get something out of it. "If we're to escape together, he'd better be commissioned. Two officers escaping together makes more sense than an officer and enlisted man. And if his background were Alsatian, or the Austrian that he is, and his supposed family was dead, some of them in a labor camp... Then his leaving would make sense."

Minten nodded, going along with him equally. "That way the woman could go as his sister."

"What woman?"

"I didn't mention a woman?" Minten was all innocence.

"You know perfectly well that you didn't." Hans was furious. Two lives and one of them Bergmann's. It was intolerable.

"You know we always send a woman whenever possible. They're so... distracting. And a woman can go places a man can't, often with fewer questions being asked. Also, she can get information from a man in so many interesting ways."

Richter grimaced and Minten sensed that he had gone too far. He'd forgotten Richter's choir boy mentality. Unbelievable in these times and given the apparently luscious Miss Henderson who was so wild about him. Or was it just an overblown sense of chivalry?

"No woman, Herr Major."

"Admiral Canaris specified that a woman should be part of the group, but of course I shall tell him of your strong objections. That's the best I can do." There will be a woman, Richter, but there's no sense aggravating you right now. Get Bergmann in and get you to a point where you can't back out and then we'll spring the woman.

"I would appreciate that, Herr Major." And he would have, if he thought Minten actually would talk to the Little Admiral about it. But he couldn't turn it down, no matter what Minten threw at him.

To be able to get to England with what he knew... But he couldn't let Minten know that. How far could Michael go? He could barter with him for one life, especially Bergmann's, but two? It had damn well better be two.

"Of course," Minten said "no trouble at all." Lord of the Manor conferring favor. Minten loved playing that role. "Why don't you find the sergeant? Did Heinrich say he'd gone off to pick up someone?"

"Yes, sir. I'll see if he's back."

"And ask Heinrich to bring me a drink. I'll wait here." Minten's eyes had strayed again to the letters lying on the table beside him. Hans noticed and it was all he could do to keep from laughing. "Fine, sir." And I'll see to it that you have plenty of time to read my mail.

Hans left him there, his hand close to the letters, and shut the door after him carefully. Best to give Minten plenty of privacy.

*       *       *

It was very late that night before Dieter finally fell into bed in an alcoholic haze. It had been quite a celebration. Fun? My God, he hadn't had that much fun in a long time. And to think that he'd been worried when the Hauptmann ... Hans ... Why was it so hard to remember that now? He had laughed and said, while they were still alone, "Look if we're going to sail off into the sunrise together as brother officers, you really are going to have to start calling me Hans."

And he was right. But it was going to take some getting used to, even after tonight. But Georg... He laughed again. To think that he'd been worried when... Hans and Georg had insisted he come to dinner with them, saying that, after all, it wasn't every day that a non-com would be commissioned. My God, they laughed. And they'd needed to. After that session with Minten... And Georg's wife – Birgid? – Had just gone back to Berlin after a three-day visit. The powers-that-be wouldn't let her stay. No housing. Ridiculous. Something could have been found.

What was it about Georg's father? Nothing had been said directly, but there was something odd. And his own father. Father wouldn't like his being an officer, not in the Wehrmacht. He didn't like it either, not really. But he'd had no more choice about that than he'd had about going. Richter had to have done it, shoved it right down Minten's throat. Dieter giggled. Too bad he couldn't have shoved it somewhere else.

At least if he had to be an officer, he'd have the name without the game, the money and privileges without the command responsibilities.

He'd never want the responsibility, at least not in the Fuehrer's precious Wehrmacht. And the family could use the extra money. He'd have it all sent to them directly. He couldn't use it in England, could he? He frowned. Would they make him pay his own expenses in England? Not bloody likely.

And how would the major handle it, sending the money? And what would his family be told about it and about him? Suddenly, the haze lifted from his brain and his mind was crystal clear. What would his family be told? Where would they think he'd gone?

It didn't matter, he thought grimly. He had to go. There was no choice. He hadn't dared to hesitate – because of them. Because of the family – not even for a moment, when Minten had asked, even though he'd seen that the Hauptmann wasn't happy about his going. That had bothered him, but despite that, he'd agreed and at once.

He shook his head, trying to concentrate, trying to remember what the Hauptmann had said after Minten had left, wondering why it was important to remember.

He'd been afraid that the Hauptmann didn't want him because he didn't trust him for some reason or because he thought he'd be no good. But it wasn't that. He'd known from the first that there was no choice, because of his father. It was the danger. The Hauptmann had been worried for him because of the danger. That had been the reason. Amazing.

Dieter considered that. The Hauptmann was right to be afraid for him. He was afraid for himself. And for the Hauptmann as well. But at least the Hauptmann was going home. There was a great deal to be said for going home. But maybe that made it harder for him? And what were their chances? Not very good. He had asked theHhauptmann about that, just before they went downstairs.

"I don't know, Bergmann," he had said. "Ordinarily they wouldn't be very good, but there's just no way to say. This isn't an ordinary mission. I guess it all depends on whether or not they believe me."

Dieter was remembering it all with great clarity. He had been studying Hans's face carefully as he asked, "And are you a good liar, Herr Hauptmann?""

Hans had met his eyes solemnly. "Yes. Yes, I'm afraid that I am. I don't like to lie and I don't do it often, but when I do, I'm very good at it, indeed."

That was what he had been trying to remember. Why was that important? It was all too much to think about right now. He'd have to think about it later, when he wasn't so tired.

Slowly, Dieter's eyes closed, and at last he slept.

# Chapter XII

"Now what the hell is this all about, Minten?" Kramer's tone was vicious. "I dislike being summoned."

"Herr Major, if you please." Minten matched his tone as he waved toward the chair on the other side of the desk. "Sit down."

"I prefer to stand, since I'm sure this won't take long."

"I said, sit down!"

Kramer didn't like this, didn't like it at all. Where did Minten get off talking to him like that? He sat.

"I have some orders for you from Admiral Canaris."

Kramer looked at him warily. Minten was entirely too pleased with himself. "Yes?"

"Within four weeks we shall have another group of agents trained and ready to go. They are to be put in place no later than September tenth, sooner, if we can arrange it."

"So?" Kramer sneered. "I helped to train the last group and I'll help train this one. But I can tell you that four weeks isn't long enough."

"It will have to be. That's all the time we have. But you won't be involved with training this lot."

"Why not?"

"Because." Minten was leaning across the desk, almost sneering himself as he paused for effect. "You will be in training yourself. You won't have time."

"Training for what?" Kramer's face contorted in anger and his heart was pounding. Minten wasn't going to do this to him. Oh, no.

"You're going to England."

"The hell I am."

"The hell you aren't." Minten met his anger. "Admiral Canaris has ordered it himself, personally, and you will disobey his orders at your peril."

Kramer was virtually apoplectic. He exploded out of the chair and leaned over Minten's desk on his hands, his face bare inches from the major's. "You arranged this. It was all your idea. But if you think you can get rid of me that easily, you have another thing coming."

"The only thing that saddens me is that I can't get rid of you permanently."

"And you damn well know why you better not try. You got me into this, now you get me out. I am not going to England."

"Oh, yes, you are. A pleasant September vacation in Britain. I understand the hills of Scotland are gorgeous then, with the heather in bloom."

"Look...!"

"No! You look. You'll be gone for three weeks. I wish it were for three years. You're to fly in via Portugal on a Swiss passport. You'll even have a legitimate business to attend to. Ladies lingerie. Representing a firm in which we have considerable interest. It's Horst's cover, actually, which will make it logical for you to spend some time with him, even travel with him.

"You'll be the liaison between Horst and the new group going in, and you'll be the only one to know them both. Horst has good connections all over the southeast coast, so once the new group's in place, he'll be concentrating on that area while they take over in London. They're much better suited to operate there. You'll be helping with the transition, as well as taking in funds. Getting money into Britain is a major problem. Our agents, the ones who were caught, were carrying a great deal of it."

"I'm no smuggler, and money is bulky."

Good. Good. Arguing points. He's getting into the inevitable.

"Drafts on Portuguese banks aren't. You'll have four or five, none of them large enough to excite comment, but together they'll make a considerable sum. We've done this periodically with Swiss bank drafts, so foreign drafts are no novelty to the accounts involved. And the office has been moved to Portugal. Not so many questions being asked there these days. The Swiss are being very cautious, trying not to offend anyone." He gave a harsh laugh. "We'd hoped to avoid this, but there is no other way now, since the new group won't be able to take any funds with them."

Kramer sat there in silence, just looking at him.

Minten went on, totally unconcerned. You and Horst will go to Scotland 'on business' and while you're there, you'll pick up the supplies they'll drop in. You will deliver the radio and set up information drops in London. That can be done only after you get there because the new drops must be of Horst's choosing. He'll have to be the one to arrange it with the radioman there. The new group is not to know either Horst or the radioman. They'll have a radioman of their own, though he won't be able to operate for a while. In the meantime, they must not be in a position to compromise each other. Horst has the perfect cover and so will this new group." Minten was smirking his pleasure.

"And just who are these paragons of virtue?" Kramer's tone was acid.

"Hauptmann Richter and Sergeant-soon-to-be-Lieutenant Bergmann and a woman who is yet to be decided." He sat back waiting for the explosion he was sure would come. He wasn't disappointed.

"Are you mad?" Kramer was astounded, horrified.

"Far from it." Minten's laugh was nasty. "It's perfect." Then he played his ace-in-the-hole. "And the orders for it are coming from Admiral Canaris, himself. Do you think he's mad?"

"Yes!"

He was startled by the vehemence in Kramer's voice. His face reddened. "Just who the hell do you think you are?"

"You fool." Kramer sounded utterly weary as he slumped back in the chair in disbelief, not even hearing Minten's spluttering rage, thinking it had to be a bad dream, a nightmare. But Kramer knew that he could never have conjured this up, even in the wildest of nightmares. It was a question of survival now, pure and simple.

Finally, the spluttering died down, and he was able to tell the major in a voice devoid of any emotion. "Richter's the leak."

Minten stiffened, staring in surprise for a moment before he burst out laughing. "Now who's mad?"

Kramer was containing himself with an effort. This would have to be handled carefully if he was going to get out of it in one piece. "He has to be."

"Why?"

"If Richter's the leak, then all the pieces fit together. And they fit far too well for there to be any other answer. Going to England to set up anything with him would be suicide."

"Oh?" Minten couldn't entirely hide his amusement. Little did Kramer realize how right he was, but it had nothing to do with Richter. And Kramer was going to be paying for his own 'suicide' with one of the bank drafts he'd be carrying. I'll be rid of you once and for all, you bastard, Minten thought, and no one will be the wiser. Horst was a past master at arranging 'accidents'. But he had to find those pictures first.

"He's the leak, I tell you!" Kramer was almost shrieking in his fury. "I'm not going to England to wind up at the end of the hangman's noose!" He took a deep breath. Calm, he told himself. Be calm, reasonable. Control yourself or you'll never get anywhere.

"That's the crux of the matter, isn't it, Kramer," Minten said. "Going to England. It scares you shitless, and you're trying to wiggle off the hook any way you can."

Kramer had himself under control. "I'm not going to go. It's as simple as that. You're not going to get away with sending me or anyone else as long as Richter is going, because whomever you send with him will be a dead man.

"And just think, Herr Major, just think what a veritable gold mine of intelligence will be sailing into Dover Harbor. Our methods. Sea Lion. All of that and more. He'll be welcomed home as a conquering hero, leaving our agents dead in a smashed network in his wake. Think what that would do for your precious career."

Suddenly Minten was uneasy. For once there was a ring of truth in what Kramer was saying. He was calm now, entirely too calm. Better listen to what he has to say. If he did have proof... "All right. Let's hear it. All of it."

"Richter's godfather."

"What about him?"

Kramer's superior air returned now that he felt he was on safe ground. "He's what I asked Horst to find out about. A hunch. But I've found that my hunches are rarely wrong." He paused, enjoying the bombshell he was about to drop. "He's a very high level officer in British Intelligence."

"So?" Was that all Kramer had, for God sake?

"Don't you see?" What was wrong with the pontifical fathead?

"All I can see is that this puts Richter in an even better position to do what we want him to do than I thought he was."

"He's been sending information for years. Can't you see that?" Kramer was sweating again. "He's the leak!"

"And just how, pray tell, has he been sending information out for years?" Minten sneered. "From his tank radio? From Abwehr's Code Room?"

"No. Of course not."

"How then?"

Kramer was getting frantic. His bombshell had been a dud, and it was finally dawning on him that he had no hard proof. He just knew and that wasn't going to be enough. But it would be even worse if you stop now. "It's the girl."

"What girl?"

"It has to be the girl. Julia Henderson. The girl he writes to in England. He sends the information in the letters he writes to her."

"You've been reading too many spy novels."

"But it's the only thing that makes sense! She's the secretary to the Third Sea Lord and Richter's godfather is ex-Navy. She's their contact!"

"Since our little... ah... session in your office, I have had occasion to look further into that leak. I thought that was what you had to be after. Trying to steal my thunder." Minten waved a deprecating hand to cut Kramer off as he opened his mouth to interrupt. "I'll grant you that part of the information could have come from Richter, but only part. They're getting sporadic but first-rate intelligence concerning all the services, not just the panzers. It has to be coming from someone either very high up in Abwehr or in the highest military circles, probably the OKW itself. The Joint Chiefs of Staff are almost the only ones with that sort of across-the-board military information. Richter isn't even close to the OKW and he wasn't with Abwehr until after the Sea Lion planning began."

"But his uncle, all the generals he knows..."

"All OKH. Strictly Army General Staff. What about the Luft-waffe? The Kriegsmarine?"

"Maybe there's more than one man involved. And this agent who suddenly 'returned from the dead' appeared about the time Richter got to Hamburg!"

"Has Richter seen anyone here he shouldn't have? Has there been anything odd in his behavior?"

"No. Nothing except his refusal to make that propaganda broad-cast." Kramer sounded sullen now. "He's kept his nose so boringly clean that it's enough to make anyone suspicious."

"So you've had him watched."

Kramer flushed. "That's beside the point now."

"I'd say it is the point, if you've found nothing."

He brightened. "It's since he came to Hamburg. It's the girl. He started writing to her about then. About the time this long-lost agent resurrected himself. It has to be the girl. Don't you see? That proves it." Kramer sat back, satisfied that he made his point at last.

"It doesn't prove anything at all. He couldn't possibly be sending out enough information in those letters to account for the leak. What's the Code Room had to say about his letters? I assume you've had copies sent to the Code Room? You've been such a busy boy about everything else." More time wasted. The Code Room's time, his time and – God damn – worst of all Horst's time and all because of Kramer's idiotic machinations.

Kramer had set his face into a mask. Fool. He had to be right. It all made too much sense for him not to be. Minten was too big an idiot to see it without proof set in rock. And since Richter was Canaris' fair-haired boy, Canaris wouldn't believe it either. Not without solid proof. He'd get proof because it was there somewhere, just waiting to be found. Richter was bound to slip up before he left. He'd want to take everything with him that he could. But he was a clever bastard to have lasted this long and so someone would have to be with him twenty-four hours a day to catch him out, someone he'd never suspect. It couldn't be Bergmann, because Bergmann would never do it.

"I asked you, Kramer," Minten was testy now. Kramer had nothing but a bee in his bonnet, the arrogant prick. "What has the Code Room had to say about his letters?"

"They haven't found anything yet."

"He writes in English, doesn't he? Does he have any reference books in English? Any books in English at all?"

"No. Almost no books at all." Kramer was studying his fingernails. "Just an old German-French dictionary and some mysteries he reads for relaxation."

Minten shrugged his annoyance. "As I said, Kramer, forget it; you're just wasting your time, grasping at straws to keep from going. It won't work."

"Listen." Kramer struggled to control himself and Minten enjoyed watching his efforts. "Listen," he said again, his voice tight, "I was onto this long before you arranged to ship me out."

That much was true. He'd been nagging about Richter since Dunkirk. But all that proved was that he was out to get Richter for some personal reason. And Kramer was a digger. If that was all he had, then he'd only succeeded in proving that Richter's record was clean, and that was encouraging. But – he almost smiled – a little salt in the wound wouldn't hurt. "If this girl is his contact with British Intelligence, then why would he stop writing to her in the middle of Sea Lion planning?"

"How did you know that?"

"I have my own sources." Thank heaven he had time to read Richter's mail. "You don't think I'd wait for crumbs to fall from your table, do you?"

Kramer gave it one last shot. "But his godfather!"

"Good grief, it means nothing! He was little more than a boy when he started out at the university here eight years ago. Look at his record. The only time he's been to England for as long as six weeks at one time since was the summer his father died. The past four years he hasn't set foot there. When could he have been recruited, let alone trained?

"And there's not a blemish on his record! You've been digging for weeks and you've come up with nothing. He fought hard and well for the Fatherland. Won the Ritterkreuz, for God's sake. And he didn't ask for Abwehr, Abwehr asked for him. And even that wouldn't have happened if he hadn't been wounded. Without that wound, he would have been sent south with his division and that would have been that. It was his uncle who suggested Richter to Admiral Canaris. Are you accusing his uncle of being a spy?"

"No. Certainly not. But..."

Minten wanted no interruption. "And he's been a gold mine of information, just as you say he would be for the British. But for us. His work has been nothing short of brilliant. He's even trained agents to spy on England, and trained them well."

"And look what happened to them!"

Minten lost what little patience he had left. "A capture in the channel? There's always a ship patrolling the area and no diversion was arranged. Our naval stupidity. And the people we sent... Grupner, that damn lush. The public keeper told Horst about it. Asinine. He was a disastrous mistake."

Kramer could see he was getting nowhere with this. Minten was right for once. All he had... He just knew. And he'd spoken too soon, but Minten had given him no choice. He'd get what he needed and soon. Richter wasn't going to put his neck in a noose.

Meanwhile, he had to complete the arrangements for the pictures. Stroke of luck to find that attorney named Kramer to hold them so that the next-of-kin notification in his file could be changed without eyebrows being raised. But until Stepfather Number Four answered his letter there was no one for attorney Kramer to deliver them to, if that became necessary. He felt a little shiver. For it to be necessary, he would have to be dead, and he had no intention of dying. And this was sure to keep him safe. He had posted the letter to #4 only this morning, on the way in. Minten was bound to be monitoring everything he mailed either from the School House or from here, but he couldn't very well monitor every postal box in the city. And he'd taken precautions even though no one seemed to be following him. And the return letter was to say only yes or no so that would be no problem. Minten would never suspect #4. A supply contract with Martin Bormann. Bless Mother for her delight in telling him of all 'her' financial coups. He smiled.

"And what brings a smile to your face, Kramer?"

He looked at Minten speculatively. "I think... I may have just the girl for the group. You've mentioned the Navy botching it..." Careful. Go slowly. Minten has to think he has you right where he wants you. "If I may be permitted to make a recommendation?"

"By all means." Minten was feeling expansive. He had Kramer in his pocket now, pictures or no.

"Annaliese Scheuermann, Kapitan-zur-See Schroeder's niece." Would Minten swallow it? She'd be perfect. Richter was besotted with her. But the bitch had gotten nothing from him lately. Protecting him? She better not be. Certainly, she wouldn't over this, not if it meant facing an English hangman's noose. Impress that on her, and she'd be sure to get the goods on Richter. No woman – no one – would risk that for anyone. And she could scarcely refuse.

"I don't know her," said Minten, thinking that whomever she was, she had to be thoroughly checked out if Kramer was recommending her. Still, Schroeder's niece would be a good bet. Schroeder was a real gentleman of the old school, not like some of the schmucks he was forced to deal with. Kramer, for instance. Minten yawned. He shouldn't have stayed out so late last night. Where had Kugelmann found that girl? Exquisite. Only fourteen. But what she knew... He brought himself back to the business at hand with an effort. "What did you say her name was?"

"Annaliese Scheuermann." What was Minten's problem? Early senility? He'd been born senile. "She's his secretary as well as his niece and she spent a year in England several years ago, so she should be able to speak the language."

Minten nodded slowly. "Is she attractive? She has to be attractive, at least."

"I'd say so."

"Get her down here." The niece would have to be all right or Schroeder wouldn't have her working for him. Schroeder was that sort of man. Besides, he'd know when he saw her.

"The only thing... I don't know how pleased Richter would be to have her along. He's... rather fond of her."

"If we want her, he'll have to take her. I'll put her through Admiral Canaris before he can object. And it would make her cover as Bergmann's sister all the more convincing if she were also Richter's mistress."

"I don't think it's gone that far."

Minten just snorted. Idiotic choirboy. "Still, if she were willing..."

"Exactly," Kramer drawled, trying to hide his excitement.

"Then get her down here now. Need to start this tomorrow, if we can." They could complete the investigation of her while she was in training. Time was too damn short to wait. "I need to see her before I can make up my mind."

Minten watched him walk towards the door. He was in a hurry. Was Kramer anxious to get to her first? If so, why? Could she be part of his own investigation of Richter? "You have something on her." It had come to him in a flash.

Kramer turned back. He was at the door. "Not really. Let's just say that I can bring some influence to bear."

"I think I'd better have Kugelmann call her down. You wait here."

Kramer gave up his pretense of disinterest. It was too important. "I want this girl, Herr Major. She would be perfect for the job. Aside from what I've told you already, she has an excellent retentive memory and can organize information and deliver it succinctly. She also has the inside track with Richter. If I'm right about him, she'll be able to find out, and before they go. Either way, you have nothing to lose and everything to gain."

He waited, barely able to stand still but unwilling to let Minten know just how agitated he was. Minten had to agree or he was done for, pictures or no. The orders were coming from Admiral Canaris himself and there was no way to get around them unless he got proof that could cancel the whole damn fiasco of a mission.

"All right. Have it your way. But remember, the final decision is mine. We can't afford to have this mission fucked up the way the last one was." And Kramer would just love to fuck it up, get it canceled before it could even get off the ground, perhaps even by having this girl plant fake evidence against Richter? Nothing was beneath Kramer when he was after something. Dunkel had shown that. And Richter was too valuable to lose, far too valuable to have him tossed out on fake evidence. Kramer needed to know that sort of thing would do him no good, at least as far as is going to England was concerned.

Kramer was smiling broadly. "I'll get her."

"One thing you have to know first," Minten barked. "Even if you prove that Richter is the leak, and granted, that would be a coup for you, you would still have to go to England. Horst needs funds and you're going to deliver them regardless."

"We shall see what we shall see, Herr Major." He turned and walked out the door at last, thinking, dream on, you fool. When I prove it, I'll be able to write my own ticket, and you'll be out for promoting Richter to Canaris. Who knows, the admiral might even be out himself. It could very well be that big.

Minten looked after him, his eyes narrowing. Arrogant bastard. He wouldn't draw an easy breath until he had word from Horst that Kramer had been taken care of. God, what a relief that would be.

\*     \*     \*

There was a moan from under the pillow where Hans' head was buried.

"Come on, Herr Hauptmann."

"Hans," came the muffled reply.

"Sorry. I'm still not used to it."

He pulled off the pillow. "You didn't have any trouble with it last night."

"Everything was easy last night."

Hans sat up, then groaned and held his head.

Bergmann smiled sympathetically. "But not this morning."

"You're right. Not this morning. Nothing is easy this morning. Thank God Minten canceled our meeting. I don't have to be in until 1330."

"That's why I let you sleep late. You wanted to review some files before then."

Hans sighed and looked at the clock. 0900. Blast. He simply couldn't face the office this morning. People coming and going, the phone ringing. He groaned again at the thought of the phone ringing. It was going to be hard enough to concentrate without that. And there was still that damn letter to decode. He should have done it last night. He should stay here and do it now. Hans considered that. Why not? Bergmann could bring him what he needed from headquarters while he took a shower, and without the interruptions he'd have at the office, he'd easily have the whole lot finished by 1300.

"Are you there?"

He struggled out of his thoughts. "Yes."

"Will wonders never cease?"

Hans yawned and stretched. "You sound more and more like Georg all the time."

Dieter laughed.

"Would it be beneath the dignity of an officer-about-to-be to get those damn files from my office so I can work on them here?"

"Not at all, but it's not the sort of stuff they like to have leave the building."

"I'll give you a note from Mother." Hans' voice was laced with sarcasm but before Dieter could reply, he sighed again. "I'm sorry. It's just that I can't face that damn office this morning. If they find out, it'll be on my head."

"Okay. And there's no problem. I know the drill."

True enough. He'd acted as a messenger almost since day one. He rummaged through the pocket of a pair of pants that were draped over the chair and came up with a key to the file cabinet.

"What will you do for a gun?" Messengers had to be armed.

Dieter took the key. "I still have the machine pistol."

"God Almighty!" Hans gave a short laugh that sent a stab of pain through his head. "Anyone would be a fool to tangle with you while you are carrying that. Where the hell have you been hiding it?"

"My room." Dieter grinned. "Locked in the armoire along with the ammunition. Do you need anything else?"

A camera, thought Hans. But there was no way to get one right now and more's the pity. "Just ask Heinrich to bring me some coffee, will you?"

"A gallon?"

"At least." His mouth felt like the bottom of a bird cage. "Tell him I'd like a shower first, though."

"Yes M'lord." Dieter swept his arm across in front of himself as he gave a courtly bow.

Hans' laugh turned into a moan of pain. "Get out of here!"

"Don't hit me, sire," Dieter squeaked as he went out the door. "I'm just a growing boy!"

"Don't make me laugh. It hurts!"

He heard Dieter's answering laugh as he shut the door after himself. It wasn't fair that anyone should feel so well this morning. Especially someone who'd been with him last night. Hans rose slowly from the bed and then sat back down abruptly, his head spinning. This was ridiculous. He hadn't been drunk in years. He hoped that it was years before he was drunk again. Stupid to get drunk, stupid and dangerous. Besides, he didn't have time for a hangover. He had far too much to do.

And then it hit him. He was going home! The thought galvanized him. He rose, swaying for a moment, then ignored it as he threw on his robe, dug a bottle of aspirin out of the top drawer, grabbed his towel and shaving kit and headed for the bathroom.

It was only after a quick shave, when he was standing under a cold shower – hot water had run out – that he permitted himself to think about it again. Going home. He still couldn't believe it. Eaton Square. Mother. The wedding. Would he be home in time for Mother's wedding? She hadn't said when it would be. And he'd be able to tell her. And James. If only James could have been there last night. It was just the sort of time he liked best. Laugh? He hadn't laughed like that in ages. And he had relaxed, totally relaxed with two good friends, a luxury he hadn't permitted himself for a long, long time.

And to have Annaliese come with him, meet Mother. Damn the war. If only this were a simple trip home and he could take her. He was surprised to realize just how much he didn't like the thought of leaving her. But he wasn't leaving Bergmann, was he? There was a sudden knot of fear in his stomach.

He turned off the water and concentrated on drying himself off.

As he walked back down the hall toward his room, he saw Heinrich coming toward him with a tray and realized just how hungry he was. And so, when he opened the door to let Heinrich in, he was delighted to see, "Croissants! I'm ravenous."

"I thought you might be." Heinrich put the tray on the desk, and at that same moment Dieter came to the open door, the dispatch case in one hand and the machine pistol in the other. "You're looking very well, Herr Hauptmann." His grin belied the formality of his words.

Hans laughed. "I'm a new man or I will be when I get some of this coffee into me."

Heinrich eyed the machine pistol warily, then concentrated on pouring out a cup of coffee before he turned to go. It was then that he saw what the dispatch case was. There hadn't been one here since the last batch of agents left. Did this mean another batch was due soon? He devoutly hoped not. "Will there be anything else, Herr Hauptmann?" More agents. More work. He knew that it had been too good to last.

"No, thank you, Heinrich."

Heinrich nodded and left, closing the door.

Hans was savoring the coffee as Dieter set the dispatch case on the desk chair and handed him the key.

"Any maps?"

"Just the one in the file cabinet with the folders. I'd've had to have a requisition for anything else."

"Right. Right." Hans was buttering a section of croissant. "Want some?"

"No. Thanks. I've already had my breakfast."

"If there isn't anything else you want me for, I thought I'd go to the gym and work out. There hasn't been time for the past few days and God knows there won't be once we start on this business."

"I'll make sure there is. Write it into the schedule for both of us. Your workouts and my exercises. This damn arm still isn't quite right."

"I'd appreciate it."

"So would I. I can do just so much paperwork without getting muzzy-brained. It clears the head. Enjoy it for me this morning."

"I will. See you at noon."

"Right."

Hans locked the door after him then moved the tray from the desk to the table by the chair and poured himself another cup of coffee. Only one more left. Best to finish it off while it was still hot. They were lucky to get real coffee. Abwehr certainly hath its privilege.

He looked out of the window as he finished his last croissant. No barges. River commerce had come to a virtual standstill. Almost everything that could float had been gobbled up by the military and sent to the French channel ports. Not many would be back. The British were bombing the hell out of those ports, concentrating on the barges. Stupid to take them there for conversion into landing craft. This should be done out of range and hauled in at the last possible moment. Thank God no one had thought of it, or at least no one with any clout.

He put down the cup and took off his robe. It was going to be a hot day.

The letter from 'Darling Julia' took only forty minutes. The message wasn't long. There wasn't much Michael could say at this point. But what he did say was sobering.

```
Concur. Go to ground. Someone checking on you. I'm
known as your godfather. Same man saw Julia. She
knows you. Safest way. Be careful.
```

So Julia knew. Just as he'd thought from the letter. And it had to be Kramer doing the checking. Julia could be part of the normal check, but not Michael. And only Kramer had asked about his godfather. That had to be what he was after when he'd written to London. How good was Michael's cover? Probably not good enough since he'd been in it for so long. But even if Kramer did know, he couldn't prove anything. He'd have nothing but his God damn suspicions. But it meant being twice as careful, especially since he was so close to the end.

Just four more weeks and he'd be home with the goods. Oh, God, if only it were over. If only he could press a button and he and Bergmann could be sitting at the breakfast table in Eaton Square, with Mother.

He shook himself angrily. No sense thinking like that. There weren't any magic buttons, and it wasn't four weeks from now. It was now, and he had to concentrate on surviving those weeks and making the most of them. Get hold of everything he could, but carefully. There was a lot to do if he were to finish everything up and get ready to go to England. He'd have to work evenings, nights. Here? Here. The perfect excuse. Bring papers here where it would be 'more comfortable' to work.

And he'd need a camera. There'd be too much bulk to papers. But even regular film was bulky. He'd have trouble hiding enough regular rolls of film well enough to get them out. One of the new miniature cameras with their miniature rolls of film. If he could just get hold of one of them. Perhaps he could convince Minten that he could put one to good use in London? He smiled at the thought. "I can't take one in with me I know, Herr Major, but couldn't it be sent with the supply drop?" Yes it would be invaluable, wouldn't it. The smile broadened. And he'd need plenty of practice with it beforehand, wouldn't he? Yes indeed, plenty of practice.

*    *    *

Annaliese stood in the middle of her uncle's office, watching warily as Kramer shut the door behind them. "My uncle wouldn't appreciate your using his office when he's not here." Or when he was here, for that matter.

Bitch. "Well then, we just won't tell him, will we? That is, when he gets back from his trip to the French channel ports."

"How did you know about that?" She had found out about the trip herself only the night before. It was supposed to be a surprise inspection and therefore had been kept secret even from her until the last moment. And to keep it secret, she was to come to the office every day. Heaven knows there was enough work to do. That wasn't the problem. But right now she wished she knew that Uncle Friedrich could walk through the door at any moment. He couldn't do anything about Kramer, but it would have been reassuring to have him there, all the same.

The lieutenant didn't answer. He just watched her, pleased to see a tinge of fear.

"Just what is it you want, Herr Lieutenant? I have work to do." Simply being in the same room with him made her almost physically ill.

"The Fatherland has need of your services, Fräulein."

Hypocrite. "Don't give me that. You have need of my services. You could care less what the Fatherland needs if it doesn't suit your purposes."

"My, my, aren't we testy this morning."

"I can only speak for myself. Not for you."

He was barely able to control his anger. Bitch! Bitch! Bitch! How dare she? "Fortunately my needs and those of the Fatherland are one in the same. Urgently so, in fact."

"Well?"

"Don't 'well' me!" Stay calm. Don't let her have the satisfaction of making you angry. That's what she wants. To keep control of the situation. "It seems, my dear, that your lover boy is a spy."

She was genuinely amused. "And for whom, pray tell, would he be spying?"

"England. Who else?"

"Is that what all this skulking around corners has been about?"

"You're supposed to be a bright girl. I thought that you would have figured it out for yourself by now."

"I'm bright enough to know that it's ridiculous."

It was ridiculous; it had to be. Kramer had to be after Hans for personal reasons. He wouldn't have to blackmail Uncle Friedrich and use her if he were doing it through channels. He was on a fishing expedition. Just to see what she'd say? "How is he getting the information out? Through those POWs he was interrogating in Dunkirk?" They were both standing, glaring at each other.

"I can't tell you that," he snapped.

"Because you don't know! Because he's not doing what you say he is!"

Kramer's face reddened, but before he could speak, she went on. "And even if it were true what would that have to do with me? You ordered me to see him, after all." How dare this man toy with all their lives this way? He couldn't be right. Oh, damn. It wailed through her brain.

"Yes, and a lot of good it's done. You've gotten next to nothing."

"Maybe there's nothing to get. Have you ever thought of that?"

He ignored her remark. "You're going to get it for me now."

Her heart turned over. "How?" Oh, Hans, dear Hans...

"You're going to prepare for a little trip."

"I can't possibly. This office is up to its ears in work."

"You could be replaced."

"My uncle won't like it."

"Frankly, I don't give a damn whether your uncle likes it or not."

She glared at him in silence.

"You're not even curious about where this little trip could take you if you fail to get what I want?"

"What do you mean, if I fail?"

"Get the information and the trip will be canceled. Then you can stay here with your precious Uncle Friedrich. Fail and you're off to jolly old England with your lover boy. He'll even throw in a hangman's noose as a bonus for being so good."

She couldn't seem to breathe.

"Struck dumb for once, Fräulein?"

She turned and walked towards the window and when she finally spoke her voice was curiously flat. "Hauptmann Richter is forming a group to replace the agents who are lost."

"Wrong. Admiral Canaris is forming the group and he appointed Richter to lead it."

"And you don't agree with the admiral's choice." The arrogance of the man.

"How can I agree with it? Richter's a spy."

"Obviously the a doesn't agree with you."

"That's only because you haven't helped me find the proof. And Richter's clever, I'll grant him that."

"And just how would my going, or rather not going to England get proof for you?"

"During training, you'd be with him almost twenty-four hours a day. He's been given a golden opportunity, and he's going to take advantage of it to try to get hold of every ounce of information he can take to England with him. Perhaps he'll even try to get you to help him, since you have access to so many naval files. I want you to catch him in the act."

"I don't believe you."

"Then do it. Prove me wrong. It's the only way."

He hates Hans, she thought. Really hates him. That's why I have to do it. I have no choice. Because even if the situation with Uncle Friedrich no longer existed, there would still be Hans. Kramer would only find someone else if she didn't do it and then he'd be free to manufacture the evidence if he couldn't find it. He was more than capable of doing just that. But what if he were right? Oh, God, what if by some horrible chance he was right? Hans would die. Kramer isn't right. But if he is, Hans would be a traitor.

She tried to think of him as a traitor, tried to conjure up a loathing for him, but she failed. He was so much fun. So few men were fun anymore. And she couldn't bear the thought of him being killed. She had to do it if Hans were to live. She was trapped. She had no choice. Uncle...

"Well, Fräulein?"

Goose flesh rose on her arms and her voice was harsh. "All right. I'll do it. But just to prove how wrong you are."

"You'd better prove me right, or it's the hangman." His smile was triumphant. "Major Minten wants to see you in his office."

"Now?"

"Yes. The final decision about your joining the group is his, so you'll have to have the right answers."

"How will I know what they are?" She folded her arms across her chest to hide the shaking of her hands.

"You'll know. I have faith in you."

"I have absolutely none in you."

"You should have, Fräulein."

It pleased him to see the fear that was once more in her eyes. "You should have absolute faith that I wouldn't hesitate to have your uncle sent to a labor camp. Possibly your aunt, as well. She could be considered an accessory after the fact since the money was spent on her. At best she would be reduced to poverty. Restitution would be demanded."

"She was sick. And he paid back every penny!"

"Too cleverly, by far. There are no records of that part of it."

"And I'm sure you looked into that justice closely."

He gave a wisp of a smile. "I'm no fool."

She looked away.

"You're especially lovely when you're angry. The SS officers would be enchanted with you."

"You bastard!" It was a hoarse, violent whisper.

Suddenly he was furious with her and he wanted her. He wanted to throw her onto the floor, hold her down, possess her right then and there while she fought him. And she would fight. He knew all the signs. The excitement of subduing such a woman, showing her what a real man was, seeing the hatred wiped off her face, her eyes widening and softening into pleasure.

It was a real effort to control the urge, but he did. There were some things that wouldn't be tolerated and teaching her that sort of lesson, here where they might be found, was one. Schroeder had some very influential friends, and no amount of pressure would hush that up. Another time. She was staring at him now, still afraid. Someday, you bitch. Some day. "Come, Fräulein."

"I'll be back in a minute."

"We are going now."

She met his glare without flinching. "Not unless you want me to have an embarrassing accident in the major's office."

"Oh," he mumbled, momentarily disconcerted. "Well," he was blustering now, "I'll be right outside the door."

"As you wish." She swept out of the office ahead of him, stopping only to pick up her purse from her desk drawer, allowing him to precede her into the hall so she could lock the door.

"I'm glad to see you observe security regulations so carefully, Fräulein."

"Of course I do, Herr Lieutenant." She turned from him abruptly and went across the hall to the ladies room, the one place where even he would have to leave her alone.

She held herself together as the door closed behind her, until she was in the tiny room that contained the toilet. The tears began as she fumbled to lock the door before collapsing onto the seat behind her, shaking with sobs she struggled for control so that no one would hear her. What was she to do?

*     *     *

Annaliese stumbled back, trembling, as Hans burst through the door she had open for him. He slammed it and stood there leaning against it, staring at her in silence.

The rest of the day had been hell after she'd seen Major Minten. She'd finally given up about 3pm and had come home to wait for the call she was sure would come. The major had said he would give Hauptmann Richter the 'good news' after the afternoon meeting.

When his call had finally come around four, all he'd said was "Wait there. I'm coming," and then he'd hung up before she could say a word.

He was still staring. She couldn't bear it. "Say something, please."

That broke the spell. Hans sighed and ran his fingers through his hair. "What the hell can I say?" The anger was gone now. He felt nothing, nothing at all except, "You're not going."

She was standing ramrod straight, her fists clenched at her sides as if she were about to face a firing squad. "I have to go. I told Major Minten I would."

"Then untell him."

"Did he give you any choice about me?"

"No. He'd even cleared it with Admiral Canaris. But you can change your mind. It's not too late."

She shook her head, no, not trusting herself to speak.

"Don't you see how insane it is?" He was pleading with her now. "How could I concentrate on what I have to do if I were worrying about you? It would be dangerous for all three of us."

"Three?"

"They didn't tell you? Bergmann's going."

"Bergmann?" For some reason the thought horrified her.

Hans nodded.

"I hadn't thought of that."

"Bergmann?"

"No. The danger to you." He was in so much danger without that. Oh, God. What to do. "I can't bear it." She looked at him and at that moment she both loved him, utterly, and knew it was too late for that.

His face softened. "You don't have to go. Even if I can't... Your uncle can get you out of it."

"He's not here." She turned away from him, unable to look at that marvelous face so full of – what was it? – concern? It couldn't be anything more than concern. Her fingers began twining themselves into the fabric of the curtain that was billowing back from the open window.

"When will he be back?"

"Three or four days. Please don't say anything about his being gone. No one's supposed to know."

"Call him."

She still couldn't look at him. "I can't. I'm not sure where he is. Anyway, he couldn't do anything about it."

What was wrong with her? "Of course he can! You can't go! He'll see to that. He'll stop it."

Annaliese turned finally, her face contorted by an agony of fear, tears streaming down her face. "He can't stop it!" She was all but shouting. "I can't stop it! Don't you see? Are you blind?" She slammed her fist into his chest, sobbing, "It's Kramer! Kramer!"

He caught her wrist and his voice was terrible to hear. "What about Kramer?"

She struggled to get away. It wasn't fair. She loved him and now she would lose him forever. But if she didn't tell him, he'd be dead.

"Let me go!"

His grip tightened. There was no feeling in her hand.

"What about Kramer?" He repeated, his voice deadly.

"He thinks you're a spy!"

She gasped as he released her, stepping back as if she'd struck him. She turned away and rubbed her wrist, grateful for any excuse not to have to look at him.

His voice was quiet now and curiously flat. "How do you know what Kramer thinks about me?"

She still didn't look at him. "Because I've been spying on you for him."

Hans couldn't seem to breathe suddenly, and when he was capable of feeling anything again all he felt was loathing. To think he had actually worried about asking her if Kramer had so much as had an appointment with her uncle, not wanting to involve her, certainly not wanting to accuse either her or him! He had been so stupid, so trusting.

Michael had said, 'trust no one,' and he was right. Oh God he was right! He'd been beginning to break that rule but he wouldn't again, not with her, not with anyone. He should have realized when he found out it was Schroeder. The bitch! And he thought that he loved her. The taste of bile was acid in his mouth.

"Why are you telling me this now?"

"Because I can't go on with it."

"Turn around, damn you! I can barely hear what you're saying."

She turned around, shouting, "Because I can't go on with it!"

"It didn't seem to bother you before." He was sneering at her.

"It bothered me before. It's always bothered me. I've never spied on anyone and I hated every minute of it."

"Then why did you do it?" His laugh was bitter. "You ought to go to London. You're perfect. Men trust you instinctively."

She was holding herself together by sheer effort of will. She was losing everything, but at least Hans would live. She had to tell him. He would never understand if she didn't. He wouldn't betray her uncle. He couldn't. Oh, God. Could things be any worse than they are now?

Kramer. He should be the one on the block, the one to die. Not

Hans. Kill Kramer. Right now she'd love to kill him. He'd taken everything. But he wouldn't have Hans. "He can send my uncle to a labor camp, and my aunt. And me and me. Me! He says he'd send me to an SS brothel. Uncle Friedrich said he couldn't go that far, but with Kramer, how can you know? It would kill Aunt Karin. It would kill him. A labor camp! He doesn't have that kind of stamina anymore. And my cousins. What would happen to them?" She was angry herself now. "And talk about trust. I'm trusting you with my life and the lives of everyone I hold dear by telling you."

"Why?" He was still furious, not quite taking in what she was saying.

"Because you'd die. Because Kramer hates you. He's out to get you. If he can't find any evidence against you, he'll manufacture it. You'll die." Suddenly she was terribly afraid. "You won't betray Uncle Friedrich. You won't, will you?"

"No, of course not." He turned away and lowered himself into a chair without looking at her.

"You haven't asked me what he did."

"I don't want to know."

He was exhausted, suddenly. Last night. Then the scene in Minten's office this afternoon. It had been one hell of a scene with all of them shouting at once. He stormed out without agreeing or disagreeing and Minten let him go. Now he knew why. Minten knew that Kramer had Annaliese by the throat and counted on her to persuade him. She had to. She was trapped, Bergmann was trapped, and so was he. He had been since Poland.

"It happened a long time ago."

"I don't want to know, Annaliese. It's none of my business."

"He made it right, repaid everything. He's a good man!"

"I don't want to know!" He yelled and in the long silence that followed, he managed to control himself enough to speak more reasonably when he finally said, "It's better if I don't know. It's bad enough that Kramer does."

"It's hell that Kramer does. If only I could kill him, it would solve everything."

He looked at her, startled. "It would solve nothing."

"Why?"

"Because everything would come out."

"I could say that he jilted me for another woman. That would make it a crime of passion, wouldn't it?"

He couldn't believe what he was hearing. "You're serious, aren't you."

"Yes."

"Would it be?"

"Would it be what?"

"A crime of passion." He was watching her intently.

"I suppose you could say that." She smiled. It was an odd little smile. "Hatred is a form of passion, isn't it?"

"Just hatred?"

"Isn't that enough?"

"Just hatred?" Why was it so important? He didn't know why but it was.

Her lip curled into a vicious sneer. "He fouls everything he touches. Look at what he's done to us."

"Does it matter?"

"Yes, it matters. Of course it matters. If it didn't matter, I wouldn't be telling you all this. I would've gone along with him and tried to figure out what it is he wants to know. And if I couldn't, I might've even helped him plant the evidence. It would've been so simple if it didn't matter." She heaved this shuddering sigh "You have to let me go to London. Don't you see?"

He folded his arms and looked at her curiously. "How do you know that I'm not the British spy he says I am?"

"it wouldn't matter if you were. I'd still have to go."

"It wouldn't matter if I were a traitor?"

"What difference could that possibly make? What difference does anything make anymore? The last few weeks have taught me a lot. Today even more. It's hard to know who the traitors really are. You're a good, decent man. Men like Minten and Kramer... They claim to be loyal Germans, but they don't serve anyone but themselves. Germany could go to hell for all they care as long as they get what they want. And because of them, Kramer at least, I've been terrified for weeks. That's no way to live, spying on people and hating it and being scared to death. And what about justice? There isn't any. People are simply carted off in the middle of the night and never heard from again. If my uncle were 'lucky' and were permitted to stand trial, you know what would happen. It would be public theater, not a public trial. This isn't the Germany I was brought up to believe in. I don't know what to believe in anymore."

Her voice was full of bitterness. "Just two things. That Uncle Friedrich is a good man and going to England would serve you both. That's all I do believe in right now. Nothing else matters."

She stopped and looked around, and when she spoke again he was amazed at the change in her she was brisk, matter-of-fact, the perfect hostess. "Do you want to drink or some coffee? I have some real coffee." She went towards the kitchen. He rose.

"Annaliese."

She looked back. "What is it?"

Couldn't believe it. She was being polite. Nothing more, nothing less. "You said that going to England would serve 'you both'. I take it that you are referring to your uncle and me. I can understand why you'd be willing to serve your uncle, but why me?" He was standing directly in front of her now.

She gave him a long, undecipherable look and then turned away abruptly, going into the kitchen where she began filling the kettle. "Because I love you." Her words were barely audible over the sound of the running water.

Had she really said that? He watched her while she turned off the water and put the kettle on top of the stove. She still hadn't turned around. "How can you be so calm about it?"

"It seems to me that I haven't been calm about anything today." She got out the coffee and began measuring it carefully into the kettle.

"First you tell me you've been spying on me. Then you insist that I let you come to England for your uncle's sake and mine in the same breath, saying that it doesn't matter if I'm a traitor. At the top of that, you tell me you can make real coffee and you love me."

She gave a bitter little laugh as she finally turned to look at him. But her face was softened by whatever it was she found in his and she really smiled at last. "When you put it that way, it does sound ridiculous."

"Do you really?"

She turned back and finished measuring out the coffee. "Do I really what? You've given me a lot of choices."

"Love me."

"Why are men so stupid?" She got out the coffee strainer.

"I have to know."

She put the lid back on the coffee tin and made sure it was tight. "Why do you have to know? You can't possibly care for me after what I've done, so what difference does it make? Besides, I shouldn't have said it. It wasn't fair."

"Then you didn't mean it. It was just a plea for sympathy."

The scorn in his voice was too much to bear. Annaliese turned on him, eyes blazing. "You don't know what you're talking about! Don't you know all this has been hell for me?""

"Hell for you? What do you think it is for me?"

She turned away, slammed the coffee tin back into the cupboard, picked up a small box of matches and tried to strike one to bite the burner. Her hands were trembling so that she broke the match before it lit. "Damn!" She fumbled with the box, trying to get out another.

"Here." He moved into the tiny kitchen and grabbed the box from her, careful to avoid brushing against her as he struck a match and held it to the burner, turning on the gas with his other hand. There was a slight 'poof' and a ring of blue flame appeared. He put the kettle on the burner and handed back the matchbox, asking again, harshly, "Did you mean it?"

There was a sob in her voice as she all but shouted, "Yes, dammit, yes! I meant it! There! Are you satisfied?!" She was glaring at him, tears streaming down her red face. "You don't understand anything at all!"

He grabbed her wrist just as she would have struck his chest again and held it away from him, shouting back in fury, "Oh, yes, I do. I understand that if you told me that twenty-four hours ago, I would have been the happiest man alive. But now it's nothing, less than nothing. Don't you understand?"

She nodded, head down, her hands numbed by his grip. Then she began struggling to free herself, to get away from him, away from everything. He held on.

"Let me go!"

Later he was never quite sure how it happened or why but at that moment something in him broke and he found himself kissing her almost viciously.

She fought him, finally tearing her mouth from his, twisting and turning as she tried to work herself free. "I said, let me go!"

"No!"

"You don't want me. You just want to punish me, pay me back."

"Aside from you, I don't know what I want at this moment."

"Not this way. You won't have me this way."

"Why not? You say that you love me." He was sneering at her now.

"You bastard!" Then she collapsed against his chest, weeping as if her heart would break.

He sighed and leaned back against the counter, content to hold her, waiting for her storm to pass as his had. When it had, she made no move, and he didn't push her away. Instead he stroked her back as he would have a child's and leaned down to kiss her hair, wishing that her hair was down, that it was her 'pleasure hair' instead of the braids of her 'business hair'. He rested his chin on the top of her head smiling, remembering the first time he had ever seen her with her hair down, wearing that clinging flame of a dress and those ridiculous, delightful shoes. How lovely she had been. She looked like hell right now. He leaned down to her ear, his voice just above a whisper. "I'm not going to let him spoil it."

"Let who spoil what?" Her voice was muffled against his chest.

"Kramer. I'm not going to let him do it. You said it. He's fouled everything. I'm not going to let him foul us, too." He released his hold with one arm and reached into his pocket for a clean handkerchief. Then he tipped up her chin with the same hand and began wiping away her tears.

He stopped after a moment to admire his handiwork and found that she was looking at him warily. He smiled and pulled her back to him, gently this time. "Annaliese." He stopped. How to explain? To say? "I just love you. I don't think I knew how much until now. If I didn't love you, I wouldn't have been so angry." She stirred and he pulled back to look down at her again, saying, "You took an awful chance telling me all of that."

"I couldn't go on with it." Tears welled up in her eyes. "Say it again."

"I love you?"

She nodded and the tears began falling. "Oh damn!" She wailed.

"What's the matter now?"

"I never cry and that's all I've been doing today. It's ridiculous. You just made me so happy and all I can do is cry!" He stood there looking down at her, helpless. And when she saw the expression on his face, she began laughing through her tears. "Oh, Hans, you are marvelous."

"I give up." He raised his hands in mock surrender as she reached for his handkerchief, then turned away to blow her nose vigorously.

"I must look frightful."

"You certainly do."

She laughed and reached for the kettle that had been boiling unnoticed, then poured coffee into each cup through a strainer. He watched her as if he'd never seen anyone do that homely task before, admiring the way the tendrils of hair curled at the nape of her neck. So much was at stake for her. She had to go. There was no way out of it for her, either. Besides, she covered his rear with Kramer. He turned away, hating himself with a thought. That was the hell of this business. He should be happy at this moment, as happy as she said she was. There shouldn't be any clouds but there were. He shouldn't take her with him. But how could he bear to leave her? She said she didn't care if he were a traitor, but what would she do when she came face-to-face with the fact that was precisely what he was, at least legally, as she was bound to if she came along? Damned if he did and damned if he didn't. He should've let her think that he hated her, that he couldn't possibly take her along. But her agony... She had been in such agony. He couldn't bear it. And her uncle... Damn it all to hell.

She handed him a cup. "Cream and sugar?"

"Yes, please." Idiotic social niceties. Vacuous at a time like this.

She got the cream from her small refrigerator and put it down next to the sugar bowl. "I'm sorry to be so inelegant, but right now it seems pointless to get everything out."

He nodded in agreement and helped himself.

"There is no choice, Hans" she was calm now.

"Annaliese..."

"There really is no choice. Lieutenant Kramer made sure of that. Besides, now that I've found you, I won't let you go."

"It will be dangerous. I can't be worried about you."

"You won't have to be. I can take care of myself."

"Be sensible."

"I am being sensible. You'll always know where you stand with Lieutenant Kramer if it's me. And besides, if we have to go, your cover in England is perfect. If you marry me, mine would be, too."

He looked at her in consternation, giving a little laugh every time he started to reply. It was absurd but she was right. Michael would never hang his wife. He could marry her and save her without even trying. She'd live. Even if she hated it when she found out, she'd live. And, damn it all, she looked so smug. Life was ludicrous. She was regarding him with amusement. Men were unfathomable at times. Honestly. "And if you're the spy Lieutenant Kramer thinks you are, they'll never hang your wife."

He started. Could she read his thoughts? My God... He put down his cup "Come here, woman."

"Yes, sir."

He held her close.

"You will let me come, won't you, Hans?"

"How can I possibly resist such an offer?" He hesitated, looking down at her with not a little wonder. "Annaliese, will you marry me?"

She was grinning. "I thought you'd never ask."

They were both laughing as he leaned down to kiss her and seal the bargain.

*     *     *

"Good, Kugelmann. Good. It can even be resealed."

"Of course, Herr Major."

Minten was so delighted that he didn't even notice the sarcasm in Kugelmann's voice. He took the letter carefully from the envelope.

"Who is this man?"

"One of the Lieutenant Kramer's four stepfathers. His mother's fifth and current husband."

"There are that many?"

"His mother has had a rather checkered career in that regard."

"When did you find this out?" Minten was glaring at him. "You hadn't told me."

"Would it make any difference if I had?"

Damn supercilious little prig. "You're overreaching yourself!" Then he subsided into the letter without waiting for the apology that he knew would come.

"I'm sorry, Herr Major." Kugelmann sighed. Really! The man was impossible! Here he'd brought Kramer's letter within hours of its being mailed, despite some difficulty with the postal department, after having steamed it open carefully enough so that it could be resealed, and all he got for his trouble was pick-pick-pick. Minten could have been a little grateful, at least.

He'd known about Kramer's mother for ages. Everyone knew about Kramer's mother. It was amazing that Minten didn't know.

But since everyone knew, it made no difference anyway. The only worthwhile information was what everyone didn't know. That was the problem with the pictures Kramer was holding over Minten's head, no one knew about the existence of those pictures except the boy's father – who had been handsomely paid off and knew too well what would happen to him if he tried anything further – the major, the lieutenant and himself. That made that knowledge a very valuable commodity indeed. And if Lieutenant Kramer chose to share that knowledge and, even more, the pictures themselves with someone who mattered in the Third Reich... That had to be prevented at all costs.

Unfortunately, Kramer couldn't be blackmailed. His life was scarcely lily white but there was nothing that would cause more than a raised eyebrow and a few tut-tuts in more prudish quarters. On the other hand, Minten had been a thoroughly self-indulgent fool, and Kramer was taking advantage of that. But Kramer had made one serious miscalculation. He thought that because Minten was a fool in his personal life, that that carried over into his professional life as well. Kramer wasn't the only one to think that. It was something Minten made good use of from time to time and was probably making use of again, though he hadn't said so. Not yet. He would.

It was Kramer who was the fool. Kramer who was blind, not seeing how much better the station was run now, how much closer and tighter the liaison was both with the mansion and the military side of the HQ. And, as usual, Minten had gotten rid of the deadwood without a second thought. But Kramer hadn't noticed any of that, had he. Not that Kramer didn't have Minten in a tight corner. He did, all right, but instead of the barnyard pig he thought he was facing, Kramer had a wild boar on his hands. Kugelmann smiled at the analogy. Most apt.

Where the hell were those pictures? Kramer had said in the letter that the 'envelope' was in safe hands. Whose?

"Kugelmann!"

"Sir?" He looked up, startled.

"God damn it, pay attention! I asked why Kramer thinks that this man could get the pictures to Martin Bormann."

"I don't know." Did Minten think he knew everything just because he wanted him to know?

"Find out. And who the hell could have 'safe hands' these days? I want to know everything, everyone in Hamburg that he knows outside of Abwehr. He wouldn't dare leave them with anyone here. Safe? Safe? Who's safe?"

"A priest?" Kugelmann yawned. Almost five. He'd missed dinner at noon, and there was no supper in sight. If Minten wasn't thinking about food yet, then he was taking this very seriously indeed. Sleep. He needed sleep, too. Supper and bed.

"It can't be a priest. I've never known that bastard to darken the door of the church. Besides, it has to be someone who could go to Berlin without exciting comments, and no priest could do that. And who takes priests seriously these days? It has to be someone who'd be taken seriously.

"And it has to be someone who would know if he died. Who would know if he died?" Then Minten was excited. "His next-of-kin. Who is listed as his next-of-kin?" He slammed his hand on the top of the desk. "Get his personnel file. Now!"

"Very well." Kugelmann heaved himself wearily out of the chair. Where the hell did Minten get his energy? 2am last night. The girl had looked exhausted and he had had to help shove Minten into the staff car at one end and out of it at the other. At least he had enough sense not to wear that idiotic corset, or getting him into bed would have been even more of a problem.

Kugelmann was halfway out the door when Minten hollered after him, "Right back! Bring it right back!"

"Of course." Idiot. What else did Minten think he would do with it?

It took only ten minutes for Kugelmann to return and slap the folder down on the desk in front of the major.

"Where the hell have you been?"

"In the File Room, sir," he replied wearily, "where I had to forge your name on the requisition slip. You forgot about that."

There was the faintest hint of reproach in his voice that Minten chose to ignore, preferring instead to riffle through the pages inside the folder.

"Here! Here!" He punched a stubby forefinger at a line on the front page. "His mother's name has been crossed out and the name Helmut Kramer put in. It's a Hamburg address. Look it up! Look it up!"

Kugelmann went to his desk in the outer office and leafed through the phone book. There it was. He returned to Minten's office and shut the door. "He's an attorney."

"That's it! That's it! What sort of address is it?"

"Class."

"Better and better. A 'class' attorney and probably related to Kramer in the bargain. That would certainly be 'safe hands'. He could go to Berlin any time. And even if they are related, he'd keep quiet. The lawyer-client relationship. Seal of the confessional, so to speak. So we have it all, Kugelmann," but Minten paused, his good humor suddenly gone. "Tell me why we didn't know about it when Kramer went to see him? Who fell down on the job there?""

"Because he went to see him before we started having him watched?" Kugelmann suggested hopefully. "And even if it's been since, if they met somewhere outside his office, at a club for instance, especially if he were thought to be a relative... I'll check the reports. At least we know about it now." If Minten went into one of his rages... He didn't do it often but when he did...

"Yes." Minten's good humor showed signs of returning. "As I said, we have it all now."

"No Herr Major, we don't." Kugelmann had relaxed. "The attorney does. Or at least, we hope he does."

"A small matter. A small matter."

Why the hell did Minten have to say everything twice?

"Nothing that a little robbery wouldn't clear up for us, eh, Kugelmann?" Minten was pleased at the thought. A little robbery, and he'd have Kramer right where he wanted him. He had to be right. It had to be the attorney.

"Shall I arrange it?"

"Of course." Minten leaned back and stretched luxuriously. "While you're at it arrange to have the reply from this..." He waved his hand over the letter, "... This stepfather intercepted. Was the woman... The address looks familiar."

"You were next door last night."

"Of course. Of course." Minten nodded his head "Then it should be easy to arrange."

"Very."

"But the... ah... lady in question is not to know why."

"Of course." Elementary. My God. Did Minten think he was a novice at this sort of thing? He'd been getting Minten out of scrapes for the past three years.

"By the way, your arrangements last night were most satisfactory, most satisfactory, indeed."

"I'm glad you are pleased. Now, if you don't mind, I want supper. I've been hard at it since I got the call about the letter this morning."

"And you'll stay at it if you know what's good for you. There will be time enough for relaxation, for supper, for everything when Kramer is taking care of."

"And your supper?" Kugelmann asked caustically.

"It will be brought in. Since you weren't here, I had to order it myself." He said it with irritated dignity. "I still have those corrections to make and messages to get ready to go out at midnight."

He should have known. That massive stomach of Minten's could not long go ignored.

"Come back here for me around nine, after you've taken care of everything. And check out this lawyer. Look at the building. Talk to people there, even if it's only the night man. And see if you can find out if he's related to Kramer."

"All right. All right." My God he was picking up Minten's repetitive habits. "Anything you say. By the way, I saw Bergmann bring in a dispatch case this afternoon, when he came back with Richter."

"So? He often makes deliveries. That's going to have to stop by the way. He'll be too busy for that. Take him off the messenger list."

"That's the point. I thought he was off it. An officer with the dispatch case and carrying a machine pistol, of all things!"

"He's not an officer. Not yet. And certainly no one will bother him while he's carrying a machine pistol."

Minten beamed at him in sudden inspiration. "Officer or no, since he knows the drill, he can carry the necessary reports and papers to and from the School House for their training sessions. The messenger service is always shorthanded. They'll appreciate the help."

"But you wanted me to take him off the list!"

"Get out of here, Kugelmann!" Minten was roaring now. "Just take this letter with you and mail it." He lowered his voice. "And eat somewhere along the line. It may improve your disposition. Be sure to get to bed early. You haven't been getting enough sleep. That always makes you testy."

Kugelmann couldn't believe it. He snapped his jaw shut in disgust. Who had kept whom out late?

"Anything you say, Herr Major." He grabbed the letter and the folder from the desk and stalked out.

"Mind the letter. Don't crumple it."

Kugelmann slammed the door.

*     *     *

For once the café wasn't particularly crowded. Dieter was sitting alone at an outdoor table, nursing a beer. But he wasn't particularly enjoying it. Oh, the evening was lovely enough. Tall trees in the park across the street were swaying languidly in the breeze, filtering the rays from the sun into dusty beams. It was the sort of evening to be with a girl, walking in the park, talking about everything and nothing, holding hands. And if it were the right girl on the right evening, he might wind up holding more than that. It had been a long time.

He sipped his beer and contemplated that. Too long. He'd been too busy until recently and now, tomorrow, after their training began, he'd be too busy again. Another sip. Lucky Richter. My God, with a girl like that... But then, he'd be leaving her, wouldn't he. And which was worse? Not to have a girl at all or to have one and have to leave her?

And where the hell had Richter gone anyway? He'd burst into the office, demanding the keys to the Kuebel, then had torn out without a word, and there'd been no word since.

Finally, he'd gotten tired of waiting around HQ, so he'd left a message saying where he'd be and had come here to wait instead, far from the maddening crowd. But if Richter didn't come before too long, he'd have to see about hitchhiking a ride back, or, failing that, take a tram, which would mean two changes and take an hour at the very least. He sighed. Decent café, close to headquarters. Too bad it wasn't close to the School House, as well.

"Bergmann!" The voice was delighted.

"Oh, Kugelmann." Dieter looked around frantically. Unfortunately the tables were filling up.

"May I sit down?" Dieter shifted his legs from the chair next to him and sat up slowly. "Of course." Shit.

Kugelmann sank onto the chair and gave him a lopsided grin as he snapped his fingers offhandedly for the waiter Dieter looked at him closely and bit off a curse. Kugelmann was drunk.

The waiter appeared. "Sir?"

"Wurst. Sauerkraut. Anything for you, Bergmann?"

"Just another beer." He had the feeling he was going to need it.

"No supper?" Kugelmann looked at him in surprise.

"I'll get something at the School House."

Kugelmann shook his head. "The kitchen will be closed." He turned back to the waiter. "Bring him the same."

"Look..."

"I insist."

Dieter shrugged. Kugelmann was probably right about the kitchen being closed, and besides, he couldn't refuse without Kugelmann making a fuss, and from what he'd heard, Kugelmann was capable of raising a considerable fuss when he wanted to. He looked at the waiter who was still standing there. "Fine."

The man nodded and disappeared.

"Where's the major?"

"Sitting behind his desk on his fat ass, working."

"So late?" Dieter was surprised. Minten rarely worked this late. "A busy time?"

Kugelmann snorted. "More for me than for him. I'm sick and tired of doing all of his dirty work for him. I don't have a moment's peace and all I get for my pains is more work and damn little appreciation." Dieter tried not to laugh as Kugelmann continued complaining. "All those lovely, unending jobs that he gives me. Without me, he couldn't survive this mess for five minutes."

"What mess?"

Kugelmann gave a sly smile. "Part of it's your mess, too."

"I'm not part of any mess that I know about." Jesus. Drunken riddles.

Kugelmann laughed raucously. "What do you call that enchanting little trip you're taking with that precious Hauptmann of yours and the little lady?"

"Lower your voice, for God's sake!" He looked around anxiously, but everyone seemed totally unconcerned. "I guess I shouldn't be surprised that you know, since you seem to have that boss of yours in your hip pocket." He gave a nervous little laugh. "Though frankly, I think you'd fit better in his."

Kugelmann gave another lopsided grin in appreciation for his feeble joke.

Then a frown flitted across Bergmann's face. "What little lady?"

"You don't know about her?" Kugelmann was delighted. He loved being the source of information.

"No I don't know about her," said Dieter with considerable irritation. That was all they needed. It was already complicated enough, but with a woman... Damn.

"Richter didn't tell you?" Kugelmann was positively smug now, enjoying dragging it out.

Was that what had upset the Hauptmann? "No. Richter didn't tell me." He was angry now and his jaw was working, twisting the scar on his left cheek. Kugelmann shivered with pleasure.

"When he stormed out of the major's office, I was sure he'd rush right in to tell you."

"Good God, man! He came in, grabbed the keys to the Kuebel and left."

A little smile came and went across Kugelmann's face. "Probably wanted to fly to his little damsel in distress."

"What the hell are you talking about?"

"The damsel. The little lady who is completing your party."

"Who is it?!" If he didn't answer and now, he'd smash Kugelmann's teeth down his throat. Then Dieter sat bolt upright. 'His little damsel in distress'. No. It couldn't be.

Kugelmann was enjoying watching the play of emotions on Bergmann's face, relishing every moment. He had no idea how closely he was courting disaster. Finally, he leaned across the table and gave the name, emphasizing every syllable. "Fräu-lein An-na-leis-e Scheuer-mann."

"Jesus," came out in a hushed whisper. Dieter felt as if the roof had fallen on him. No wonder the Hauptmann was so upset.

He was saved from having to see anything more by the arrival of the waiter with their order. Why should she do it? It was insane. And it was going to be hard enough for the Hauptmann as it was, without having her along to worry about.

The waiter was gone and Kugelmann had started on his wurst. He kept glancing at Dieter as he shoveled his food into his mouth, thinking that Bergmann had a marvelously sinister face, knowing that he was upset. Finally, Dieter started eating, as well.

It was Kugelmann who broke the long silence. "You don't approve." He snapped his fingers and pointed to his empty beer glass as he caught the waiter's eye.

Dieter's head jerked up. "You're damn right, I don't. It's the last thing we need. And from what I saw, Richter thinks so, too." Damn. He ought to keep his mouth shut about what Richter thinks about anything to this jerk. He'd run home and tell his Daddy Minten everything.

"I must confess that the Hauptmann's attitude surprised me. I should have thought he'd enjoy the prospect of having his little..." He caught the flash of anger in Dieter's eye and amended the word to "friend" – the word was delivered with a leer – "with him."

"I seriously doubt he feels that way about it."

The beer was delivered. "Another for you, Bergmann?"

"No... Yes. But you'd better go easy with the beer if you plan to drive the major home."

The waiter had gone.

"The hell with the major."

"That's what he'll say about you if you wrap that Mercedes staff car of his around a pole."

Kugelmann dismissed that possibility with a flick of the hand. "I could drive that car in my sleep." He giggled. "I've come close more than once."

Dieter's beer arrived, and Kugelmann raised his glass and a salute, which was honored in a most perfunctory fashion. He took a long swallow, then leaned across the table, speaking softly at first, then rising to a crescendo, "You sound like my nursemaid. How would you like to be my nursemaid? I'd love to have you for my nursemaid. You'd make a delicious nursemaid."

Dieter sat absolutely still, just staring at him.

"Oh, come on, Bergmann. Don't get on your high horse with me. You were Richter's nursemaid for weeks. I'll bet you're very good at it by now."

Dieter pushed his empty plate away. "Damn right I am." He was disgusted. "But being a nursemaid really isn't my line. Sorry." He rose abruptly and reached into his pocket for the necessary change.

"No, no, Bergmann. It's mine." Kugelmann swallowed the last of his beer and staggered to his feet. "Besides, Richter has your keys."

"So?"

"So you have a long tram ride back." He managed to pull a handful of Mark coins out of his pocket and threw them on the table as the waiter rushed towards them. He backed off discreetly when he saw the amount that had been left for him, thinking as he did that more of his patrons should get drunk more often.

"I'll get you there, Bergmann."

"That's all right." He wasn't about to commit his body to be smashed, at least not if he could help it. Let Minten do that. He was so fat he'd probably just bounce out of the car if anything happened.

They were on the sidewalk now, Kugelmann weaving toward the staff car which was parked on the street in the direction of the tram stop. Dieter was gradually pulling ahead, trying to be unobtrusive about it, when he made the mistake of glancing back just as Kugelmann leaned against a tree and deposited his dinner not quite in the gutter. He turned away disgusted, then looked again just as Kugelmann slid down the trunk of the tree, fortunately missing the remains of his supper as he hit the ground. Served him right. Sauerkraut and wurst, for God sake, on top of what had to have been a lot of beer.

Kugelmann would never get back to the car, let alone drive it anywhere. He certainly couldn't be left here to be collected at someone's leisure. Dieter sighed. There was nothing for it but to get him and the damn staff car back to HQ.

Kugelmann was on his hands and knees, shaking his head like a wet dog. "All right," Dieter muttered. He grabbed the corporal under the arms and hauled him backwards, heels dragging on the pavement, to the car.

When they arrived at headquarters, there were puzzled glances from the guards at the gate. They recognized both Dieter and the car but knew they didn't belong together. He pulled to a stop and jerked his head towards the back seat. "Can either of you take this... down to the driver's lounge?" There was a sofa down there where Kugelmann could sleep it off and a shower for the morning.

"Sorry, Bergmann." The taller guard grinned. "You'll have to tend to him yourself. Neither of us can leave."

"Thanks," came the sardonic reply, and he pulled on into the courtyard, stopping by the steps leading up to the door.

The guard ran out from behind the reception desk as he got out. "You can't park here, Bergmann!"

"Oh yes, I can."

"No, you can't!"

"Look, Schwartz." It was Dieter at his most menacing. "It's been one hell of a day, and I'm finishing it out by having to haul Kugelmann down to the driver's lounge to sleep it off. I'll move the car when I get back."

"Okay, okay, but hurry it up."

"Don't worry. I won't take any longer than I have to."

The man nodded, then chuckled sympathetically and disappeared back through the open door.

Dieter hauled the now inert Kugelmann back across the seat by his feet, then gave a grunt as he threw him across his shoulder, slammed the car door and started up the steps.

"Dieter!"

He turned. It was Richter running up the steps behind them. "What have you got there?"

"Kugelmann," came the acid reply. And then they were both laughing.

"Do me a favor, will you... Hans?"

"If I can."

"I have to take him down to the driver's lounge and Schwartz doesn't want the car left here."

"Fine. And I'll take the keys down to Minten's office. If you have Kugelmann, he must still be here, and I need to see him for a few minutes." He paused, not liking to think about seeing Minten. "I'll meet you back here."

"Major Minten will be so pleased with this bit of news. I wonder if he knows how to drive himself?" They were both chuckling as Dieter struggled into his pocket and pulled out the keys, handing them to Hans. He threw a "Thanks!" back over his shoulder as he went through the door.

He had crossed the entry hall and started down the stairs along the side of the open, wrought iron lift shaft when he felt a probing hand. "God dammit, Kugelmann, cut that out." Jesus. That was all he needed.

There was a mumbling and a giggle from behind his back, but the hand was removed. The door to the driver's lounge was propped open so he was able to walk straight in and dump Kugelmann unceremoniously on the couch. No one was there, for once.

Kugelmann was giggling again after the gasp on his landing. "Beautiful."

"What's beautiful," he asked in irritation as he pulled off Kugelmann's boot.

"You, Bergmann. Too bad."

"What's too bad?" He asked it almost absently as he concentrated on pulling off the other boot. That was enough. He started towards the door.

"Kramer."

Dieter stopped and turned, interested suddenly. "What about him?"

"He thinks your precious Richter is a..." The word trailed off.

"What?"

Kugelmann was muttering to himself.

"Is a what, Kugelmann?!" Dieter was standing over him now.

He giggled again. "But Kramer's going, too. Kramer's furious. But he has to go."

"Where? Where is Kramer going?"

"England."

Oh my Lord. "With us?"

"No. No. Later. Supplies."

"What does he think about Richter?"

There was a hiccup and more mumbling. Dieter repeated the question, trying not to sound as frantically interested as he was.

"Spy."

"What about a spy?"

"Richter's a spy!" Kugelmann was shouting now.

Dieter virtually leapt towards the door, slamming it. "You're crazy." He was back at the couch.

"Kramer. Kramer thinks..." His voice trailed off again.

"Why?"

There was a vague shrugged as his eyes closed.

Dieter shook him "Why! Come on you bastard! Wake up! Why?!"

"Why what?" Kugelmann's voice was barely audible

Dieter tried to control himself, to be patient. It wasn't easy. "Why does Kramer think that Richter's a spy?"

"Godfather."

"What about his godfather?" Kugelmann wasn't making any sense. But then he was drunk and if he weren't drunk...

"Intelligence."

"What about intelligence?"

"Godfather in British Intelligence."

Dieter sucked in a breath.

"No one to know. Shhh."

"I won't tell anyone," he said drily. That was certain. Jesus. "Don't worry."

Kugelmann gave a slight nod as Dieter walked slowly towards the door. It was crazy. Richter a spy? Insane. He would've known. They have been together almost constantly for well over a year. Impossible. And what could he have been spying on for God sake?

Dieter propped the door open.

Except here. There was plenty to spy on here. His heart sank but then rose again. Richter hadn't asked to be posted here. There had been no one, nothing suspicious since he came here. Kramer was crazy. He hated Richter. He was out to get Richter anyway he could.

Dieter walked back to the couch again. Better find out all he could while Kugelmann was still drunk. He'd never talk like this if he were sober. Kugelmann rarely talked much about anything when he was sober.

Dieter shook him again. There was no response.

"Kugelmann!" His voice was harsh as he shook the corporal again. "What's Kramer up to?!"

The words were thick and slurred. "Get Richter."

Yes. Yes. He knew that already. "Why?" There was no sensible reason for it.

Kugelmann muttered on, "... you'd hang. Too bad." There were tears in his eyes.

"Why would I hang?!"

"If Kramer's right. You'd hang. Watch..."

Watch who? Kramer? Richter? He shook Kugelmann again but there was no waking him.

Dieter stood there looking down at nothing, his mind a blank. Finally he turned and walked slowly out through the door.

*       *       *

Hans ambled into the entry hall.

"Thank you, Herr Hauptmann." It was Schwartz. "I really catch it when there are any unattended cars out there."

He grinned. "Bergmann had his hands full."

Schwartz's laugh followed him down the corridor. The place was nearly deserted for once.

He went in through Minten's outer office where Kugelmann's desk was. The door to Kramer's office was shut and there was no light coming out from under the door. He must be out. One blessing, at least. He tapped on Minten's door. No answer. Could he have gone? No. There was light coming from under the door. And where would he have gone without his car?

He tried the knob. It turned. He pushed the door open and peered in. No one was there. He snorted. Minten certainly didn't believe in security regulations. Not only was he not here but there was no one in the outer office and neither door was locked. Good grief! The wall safe was open, and there were papers scattered all over the desk. The remains of a dinner littered a low table in front of the sofa. The place was a mess. Where was he? Leave the keys and a note with Schwartz. Minten was bound to be back any moment. Suddenly he didn't want to see him. Let it wait.

Leaving the door ajar, Hans moved behind the desk looking for a scrap of paper and shuffled through the clutter for a pen. How did Minten find anything? A pen. Then he saw it. The folder was stamped Top Secret and the label said 'Aufbau Ost.' He put the paper beside the folder before he opened it, keeping the pen in hand and his ear cocked.

His finger ran down the first page and what he saw made his blood run cold. Russia. He stopped. Russia. And in the spring. They must be counting on Britain being finished by then. They wouldn't be so foolish as to turn east before things were settled in the west. Russia. Winter. He shuddered. There was a sound in the outer office. Hans slammed the folder shut, covered it with some papers and began scribbling hastily.

The door opened slowly. Hans concentrated on his writing, his heart pounding.

"Well, well, Richter. When the cat's away, the mice will play, I see."

Hans looked up, managing to keep his tone casual. "Oh. Kramer. Minten's not here. I'm leaving him a note."

Kramer's eyes took in the open safe. "What's so urgent that it couldn't wait?"

Hans finished writing. "Kugelmann's drunk. Bergmann took him down to the driver's lounge to sleep it off. I'm leaving the car keys."

"And doing a little snooping on the side?"

Hans threw the keys onto the note and then looked Kramer in the eye, giving a little smirk that was not pleasant to see. "That's more your style than mine, I'd say."

Kramer reddened.

Minten picked that moment to come barging in. He stopped when he saw them and looked from one to the other. "Well. Isn't this cozy? Can't I even go to the can without having my office invaded?"

He turned to Hans. "Just what are you doing in here, Richter?"

"Kugelmann is dead drunk and sleeping it off in the driver's lounge. I brought you the keys, and since you weren't here, I was leaving you a note." He reached down, took the keys from the desk, and handed them to the major. "Your door was open and light was on." He thought it the better part of valor not to mention the safe.

Minten flushed as he took the keys. "Thank you. But the next time, leave them at the reception's desk. If there is a next time. If Kugelmann knows what's good for him, there won't be." Damn idiot. He had better have finished what he had to do. "And you Kramer?"

"I saw the light on in the door ajar, so I came in to say good night, Herr Major."

"Very thoughtful," Minten said acidly. "And since you're here, Lieutenant, you may drive me home."

"Certainly, Herr Major." He hid his annoyance well. "And would you like me to pick you up in the morning?"

"How else do you think I'd get here? That fool Kugelmann deserves what he gets. Let him sleep it off here. You may go, Richter."

"Thank you, Herr Major. Good night. Lieutenant." He gave a bare nod in Kramer's direction. It was returned in like fashion.

"Richter."

Hans turned in the doorway. "Yes, sir?"

"What did you and the Fräulein decide? I take it that's where you went."

"She will be here in the morning."

"Good. Good. I thought you'd see it my way."

Hans turned to leave.

"And Richter…"

He sighed and turned back again. "Yes, Herr Major?"

"Tell that man of yours, Bergmann, to get a sidearm. He was seen bringing in a dispatch case today, and he wasn't wearing one."

"He has a weapon, sir. But he must not have been carrying it. I'll speak to him about it. Is he to be relieved for messenger duties since he'll be going into training?" Hans devoutly hoped not. It hadn't occurred to him that he might until this minute.

"He can handle the documents for the School House since he knows the form. Easier that way."

Hahn suppressed a sigh of relief. "Fine, sir. Is there anything else?" All he wanted to do was get out of there.

"No. No." Minten dismissed him with a brisk wave and walked behind his desk.

Hans shut the door and wiped the thin film of sweat from his face with his handkerchief before he went out into the hall.

\* \* \*

"I'll be with you in a moment, Kramer. I have to clean up some of this."

"I hope that there's nothing important there, Herr Major."

Sanctimonious bastard. Minten glanced up sharply but Kramer was wearing a look of complete innocence. He went back to his papers.

"I found Richter back there, Herr Major."

"So I see. Here's the note." He gave it a vague wave before consigning it to the wastebasket, then he paused almost imperceptibly. God. Had he left that out? He turned his head slightly, noticing that he had left the safe open. His forehead was beaded with sweat as he shoved the folder into the safe and shut the door, twirling the dials before he replaced the picture that hung over it. What if Richter had looked at it and was captured when he got to England, and they made him talk... He was shivering despite the sweat.

"Anything there that would be of interest to the English?" The tone was just a shade too casual.

"Not really," he muttered as he shoved the rest of the papers willy-nilly into a desk drawer.

"Then why are you sweating, Herr Major?"

Minten slammed the door shut savagely. "Because it's hot in here, you fool!" It was going to be pure pleasure to get rid of Kramer. Minten threw him the keys. "Get the car. I'll be right out."

Kramer paused at the door. "I hope that our 'friends' across the Channel enjoy hearing about whatever it is."

He slammed the door behind himself before Minten could say anything.

The major looked after him. Damn. What if he were right? He snapped off the desk light. Ridiculous. Still... He shouldn't have left that out, the safe open. No sense worrying about it. Richter probably hadn't done anything but write the note and the folder had been under the paper. He probably hadn't even seen it.

Lock the damn office to go to the bathroom? It had taken too long, far too long. He needed more exercise. He frowned. He hated exercise. Then he smiled. He'd gotten plenty of exercise last night. Now that was the way to exercise! But not every night. He had to be realistic. Prune juice. That would take care of things between times.

He was careful to lock the door this time, first to his office, then to the outer office before he walked down the hall towards the entrance.

                    *        *        *

Dieter didn't speak until they were through the gate. "Kugelmann had some odd things to say."

"That isn't surprising. He was completely soused."

"I think we'd better be glad that he was. Ordinarily, he's pretty closed-mouth."

There was something about the way Bergmann had said that... "What did he have to say?"

"Kramer's out to get you."

Hans snorted. "So what else is new?"

"He's circulating some story that your godfather is with British Intelligence and that you're a spy." They had stopped for a stop sign, and as Dieter looked both ways he made sure that he caught Richter's profile. It was unreadable. He started across the intersection.

"That explains a great deal."

"What do you mean?"

"Annaliese told me this afternoon that he had made her spy on me."

Dieter started visibly and slammed on the brakes. "But she's going to England with us!"

"How the hell did you know that? I just found out this afternoon, myself."

"So that was what sent you tearing off." It was a honk behind them. Dieter started up slowly.

"I was hoping to talk her out of it. Instead... How did you find out?"

"Kugelmann."

"He has to be the most talkative drunk in town."

"It was at dinner before he got sick and passed out. He thoroughly enjoyed being able to tell me about it." Dieter hesitated, looking over at Hans briefly. "Spying on you?"

"She had no choice."

"And she's not going?" He sounded hopeful.

"Oh, she's going all right."

"Jesus."

"Jesus is right. She didn't have any more choice than you do."

"Kramer?"

"Right you are."

"Jesus."

"Right again."

"And you don't know the half of it. Kramer is going to England, too."

"Jesus." Came out in a low whisper as Hans sank down in the seat.

"Not with us. At least I don't think so. Kugelmann was pretty well out of it when he told me. All I could get out of him was 'later' and 'supplies'."

Hans groaned. "Someone is coming over after we get there to set up a liaison with someone who is already there and to bring the supplies. But Minten didn't say who. If it's Kramer, I can see why. He knows there's no love lost between us."

"Is your godfather in Intelligence?"

"He's in the Foreign Office." The truth. At least it was the truth as far as it went.

Dieter nodded, satisfied. "What's to be done?"

"That will take some thought. It's been one hell of a day."

"And Fräulein Scheuermann? There was an 'instead' back there somewhere."

"We're going to be married."

The car slammed to a halt, nearly throwing Hans into the dashboard. Dieter was sitting there, gaping at him. Hans burst out laughing at the expression on his face. It was a moment before he could go on. "It's the only good thing to come out of this whole mess."

"Married?!"

Hans was grinning. "As the lady put it, 'your cover in England is perfect. If we were married, mine would be, too.' Or words to that effect."

That was Dieter's turn to burst out laughing as the car that had been behind them, honking, edged cautiously around the Kuebel, the driver giving them an exceedingly irritated stare.

Finally, he started up again without saying a word. He didn't know what to say. Married. He began grinning and they were both grinning and chuckling as they drove through the gate and up to the School House.

Later, when they were settled in Hans' room, each with a glass in hand, a bottle of schnapps on the desk, Dieter raised his glass in salute. "To you and your lady."

"Amen to that."

Dieter sipped solemnly.

"But not a word about it to anyone. It would give too much away right now. We have to be careful. I don't want Kramer to get wise to the situation."

"The less he knows about anything, the better."

"Amen again." Hans sighed. "As I said, it's been one hell of a day."

Dieter gave a little laugh. "I'll drink to that."

They both did, and to quite a few other things, as well, including the start of their training at 0900 the next morning and the fact that Hans had also heard that another group was coming to the School House to train to go to the United States. That had surprised Dieter, but he didn't know why it had. Nothing that went on these days should be surprising. Their final toast was to the damnation of their enemies in general and Kramer in particular.

Dieter floated to the bed in an alcoholic haze. He was almost asleep when his memory nudged him and he could see, in his mind's eye, Richter standing before him as he asked, 'Are you a good liar, Hauptmann?', and hear his reply, 'Yes. Yes, I'm afraid that I am, Bergmann. I don't like to lie and I don't do it often, but when I do, I am very good at it indeed.'

Now why the hell had he thought of that? No answer came and he drifted off to sleep.

# Chapter XIII

Hans yawned and then stretched luxuriously. "Five more minutes of the good 'Herr Major' would have finished me off."

Annaliese laughed. "How have the two of you stood him all these months?"

Dieter's snort spoke volumes. It had been a long day and Minten had made it even longer. He sighed. They still weren't through. They had to be back at the School House in 40 minutes for dinner and after that there was to be an evening session. Minten was setting a fast pace. But as he had said over and over during the day, four weeks wasn't much time. It wasn't. Look what happened to the last lot.

Dieter looked around. They were sitting in the same café where he'd had dinner with Kugelmann the night before. He shuddered faintly at the recollection.

And Alsatian. God. This new background business. Would he ever fall into it? Would it ever fit like a 'second skin' as Minten had said that it must? Hans didn't have that problem, lucky bastard. But he did have to know theirs almost as well as they knew them, themselves.

But he had never set foot in Alsace. At least it would account for his German accent. And of the new last name. Kerrmann. What a pain. At least he was keeping his own first name. Mrs. Richter was going to be a problem. He'd have to be constantly on his guard with her. Mrs. Richter knew something about Dieter Bergmann. He'd have to be careful not to let anything slip, especially about Poland. No Alsatian would have been in the Wehrmacht in 1939. France either, for that matter. He wished that he could be going as himself. It would be so much easier. There was no compelling reason for an Austrian to escape the Third Reich these days. Austria was part of Germany now, a 'voluntary' part. Anyway, it wasn't his decision to make.

He smiled across at Annaliese. "Tell me, dear sister, how do you

307

like your new family?"

"Brother, dear," she laughed, "it's a privilege. I've never had a real brother of my own before."

"What about your cousins? You were all raised together."

"I suppose they're like brothers. At least Helmut is. But Reinhard was already away at school when I came to live with Uncle Friedrich and Aunt Karin, so I've never been close to him. He's a good sort. They both are. It's just that I've never had an 'official' brother before." She smiled. "It's rather nice, really."

Dieter gave an airy wave of the hand in Hans' direction. "If you have any trouble with this one, let me know. That's what big brothers are for."

"Pooh. You and I are almost exactly the same age."

"I didn't say older. I said big, and unless my eyes deceive me, I am considerably bigger than you are."

"I should hope so!" She managed to look properly horrified which made both men laugh. "And you are older. One year. At least that's what our papers will say."

"Come on, you two," Hans grumbled. "You're making me feel left out in the cold with all of this family talk."

"Never, darling."

Dieter's eyes narrowed slightly at this endearment. She was oblivious to everyone and everything but Hans at the moment. Then he smiled to himself. That was the way it should be. Hans was damn lucky and he'd better appreciate it. Was he really turning into a protective big brother? Already? God knows, he'd really felt that way about his own sister. She was a big girl, a large girl, and she had always insisted that she could take care of herself. And now she was getting married. At Christmas. At least he knew the boy. A good boy. He wished he could be there. December. What would've happened to them by December?

He looked over at them again as Annaliese covered Hans' hands with hers. "You'll be my husband and Dieter's brother-in-law, so it's all 'family talk'."

"Hush!" Hans looked around.

"Don't worry. I've already laid the groundwork for it."

He looked back, startled. "When?"

"During our afternoon break for coffee."

"Is that where you went? Why didn't you tell me?" He sounded a little plaintive. He did feel a little left out. She was so terribly efficient and seemed so able to take care of herself. He supposed that he should be grateful. God knows, he couldn't bear the thought of a clinging vine, but still, at least she could've told him.

"I'm sorry, darling." And she was. "But it was one of those things. He gave me the perfect opening and I took it. You know Kramer. You have to take the openings he gives you because he doesn't give very many."

He nodded, trying to smile at her. He was being unreasonable and he knew it. He knew that her having to deal with a slippery bastard like Kramer couldn't be helped, but that didn't mean that he had to like it.

"And there hasn't been a peaceful moment until now to tell you about it. The major was hovering in the background every minute, the Kuebel was too noisy, and it was too chaotic in my apartment. Thank heaven I took your advice and packed up what I needed after you left last night. Going to be a real job to clear my things out of there. I didn't realize how much I had." She was talking rapidly now, worried that he was still annoyed with her. "Maybe Helga will want to move in. It would save me a lot of trouble if she did."

"You think she will?" He was handing her an olive branch.

Annaliese relaxed a little. "She just might. She really does need a place of her own. And Karin is awful free with 'advice' that's not always easy to take. She'd have a place to call her own, she and the children, but she'd be close to them if she needed them."

Dieter was restless. "Come on, Annaliese. What happened with Kramer?"

Hans looked around again. No one seemed to be paying any attention to them, but one never knew these days. Especially since Kramer was on his tail. He was so close to being done with it, so very close. He couldn't let anything go wrong, not now, especially since Dieter and Annaliese were in it, as well. He'd never had anyone else to consider before, and he didn't like having anyone else to consider now. During battle, they all needed each other. It was different then, but now... It was hard enough keeping his own rear covered without having to worry about someone else's.

His mouth tightened to a grim line. He was being ridiculous. Without Annaliese, his tail would be flapping in the breeze, completely uncovered. Kramer could plant whatever evidence he wanted to plant, and no one would be the wiser. He needed her. That's what he didn't like, the fact that he needed her. He had never needed anyone the way he needed her, and not just because she covered his rear.

By God, he'd be glad when this war was over.

"Hans!"

He came to, looking at her quizzically. "Sorry."

"Where were you?"

"Just thinking. You were saying? About Kramer?"

Dieter was looking at him, thinking he was as strung and tight as a piano wire. But then who wouldn't be? He was between a rock and a hard place.

She had been so sure that she'd done it all well, but now, with Hans annoyed, even though he... Why hadn't she seen how hard all this would be for him? At least Dieter knew what she had done and that she had to do it, even if he didn't know precisely why. He accepted that. She took a deep breath.

"It was easy really." Had it been too easy?

"He's so full of himself." Her lip curled into a faint sneer as she got caught up in remembering.

"He's so sure he has us all where he wants us. Especially me. I told him that since your cover was perfect, Hans, that mine would be too if I talked you into marrying me. He laughed." Her sneer was full-blown now. "He told me that I must really be desperate if I was willing to marry you. It was easy to tell him that I didn't want to hang, no matter how this turned out. And since Dieter was to be my brother, it would be safer for him, too. Would make all of us coming together logical. There wouldn't be any need to explain it."

"Perfect," Hans broke in, his voice dripping acid. It was perfect. Jesus. She'd been right. Kramer fouled everything, even his marrying her, especially his marrying her.

"Just don't fall into that same trap yourself Annaliese."

"What trap?"

"The trap that Kramer is apparently falling into, of believing that things are going your way and that there is no other way for them to go. There is another way for things to go for Kramer and there could be for you, too, for all of us. If you don't remember that, it could make you careless."

Her face reddened and she looked down for a moment, then nodded slowly before she looked back up at him again. "You're right, of course. I was too pleased with myself by half. After all, this is just beginning. Pride goes before the fall. Is that what you mean?"

"Something like that." He shifted in his chair. She had done well. Why couldn't he tell her that?

She nodded again, soberly. But then she had to smile. "Still, I wish you could've seen his face. He was so angry because it was perfect, and he hadn't thought of it himself. He would have loved ordering me to marry you."

"But what did he say about it"? Dieter was beginning to wonder if she'd ever get it all out. He was getting restless and some of Hans' concern was beginning to rub off. Now it was Dieter who was looking around to see if anyone was listening. They were in a back corner under the awning, still well away from the rest of the early diners. "Didn't he suspect anything?" He kept his voice low.

"No. That's what I meant when I said that he desperately wants to believe that everything is under his control." She looked back at Hans.

"He did ask if you had already asked me to marry you. I told him that you hadn't, not yet, but that I was sure that I could bring you to that point fairly quickly, especially since I would be in the School House. I'm afraid, darling," she was almost pleading for his understanding now, worried because of the way he was reacting, "that I had to make you look a bit the besotted fool."

Hans smiled wryly. "The more the fool he thinks I am, the better." Then he gave a harsh laugh. "Besides, where you're concerned, I am a besotted fool."

That was too much for Dieter. This was getting to be too private a conversation for him to be listening to. They needed to be alone to sort it out. He rose. "Excuse me. I'll be back in a minute." Then he made his way to the door of the café and disappeared inside.

Annaliese looked after him fondly. "Where did you ever find him?"

Hans shrugged. "Driving my tank." He couldn't get rid of his irritation.

"You were lucky that he was. There aren't many like him."

He looked at her closely. "Yes. Yes I was."

"He knows that I need to talk with you alone."

"Do you?"

"Yes."

"Then he reads you better than I do. Are you sure it's not just a trip to the loo?" He didn't like having Bergmann understand her. He didn't like much of anything right now.

"Not unless he has a problem. He used the loo at my apartment."

"Then by all means, don't let his 'sacrifice' be in vain."

She flushed slightly and looked down, fidgeting with her beer glass.

"Come on, my darling. You were scarcely shy yesterday."

She looked up sadly. "What is wrong, Hans? I thought that I had handled it well."

He sighed. "I'm sorry. I know I'm being a bastard. I can't seem to help it. I hate this whole situation. I hate your being involved in it. I hate the secrecy and the plotting, and for some reason I hate the fact that you're good at it. You have to do so damn much of it yourself and why you're doing it, all I can think is to be your rearguard and go along with whatever it is. I want to marry you more than anything in the world, but even that has to be part of this damn conspiracy. I just don't like it." Then it was his turn to look down and fiddle with his beer glass.

Her face softened. "Would you rather I weren't good at it?"

He looked up sharply and then back down when he saw the expression on her face. Love? Concern? He couldn't tell. His laugh was brief and harsh. "No. Of course not. It's just..." His voice trailed off.

She drew a deep breath, thinking that she was holding something fragile in her hands, and she would have to be very careful with it. She so desperately wanted to hang onto it, to keep it from slipping away, but if she held on too tight she would crush it. Oh God, let me say the right thing. He looks so miserable. Suddenly her loins were aching for him so that she had had to shift in her chair. It was almost overwhelming. "Darling Hans, I would give my life simply to be going to a country cottage in England where we could raise our babies and live happily ever after." She stopped for a moment, searching for his face.

Babies. The word made him think of only one thing. Babies. God. His baby in her. But he said nothing.

"But this damn war and our 'friend'," she spat out the word, "Kramer have taken care of that for the time being. We have our own personal war to fight now in addition to the other one, and neither of us can fight it alone. Separately, we'd be too vulnerable. It will take both of us, together. Usually it's still the same old thing. A man goes off to war, his woman waits at home for him to come back, either on his shield or carrying it. I'm afraid, my darling, that I wouldn't be very good at that, anymore. I did it once for a man I only thought I loved. I will never put myself through that again if I can help it."

He looked up at the sudden ferociousness in her voice. What was his name? He had died in Poland. Strange. He had never understood before how hard it must be for a woman to wait. But then there had never been a woman waiting for him except for his mother, and he was used to her waiting and worrying. He knew that he would never be quite so used to it again.

"I'm lucky in this fight," she went on, ferocious still. "I can stand beside you, and I have my own shield and armor and some weapons. I have my wits but even more, there is the love that you have for me. And that makes me far more formidable. I am fighting for you and for me and for both of us together, and I won't be beaten. There are two of us armed and armored, fighting for each other together. That's something far different than one of us alone, because we can cover each other. I just have to remember that there are two of us now, that I'm not alone anymore."

"But you always had your uncle!" He was angry with himself. Why was he making things so hard for her? She was right, and by God she loved him, really loved him and she would fight like a tiger. Formidable. She had used that word and it described her to a tee. Suddenly he felt humble. How had he been so lucky?

She was going on, explaining, almost pleading again for his understanding, his acceptance of what could not be changed.

"But Uncle Friedrich couldn't help me. He loves me and it's been tearing him apart that he's the reason I got caught up in all of this. He hates it. But he has Aunt Karin to worry about, and the boys. There wasn't much he could do. There still isn't. When he gets back and hears about my going to England..."

She sighed. It was an effort to get back to the point.

"Anyway, I had to fight for Uncle Friedrich and myself by myself, and in a way fight for you, too, without letting you know what Kramer was trying to do, what I was having to do for him. It was hell. It's such a relief that you know now and that I can count on you. I have to get used to it. I've always had to fight my own battles; there's never been anyone to help me with most of them. Uncle Friedrich was away so much of the time. I love you so."

She was speaking rapidly now, trying to get it all out.

"You understand? Can you understand? I'm glad we're together. I'm glad that I can serve you. I love you and I serve you, but I will hate it if instead of helping, it gets in our way because there is no other choice really, for either of us. Help me. Please help me to do it right, to do it the best way for both of us." There were tears in her eyes.

He leaned forward and took her hand. She had been fiddling nervously with a napkin. "Hush. It's all right. It will be alright. I'll be alright. It's me, not you. I hate having anyone fight my battles for me. Happened too often when I was little. My brother James... And Dieter. Dieter saved me twice." Hans shook his head. He was pleading with her now.

Saved him twice? She looked at him quizzically. "I knew about your arm. When was the other time?"

He shook his head, not liking to remember. But then he spoke. "In Dunkirk."

She tensed. Kramer had said...

"One of the prisoners jumped me. He had me on the floor and was choking the life out of me, literally. It was a near thing. That damn cast. I couldn't do a thing. Anyway, Dieter hauled him off me and threw him against the wall. Broke his neck." Hans was studying his beer glass. His face was bleak.

"God." It came out as a sigh. Then her voice hardened. "Kramer implied that Dieter... That you and he... That you were too rough with him while you were questioning him and that was how he died."

Hans stared at her. "He told you that?!"

"No. Not really. He just implied it. You know how he is."

"Bastard!" He looked at her, hard. "Did you believe him?"

She snorted. "I don't believe anything he says. But..." She hesitated.

"But what?!" He was getting angry again.

"You know how he twists things. For just a moment... But Dieter's not that sort. I knew that even then. But he looks so tough. For a moment, just for a moment... And I knew you. Even then I knew you couldn't have done anything like that." She shrugged helplessly.

Hans sighed. "Darling, forget it. That's Kramer's strength. He can make white seem black sometimes." Then he smiled. "But we'll beat him, and together, all three of us. You're really something. You're tough." His eyes were twinkling and then he laughed. "Kramer can't possibly know what he's up against. Armed and armored. By God, we are. Just that. I've never dealt with a woman in armor before and that will take some getting used to."

Her eyes lit up. This was Hans. He was himself again. Thank God. It was going to be alright. His face said that it was. It had to be. "But from what you've said about your mother..."

"Touché." He grinned. "Though, somehow I had never thought about it quite that way, Mother wearing armor, I mean. I suppose that she does, but like you, she conceals it very well indeed. And she is a good infighter when the chips are down."

She hesitated, looking worried again. "After this I almost hate to tell you... It sounds so... calculating."

"Out with it. Right now I feel ready for anything."

"I let Kramer think... Well... he thinks that I'm going to... actually probably get where you have... Oh, Hans. It makes me feel so dirty."

Aha. So that was rearing its head. How to let her off the hook? Amazing. Now he wanted her off the hook, wanted to help her, was willing to help her as she was helping him. The light touch. That was what was needed. "Are you trying to seduce me?"

Her face was beet red. "Well, at least the appearance of it."

"You mean you don't want to seduce me?" He managed to look crestfallen.

"Well, no. I mean, yes." She gave a little laugh, still red-faced. "That's a 'when did you stop beating your wife' sort of question."

"Tonight?" He was watching her with considerable amusement.

"No. No. That would be too soon. Maybe in a few days. It should be easy since my room is just down the hall. Thank God it's not next to his. Some night when he's there."

"You know, you really are a heartless, calculating wench."

"Why?! I told you..."

"I know. This is all for my own good. To keep me safe." He put on a sorrowful look. "I shall make the considerable sacrifice. But just to preserve the mission and do Kramer in the eye, mind you."

He was grinning now. "There is one problem, though."

"Oh? And what could that possibly be?" She was giving him back tit for tat.

"How am I supposed to work my way through all of that armor?"

Her eyes were laughing at him over the rim of the beer stein. "I am sure that you could find a way. You are so resourceful." Then her expression turned to one of malevolent sweetness. "But you know how clunky armor is, especially two sets clanking together, and we have to be discreet. At least there are two beds so you won't have to sleep on the floor. In armor that would be intolerable."

He had been chuckling, but he stopped. Was she serious? Two beds? Could he bear sleeping in the same room without her... God, how he wanted her. At this moment she was infinitely desirable. She was at any moment. But he would have her on her terms, on their terms, not Kramer's terms. That bastard would openly foul this. By God not this.

"You look so grim."

"I'm sorry, love. Kramer."

She made a face. "It always seems to come back to Kramer, doesn't it?"

"Self-seeking, self-centered, power-grabbing, arrogant son-of-a-bitch."

"Foulmouthed, dirty-minded prick."

"Annaliese!"

Then they were laughing. She stopped to catch her breath, relishing his face, relaxed and happy at last. Dear Lord, please let me keep it this way.

There was a catch in his throat. "If you don't stop looking at me that way, I shall throw you bodily into that Kuebel and cart you off somewhere. Then Kramer would have no doubt whatsoever that you were successful and it might blow everything."

"Perhaps not." She was grinning mischievously. "You never know until you try."

"Don't tempt me."

"And do I?"

"Witch. You have to know that you do."

"Then Lieutenant Kramer can go straight to hell."

"I'll drink to that." He smiled at her and then caught sight of Dieter's face peering around the doorjamb. He started. He had forgotten all about Dieter. Hans beckoned to him and when he reached the table, looked up to say "We got it all settled. Thank you."

Dieter was smiling as he sat down. "I didn't think that I was that obvious."

"The lady read your mind."

"Then I shall have to be careful what I think."

"We both shall."

"You mean that she can read yours as well?" Dieter shook his head. "My God, Hans. That bodes ill."

They were all laughing as the waiter brought the second round of beer that Dieter had ordered. They still had about ten minutes.

\*       \*       \*

```
Dear Michael,
So you finally cornered her. Congratulations! I
trust by now that you know you have a tiger by the
tail. But hold firm. She's worth the struggle.
I just wish that I could be there for the nuptials.
She will be a gorgeous bride. And it would be good
to see her as happy as I know she'll be, as she
already is.
Keep her safe and watch out for flying books.
Love to you both,
John
```

He looked up and grinned. "Impudent pup. Did you read this?"

She was glad to see his grin. He had looked exhausted and positively grim when he came in. "No." Then, "Yes." She flushed as she sat on the arm of the sofa beside him "I shouldn't have. I'm sorry. But I was a little nervous about what he might have to say to me. It was just easier to read yours first."

He laughed. "Is that a portent of things to come?"

"Certainly not!" She was indignant. "It was in an envelope addressed to me. Your envelopes are sacrosanct."

"Turnabout's fair play. What does yours say?"

She handed it to him and walked over to the chair opposite, so that she could watch his face as he read.

```
Dearest Mother,
```

He looked up.

"Bad grammar. But I appreciate the sentiment."

"A standing joke."

Michael nodded as he turned back to the letter.

```
Good for you! About time Michael got into the
family officially.
I assume that James will give away the blushing
bride. Just wish that I could be there to hold up
the train or the bridegroom, whichever needs the
most. He hasn't been through this before. But from
what I hear, the first time is the worst time.
Give old James my best whether he wants it or not.
I'll be glad when all this is over.
My love, John
```

Michael cleared his throat. "Nice boy."

There were tears in her eyes as she nodded in agreement.

"But what's this 'watch out for flying books' business?"

She groaned, then gave a little laugh. "I was hoping that you wouldn't ask about that. It was the only knock-down-drag-out fight Gerhard and I ever had. Gretl had written him, saying that I was up to no good with her husband. You remember. I told you about it."

He nodded, unwilling to interrupt the flow. She had mentioned it once, briefly. He smiled as he settled back. This was bound to be good.

"Anyway, Gerhard was furious and I was even more furious. Gretl was always a bit of a troublemaker, a thoroughly spoiled little sister in some ways, I'm afraid. She's the baby of the family. I was so frustrated and angry... We were in the library at the time, the music room now." She grinned. "Most remarkable things tend to happen to me in there. I love you."

"Go on. I refuse to be distracted, even by that!" He suppressed a grin.

She laughed, unembarrassed at having been caught out. "The books were the only thing at hand and so I started throwing them. He just stood there and either ducked or caught them until I couldn't throw anymore. It was the smartest thing he could've done because I got everything out of my system and because it made us both laugh. It was also ridiculous. John came in and found us both sitting on the floor laughing our heads off. He was terribly confused, poor boy, because he knew what would've happened to him if he'd thrown the books. It was years before I could explain it to him."

"Then by all means, I shall watch out for flying books." He was laughing, picturing it all in his mind. Her smile was just a little wicked. "It's nice to know that when I grow fat and contented and your eyes begin to wander, that I'll have something to hold over your head."

"Then you'll be sadly disappointed. I've had my fill of wandering. It's not what it's cracked up to be. I'm afraid that I'll be the one to get fat and contented and you'll be the one with the wandering eye."

"Don't worry, I'll see that you stay thin."

His eyes were sparkling. "You certainly have seen to it that I've had plenty of exercise lately. If you keep that up, there's no danger of my ever getting fat."

She stuck her tongue out at him. "That's all it's good for, keeping you thin?"

His only answer was a slow smile.

It took a moment for the blush to work its way up to her face and by then she was looking at her hands as they worked themselves in her lap. "There's only one thing about it that really bothers me."

"That I haven't made an honest woman of you yet?" He sounded faintly surprised.

"No." She managed a faint smile "I asked you the first time, remember?"

"I remember it very well, indeed." Oh my, how he remembered.

She was looking at her hands again. "It's just that in one way it isn't good for anything except keeping you thin." She looked up, clearly troubled.

"I'd so like to give you a child, Michael, but I can't."

"Please, Anne. Don't. It never occurred to me that you could. By God. In one way you've already given me two." He gave a nervous little laugh. "Actually, it's a bit of a relief."

"A relief?!" She was genuinely surprised.

"If I were interested in having children, I could have married a dozen times over in the past 25 years. James and John are enough and my brother's children. I honestly don't think I could go through raising one of my own after seeing all of that, especially now.

"Besides," he was chuckling now, "who says that I don't have one running around somewhere. I'm very afraid that I had a misspent youth."

"No misspent middle age?"

"My darling, as I said, my wandering days are over and have been for several years, ever since I realized that every woman I saw was nothing but a substitute for you. The original is all that I want. So quit that sort of talking and come here."

"Aye, aye, sir." She settled on the couch next to him, nestling into the curve of his arm, her feet tucked under her.

He put his cheek against her hair. "That's better."

"Infinitely." She hesitated but when she went on her voice was firm. "When are you going to make an honest woman of me?"

His face clouded a bit. "It's hard to say. September." Then he looked alarmed. "You don't want a big wedding, do you?"

She laughed. "The thought frightens you?"

"Not really. It's just that big weddings have always seemed so... theatrical. I want to be sure that it's you and I getting married and not two characters in some sort of extravagant play."

"Can James come?"

He laughed. "Of course. He can give you away and be my best man, too." He frowned. "But it depends on whether he can get away. And it would have to be on awfully short notice, if he could at all."

"Why couldn't we go to him?"

"To Dover? I suppose we could, but it's not the safest place in the world these days. They're getting the hell knocked out of them."

"Everything in the south seems to be getting the hell knocked out of it," she said gloomily. "I'm not going to let those damn Nazis interfere with his wedding anymore than they have already. They have one of my sons, and I'm not going to let them keep the other from my wedding if I can possibly help it. You could get us clearance to go down there, couldn't you? You've been down there. I know you have. That time Annabelle saw James. She was with you. She had to be. Actually, she was down there twice. I know I can't ask why or when or where you go, so I won't. But there is a lovely ancient church up there within the castle walls. It would be a perfect place for a wedding."

"All of that is under army control."

"But it's well above the harbor, so it's bound to be safer. The Germans aren't interested in that. They want the harbor, not the old castle. What possible harm can that castle be doing them?"

For the radio station beyond it. He kept that thought to himself.

"Will you see about it?"

"You really do have your heart set on it, don't you."

She nodded eagerly. "I could stay at the Watsons. We both could. It's well out in the country. They've come back to London now, but the caretaker is down there with his wife, and with Hannah and Max..."

"You've already planned all of this out, haven't you?" He started to laugh. "Have you asked the Watsons yet?"

"No." She was laughing back at him. "I wouldn't go that far without checking with you."

"What am I to do with you?"

She wrinkled her nose at him. "Marry me on my birthday. It's all I want, especially since you were so terribly extravagant with this lovely ring." She held up her left hand, admiring yet again at the deep blue of the large square sapphire set with a diamond baguette on either side, all in yellow gold.

He smiled at her obvious pleasure. "You do like it?"

"How many times have I told you that I do. You have marvelous taste."

"Since I happen to marrying you, you couldn't very well say anything else."

She laughed. "As I said, you have marvelous taste."

"Your birthday?"

"My birthday."

"September eighth."

"September eighth."

"And pray tell, what happens if the Germans decide to celebrate the event by coming to the party as well."

"They're not coming."

"Oh? The powers-that-be will be delighted to know that. I shall call and tell them at once." Actually, she might be right. The Wehrmacht and the Kriegsmarine were still bickering, and the date had been put back once more, to early September.

"Then tell them. They can't come."

Fortunately, he was not confused about which 'theys' were meant. "Why ever not?"

"They just can't. The Royal Navy and the RAF would never let them come."

"I pray God that you're right. But if they do?"

"The posters say to stay put. If they stay put, if everyone stays put and don't clog the roads as they did in France so the army can't move... We'd have to do it, too. We'd simply stay at the Watsons and have a long honeymoon."

He had to laugh. He wished it were that simple. "I can't possibly."

She shrugged. "Then we'll come back. They won't land at Dover anyway. The cliffs. Max would get us back. I have the distinct feeling that Max could get you anywhere you really want to go.

She had Max pegged and she certainly was right about the cliffs. "We'll see. I'll try. But we'll have to wait until closer to the time and see how things are."

"Will you start about the church, with the Army? You know how military red tape is."

"All too well. I'll see what I can do. The deputy constable is a friend of mine."

"That's all I can ask." She leaned up and kissed his cheek. "Anytime, really. Just so James can be there and Annabelle for James."
He smiled down at her. "You don't want much, do you."

"No. Just for everyone to be as happy as we are."

"That, my darling, is impossible. No one could be as happy as we are."

"You really are, aren't you."

"What?"

"Happy."

"Blissfully." He kissed her nose.

"Even without children."

"Especially without children." Then there was a wicked gleam in his eye. "I feel fat."

"We can't have any of that, can we."

"No indeed. Where's Hannah?"

"I think she and Max are in the kitchen."

"Do you think they'd like the evening off?"

"Shall I tell them that we'll be staying in and they can go out if they wish?"

"Why not?"

"Think they'll go out together?"

"If I read the signs right, I think so."

She nodded. "I think so, too. Hannah bought a new hat and threw out her old one."

"What's that got to do with anything?"

"She'd had that horrible thing since before the flood. It was her favorite. I think Max told her that he didn't like it."

"I see."

"Anyway, I think that she'd see that Max got himself out of the way, whether they went together or not."

Michael's eyebrows flew up.

"Hannah wasn't born yesterday. She's an incurable romantic and she adores you."

"Well, well. Maybe my eye won't need to stray so far from home after all."

The idea of Michael and Hannah as a pair set her off laughing again.

"Come on now, Anne," he said, playing her along, "she's a fine figure of a woman."

"Indeed she is. And I think that Max thinks so, too. But her scones would make you fat."

"I think that the two of you are in a conspiracy. She feeds me scones, and you make me work them off."

Her face turned a fiery red.

Michael roared with laughter. "Anne Richter," he hugged her to him, hard, "I'm beginning to think that there really is a conspiracy."

"Are you enjoying this alleged conspiracy?"

"Every minute of it."

"Then don't ask any questions." Why on earth had she blushed? He made her feel like a schoolgirl. Infuriating. Then she smiled and settled herself against him once more, thinking that actually it was rather nice to feel like a schoolgirl as long as she didn't have to be one again.

"Not a question. I'm no fool." He rubbed his chin on top of her head.

"Then I'll go see Hannah, and send Max in to you."

"I'll tell him that I'll take a cab home."

"What time?"

"Who knows?" He pursed his lips, considering. "As late or as early as possible, depending on how you look at it. Hurry up!" He pushed her to her feet.

She stood looking down at him, laughing. "Getting anxious?"

"Go, woman!" He commanded imperiously. "Your lord and master awaits his pleasure." His voice softened. "And very impatiently, if I may say so."

"Indeed, you may say so. Any time." His face mirrored her delight, and she was smiling as she walked quickly out of the drawing room.

*       *       *

"Roll on the peace!" shouted Colin as they dived into the shelter.

"Amen," grunted James as he blinked his eyes to adjust to the relative gloom after the bright sunlight outside. Miserable business this, something like being a mole. Apparently there were some people who had all but set up housekeeping in the shelters. Idiotic. How could they stand it?

There was a slight tremor under his feet, and the faint haze of dust disconnected itself from the ceiling. Fairly close. He looked around. All of these damn places smelled the same. How could anything smell dusty and musty at the same time? And the smell of sweat and fear... The smell of fear was definitely there, hanging in the air like the dust.

James sighed as he sat down next to Colin and leaned against the wall. At least the place wasn't jammed with people for once, so it would stay relatively cool. He groaned. The crowd was pushing its way in. Where had they come from? He hadn't noticed that there were many people on the street.

There was a commotion at the doorway, at the rear of the crowd. James' head turned in irritation which changed to laughter when he saw Rafferty and Kennedy burst in and fall laughing on the last two places open on the bench along the opposite wall. They hadn't noticed their officers.

"Good spirits," Colin commented.

"Better than a couple of days ago certainly."

James let out a long breath. "That's true of all of us."

The eighth of August. The date had been burned into his brain. Just a couple of days ago. What was it? The eleventh? The tenth? It was all running together again. Convoy escort. A predawn E-boat raid with about three ships sunk. Then the Stukas came, seemingly hundreds of them, wave after wave of Stukas stacked up in the sky covered by a swarm of ME-109s, with the hopelessly outnumbered Hurricanes and Spitfires wheeling and swooping through it all.

The toll had been dreadful. The convoy had closed and re-closed its ranks, leaving disabled ships, downed planes, men living and dead and a veritable junkyard of debris in its wake. It had been bad before but never that bad. *Vectis* had been damn lucky to escape unscathed. The only consolation was that the Luftwaffe losses had been heavy, especially among the Stukas, far heavier than those of the RAF. Incredible to watch those fighters in their intricate dance of death, sometimes nearly standing on end to climb up and away from someone on their respective tails.

What was happening on *Vectis*? It was hell sitting here with the ship in danger. Tired. Was he destined to spend this whole damn war being tired?

He looked around. Colin was standing, looking down at him.

"All clear, James."

Rafferty was grinning back over his shoulder as he went through the doorway. 'Probably wondering why I'm sitting here wool-gathering,' thought James irritably. He rose slowly and dusted off his trousers.

They had walked into Dante's inferno. The raid had been brief but savage. Something looked odd. The barrage balloons. Only three left. Maddening. They were harmless enough, but the Luftwaffe seemed to find great sport in shooting them down.

The fire hoses were spraying on the burning buildings already. The firefighters had probably never seen the inside of the shelter. They were always hard at it when he came out. Since when were three times always? He snorted, wondering how many times he would have to go down into the shelter before he would lose count of how many times it had been. Three wasn't nearly enough.

They were picking their way through the debris now, on their way back to the harbor. So many familiar landmarks were gone, but somehow he always seems to know which way to go to the harbor.

While they were waiting for the motorboat to collect them from the jetty, Rafferty approached him, saying tentatively, "I called my sister, sir."

"Oh?" James was in no mood to be helpful. Inconsequentially, he thought that Rafferty's brother-in-law must be sending most of his pay home and then some if they were able to have a phone. Did Rafferty's sister work? He couldn't remember.

"She says that Suzanne and the baby are fine and that Suzanne is learning English fast. You notice that you haven't had to read any of my letters lately."

As James considered that. "Yes. Now that you mention. I haven't. Is she still writing to you regularly?"

"'Course, sir!" Rafferty looked slightly offended. "Regular as clockwork, she is. Sent this picture. See?" Rafferty thrust out a picture, which James took reluctantly.

It was hard to believe that it was the same woman he had seen in Dunkirk. She was smiling and her hair was shorter now, curling softly around her shoulders. A blouse and skirt. Much better than that frumpy old French field uniform. And whoever had taken the picture had stood close enough so that her face could really be seen and that of the baby, whose hand was in the air. The baby was growing.

His irritation evaporated and he smiled as he handed the picture back. "A fine looking woman, Rafferty, and the baby looks fat and happy."

"She's really grown, hasn't she?" he asked eagerly as he put the picture carefully back away in his savings book.

"Banking?" He'd never thought of Rafferty as a particularly thrifty person. Probably a withdrawal.

"A deposit, sir." He was looking at James steadily, thinking that he looked tired, more tired than usual. Everyone looked tired these days.

"She sent me another postal money order and I wanted to put it into my savings. I wish she wouldn't." He shrugged. "But there seems to be nothing for it but to let her."

"Wise man, Rafferty." James was smiling as they both turned to watch the motorboat come up the jetty.

Colin was glad to see it. Three mail calls without James having a letter from Annabelle, and he hadn't been able to get through to her when he'd tried to call. James' mood had not been the best. He sighed. There had been a letter from Julia, but her letters were something less than satisfactory. Actually, it was amazing that she wrote at all, considering the fact that they had seen each other only once. And God alone knew when he might get to see her again. Or Annabelle, for that matter. War was indeed hell. He shuddered, remembering the Stukas a few days before as the motorboat pulled alongside the unscathed *Vectis*.

Vickers met them on the deck, grinning as he held out an envelope, presenting it to James with a flourish. "James, old sod, as ship's doctor I believe that this is the remedy for what ails you."

James grabbed it with a laugh and went off to his cabin to read it and change. He was due on watch in 20 minutes. Colin left him to do his reading.

Later, he had to smile when he saw James come out on deck. James was whistling. That letter must've been just what the doctor ordered.

\*     \*     \*

For once, all Major Minten wanted was to be home in bed, alone. He was bone weary. Damn Kramer, anyway. He looked up at him from the depths of the wing chair in the School House library with considerable malevolence. "Make it fast."

"Fräulein Scheuermann is being most cooperative."

"Almost too much so, if you ask me. Her billing and cooing over Richter at dinner was discrete but nauseating. She's in love with him."

"Nonsense." Kramer looked smug. "It's all an act. She's going to get him to marry her."

"God. That's all we need. A wedding. Grand. Just grand."

The major was such a fool. "It's perfect." He didn't quite keep the contempt out of his voice. It made Minten look up again, sharply this time. Kramer went on, oblivious to everything but the sound of his own voice. He was pleased. Things were going his way again, in spades. He really was on the right track. "She says that she can convince him that, since he has the perfect cover, if he marries her, she will, too. If he turns up a spy, an annulment can be arranged. If he doesn't, she'll feel safer about going. It would also give greater credence to Bergmann as her brother."

"That part of it is true enough," said Minten acidly, "but what if she really does love him? Could she be marrying him to protect his ass? She'd scarcely be willing to throw him to the wolves if she loved him. And what makes you think that he wants to marry her anyway?"

"He's besotted with her," scoffed Kramer. "Even a blind man could see that. And that conniving little bitch wouldn't let herself love anyone. She's looking after her own hide and her precious uncle's in the bargain."

"I thought that you said she wouldn't let herself love anyone." Minten yawned. Idiot. Didn't he realize that he was contradicting himself all over the place?

It was all Kramer could do to contain his anger. "You missed the point. He's like her father, for God's sake."

Minten just looked over at him. There was no point in aggravating him any further or Kramer would never get to the point, and he'd be sitting here all night. Since when had Kramer been so concerned about any of his stepfathers, or his mother, either, for that matter? What could he possibly know about it?

Kramer mistook Minten's silence for acquiescence and plunged on. "They'll be together constantly, especially if they're going to be married. If he is collecting information, she's bound to find out about it, and even if she fails there, he certainly couldn't code it and send it without her knowing." Kramer was very pleased with himself.

"But if he is what you say he is, he's too clever by half to try and send it now. He wouldn't want to take any unnecessary risks. He'd simply store it up and take it back with him."

Minten shifted his bulk into a more comfortable position and decided that he was beginning to enjoy this. Kramer and his machinations. Let him play out his string. Keep him happy. Lure him into a false sense of security, at least until those pictures were safely in hand, in a week or so. Kugelmann was working cautiously. It had to be done cautiously. But credit where credit was due. Kugelmann would get the job done. He always did. Kugelmann had arranged for a client to lease some bearer bonds with attorney Kramer. It was natural for a man leaving anything as negotiable as that to want to check into the security arrangements in the office. If necessary, the bonds could be stolen and the pictures taken as part of a general 'robbery'.

Kramer stared at him. He hadn't thought of that.

"You're right." The words came out slowly.

Minten looked up in surprise.

"That's why, Herr Major," he rushed on, his brain in high gear. Something clicked. That was it. Even better.

"I want you to help me give him an opportunity to get ahold of anything he wants in a way he could transport it secretly."

Minten was annoyed again. "What the hell are you getting at?" Enough was enough.

"A miniature camera. He should be given one and trained to use it."

"How original of you to think of that," Minten said sarcastically.

"My God, Kramer, of course he's going to be, and Bergmann is going to be, as well. Bergmann is also going to be taught how to develop the film. The stuff that Richter should be able to send us, if he's half the man I think he is, demands on that. It's far too much and far too complicated to be transmitted. And maps can't be transmitted in any event. Neither can pictures." He leaned forward, menacing now. "Don't try to tell me how to do my job."

"No, Herr Major." Kramer backed off hastily. He wished that he didn't need this old fart's cooperation. It would be far better, far easier if he had a free hand. But he didn't. And since he didn't, why the hell couldn't Minten be sensible and quit getting his hackles up all the time. "It's just that if Richter did have one at his disposal, and if he were left in an office with a safe was open, your office for instance, at a time when he thought he could be undisturbed and could therefore safely photograph documents, then he could be caught in the act."

Minten was livid but silent for once. How dare Kramer bring that up!

Fools rush in where angels fear to tread. "The idea occurred to me when I found him in your office."

"Why not your office, Kramer?" Minten sneered. It was Kramer's harebrained idea. Let him take the risks. Let him suffer the consequences if he were caught breaching security regulations.

"Because I have no safe, and besides, I don't have any personal access to the high-level secret documents that you do."

He grudgingly admitted to himself that Kramer did have a point. Play along. Keep him happy. "All right. All right. Say we lay this little trap. What then?" He gritted his teeth. This playing Kramer along was getting to be a pain.

"We set it up." Kramer's eyes were gleaming at the prospect. "Give him five or ten minutes and spring the trap. We could wait in my office with the door locked and the light off. Make him think we were somewhere else."

Minten was unenthusiastic. He couldn't suppress another yawn. "Why not let Fräulein Scheuermann spring it for you? She could report."

Kramer gritted his teeth and had to resist speaking to them. "Because I don't want to tell even Fräulein Scheuermann about this." Calm. Stay calm. "And I want you there when he's caught so that you don't have any doubts about it. I want you to know that it's true." Yawning. The bastard was yawning. Didn't he understand? Didn't he see how important this was, what a coup it would be if they succeeded, how disastrous it would be if they failed? He was angry and it showed. "Just remember, if I go to England and if I hang, it will be the end for you, as well."

"I haven't forgotten." Minten was looking straight at him now, his eyes steely. 'You had better know that I haven't forgotten, Kramer,' he thought. 'You'd be surprised to know just how much I haven't forgotten. How I'd love to be on that London street watching when Horst does you in. That would be pure pleasure to watch. String him along,' he reminded himself. 'Remember, he thinks that he has you where he wants you, and indeed, he does until those pictures are safely out of the way.'

Minten made his voice positively obsequious, his face penitent. "All right, Kramer." He even managed at a sigh. "Have it your way."

For the moment, Kramer, for the moment. Besides what could it hurt? Kramer was wrong, a fool, but if he had this bee in his bonnet, it wouldn't hurt to test it out. He had been persistent, amazingly persistent about it, and if there were even the faintest chance that he was right... Minten shuddered. No, it wouldn't hurt. Actually, it was probably a good idea. He brightened. And if Kramer was right, it would be quite a feather in his, Minten's, cap to catch Richter. He smiled. That would be one in Canaris's eye. His fair-haired boy a spy. Ho ho. That would be rich. He shook himself. He was living in a fool's paradise with this. Kramer wasn't right. He couldn't be.

Kramer had been watching the emotions play across Minten's face with considerable satisfaction. "Then I'll set it up."

May well get something in exchange for giving in. It wouldn't do to let Kramer think he was 'cooperating' that easily. "Just one thing, Kramer." Minten was studying him closely now. "If I go along with you in this, at considerable risk to my security clearance I might add, but if I go along with you and you're proven wrong, will you give up? Will you let Richter alone and go to England and do your job there without any fuss? I'm damn sick of your fighting me on this business. You've become a real pain in the ass about it." And it is the only place, dear Kramer, where you can be safely eliminated without any questions being asked.

"Of course, Herr Major," Kramer said easily. Why not agree? It cost him nothing. Get Richter taken care of and England should be easy.

"Your word as a gentleman." Minten gave a nasty little laugh.

"Of course, Herr Major." He repeated blandly. "My word as a gentleman is just as good as yours."

Minten stared at him for a moment, then gave a little smile as he rose. "Just so we both know where we stand, Lieutenant."

Kramer sprang into a perfect Nazi salute to which Minten responded in a most perfunctory fashion.

At the door, Minten was all business. "Equipment issue in two days. Let me know when everything is ready, Lieutenant."

"Of course, Herr Major."

My God, was that all he could say? 'Of course, Herr Major'. Minten walked briskly down the front steps and entered the staff car as Heinrich held the door open for him. Kugelmann was already in the driver's seat with the engine running.

Kramer turned from the door as the car pulled away, barely able to hide his jubilation. It would work. It had to work. He fairly bounded up the stairs. As he passed Richter's door, he saw a strip light coming out from underneath. Damn bitch would have him well in her by now even, if by some strange chance he hadn't been there before.

On impulse, he tapped the door. No answer. Was Richter asleep with his light on? Hardly. Just as well that he hadn't answered. Kramer had regretted the impulse as soon as his hand touched the door. What would he have said? Why was he doing this anyway? Checking?

Curious. If the lights were on, he should've been there, reading or some such. Coding letters? Kramer smiled. Not sleeping, at any rate. It was too damn stuffy in these rooms with the blackout up and the door shut. No one could sleep long enough. Up the RAF. Bomb Hamburg, would they? They hadn't done much damage but how the hell had they gotten through? What had the Luftwaffe been doing? Sleeping on the job. That seemed to be their favorite occupation. Glamour boys. This new campaign of Goering's had better work. They had been diddling around with this invasion business far too long already.

Well, at least the RAF hadn't been back. Maybe the Luftwaffe had gotten to them on the way home. From all the reports, British losses had been tremendous. But could you believe the reports? What could you believe these days?

He stared at the door. Was Richter there and just not answering? He turned the knob, cautiously. The door swung open. Kramer peered in. No coding. Nothing. Richter wasn't there. So she hadn't wasted any time. He smiled his satisfaction as he shut the door without turning out the light. Let Heinrich get it on his night rounds.

He caught himself whistling tonelessly as he opened his own door and stopped abruptly. No sense disturbing the 'lovers', if indeed they could be disturbed. He laughed out loud as he shut the door behind him.

\*     \*     \*

Hans had come upstairs, leaving Minten and Kramer alone in library. Annaliese had gone up a half an hour before, pleading the press of unpacking. Lucky Bergmann had escaped immediately, right after the evening session.

He paused briefly outside Annaliese's door, then turned and went resolutely into his room, shutting the door behind him. One of the girls had lowered the blackout curtains. It was stuffy as hell.

He sighed as he snapped on the light and took off his jacket, throwing it on the chair by the window. He stood there staring at it without seeing it. It was no use. He had to see her. She was there, just down the hall and across the landing. She was too close for him not to see her. He hadn't been alone with her, hadn't touched her, held her since yesterday. And yesterday... So damn much had happened yesterday. Today had cleared the air. Now...

Hans slammed the door behind him, forgetting the lights as he strode down the hall, cursing himself for his adolescent behavior. He was being ridiculous.

His heart was pounding as he tapped on her door without giving himself any time to think about it.

"Yes?"

Just the sound of her voice coming through the door turned his knees to jelly. "It's Hans."

There was a brief pause before the door opened. She must have just bathed. Her face was shining and slightly flushed as she stood there wearing a blue wrap-around that matched the color of her eyes precisely. And her hair, her wonderful hair was brushed to a sheen, hanging free around her shoulders.

He cleared his throat, but his voice was still husky as he said slowly, "You are beautiful."

Her face lit up and her smile was enchanting. "Come in." She laughed as he shut the door. "I shall never dress up for you again." Then she was looking at him, and her laughter stopped abruptly as she saw the intensity of his gaze. His eyes seem to be boring right through her.

She drew a sharp breath. "What is it?"

Mentally he shook himself, trying to relax, trying not to... He refused to frame the words, even in his mind. "It's you, I'm afraid. I still can't believe it." His laugh was short, self-conscious. "You make me feel like a schoolboy."

She came to him and put her arms around his neck, leaning back to look up at his face. "I'm glad I can make you feel like a schoolboy. I hope I always can."

He pulled her to him with a groan and suddenly his whole body was electrified. "You don't have anything on under that thing!"

She really laughed then. "It was stuffy in here. I had just had a bath and there were a few things left to put away. It was cooler without anything on. I was just going to put on my nightgown when you knocked. See?" She pointed toward the bed which was already turned down for the night.

He glanced around and the flimsy garment he saw made him laugh. "Fat lot of difference that would have made."

Her eyes were shining. "When you knock on the lady's door at this hour, you have to take what you get."

"Are you a lady?"

"I must confess, I don't feel very much like one right now."

"You do to me."

"A lady or a woman?"

"Let's see." He leaned down and kissed her. He had meant to make it a light kiss, teasing really, but by the time it had ended, it was anything but that. When he finally lifted his head, his heart was pounding and his breath was coming and harsh rasps. He forced himself to release her and tried to be casual, humorous, as he said, "A woman. Definitely a woman." His hands were shaking. He was shaking all over.

Annaliese had to step back when he released her, breasts heaving visibly under the fabric of her wrapper. She was as breathless as he was, trembling, as well. Even her voice trembled a little. "Will you take down the blackout while I turn out the light? I'd like to sit in the chair with you and watch the night for a while if you don't mind." All sounded so formal. Why was she sounding formal?

"I'd like nothing better but I'm afraid that if we do, I might be tempted to, how did you put it?... 'take what you get'."

She looked down. "I'm not afraid of that."

He stared at her for a moment. She looked up, regarding him soberly. Then he nodded solemnly as he moved towards the window, waiting for her to switch off the light before he unhooked the shade at the bottom so he could push it up in the special

tracks attached to the window frame that kept the room light-tight.
Luxury fittings these, he thought idly. The light went out and he
raised first the shade and then the window. The evening breeze that
wafted through the window was like a tonic in the stuffy room. He
pushed the large overstuffed chair right next to the window and sat
down. Faint moonlight cast an oblong patch on the rug.

"Come here, Annaliese."

She had hesitated by the light switch, watching, listening to the
chair scrape across the floor, her heart still pounding.

She had said that she wasn't afraid, but she was. Why? She
wasn't a virgin. God knows, she wished she were, for him. But she
wasn't. 'Blast you, Ernst,' she thought, 'why did I have to think
that I loved you, was going to marry you?!' Would Hans know?
Would it matter to him? Was she making the same mistake again? It
couldn't be a mistake. She'd never known what love was until now,
until Hans. She loved him so, and she was afraid. But it was more
than Ernst. England? She'd be a fool not to be afraid of England. A
baby? Oh God. A baby. The thought of carrying his child inside her
made her tremble again. She wanted him, wanted his child, wanted
everything that had anything to do with him.

Then what was it? Was she afraid that she might disappoint
him? She sighed and gave it up, moving slowly towards the chair
in the darkness.

He took her hand and brought her around so that she could sit
on his lap. She sank down on his legs and leaned against his chest
gratefully, her head on his shoulder, his jaw against her hair.

They sat that way for a long time before he finally broke the
silence. "Will it be like this when we're married?"

"I hope so. Sometimes, anyway." She smiled to herself, relaxed
now, happy, a little sleepy.

"The stars shine this way in England. But they're hard to see on
Eaton square. It's the moonlight there. It filters through the trees
and the shadows play on the floor. I loved watching them when I
was little. I wish I'd known you when you were little."

"I wish I'd known you when you were little. You're not little now."

He laughed. "How do you know?"

"Well..." Then she was laughing, too.

But he went back to the point, serious now. "I've always envied James, always wanted to be as big and strong as he was and is. James and Dieter are about the same size."

"Will I like James?"

She could feel his nod. "Oh yes, and he'll like you too. Very much. So will Mother."

"What's she like?"

He laughed. "I've already told you about her."

"Tell me again."

He smiled. This must be what it was like to be a father with a child on his lap who wanted a bedtime story. Then the scent of the perfume in her hair was in his nostrils and the image of a child evoked different thoughts entirely. Her child. Their child. His arms tightened around her. "She's indescribable." He gave a little laugh. "Which means, of course, that I'm going to try to describe her. Small. Fine-boned like you. And fun. A rather bawdy sense of humor under what at first glance is an exceedingly elegant exterior. Frank. That's like you, too. You always know where you stand with her if you want to know, but she doesn't impose it if you'd rather not."

"How objective you sound!"

"Four years away gives a certain perspective."

"Are you anxious to see her?" Four years was a long time.

"God, yes!"

"So am I."

"I'm glad." He smiled to himself. "She may have married again by the time we get there."

"Really!"

"My godfather."

"Are you glad about that?"

"Yes. Yes, I am. She's been alone long enough. And he's a good man. You like him, too."

"Is there anyone I won't like?"

"I doubt it. Not anyone in the family, at any rate. Certainly not Hannah." He laughed again.

"Who's Hannah?"

"Our maid of all work. She'll fuss over you like a mother hen, and probably ply you with scones. She makes the most marvelous scones. They're the pride of her life."

"I love scones."

He kissed her on the top of the head. "I'd forgotten that you probably had them. That will make Hannah very happy."

"What about the spying?" She sounded very sad, suddenly.

He wriggled restlessly, shifting his position. Light as she was, the pressure of her body was making his legs go to sleep. "Let's not talk about that now. It's not a night for spying."

"But we're spies!"

"Not tonight."

"Then what are we tonight?"

He tipped her head back with his chin. "This." He was kissing her. Holding her to him. It was quite some time before she could speak and when she did, there was a catch in her voice. "Oh God, Hans. I do love you so."

"Then love me. Let me love you. I never knew what it meant to want a woman before. God dammit all, Annaliese, I love you."

He sounded almost angry about it, but before that had time to register in her brain, his mouth was on hers again, rough, demanding, seeking.

She was clinging to him, her fingers digging into his back, wanting to become a part his very being. He pulled away savagely and rose, literally setting her on her feet.

With her last shred of sense she asked, "What about Kramer?"

"The hell with Kramer," he said fiercely. "He has no business here." And then he was kissing her again and it was the end of sense. There was a fearful urgency in him, an overwhelming desire he'd never known before. All thoughts of life beyond this moment, beyond her, had evaporated in the fire set by the touch of her skin, the smell, the feel of her.

Much later, as she lay blissfully in the curve of his arm, her head on his shoulder, her arm across his chest, she said sleepily, "You are the perfect size, you know."

He chuckled. "Where?"

"Everywhere. Everything." She trailed her fingers across the smooth skin of his chest. "I'm glad that you're not James' size."

"Why?" He was genuinely surprised.

"Big men worry me."

"Why on earth!"

She giggled. "I'm afraid of being squashed."

He shook the narrow bed with his silent laughter and hugged her to him. And an old, old feeling that he was only barely aware that he still had fell away. 'Grow, James, damn you.' He thought, 'Seven feet tall if you'd like. I never have to envy you again. I have everything I want, everything. Right here.'

"I love you." He held her even tighter as he started laughing again. "Oh, my God, I love you."

She was enchanted by his happiness, knowing that she was the cause, and so she lifted herself to lean over him and kiss him again.

After a moment, she raised her head and he looked up at the faint white oval of her face. Her hair fell around his face like a curtain shutting out everything else.

He smiled. "We weren't going to do this. At least not tonight."

He could see the gleam of her teeth as she smiled back at him. Her voice was soft as her hand brushed his cheek. "Are you sorry?"

He chuckled and hugged her briefly. "What do you think?"

"Is this why you knocked on my door tonight?"

"Probably, but I didn't know it at the time. I just wanted to put my arms around you, make sure that you were real and really wanted to marry me."

"Any doubts about that now?"

He shook his head. "You?"

"No. Thanks heavens, no. All the nameless fears of the night are gone. You've chased them away, poof!"

"Fears? What fears?" He ran his fingers through the silk of her hair.

"I don't know. I wish I did. Not about you. Just... I don't know." She lay back on the bed at his side.

"We'll work it out." He was leaning over her now speaking with a confidence he didn't feel.

She sighed. "Even Uncle Friedrich?"

"Even Uncle Friedrich." His voice was grim. "Kramer hasn't managed to beat us with each other, though God knows he tried. He won't beat us with that, either." If anything happened to Uncle Friedrich... He shuddered, not liking to consider the possibility. But as long as Kramer didn't know that he and Annaliese were together in this, there was a chance.

Her hand was on his cheek. "We can do it together. As long as we're together. An there's always Dieter."

He nodded. But how far would Dieter go? Could Dieter go? Dieter had a great deal to lose and almost nothing to gain.

She felt him tense, saw the moment slipping away and couldn't bear it. So she pulled his head down to hers and then for hours, there was no more time for thought. There was nothing but Annaliese and a deep dreamless sleep till after dawn.

# Chapter XIV

Dieter leaned back in the hard wooden chair and stretched. His head was spinning. Two hours. He had been at that fool radio for over two hours without a break, taking it apart and putting it back together. He could do it in his sleep now, if he had to. He knew every part almost by touch alone, could repair anything that went wrong with it short of someone taking an axe to it. It was just as well. It was his last day with it.

Before this session with the radio, there had been a twenty minute break, and for the hour and forty minutes before that, he had been in the code room working on both radio and letter codes. Picky work. Tedious. Before that there had been, thankfully, a whole hour for lunch. His head had been spinning from the two hours of transmitting that had gone before. It had taken that hour to clear the dots and dashes of his brain. Blocks of four numbers. Jesus. He was seeing numbers in his sleep and hearing dots and dashes at the same time.

At least it was his last day with radio. He'd had it with the damn thing. It was clever, though, fitting as it did into an unobtrusive looking suitcase. A specially constructed suitcase. The radio was heavy.

Camera work. Darkroom. Film processing. That was next on his list. Worrisome. It meant that there was going to have to be a darkroom in London, and a darkroom would make him vulnerable. The radio could be shut up in the suitcase and moved in a matter of minutes. The darkroom couldn't be. And while he was there with the door shut, a whole armored division could move in without his knowing a thing about it. And a darkroom was hard to hide. All of that stuff fit into another suitcase, or so he'd been told. He'd believe that when he saw it. Even so, it meant setting it up and taking it down and that took time. A bathroom with blackout curtains would be the best, probably, but would he be able to have his own bathroom? He'd have to arrange it. That may not be easy, and it certainly would be more expensive.

No sense worrying about it. He'd been at it for two weeks, and there were two weeks left. It had been two weeks of England being bombed to hell. Not London, though. London hadn't been touched. The Luftwaffe seemed to have been avoiding it like the plague. Why? Hamburg had been bombed. A couple of times. Not much damage so far, thank God. Was London to be immune? Damn well better be. He smiled to himself. All he needed was an air raid while he was in the darkroom.

"All right, Bergmann," Reifschneider's stentorian tones were apparent before he was. "Quit goofing off."

Dieter yawned, and then stretched again. "Time's up, thank God."

Riefschneider grunted. "So it is. And it's your last day."

"Right."

"You've done pretty well," he admitted reluctantly.

"From you that's high praise, indeed."

His laugh was something of a deep throated honk. "Doesn't pay to let you boys get too cocky."

"I suppose not, but an occasional pat on the head wouldn't hurt."

Riefschneider's grin was positively evil. "I thought that you got all the pats you needed elsewhere from Kugelmann."

Dieter nearly choked. How the hell had he heard about that!?! No one had been around, or at least he thought that no one had been around. And the only one person he had told was Richter, and Richter was scarcely the sort to tell anyone. "Once was more than enough."

The big man laughed raucously. "Somehow you didn't strike me as his sort."

"That would be the day!"

"But from what I hear, you don't chase tail either."

He shrugged. "Not averse. Just no chance."

"Interested?"

"Any time when there is time."

"Tonight?"

Dieter shook his head. "Classes." It was probably just as well. He didn't trust Riefschneider's taste in women.

"Night too?! Jesus!"

"Jesus is right."

"Well then," he walked to the door and closed it carefully, "we'll celebrate here."

The windowless room in the basement was crammed with radio sets in various stages of repair and development. It was Riefschneider's domain, and usually there were two other men who worked under him. But they had left for home about twenty minutes before.

Riefschneider pulled out a ring of keys and unlocked a cabinet full of parts, which was under the counter by the door. He grunted with the effort of bending his bulk nearly double as he reached into the dark recess of the cabinet, coming up red-faced and triumphant, a bottle of schnapps in his hand. "This," he said grinning, "is the real reason why the cabinet is locked. No one gives a damn about the parts."

Dieter didn't really want to drink, but there seemed to be nothing else for it in the face of such good-natured goodwill. "Just a short one. Richter and I are doing the gym in about 20 minutes."

Riefschneider nodded then concentrated on pouring out a generous two fingers, generous because his fingers were thick. The glasses were water tumblers from beside the sink and they were none too clean.

"Half that."

He nodded again and poured a careful half. "How is the Hauptmann's arm?"

Riefschneider handed him his class and then raised his own. "Prosit."

"Prosit," echoed Dieter taking a sip. Terrible stuff. It was hard to keep a straight face as it burned its way down.

"Are you learning that Japanese style of fighting? What's it called? Jiu-jitsu?"

"Right." How the hell did he know about that? Dieter had been consistently surprised by what Riefschneider knew. That Kugelmann business for instance. Had Kugelmann mentioned it to someone? He shrugged. It didn't matter.

"Does it work?"

"Seems to. Yesterday Richter had me on the floor before I knew it was happening."

"Richter did?" Riefschneider was impressed. Bergmann was half a head taller than Richter and probably twenty kilos heavier. "I'll have to watch out for him."

Dieter laughed. "I wouldn't worry. Generally, he's pretty easy-going. But when he does get mad... I wouldn't make him mad, if I were you."

"A temper?" Riefschneider took a healthy swallow of schnapps and then wiped his mouth on the back of his hand.

"I've seen it just once."

"How long have you known him?"

"A little over a year. We went through Poland and France together."

"Jesus. He really is easy-going if he lost his temper only once through all of that."

"Oh, he gets annoyed like anyone else, but furious just once. It was in Poland and the ass of a Hauptmann who was our squadron commander didn't use his head in deploying the tanks, and one platoon got caught in an ambush. We had to go in and get them out. That's where Richter got his Ritterkreuz." His jaw tightened at the memory. "He was brilliant."

"Is that where your Iron Cross First Class came from?"

Dieter nodded. "What Richter had to say to that Hauptmann later isn't fit to print." He laughed. "I thought he was going to have apoplexy."

"Richter?"

"Both of them, actually, but mainly Hauptmann Schweigert."

Riefschneider gave a low whistle. "And he got the Ritterkreuz and made Hauptmann after that?"

"I was the only other one there and that idiot wasn't going to complain. It was all his fault and he knew it. I'm sure he felt the less said, the better."

"Richter didn't hit him, did he?"

"Hell, no. But I wouldn't have blamed him if he had. And in the mood he was in, that jackass wouldn't have stood a chance. But Richter's too smart to set himself up for court martial over someone like that."

Riefschneider leaned back and yawned hugely. It had been a difficult day and the schnapps was having its effect. "And tell me, Bergmann, how do you like being an officer?"

Dieter looked down at his uniform and grinned. "And a gentleman?"

He laughed appreciatively. "You bypassed Faehnrich and went straight to lieutenant. How come?"

Dieter shrugged again. "I'm not sure. Richter, I think." Actually it had been his age. He was too old to be a Faehnrich, and Richter had pointed that out, insisting that a straight commission would be better. It was certainly more money.

"He seems a good sort."

"He is. The best. I was damn lucky to have him for a tank commander." Dieter finally managed to swallow the last of his schnapps. He put the glass down forcefully as he rose to go. "Thanks. I wish I didn't have to go but I do have the gym."

Riefschneider stayed where he was and looked up at Dieter debating with himself. When he spoke, he kept his voice low. "Look, Bergmann..."

Dieter stopped and waited.

"I see a lot. Hear a lot. And make it a point to keep my ear to the ground."

He nodded. That was the understatement of the year.

"And I have reason not to like Lieutenant Kramer."

"Who doesn't?" Kramer was scarcely popular these days. He had ridden roughshod over too many people.

"Kramer's up to something."

Dieter's laugh was short and sharp. "Isn't he always?"

The sergeant's face was sober now. "It's serious. All your mail is being monitored, and you've been followed for weeks. Or rather, Richter has. And the phones are probably tapped."

Dieter stared at him. "Followed?!"

"Not by Abwehr people, or if they are, I don't know them."

"How do you know? I haven't noticed anything."

It was Riefschneider's turn to shrug. "I just know. Never mind how."

"They're on a fool's errand, whoever they are."

"Then you don't have anything to hide?"

"God, no!"

"Better keep it that way."

Dieter laughed uneasily. "No time for anything else."

Riefschneider rose and put out his hand. Dieter shook it warmly. "Then consider yourself warned. It's been a pleasure having you, Bergmann. You're good company, and you've worked hard and taken it seriously. That's more than I can say for some of them who come through here. Good luck," he paused, "with everything."

"Thanks. And thanks for the warning. I'll keep my eyes open." Then it was his turn to hesitate. "If you hear anything else..."

"Why not stop down in a week or so?" He laughed. "I don't think you liked my schnapps much, and I can't say that I blame you. Why not bring some of your own, and we'll see if it's any better."

"With pleasure." He smiled, thinking that it might prove well worth his while to do just that. Two bottles , for that matter.

Then he was off down the hall with a wave of his hand. Credit where credit was due. Whoever was handling it for Kramer was doing it well. He hadn't suspected a thing. Neither the mail nor the phone surprised him. That was to be expected these days. But followed? Jesus. Kramer meant business. Dieter shivered. He felt as if there were eyes boring into his back as he took the steps two at a time. He didn't want to keep Richter waiting.

*     *     *

"It's about time, Kugelmann, for God sake. Two weeks! More than two weeks!" He grabbed the envelope eagerly and took out the pictures, his face relaxing as he went through them one by one, counting them carefully. When he looked up, he was beaming. "All here."

"Of course, Herr Major," said Kugelmann, trying to keep the exasperation out of his voice. Good grief, didn't Minten think that he would have checked that out before he brought in the pictures? Elementary. The idiot.

But Minten missed the irritation in Kugelmann's voice and the expression on his face, as well, for he had leaned down to pull out the omnipresent brandy bottle, saying gleefully. "A little celebration is in order!"

"I think that you might want to look at the other envelope before you do that, Herr Major."

Minten sat up and plunked the bottle onto the desk. "What's this?" He looked at Kugelmann quizzically without taking the envelope he was holding out.

Kugelmann shook it slightly and finally Minten took it, looking it over back and front. The inscription read 'For Admiral Canaris'. He looked back at Kugelmann again. "What is this?"

"Something I think might interest you. It was the only other thing in Kramer's special box beside his will."

"Special box?"

"That's why it took so long. Attorney Kramer," Kugelmann thought again how silly it sounded to refer to the man that way but it was the only way to avoid confusion. He started again. "Attorney Kramer has a carefully coded file system for some of his boxes, the ones that contain highly confidential information, or real valuables. It meant our... ah... cultivating, shall we say, one of his junior clerks who had a great deal to say once he'd had enough to drink and once he got started." Apparently it had been almost impossible to shut the man up. "Even then, all he was able to tell us about it was that the key to the system was in the safe. That was when Ostermann took in the bearer bonds. He really raised a fuss, wanting to make sure that they couldn't be stolen."

"Did our man steal the bonds?"

"He didn't have to. Ostermann can go back and collect them any time and no one will be the wiser. In fact, unless Kramer goes in there to check things out or put something else in the box, no one will know that anything is gone. It was a good clean job." Kugelmann was pleased about that. Nothing had been left out of place. Ostermann had done the job himself, but Minten hadn't wanted know anything about that. He wanted to keep his nose clean. Ha!

It had been the sensible thing for Ostermann to do it. He knew the layout of the office and was the best safe man they had in the bargain. He had said that the safe was a piece of cake. A baby could have opened it, or so he'd said. Once he had the booklet with the code key in it, finding the box had been a cinch.

Minten was opening the envelope. "Then you've done well Kugelmann. It's even better that way. Kramer's suspicions won't even be aroused."

"Lieutenant Kramer's?"

"Either Kramer." He put on his monocle and took the papers out of the envelope. Good man, Kugelmann. Resourceful. But it wouldn't do to say too much about it. Couldn't risk letting him get a swelled head. He unfolded the papers. Now what was this?

There was a grunt of surprise. Kugelmann had thought that there would be. Minten took off his monocle and stuffed it back into his breast pocket, contemplating the papers again for a moment before he finally said, "Sit down, Kugelmann. Sit down."

There was a further silence before he spoke again. "That explains a great deal."

"Indeed it does."

"He had Schroeder by the balls. Still does, for that matter. If he got hold of this stuff once, he can again, even if he does find out that it's gone."

"Hmmm." Kugelmann's response was noncommittal. Minten was thinking, and it never did to disturb the 'master' at his work.

"And just what does 'Hmmm' mean?" asked Minten testily.

So he wanted a comment on this. One never knew. "If Schroeder had that," Kugelmann jabbed his forefinger toward the papers, "he'd know just what Kramer had and where it came from. And if he knew that, and had the papers, he could cover his tracks and get out from under it."

"Oh, but Schroeder is an honorable man." Sarcasm oozed from every syllable.

"I wonder if there's any evidence that he paid it back."

"The long-term books must've balanced, or he would have been caught out. There would have been a full-scale investigation of any irregularities, and that couldn't have been hushed up."

"I don't know about that. Schroeder was pretty clever. I'm amazed that Kramer was able to figure it out. He must've been tipped off by someone. In fact, if there hadn't been a summary in there... But I would guess that he did pay it back, Herr Major. He's that sort of man."

"I agree, and more the fool Schroeder."

Kugelmann gave a sharp little laugh but said nothing.

"I think, Corporal Kugelmann, that for once I'm going to be 'Mr. Benevolence' himself."

"That I find hard to believe." Minten didn't have a benevolent bone in his body.

"Why do you always expect the worst of everyone, Kugelmann?" Minten gave him a simpering leer.

"Because that's what I always find, and it's best to be prepared."

"Well, this time we shall do the right thing." He was positively sanctimonious. "We shall give this to Kapitan-zur-See Schroeder."

Kugelmann was astounded. "Give it to him?! For nothing?! Why?! If Kramer has him by the balls with this, then so do we."

"That shows you what you know." Minten leaned across his desk, speaking quickly, the teacher lecturing the recalcitrant pupil. His eyes had receded into little slits. "Very best way to have a man like Schroeder by the balls is if he lets you hang on to him there. Hold something like this over his head and you have an enemy.

Show him a little respect, treat him like the 'gentleman' he thinks he is, save him from ignominy, and his gratitude, his sense of 'honor' will demand that he give a recompense. Especially if he's convinced that you think that he really is an 'honorable man' and are sure that he 'did the right thing' and paid the money back. Why, Kugelmann," he went on, warming to the subject now, "you and I know that he had to have paid it back." Minten snickered.

"I can't imagine what possible good Schroeder could do for us in the future, but something will turn up. Besides," he concluded briskly, "we shall make photocopies. See to it."

Kugelmann laughed. Bloody marvelous. He knew that Minten wouldn't let him down. 'Mr. Benevolence' indeed.

"However," Minten leaned back in his chair, enormously pleased with himself, "my 'benevolence' only goes so far. If Schroeder gets ahold of this now, he'll raise hell and get his niece out of this English venture. We can't afford that. There's no time to put anyone else in and Kramer would be mad as hell, in the bargain. He's convinced that she's going to get Richter right where he wants him." Minten stopped, remembering the fuss that Schroeder had raised when he had come back from inspecting the French channel ports and found his niece in training to go to England. My God, he must love that girl. It certainly took courage with this hanging over his head. Courage. That was the word. The fool. But far better to have a man like that on your side.

Schroeder and the girl had been closeted in Schroeder's office for more than an hour, and after she'd come out, no more had been said. What could she have said to Schroeder? There was more to all of this than met the eye. Far more. "No. We can't have another of Schroeder's fusses. Things are going far too well, far too well indeed."

"Tell me, Kugelmann, just what has Kramer been up to?"

"He went to see Attorney Kramer after the letter came from his current stepfather."

"Yes. Yes. I know about that. The old man agreed to do as he asked."

Old man indeed! Kugelmann all but snorted. He's only six years older than you are, you old fart, from the picture I saw, and in far better shape. He held his tongue about all of that, saying only, "He goes to all the usual places, or did until last week. He doesn't have time to go anywhere now, not even to see his precious Sonya. He's up to his ears between his training and his usual duties."

"Good. Good. But keep up the watch."

"He's still having Richter followed."

"Anything there?"

"Kramer's wasting his time. I have one of his men in my pocket. Private group. Good. He must have plenty of money to throw around."

"He does. And?"

"And nothing. Kramer's men are bored to tears. They can't believe it. The one I talk to says that no one can lead that clean a life."

"But apparently Richter does. A real choirboy." He shook his head. It was beyond comprehension. Hamburg was a gourmet's delight, and in more ways than one. "What about Bergmann?"

"The same."

"What a waste, eh Kugelmann?" Minten laughed as Kugelmann sat there, stony-faced.

Honestly, Minten was the limit sometimes.

Minten was relishing Kugelmann's discomfiture, so much that it took him a moment to recover. He had to remind himself that if it didn't pay to praise him too much, it didn't pay to rub things in too much, either. He got back to the subject at hand. "So Kramer's wasting his time and his money. Well, let him. It will be all over soon enough."

"So it's arranged?"

Minten shot him an angry look. "I shouldn't have told you."

"Why not? It's a pleasure just knowing that Kramer is going to get his. And it is a clever plan, Herr Major, damn clever. One of your better efforts, if I may say so." The 'Herr Major' loved flattery. And it was clever. Minten could be damn clever at times.

The major's smile was smug as he rose and began turning the dials on his safe. "I'm glad that you appreciate that little plan of mine, Kugelmann. It's always nice to have one's artistry appreciated. Now." He pulled open the door and put Schroeder's envelope inside the safe, and then shut it carefully and twirled the dials to lock it. "That's that. You'll have to bring a camera up and photograph those later. Then, once our little Fräulein is safely ensconced in England..."

He picked up the pictures and the envelope. "Come with me while I burn these in the incinerator. I don't want to get caught in the act up here. It would take too long, and it would be just like Kramer to come barging in in the middle of the proceedings." He looked around. "Anything we ought to take?"

"No."

"Let's arrange a celebration."

Kugelmann groaned to himself. What Minten meant of course was that he, Kugelmann, should arrange a celebration. Shit.

"And Kugelmann, make it an early one this time, if you please," he said archly. "I was out far too late last time."

My God. The nerve of the man! "Of course, Herr Major. We'll arrange something suitable, I'm sure."

"You always do." Minten's smile was seen as he turned to lock the office door behind them.

*       *       *

"Marry him?!" Kapitan Schroeder was shouting, furious.

She shouldn't have told him first thing in the morning. He was never at his best then. But she'd had no choice. He would be tied up for the rest of the day, and she needed to tell Kramer, needed to get it over with. She had to tell her uncle first. If he heard from Kramer... And she had to make him understand. So she leaned across her desk on her fists to emphasize her point. "I want to marry him. I love him."

"But the danger, Annaliese. Think of the danger. If you're married and he's caught, they will presume at once that you're in it with him. He wouldn't have a chance."

"It would be that way anyway, since we came together. For all three of us. If any one of us is caught, it's the end for all of us." And she paused and straightened up her voice softening. "Don't you like him, Uncle?"

"Of course I like him. He's a fine boy. That's the point."

"It is the point. That and the fact that I love him and want to marry him. And if I do, it will be far safer for me in England. His cover is perfect. If I were his wife, mine would be, too, and so would Dieter's as my brother. That's the one thing I don't like about it." She made a face. "It's the politic thing to do, as well." Then she sighed. "In fact it's so politic that it almost spoils everything. Lieutenant Kramer thinks it's a wonderful idea, damn him."

"Kramer does?!" Her uncle started visibly, and his face turned a dusky red. "If that bastard thinks it's a wonderful idea, then that's all the more reason not to like it." He looked at her, hard.

It had been an exceedingly difficult two weeks for Friedrich Schroeder. He had not been pleased with what he had found during an exasperating and exhausting week inspecting the Navy's state of readiness in the French channel ports. The barges were there and they were being converted all right, but not fast enough. And the British were bombing the hell out of the ports. The idiots in charge had concentrated the barges right in the harbors rather than spreading them out along the nearby inland waterways as they should have done. Nose to nose, strung out along the canals, it would've taken more bombs than the British possessed to make a dent in the barge supply. As it was, the bombs were taking a heavy toll.

And there had been that fiasco of a training exercise with part of the sea aflame. Thank God he had seen only the aftermath of that. Aftermath was bad enough. And the casualties... So many of them. And those who had survived were horribly burned. A ghastly mess. If the British got ahold of that information... But maybe they had.

There were noises coming from Berlin that Churchill was having gas lines run down to the beaches and into the water and likely landing spots to set the sea aflame to 'welcome' the dreaded Hun. The thoughts of the consequences of that shook into the core. Well, not to worry. As things stood now, the Kriegsmarine couldn't guarantee the safe landing of a kindergarten class for a picnic on British shores, let alone however many divisions the Wehrmacht would finally decide to send.

The trouble was the planning for Sea Lion should have been going on for months, not weeks. Nothing replaced careful long-term planning. How could the OKW have been so blind? Ridiculous. Planning for such a large-scale operation simply could not be compressed into weeks, no matter how hard everyone tried. And to make matters worse, because they were under so much pressure, tempers were exceedingly short, his own included.

And then he had come back to find Annaliese up to her eyeballs in training for going to England as a spy. He had hit the ceiling. In fact, if he had thought that it could do any good, he would have cheerfully wrung Kramer's neck with his bare hands, slowly, relishing watching that supercilious face turn blue. But Canaris himself signed the orders, and after an awful row with Annaliese in his office, he had grudgingly given in. She had stood firm, insisting that she would go no matter what he did, that there was danger not only to him, but to Hans if she refused. She had said that she loved Hans and that without her, Kramer would be able to manufacture enough evidence to send him to the dogs. She had not mentioned marriage. Had that been in the wind even then?

The weight of her going sat in his chest like a stone. Prison, losing everything, would be nothing compared to losing this maddening, enchanting, golden-haired niece of his, for she was secretly the delight of his heart. She was the only person in the world that he could really talk to now that the Bleucher and the Graf Spee had been lost, each taking one of his two best boyhood friends.

Kramer. Damn Kramer and his blind ambition.

And Richter. Damn him as well. Damn her loving him. It was

Richter she was doing this for now, even more than for him. 'The only two people I love in this whole world,' she had said. Not Karin. She didn't really love Karin. It was easy to understand why. If it hadn't been for Karin insisting that Ernst was unsuitable and shipping Annaliese off to England, she would have been safely married to him. He might not have had to go to Poland. He might be alive. There was a welling up of bitterness against his willful wife. It was not the first time. The boys were Karin's. She had made them so while he was off at sea. But Annaliese was his, even though she wasn't really. Oddly, she was more his than his own sons.

Annaliese watched him sadly. It was so hard for him. He hated it. Hated the danger to her. Hated knuckling down to a man like Kramer. She wished that she could've told him about marrying Hans right away but it wouldn't have been safe. He had been too upset and might have let something slip to Kramer. The two men had had a real set-to about her going to England, before she had got to him in his office. Kramer had been furious. But then so had Uncle Friedrich. And she had told him that she had confessed her dealings with Kramer to Hans and that Hans had understood and forgiven her. Uncle Friedrich had been floored by that, especially when she had told him that Hans did not want to know what it was Kramer was holding over their heads. He had thought that quite remarkable, the sign of a man of honor, the highest accolade he could give to anyone.

She should've told him then. It had been the perfect opening. She sighed. It was safer for her to tell him now only because it was logical for her to have 'snared' Hans; it was safe for Kramer to know about their marrying, to tell him about it.

Tell Kramer. She hated the thought, but she'd have to do it. She sighed. It was like pouring grease on your wedding dress just before you walked down the aisle. Telling Uncle Friedrich was different. That was right. She could tell him the truth, that she loved Hans. She would have been telling Uncle Friedrich even if it were ordinary times and he would have been so happy for her. Oh God. Ordinary times. Oh, Hans. If only these were ordinary times.

And now that Uncle Friedrich knew. Even if he slipped up and told Kramer that she really did love Hans, Kramer would be delighted, feeling that she had been wise to 'convince' her uncle that she did so that he wouldn't raise a fuss. Kramer had had more than enough of her uncle's fusses. So the truth was politic, just as their marriage was. Damn Kramer. Damn him to hell. Along with everything else, he was spoiling her telling her uncle the happiest news of her life.

"Uncle." Her voice was gentle.

He looked across the desk at her, aware again that she was there. "I'm sorry, Annaliese. You were saying?"

"Where were you?"

He smiled a little as he shifted in his chair. "Off somewhere, trying to make sense of all of this."

"Did you find any?"

"I'm afraid that I did. It makes a horrible kind of sense."

She nodded slowly, glad that he could see that. It made it easier to take.

"I shall have to tell Lieutenant Kramer. I shall have to convince him that I've lured Hans into my trap, that I'm marrying him to protect you. He'll be delighted. He thinks that it's the perfect opportunity for me to find out what he wants to know." She laughed, bitterly. "I told him that if I did, the marriage could be annulled. And if I didn't, the worst thing could happen to me is that I would go to London with a better cover, and furthermore, a cover that would help me get the kind of job that would help Abwehr the most."

He looked at her sadly. "How devious you've become. And what's more," he managed a wry smile, "you are so very good at it." Her return smile was bleak.

"There doesn't seem to be anything else for it but to be good at it. I just hope that I don't get to like it."

"God forbid!" And then there was the suspicion of a twinkle in his eye that surprised her. "Our Lieutenant Kramer picked the wrong woman. He thinks that he's dealing with the pussycat." He began chuckling out right. "He doesn't know that he has a tiger by the tail."

"A tiger!" She met his mood. "Goodness, Uncle!" What he had said pleased her to an absurd extent. A tiger was a formidable animal and that was what she had to be, formidable. Armored. Now clawed. She smiled.

"Yes, a tiger. Does Hans know that's what he has?"

"He knows."

"Then he's an even better man than I thought he was."

"Even if he is a spy?"

"Why not? Our spies are good men by and large."

"And British spies? Are they good men too?" Now why had she asked that?

"By their own rights, they're good men, too. There are good men on both sides. That's the hell of it." Among other things. He had stopped abruptly.

"What is it?"

"A stray thought. One you won't like."

She knew what he was going to say before he said it. "Go on."

He began fiddling with a pencil on his desk. Then he stopped and looked up at her. "What if Hans Richter is precisely what Kramer says he is?"

She met his eyes with that disconcertingly level stare of hers. "I really don't care if he is."

"Annaliese!"

She had to smile. It was difficult to shock Uncle Friedrich but she had succeeded. But then she sobered. It was all so complicated. "Why should I care? Can you give me one reason why I should?"

"Because you're German." It wouldn't be enough of a reason for her. He knew that. But he didn't know how to explain it any other way.

"German?! Know what it means to be a German in Europe today?"

Before he could answer, she began pacing, then turned to him in sudden anger.

"The Czechs, the Poles, the French, the Belgians, the Dutch – ask any of them what a German is. And the people who have disappeared in the night. What would they say a German is? The world hates us, fears us. And look what being a German has done for us, for you and me. We're quaking in our boots, under the thumb of an arrogant, underhanded, self-seeking son-of-a-bitch. And that's the sort of man who runs Germany these days. That nearsighted chicken farmer Himmler, that fat satyr Goehring, and all the rest. Are they the men who you want leading Germany? Are they the men you want to serve?" She lowered her voice as her uncle looked around nervously. "And our precious Fuehrer? Enslaving the world. Speaking peace and making war. I hate it. I hate hypocrisy, all of it, and what it's doing to us. Look at you. Looking around as if the walls have ears, and they may! They may indeed!

"Do you know what I really want from life?" She didn't wait for an answer. "All I want is a little house to take care of for Hans. I want his babies to raise and a garden to tend, all those ordinary things that don't seem to exist anymore for anyone, anywhere. Will I ever have a chance of any of that?" She snorted to reply to her own question. "So tell me. Give me another reason." She leaned on her fists on the desk once more, all but shouting. "Why should I care?!" She was glaring at him.

He sat there looking at her, saying nothing. What could he say to that? She had a right to pursue her happiness. He remembered reading that in the American Constitution years ago in school. At the time he had thought it an oddly whimsical thing to put into a constitution. At last it made sense, a great deal of sense. But that wasn't in any part of the document that had brought the Weimar Republic into existence, to say nothing of the total lack of documentation that was the 'basis' for the Third Reich. She wasn't going to get a chance. At least not now. Kramer was seeing to that.

Her face softened at the sight of the struggle in his. "Don't worry Uncle Friedrich. Somehow, I can't see him as a spy. He's not that sort."

"You'd better be able to," he reminded her harshly. "That's precisely what he's going to be."

A spy. She took a deep breath. She had been too caught up with Kramer to really think about it. It had seemed like some sort of elaborate sort of game. "Yes," she said slowly. "That's what he's going to be. That's what all three of us are going to be. I hadn't realized the implications of that until right now. It was just a word."

"One hell of a word. I'm glad that you are thinking about it. It's still not too late to get out of it if we really work at it."

"Oh yes, it is." Too late for her and too late for Hans. Hans a spy. He would be betraying his mother and his brother and his godfather while he was living under his mother's roof. How could he do that? Could he do that? He wasn't that sort. He wasn't underhanded, except in his dealings with Kramer. And there was no way to be anything but underhanded when dealing with Kramer.

He was raised in England. What would real betrayal be for him? Germany or England? To betray Germany would be easier. He loved his mother; it was easy to see. But he loved her, too. Even if he didn't, there was Dieter. Dieter was his friend. Dieter had saved his life, twice.

So who would he betray? She shivered.

"I'll call Admiral Canaris right now." He reached for the phone.

"No! Don't. It wouldn't do any good. I have to go. There isn't time enough for them to train anyone else."

"But you don't have to marry him."

"I love him."

"But you're terrified. Any fool could see that."

"I'll be alright. It's just that you know me so well. And you made me realize the implications of all this. It just takes some getting used to. I trust him, Uncle. He is a man to trust, spy or no, and there are all too few of those around these days." She clasped her hands behind her to hide their trembling. She was alone again. She couldn't bear it. She had to go on just as if she had never thought these thoughts. She couldn't ask Hans. If he were what he seemed, he would be devastated by her lack of trust. And if he weren't, he'd have to lie. He had asked her, 'What if I were just what Kramer said I was?' Or words to that effect; had he been trying to warn her? He couldn't tell her the truth if he were spying for England. It would be too dangerous for him. And for her. It took only a moment for the thoughts to race through her brain and she showed none of it on her face.

Schroeder shrugged. He was surrendering. There was nothing more he could say. Knowing Annaliese, even if there were more he could say, there would be no sense in saying it. When she had made up her mind, it was made up and that was that. "If you trust him, that it will have to be enough for me." She looked so small to him suddenly, so vulnerable. He rose and went around his desk to her, putting his arms around her gently, wanting to take care of her, wanting her to be his little girl again, wanting to return to a time when her problems weren't so complicated, when he could wipe away her tears and win a smile. She was leaning against him gratefully. He went on. "And I shall be happy for you because you love him." He suppressed a sigh. "At least you'll have that much out of this mess."

Annaliese could only whisper her 'Thank you' through the lump in her throat. She drew back and looked up at him. It was her undoing. She leaned against his chest again. There were no sobs, but tears were streaming down her face.

"Darling girl!" His heart was breaking.

"I'm sorry, Uncle. It's just that I love him so much, and everything should be so simple. But it's not." She had herself under control now and was able to look up at him again.

He wiped away the tears on her cheeks with his handkerchief. "I know. It's been a hell of a time for both of us."

She started. Uncle Friedrich had never sworn in her presence before. She had to smile, just a little. It was the precise word to describe the situation.

And he was smiling down at her. He had wiped away her tears and won a smile, by God. And there was at least one redeeming feature. He started chuckling. "There's going to be a wedding! When will you tell your Aunt Karin?"

She groaned. "Oh, dear. She'll want to make a fuss about it."

"Indeed she will! She'd been waiting to give your wedding for a long time."

Annaliese made a wry face.

"I know," he said in contrition, "I shouldn't have mentioned that. She made your life miserable when you wanted to marry Ernst."

"But Hans is suitable?"

"Eminently, I'm afraid."

"Despite his British connections?"

"His German connections are impeccable."

"And that's all that matters." She was bitter.

"Not at all. He is a fine boy."

"But she's never met him!"

"I've told her."

She gave a little laugh and hugged him. "Thank you, Uncle Friedrich. That will make things easier when I tell her. And it may soften the blow of having to do a simple wedding."

"Do you mind that?"

"Uncle, I'd marry him on a harbor tug at high noon during a gale if that was the only way."

He smiled. Now she looked the way a bride ought to look. There was a glow about her. Please God, let it last. "Does anyone else know?"

"Just Dieter Bergmann. Hans told him. But he's the only one." She grimaced. "I shall have to tell Kramer, of course."

"When?"

"Later today."

"It's well not to delay. Better to get it over with."

I know. Besides, telling him is politic." She said the last word viciously.

"You'll have to be a good actress."

"I will be. It's surprising how easy that's getting to be. I'll be what I have to be, for him and for you. I guess that's what makes it easy."

He leaned down and kissed her forehead. Then he let her go.
"I'm all right now."

"I'm glad."

"Remember me in your prayers."

"I always do."

"And Hans, too."

He hesitated but his voice was firm as he said, "I will."

She nodded, understanding his hesitation but grateful that he
had agreed. They would need all the prayers given for them. "I must
go. I'm late already."

"Gruss Gott."

She stared at him for a moment and then smiled. The old
Bavarian greeting. It suited the moment. "I shall."

He smiled back, his heart lifting as she turned and left.

*       *       *

"Fräulein Scheuermann."

She looked up to find Lieutenant Kramer leering down at her.
She looked down again. She hated working on these codes. It was
such picky work, and the Code Room wasn't the quietest place in
the world. But it had to be done. Dieter would need help from time
to time when they got to London.

"Fräulein Scheuermann!"

"I'm sorry, Herr Lieutenant, I was afraid I'd lose my place." She
looked at the papers before her and took quick notations, one on
the text and the other next to the last number on the coding sheet.
If she'd lost her place, it would have meant decoding at least five
sets of numbers to find it again.

"Commendable, I'm sure." He was angry. Bitch.

"Did you want something?"

Kramer looked around. He couldn't talk to her here, in the
middle of everyone and everything. There were too many people
around. And Bergmann. He was sitting there watching everything,

and he wouldn't stop watching. The office door was open. Empty? Probably. Whose was it? Never mind. "Come with me." It was a command.

Annaliese steeled herself and rose, catching Dieter's eye. She managed a smile and he nodded soberly in reply. It was good to know that he was there. She was able to turn to Kramer easily now. "Of course, Herr Lieutenant."

She felt Dieter's eyes following her.

Kramer shut the door behind them. "Well, Fräulein?" He was facing her now.

"Well, Lieutenant? You asked to see me after all. And this is Hauptmann Fenstermacher's office."

"I'm sure he won't mind."

"You always seem to assume that with someone else's office."

Bitch. Bitch. His smile was nasty. "That's because it doesn't matter with someone else's office." Then he was brisk, businesslike. "Don't you have something to report? It's time there was something."

"As matter of fact I do."

"At last," he said caustically.

"I've done what I said I would."

"You have the proof?" He was jubilant.

"No. But if it's there, I shall have an opportunity to get it. Hauptmann Richter has asked me to marry him."

"Is that all?!" Damn.

"What you mean, 'Is that all'!" She was really angry now. She would have hated his taking pleasure in the fact that she and Hans were to marry, but somehow this was even worse. "Do you think that any of this has been easy for me?"

"Oh, come now, Fräulein. I know your sort all too well. There is nothing you like better than making a man do precisely what you want him to do without his realizing. It gives you a feeling of power. It's like a game, and you're a very good player. It never occurred to me that you wouldn't succeed."

She lifted her chin defiantly. "I'm so glad that I didn't let you down."

Her sarcasm wasn't lost on him. "If you know what's good for you, you won't let me down, ever. And most especially not in this." There was menace in every line of his body, and she hated him.

"And to think that I thought that you'd be pleased."

"Oh, I am pleased." Bitch. She ought to be pleading for him to be pleased. She ought to be groveling, begging for his pleasure. Damn that steady gaze of hers, anyway. He sneered. "But only because of what this can lead to. You really want to please me? Then bring me the proof I want."

Her jaw was set now and she spoke through clenched teeth. "If it's there, I'll find it, and not to 'please' you either."

Bitch. Exquisite little bitch. His lip curled around his words. "It is there and you will please me when you find it. It's just too bad that you will be pleasing a little prick like Richter so much in getting it."

Her eyes were flashing. Careful. Careful. It was a struggle and she was not successful. "How can you be so sure that he is a little prick? And how do you know that he's not pleasing me?" She was leering at him now, throwing caution to the wind.

"Because you can lead him around by the nose. You'll never be happy with a man like that. That's why you fight me so hard. You know a real man when you see one. You know that you could never tame me as you tamed him."

She didn't like this. Not at all. She looked around, wary now. The door was shut.

Fear? Was that fear he saw her face? Good. That was more like it. He reached out and took her arm, slowly tightening his grip, drawing her toward him. "You don't know what pleasure is, and he can never teach you."

"Let me go, Lieutenant." Her voice was deadly.

He held on, grinning now as she began to struggle. "That's it, you little bitch. Fight me all you want. When all this is over, I'm going to enjoy taming you."

"You bastard!" She spit at him and he laughed as the spittle ran down his face. And then he was grabbing her with his free hand squeezing and kneading. It hurt dreadfully. Oh, God. Dieter. You're out there. Come in! But she struggled in silence, trying to slap him. He gripped her wrist, laughing even harder. At least he had had to take his hand away to do it. Filthy. She felt filthy, used. Dieter! It was all she could do not to scream his name. They couldn't fight. Dieter would kill him.

The door burst open. "What the hell...!"

Kramer grunted, surprised, and released his grip. She jerked away and stood there glaring at him rubbing her arm, her face red, and her chest heaving.

Fenstermacher looked from one of them to the other, then turned on Kramer. "Use someone else's office for your fun and games, Lieutenant." He was furious. Kramer was Minten's fair-haired boy. But enough was enough and this was more than enough. He had been all but assaulting the Kapitan's niece, for God sake. Who the hell did he think he was? Who the hell did he think she was? "Besides, the Fräulein has work to do." He worked to keep his temper under control. It would be a pleasure to beat that overbearing, sanctimonious sod to a pulp. "I'm sure that Major Minten," he emphasized the name carefully, "would not be pleased to hear that you are interrupting her training time."

Kramer had recovered himself quickly. Minten wouldn't do one damn thing. But still... His jaw tightened as he forced himself to say, "Certainly, Hauptmann. I'm sorry we trespassed but there was something I... ah... had to straighten out with the Fräulein."

"Then do it on your own time."

Just who did Fenstermacher think he was talking to? He managed to smile obsequiously. No sense irritating him further. "I am sorry, Hauptmann."

Fenstermacher didn't want to press things too far and besides, he had to get Kramer out of there and give the Fräulein some time to collect herself. She was clearly upset. She had a right to be. "Just see that it doesn't happen again." He turned to Annaliese. "I need to see you for a moment, Fräulein."

"Certainly, Herr Hauptmann." Her voice was steady but she still was carefully avoiding looking at Kramer.

The lieutenant saw that he was being dismissed. He drew himself to attention, clicking his heels. "If there is nothing further, Herr Hauptmann?"

"Nothing."

"Fräulein." He gave a stiff bow in her direction.

"Lieutenant." She spoke through her teeth.

"I shall wait for your report on that matter."

"If I have anything to report." And never alone, you bastard. Never again behind a closed door.

He stared at her, hard, then turned and strode out.

Fenstermacher shut the door behind him and stood looking at her. "Sit down, Fräulein."

"Thank you, Herr Hauptmann." She sat gratefully in the nearest chair. Her knees were still shaking. Only then did Fenstermacher sit down himself. He was still looking at her, his face full of concern. "Are you all right?"

"I am now. Thank you."

"He was playing rough."

She looked at him squarely. "Let's just say that I am very glad that you came in when you did."

"What did you want me to do?"

"Nothing!" She looked at him in surprise. "What is there to be done?"

"I could report him to the major."

She snorted.

He nodded then took a deep breath. It was most decidedly time to change the subject. They were getting into dangerous waters. "I hear that you're doing very well with the codes."

"Thank you, Herr Hauptmann. I'm doing my best. I must confess that it's not my favorite occupation."

Her dry tone made him laugh. "It's tedious work."

"You're right." She was smiling and he was glad to see it. When she went on, it was in a very different tone. "And thank you."

"For what?"

"For letting me sit down."

He flushed slightly and then gave a nervous little laugh. "You looked as if you needed to. But I think that the person you really have to thank is your friend, Lieutenant Bergmann."

She looked at him, not understanding.

"I think that he was about ready to break the door down himself. He was standing by the water cooler just outside the door and must've heard something he didn't like because he had murder in his eyes when he caught sight of me. God in heaven," Fenstermacher shuddered, "I wouldn't want to tangle with him any time, but when he looks like that..."

She nodded, knowing precisely what he meant.

"I was on my way through into the conference room when he stopped me and told me that I was wanted in my office at once. There was something about that expression and the way he said it... Anyway, when I opened the door, I knew what he meant."

"Did anyone else see?" she was horrified at the thought.

"I doubt it." He laughed. "I do rather fill up the doorway."

She smiled at this reference to his bulk. At this moment it was a very comforting bulk. "I..." He deserved some sort of an explanation, even if it wasn't the truth.

"I am engaged to Hauptmann Richter." Well, that much was the truth.

"Congratulations!" He beamed. Richter was a good man. Then the light dawned. "And Lieutenant Kramer's a disappointed suitor." It was not a question.

"You might say that." She was relieved that she would have to say nothing more.

"You'll need to be careful with that one, Fräulein." He looked around nervously, surprised that Kramer had even been in contention at all. She was clearly out of his class. Even though the door was shut, he lowered his voice. "He can be a very nasty customer."

"Indeed."

The sour tone in her voice made it very difficult not to smile. "Don't let him get you alone again."

"Don't worry." She rose. "I won't." He stood and came around the desk to the door. She put out her hand and he shook it warmly. "Thank you again, Hauptmann. I've taken enough of your time."

"Glad I could be of help." He did smile down at her now. "You had better let Lieutenant Bergmann take you to the canteen for coffee. He could use a break, I'm sure, and I know that you could."

"But the coding..."

He opened the door. "It will still be here when you get back. Besides, as I said before, you seem to be doing very well with it. So is Lieutenant Bergmann. Consider the time off a reward."

Her smile was dazzling. He was enchanted. Richter was a lucky man.

"Thank you, Herr Hauptmann." She laughed. "I seem to be thanking you a great deal this afternoon."

"You're welcome," he was actually grinning, "a great deal."

And then she walked out the door and toward Bergmann's desk. He saw the relief in Bergmann's eyes before he shut the door and walked slowly back to his desk. "Damn Bergmann's eyes anyway." He said it aloud as he stood there, staring at the wall. Someone was going to have to take care of that bastard one of these days. The sooner the better. He was long overdue.

The conference room. Fenstermacher was galvanized into action. My God. He was late. He burst out the door and all but ran through the code room. There were a few stares as he went by. Hauptmann Fenstermacher was not ordinarily a fast-moving man. He didn't even see Annaliese and Dieter going out into the hall.

*     *     *

Dieter looked up in relief as she came out the door. He had gone back to his desk after Hauptmann Fenstermacher had gone into his office, but he had been unable to do anything. It had been impossible to concentrate. He had just sat at the small desk, his brain racing. Thank God Kramer hadn't noticed him sitting there when he stormed out. And he really had stormed. Jesus. What a mess.

Still no Annaliese. What had gone on in there, anyway? He had heard scuffling and had been ready to break down the door when he caught sight of Fenstermacher. Thank God he had come in when he had. If he hadn't... Dieter shuddered. He would have rammed Kramer's teeth down his throat and there would've been a court martial. True, he was a lieutenant. now, just as Kramer was, but a very junior lieutenant. Certainly junior to Kramer. It would have meant a court martial and he didn't like to think of the long range consequences of that. His family... Jesus. He hated it. He should have been able to go into that office without a thought. But it had been a choice between being a coward or a fool. Some choice. Yes it was a very good thing indeed that Fenstermacher had come in when he did. Apparently he had been able to take care of it. But where was Annaliese?

And then he saw her, and he was flooded with relief. She looked just the same. He almost laughed. What had he expected? That was the problem. He hadn't known what to expect.

She stopped, standing over him, her heart filling at the sight of the concern in his face.

He rose slowly, keeping his voice low, hoping that it would be covered by the clack of the cipher machines. "Are you all right?"

She nodded. "Hauptmann Fenstermacher suggests that you take me to the canteen for a cup of coffee."

"Good. I could use one myself."

She smiled up at him. "The Hauptmann thought you might." She looked down at the welter of papers on his desk. "But don't you need to mark your place?"

"I lost it when Kramer came in."

"I'm sorry." What a mess for him.

He shrugged. "It won't be too hard to find when I can get my mind on it."

"It would be for me."

They were in the hall, walking toward the canteen. "Then it's just as well that it was my place and not yours it was lost. I saw you mark it."

She had been cool with Kramer standing over her, very cool. But what could've gone wrong?

"What was he doing to you in there?"

"Did anyone hear?" she asked anxiously, looking around. The hallway was deserted.

"No. I was at the water cooler, listening," he smiled ruefully, "or I wouldn't have heard as much as I did."

"I'm glad you were. Hauptmann Fenstermacher said that you sent him in."

"Not exactly sent."

"No, but you know what I mean." She looked up at him. His face was set and he was looking straight ahead. Only his profile could be seen, with that long scar on his cheek. Funny. He didn't look at all sinister in profile. In fact, he had a handsome profile.

Finally, he turned toward her and gave a sad little smile. "I wish I could've come in myself. But I'm afraid if I had, I would have removed his teeth, permanently. It was better to let Fenstermacher handle it. Besides," he added with a trace of bitterness, "Fenstermacher outranks him."

She shivered, grateful to the Hauptmann all over again. "I wish I could have."

"What? Handled it?"

"Removed his teeth. Permanently." She sighed. "Or handled it. Either one. He... he surprised me."

They were at the door of the canteen now. There were several drivers inside. He stopped her, his voice very low now. "How?"

"Well..." She flushed. "He... I..." She didn't want to go on.

She didn't need to. Dieter's face darkened. She had never seen such a look on his face. It was frightening, especially since it was at such odds with the sort of person she knew he was. It must've been much the same sort of look that Hauptmann Fenstermacher had seen.

His voice was harsh. "Did he hurt you?"

"No. Not really." She could scarcely tell the truth, not while he was looking that way.

"If he touches you again, I'll kill him."

She was trembling. He just might. "Dieter, please." She put a hand on his forearm, surprised by the size and hardness of it under his shirt sleeve. This was a powerful man. "I'll never be alone with him again. I'll be careful. Don't worry. He had never... never shown signs of anything like that before. Besides, he won't dare again. If only I thought to mention Major Minten's name..."

"You shouldn't have had to mention anyone's name!"

"I know. But when Hauptmann Fenstermacher said the major's name, indicated that the major would be less than pleased, that stopped him cold. He didn't want to show it, but it did." Was that the truth? It had been hard to tell.

"Because you're too valuable a commodity to the good major these days?"

She nodded grimly and went on to the doorway. "Exactly."

"I'll be watching him."

She twirled around. The drivers were watching her appreciatively. Dieter glowered at them and they returned to their beer. "Don't tell Hans."

"You're not going to tell him?" He couldn't believe it. Jesus. She had to tell him.

"Yes. Yes, I will." Actually she wasn't at all sure that she would. Things were bad enough between Hans and Kramer without that. But then, what if Fenstermacher said something? She had better tell him. In his office. When Kramer wasn't around. "Before he goes to the gym?"

Dieter nodded then started to laugh. It was all he could do not to hug her. Oh my, Richter was in for a time with this one. His eyes were laughing as well. "So that he can work it off on the punching bag or the jiu-jitsu instructor?"

She grinned. "Can you think of a better time?"

They were at the counter now. The woman behind it looked up from her knitting. Things must be really slow right now. "Two coffees." Then he turned back to Annaliese. "No, I can't."

The coffee appeared on the counter, and he reached into his pocket for some coins.

She started to protest.

He grinned. "I'm flush now. I'm an officer. Remember?"

"And a gentleman."

"For the moment. Only for the moment."

He was delighted to see the way she smiled up at him. That was better, far better. She was herself again.

*      *      *

Hans looked up when he heard the tap on his door and his eyes caught the clock on the wall. Nearly time to go to the gym, thank God. Then there was his appointment with Kapitan-zur-See Schroeder to ask for Annaliese's hand. He smiled. It all sounded so formal. Well, it was. He didn't know whether he was glad that Annaliese had seen him first or not. But she had asked him so earnestly.

As he stretched, he looked down. The camera! He had forgotten the camera. A beauty. He picked it up. Tiny. It would be perfect. Now if he could just get the extra film.

There was another tap at the door, louder this time.

He slipped the camera into his narrow middle desk drawer. "Come!"

Annaliese! His heart gave a lurch as did hers at the sight of the delight on his face.

"I was beginning to wonder if you were here." She shut the door carefully as he came around the desk. Then she was in his arms, sinking into the warmth of him.

"How good you feel. My God, Annaliese..." He kissed her, then lifted her head to look down at her face. It was too much and he hugged her to him. "What kind of day have you had? What did your uncle say?" He felt her hesitation and pulled back. "What is it? Was your uncle upset?"

"No. He was a lamb really. That is he was after I convinced him that I really do love you."

"And do you?"

The look on her face was the only answer he needed. He kissed her again, and this time it was quite a while before either of them could speak.

"I'm going to see him right after our workout. Will I be well received?"

"Oh, yes."

"Then what is it? Something's bothering you?"

She hesitated again and the words came out slowly when they finally came. "Kramer, I'm afraid."

Damn. It was always Kramer. He released her and sat back on the edge of his desk, his arms folded across his chest. She felt deserted.

"What's he done now?"

"He came to see me in the Code Room."

"Was he 'enchanted' with our news?" He hated the sneer in his voice, but he couldn't seem to help it, not when Kramer was involved.

"Not exactly. It was rather odd."

She was beside him at the desk now, watching her finger trace the pattern on the glossy surface. "He said that he had been expecting it or at least that was a general sense of what he said. I think his exact words were, 'It never occurred to me that you wouldn't succeed.'"

"How charming."

"Exactly. But that's not all."

He waited.

She couldn't look at him. "He grabbed me."

All breath was suspended. His voice was deadly. "What do you mean, 'He grabbed me.'?"

She looked up at him in anguish. "Please, Hans. He just... Grabbed me. It was awful. Could've gotten nasty but..." She couldn't go on. He looks so... dangerous. She had never seen him like that.

"Where were you?" It was the same dreadful tone.

"In Hauptmann Fenstermacher's office."

"And just what was he doing during all of this?" Hans could barely contain himself. That filthy bastard had touched her, had laid his hands on her. It was worse than she was willing to tell him, of that he was certain.

"Nothing, Hans. Please." She was pleading with him now. "He wasn't there. Then he came in. Thank God he came in." She wasn't doing this well. But she couldn't stop now. That would only make things worse. "Dieter was right outside the door by the water cooler. Was about to commit himself when the Hauptmann came through the Code Room. Dieter caught him and told him he was needed in his office." She drew in a shuddering breath. "My God, he was needed."

"I'll kill him."

"Please, darling." She shouldn't have told him. Or at least she should have waited until she could find a better way, if there was one. "I'm all right. There was no harm done except to my pride." She put on a smile. "Do you think you could arrange for me to have some jiu-jitsu instruction?"

"I'll take care of that part." His voice was grim.

"Then I shouldn't have told you."

"You shouldn't have not told me."

"I thought about it."

He was angry at her now. "What made you decide to?"

She was angry now as well. "Because I would rather you heard from me now than from Hauptmann Fenstermacher some time when Kramer was in sight."

"So now you're protecting that bastard!" He was being unreasonable and he knew it.

She recoiled as if he'd struck her.

He bore in. "You'll never keep anything like that from me. I'm

a big boy. I can take care of myself. You don't have to protect me."
He was sneering at her now.

She turned away, not able to bear it. Why was he doing this?

He couldn't bear it, either. All his life... All his life, people had
fought his battles for him. James. Dieter. Dieter again. And now
Annaliese. He would fight his own battles. He had always been able
to. What was there about him that made people want to protect
him, take care of him? He was damn sick of it, sick of her, sick of
everything. God! Didn't she understand?!

When she turned back, her eyes were flashing. He wasn't going
to sneer at her. "Just go on over to your stupid gym and take it all
out on the punching bag, and quit taking it out on me. I've had quite
enough for today, thank you."

"So that's why you decided to tell me now, so that I could go
over and take it out on the punching bag instead of Kramer's hide."

"That's right." She looked at him defiantly. "Because if I were
what Kramer thinks I am, I wouldn't dream of telling you."

"You're right, of course. Why the hell do you always have to be
right? Will I always wind up going along with what you decide to
do?

She turned away so that he wouldn't see the tears in her eyes.
Given the mood he was in, he'd think that she had turned them
on to win his sympathy. God damn crying anyway. She'd spent the
better part of the last two weeks crying. No one, nothing was worth
that. After all of this was over, she would never cry again. Damn
him! Damn him!

But he was right. It had been that way. She didn't like it either.
Didn't he know that?! Why the hell couldn't he understand that?!
What else could she have done? What could she do now? Oh God,
dammit all.

He stared at her back. Damn bitch. Then his breath caught.
What was he saying? What was he doing to her? He loved her,
for God sake. Before he knew what he was doing, he had swung
her around and was holding her, so tightly this time that she could
scarcely breathe. "Look. I'm sorry. I love you and I hate you doing

battle with the likes of him. I should be doing that. Not you."

"Oh, Hans! What am I to do?" It was almost a wail and it caught his heart.

Why hadn't he thought? Why hadn't he taken the time to realize that she didn't like this any better than he did. That this was just as hard on her, if not harder. After all, she had to deal with that bastard Kramer; he didn't. At least not very much of the time.

His hands were on either side of her face now, and he was looking down at her. "I'm sorry. Just let me love you."

Her arms went around his neck as she studied his face. She liked what she saw. It made her laugh a shaky little laugh. "Here? Now?"

He grinned. "Scarcely." Then he was laughing. "I can just see Dieter walking in in the midst of it all. He's due any moment."

"He asked me to tell you that he'd meet you at the gym." Her look was one of total innocence. "And you could always lock the door."

Hans cocked his head. "Did you arrange that?"

"I just told him that I wanted to talk with you. I didn't think about... the other." She blushed and that made him laugh again.

"All right. All right. I give up. I know when I'm beaten. But we'll have to wait for," he mimicked her hesitation, "the other. I'll take it out on the punching bag." An edge had come into his voice. "But if he ever so much as lays a finger on you again..." His face was hard, his eyes steely.

"I love you."

His face softened. "What has that got to do with it?"

"Nothing. Everything. How long?"

"How long for what?"

"Will you wait for... the other?"

He laughed, delighted. "Any time beyond the next two minutes too long."

"Two hours?"

He looked at his watch. "More like seven hours. No, six."

"I'll be waiting."

"Anxiously?"

There was only love in his face now. Oh God, she loved him so much, so much that she could only nod.

He didn't kiss her again. Instead he let her go and backed away. "Then, love, let me get to the gym. The trouble is," he was grumbling a bit, "I have more than that... ass," the word was totally inadequate, "Kramer, to work off now."

She was laughing back over her shoulder as she went out of the room without a word.

# Chapter XV

The intercom. Michael looked up wearily from the folder he had been studying. He had a red pencil in his hand.

It was a moment before he could bring himself to press the button. It buzzed again. "Yes, Miss Trimby?"

"I have Colonel Fitzhugh on the line, Sir."

"Thank you." Michael was grinning as he picked up the phone and leaned back in his chair, running his fingers to his hair. "Hallo, Charlie!"

"Good news, Michael!"

"I can use some."

"Can't we all these days? It's laid on for the church on the eighth if you still want it."

"I do, indeed!" Anne had been right. The Germans weren't coming, at least not before the middle of September, if then.

"But..."

"No buts about it, thank you."

He laughed. "But you can't have it in the morning."

"Why ever not?"

"It's Sunday, Michael, and I'm afraid that the place has been booked solid on Sunday mornings since time immemorial."

"That's what I get for dealing with the *Deputy* Constable of the Castle."

"Ha! Not even the Grand Poobah could change that one for you."

"All right, Titty-Poo."

Charlie groaned and then laughed again. "God almighty, Michael, am I never going to live that one down?"

"You brought it up!"

"So I did. So I did." He was still laughing.

Michael smiled into the phone. What was it, forty years ago?... Forty-one?... since the upper school had put on the Mikado? They'd had to get special permission to put it on without paying royalties.

Charlie had played Titty-Poo, the female lead. He'd had a gorgeous soprano voice then. Hard to realize that now, with that basso profundo coming out of the receiver. "And may I say, you were gorgeous."

"Still am, old man, and speaking of that..."

"Careful." Michael was grinning.

"Gorgeous as you are, aren't you a bit... ah... antiquated to be taking the plunge? The water is cold, you know, especially the first time. A real shock to the system."

"You've done it, what, three times? And you're not back singing soprano. At least not yet."

"Low blow!" he snorted. "All that means is that I'm in good training for it. I can knock off a wedding with my eyes closed."

"With your track record, it would have been better if you'd kept your eyes open."

"Come to think of it, that may have been the problem. I'll remember that. Forewarned is forearmed. Are you going to need propping up?"

"Then you're coming up?"

"Of course! Who could resist such an invitation? I'll arrange a spread after."

"Well, well." Michael was genuinely touched. "We hadn't gotten around to that yet. Thank you. I'm sure that Anne will be pleased. I already am."

Fitzhugh's laugh was slightly self-conscious. "Don't thank me. It's I who should be thanking you. We can all use a little cheer down here, and who better to do that than a beautiful, blushing bride. She is beautiful, I take it."

"You could make a book on it."

"Good man. Say," he hesitated, "you wouldn't want an honor guard, crossed swords and all that, would you?" Before Michael could say anything, he rushed on, "I know, I know, they'd have to be naval, but I could see about it, if you like. It's a mutual aid society down here."

Michael chuckled and then it grew to a full-blown laugh as he pictured Anne's reaction. "Why not, by God. And her son serves on *Vectis*. Could they...?"

"I'll see." Michael could almost visualize him rubbing his hands in glee.

"Commander Fredericks seems a good sort. Couldn't all be from *Vectis*, of course, but some anyway. We'll really do it up." Charlie was warming to the subject. "Swords. Have to dredge up swords. Always round in peacetime with all those formal 'dos'. But haven't seen the sword in ages. We'll find some." He was talking almost to himself now. "Yes, we'll find some. What else? A nineteen gun salute?"

"Now Charlie..."

"I know. Just teasing."

Michael wasn't entirely sure. Charlie Fitzhugh enjoyed a good show.

"You need a driver, Michael? I can arrange a car."

"The car would be an enormous help. If we had one there we could take the train down. But Max will be along."

"What about Carter?"

"Carter is retiring. I think the idea of coping with a full household was more than he could bear."

Charlie laughed. "It's women. Carter doesn't approve of women."

"Amen."

"And he is as old as the hills."

"Older."

"But Max?" Fitzhugh laughed. "I can't quite see him as a 'gentleman's gentleman.'" He'd had what he found to be the rather dubious pleasure of being driven to dinner at Michael's by Max two weeks before when he had been in London. "Been to any good fights lately?"

"Max is a pussycat."

"Ha!"

"Speaking of fights, how are things in Dover?"

"Still pretty one-sided, I'm afraid. Jerry is having a field day. Though actually it's been rather quiet the last three days, since the nineteenth. If this miserable weather will just hold... In fact I hope it holds for a year. You do live the soft life up there. My God, London barely knows there's a war on," he grumbled.

"God's saving the king."

"Indeed. He seems to be. I just hope that he saves the RAF in the bargain." His voice was gloomy.

"They seem to be doing a good job of saving themselves," Michael replied. So far, anyway. "And us."

"Don't try to con a con man, Michael. There aren't enough of them by half, and there are fewer of them all the time. The replacements are green. Some of them haven't even finished a proper training course. And the airfields are getting the hell knocked out of them. Magnificent, those young bastards." There was a choke in Charlie's voice, and then Michael remembered that Charlie had a son, a squadron leader in the RAF. No wonder he welcomed a celebration to keep his mind off things.

"How's Hillary?" He tried to keep the concern he felt out of his voice.

"Exhausted. They all are. I talked with him last night. The weather's been a godsend. He's getting some sleep finally. Don't know how he stands it, living from minute to minute. All that waiting. At least in an infantry battle you know when it begins and when it ends and there is something going on in the middle." His voice was gloomy again. "They've lost half the original squadron. McKenzie's boy for one."

Michael sighed.

"The replacements are getting killed off almost as fast as they come in."

"Charlie!"

"I know. I'm sorry. Unsecured line and all that. Should keep my mouth shut. You shouldn't have let me rattle on like that. At least we get our boys back when they bail out. That's more than Jerry does. Listen Michael," he said, recovering himself, "I'll get ahold of that boy of hers. What's his name?"

"James Richter. The lieutenant on the *Vectis*."

"Right." Charlie was obviously scribbling hastily. "I'll get hold of him. Leave it all to me, that is, as long as you're footing the bill."

Michael laughed. He should have known. "Within reason!" Charlie loved to spend money, especially when it wasn't his own.

"How far can I go when it won't be for more than twenty including an honor guard? And Beluga caviar isn't coming in from Beluga, or wherever it comes from, anymore. By the way, do you need a place to stay?"

"That's fixed. Friends of Anne have a country house down there. That's why we'll need a car."

"When are you coming down?"

"Saturday morning."

"Right-o."

"Business all day."

"It never ends." There was a sudden commotion on the other end of the line. Michael could hear Charlie's startled "God!" And then there was shouting. What the hell was going on?

Finally Charlie was back on the line, a bit breathless now. "Got to ring off. God damn Jerry. Long-range guns from France. Big ones. My God!"

My God indeed. "Roll on the peace, Charlie."

"Damn right." His voice was grim and there was a click as he rang off.

Michael hung up the receiver slowly. Coastal guns. That was all they needed. It would be better if James were stationed in Scapa Flow.

Dover. He didn't like the idea at all. He'd have to check with Charlie about conditions down there closer to the time, but it wasn't likely that they would get any better. They had forgotten to set a time, and he'd have to see about a license. Good grief! He hadn't even thought about the license! They couldn't get married without a license!

He slumped back in his chair. There was time to get it done, of course, but he should have tended to that first thing. He had certainly tended to everything else. Why not the one thing that could prevent their getting married if it was not tended to? Didn't he want to get married? Dammit all, of course he did. He loved her.

His eye caught the folder lying on his desk. The folder. He stared at it with considerable distaste. He had been going through it, reading the list, when the phone call had come. It was a long, tedious list of every person who had been in the Dungeness area for two days before and after the spies were captured who was not ordinarily there. Six spies captured. Three of them were due to be hanged and one of those was. He shuddered.

Stupid. That man. What was his name? Stupid. What the hell could Canaris have been thinking to send an idiot like that? He should have been sending the very best Germany had to offer. Maybe this was the best that Germany had to offer. He gave a harsh little laugh. He couldn't permit himself to think like that. He knew better.

Britain's best. Was Britain sending her own best? Not always, unfortunately, and now all of them were gone and not yet replaced, though they were making a beginning. Gone. All but John. He gave a wry smile. John. And in the end, it all comes back to you, doesn't it? I have your blessing when I marry your mother and that is beyond generosity, under the circumstances. If you can be generous with me, why can't I be generous myself? Because I'm not being generous with your mother, that's why. I've robbed her blind, taken her younger son from her, and all I'm offering in return is myself, a poor substitute at best.

So what happened, old John? You told me all six would be landing at the same place and you'd been definite about it. That had made sense at the time. A mistake? Was someone deliberately giving you the wrong information, trying to check you out? No. Who the hell would be willing to jeopardize a mission to do that? It must've been a change in plans and a sensible one at that.

Michael's mouth was a grim line as he returned to the list. He'd just finished the first page when Charlie's call had come through. He turned to the second page, picked up his red pencil and began tracing down the line with the index finger of his left hand, and stopped and underlined a new name. Harold Cummins. Harold. There was a brief summary by the name. Michael's eyebrows flew up. A traveler in ladies lingerie, undergarments, corsets, etc. Hardly a suitable occupation for a spy. But then, what was? And maybe it was the perfect cover. He'd probably traveled back and forth along any coast he wanted for years, getting to know the people, the terrain, making maps, and if he had been doing it for years, he'd have no trouble getting the permits he'd need to move just as freely now. And who would take a traveler in ladies scanties seriously, let alone suspect him of anything? There was the name too. Harold. He read on. The description could make it the same man. Did he have that odd smile? They'd need a picture, or better yet, the man. Ms. Henderson and the Vicar would know. He scribbled a note on a pad. This bore looking into. As far as he could see, it was the only name on the list that did. At least so far.

He traced down the column. Jones, John. John. Too damn many Johns. He flipped over to the next page. Why had he asked for this? It was MI5 business, counterespionage, not his. But he knew why. These were John's spies. The woman who was to be hanged... She haunted him somehow, though he'd never seen her.

Stupid. What difference should her being a woman make? A woman was as dangerous a spy as a man. Perhaps even more so in ways. But still...

The license. He had to tend to the license. Why didn't he just press the buzzer and ask Miss Trimby to look into it? He stared at the buzzer button, knowing that he was being difficult, and knowing, too, that whenever someone was being difficult, he had something on his plate he couldn't cope with. His lips twitched into a brief smile. "Mr. Compton," he could still hear his sixth form English master, "do not a sentence a preposition end with." Ridiculous grammatically, but he had made his point. Michael's smile broadened. Apparently he hadn't made it all that well.

At least he knew what was on his plate. John. And you're giving me indigestion, old son.

He pressed the intercom button.

*      *      *

Hans opened the door to his room and began to laugh. Dieter was standing in the hall, dispatch case in his left hand, the machine pistol in the right, and a formal glower on his face. Oddly, instead of the menace of his usual expression, the glower only made him look ridiculous.

Dieter's face lapsed into a grin. "Just trying to look official." He lifted the machine pistol for emphasis as he came through the door.

Hans took the case and put it on the desk. "You only look official when you're trying not to. When you try..." He shrugged his shoulders. "A schnapps to end the day?"

"Why not?" He sprawled into the overstuffed chair by the window and laid the machine pistol on the floor beside.

Hans reached into the bottom drawer of the desk and pulled out a bottle.

"You and Minten."

Hans stopped pouring the schnapps at two fingers. "What about Minten and me?"

"The world famous brandy bottle in his bottom right desk drawer."

Hans gave a short laugh as he handed Dieter one of the glasses. "I certainly hope the resemblance ends there!"

Dieter didn't bother to comment on the obvious as he sipped the schnapps appreciatively. "Where's the bride?"

"At dinner with her aunt and uncle."

"Why aren't you there?"

Hans waved toward the dispatch case as he drained his glass. He looked into the bottom, wishing that he had an ice cube to chew on."Besides, I was just there the other night."

"Ah, yes. I remember. And I also seem to remember that Frau Schroeder isn't exactly on top of your list of delightful, interesting people."

Hans flushed slightly as he reached for the bottle, raising his eyebrows in an unspoken question. Dieter shook his head and Hans put the bottle back on the desk as he said, "She's nice enough, really, and she certainly went out of her way to let me know how pleased she is that Annaliese and I are getting married."

"She doesn't know about England?"

"Damn right, she doesn't."

"How's the Kapitan going to handle it after the wedding?"

"Annaliese says that she's to be told that I've been posted to Warsaw and she's going with me."

"Warsaw? Why Warsaw?"

"Who knows? Aunt Karin probably doesn't know anyone in Warsaw."

"And just when is the happy event?"

"Next Friday."

"But that's a work day."

"What isn't? We leave for Dunkirk on Sunday, so in all their munificence the powers-that-be said we could have Saturday for a honeymoon."

"When was all this decided?"

"Today. That's why Annaliese is at home tonight. Going for a special license in the morning. It's been arranged."

"Why Dunkirk? I thought we were leaving from Calais." He paused. "Jesus. A week."

"It doesn't seem possible."

Dieter nodded his agreement, then repeated, "Why Dunkirk?"

Hans reached back to the bottle and poured a dollop of schnapps into Dieter's class. He didn't protest. "Because we're supposed to be stationed there with the occupation forces in northern France. That's the reason we're able to escape." What on earth possible difference could make? "And Dunkirk is better than Calais because we really were stationed there and know the city well. It would be fairly easy to trip us up about Calais, even if we spent a week there."

"But Calais is a straight shot. Far closer to Dover. Couldn't we go to Dunkirk for the week but really leave from Calais?"

Hans was getting irritated. "It's all laid out. Look, we'll be in an E-boat, the kind that's been converted to lay mines. With the ramp on the back, they can launch the sailboat close to shore on the other side. These boats can move, and it's not that much farther." He looked at Dieter closely. "What the hell possible difference could it make to you, anyway?"

He seemed upset. "Herr Hauptmann…"

Hans was startled. Dieter had not called him that in weeks.

"I can't swim." He sat there staring down at his glass.

No wonder it mattered! "Have you ever been in a boat?"

"No."

"Good grief! We'll have to get you some swimming lessons. Here and in Dunkirk. Two weeks should be enough to keep you from drowning, especially since you'll be wearing a life jacket." Hans was thinking out loud now. "There's a pool at the gym." He shook his head. "Why didn't you say something sooner?"

Dieter shrugged. "No one ever asked me and I honestly didn't think about it until I looked at the map today, really looked at it. It's got to be 20 miles across the channel!"

Hans laughed. "I promise. The E- boat won't go unless it's safe for the sort of sail we'll be taking. We'll start tomorrow. Meet me at eight and we'll go over to the gym to see about it."

"But you have to go for your license."

"Our appointment is at 10. There will be time."

"I'd appreciate it more than I can say."

"I'll bet." Hans grinned at him. "Are you ready for all that transmitting to do when we're in Dunkirk?"

"God!" Dieter groaned. "All morning for four mornings. It will do me in."

"It can't be that bad."

"You try it. All those numbers and nonsensically combined letters drive me crazy after ten minutes. And I'll have to spend the afternoons coding and decoding. It's no way to spend summer days in Dunkirk, not with those beaches."

"Cheer up. They're probably mined by this time anyway."

"What will you be doing?"

"Sailing." Hans tried not to grin.

"At this moment I don't envy you in the least. But maybe I'll feel differently about it when I can swim."

"I hope so. At least by the time we leave, I ought to be able to get us where we're going so you won't have to worry about swimming."

Dieter gave a nervous little laugh. "Will Annaliese be sailing with you?"

Hans nodded. "She learned something about sailing during her summer in England. In the Lake District. It's easier if there are two of us."

"Picnic lunches?"

"Possibly. We'll have to eat some time."

"Then enjoy it and think of me. Slaving over a hot transmitter, sending coded messages I don't understand to the Abwehr radio room just so they can learn my 'fist'."

"They do that with everyone so they'll know if the other side is trying to run a ringer in on them."

"Comforting thought, considering where I'd be if they were trying to run in a ringer."

Hans shrugged. "You could always defect. Then there'd be no need for a ringer." He did his best to sound casual, humorous.

But there must've been something in his voice, for Dieter looked up sharply and shook his head in a definite no. "I can't imagine eating mutton for the rest of my life."

They had eaten a lot of mutton during the training of the now defunct British groups. Agents training to go to America were the current residents of the School House and so they were eating ham and fried chicken until it came out of their ears. Hamburgers, too. That name had made Dieter laugh when he'd first heard it, and it still struck him as an odd name for ground beef. Two of the group, who were from Hamburg and thus called Hamburgers, had actually been offended. But when it had been the turn of the Frankfurters... He smiled.

"Who's going to be at the wedding?" It was time to talk about something else.

"You are, for one."

"A pleasure." Dieter nodded. "Since I hadn't been asked, I wasn't sure."

"How can I possibly get married without you there to hold me up?" He hadn't decided until that moment. "I want you for my best man, if you're willing to do it."

"Of course! Delighted!" And he was, both delighted and touched. "I thought you'd want either your uncle or Georg."

"Uncle Karl won't know until the last minute whether or not he can come. I talked with him just before you came back." It had been between Dieter and Georg, and God knows, this was no payment for being 'done unto', but it was all he had to offer.

"You've already saved my life twice. If it needs saving again on Friday, I'd just as soon have you as close at hand as possible."

"Nervous?"

"Just covering my rear."

"Are you being married in the church?"

"No. At the Schroeder's."

"Frau Schroeder must be in seventh heaven."

"Not really. There isn't time to plan the sort of bash she'd like to have."

"What does Annaliese have to say about it?"

"She says she doesn't care where she marries me as long as she does. And that she's glad it's at home because it's the only way to keep Aunt Karin from inviting everyone she knows in Hamburg, short notice or not." But Hans wasn't happy about it. Annaliese had said all the right things, but something was bothering her. Premarital jitters? Pray God that's all it was.

"How many people will be there?"

"You getting nervous?"

Dieter shook his head. "No. Just worried about you getting nervous in front of a big audience."

"Not to worry. Just her family, my cousin Guenter," he rolled his eyes in disgust, "you, Georg, the HQ Commandant, maybe Uncle Karl, and of course, Major Minten."

"I guess there has to be a skeleton at every feast."

"I wish he were that insubstantial. She'll have to lay in food for three extra, at least, if he's to be fed in his usual fashion. He's Frau Schroeder's idea. Her substitute for Admiral Canaris."

"She asked him?"

"Damn right, she did. Called him herself." Hans shook his head in wonder. "Kapitan Schroeder was furious. She's not supposed to know who he is! And maybe she doesn't. Maybe she thinks he's just an a. I don't know. Thank God he can't come. He'd be all I needed." In more ways than one.

The thought amused Dieter no end.

"But it does mean that Minten will be there." There was nothing to be done about that. After all, Minten was his boss.

"Kramer coming?"

Hans almost choked on the last of his schnapps. "God, no!" Every time he thought about how Kramer had cornered her, handled her in Fenstermacher's office... And not to be able to do anything about it. How had she put it? 'If I were what he thinks I am, I'd never have told you.' And she was right. That was the hell of it. But it did make it easier to take. Was that what was bothering her? His attitude about what she had to do?

Dieter had stood and was stretching. "Somehow I didn't think he would be." He leaned over and picked up the machine pistol. "I'd better turn in if I'm going to learn to swim in the morning. It's going to take every ounce of energy I can muster." He grinned. "Besides, you have work to do."

As he got to the door, he turned back. "Oh. There's one piece of news in the rumor mill that might interest you."

"What's that?"

"Kramer is having a quiet fit about the way Hektor hands out film for those miniature cameras."

Hans' heart was beating fast. "He has a right to. Hektor was pretty casual when I went in for mine. He was busy unloading something or other and told me just to take what I needed and sign for it on a sheet that was on the bin." It had been absurdly easy. He had signed for six and taken twelve. The cartridges were small. "Still, it's surprising that Kramer would have a quiet fit about anything." And what kind of fit would Kramer have if he knew about the missing camera? Or had Hektor managed to cover that up? "A lot of stuff's gone missing from time to time. The last fuss was about toilet paper, of all things, and that was scarcely quiet."

"Will Kramer think you took it?"

"No telling what he'll think, but he could very well try to pin it on me. How many rolls were missing?"

"Twenty-one."

Hans tut-tutted, relieved that he wasn't the only one, and Bergmann left.

It had been a calculated risk, taking that extra camera. But it should be all right as long as he wasn't caught carrying them both at the same time. And he did have a good place to hide it, wrapped in a piece of oil cloth and wedged into the pipe behind the water tank high on the wall over the toilet. It was wedged in so tightly that he had to use the thin handle of the toilet brush to pry it loose. No danger even if someone dusted up there, which, from the looks of things, no one ever did.

Too bad he couldn't put the film up there, too, but the moisture was bad enough, even for the camera.

This was getting him nowhere. He locked the door as quietly as he could, gritting his teeth as the deadbolt scraped along. Then suddenly, he was standing back from the door, shaking his head. He was being ridiculous. Given the material in the dispatch case, he would have had to lock the door, anyway.

He moved quickly. The camera was ready in the desk drawer, complete with a fresh film cartridge and there was a second one in his pocket. He opened the dispatch case and riffled through the files. There it was: Sea Lion.

He put the bottle of schnapps back into the desk drawer, raised the gooseneck lamp and turned it on, opened the folder and laid out the first three sheets.

It was twenty minutes before he was able to gather up the papers and put the lamp back into its normal position. He'd used both film cartridges. That meant he was going to need more than the four he had left. And with Kramer raising a fuss, it wasn't going to be easy. He'd probably just have to make do and be more selective about what he photographed in the future. But selectivity took time and time wasn't something he had.

That business about Japan was a real shocker. The Tripartite Pact. Germany, Italy, and Japan. Italy was nothing. But Germany and Japan... The way Japan was going, and with the invasion of Russia on the horizon... He shuddered. World domination. That was what Germany and Japan wanted and Italy was going along for the ride.

The Italians could raise a considerable fuss in North Africa. The sheer size of their army might well make up for its ineptitude. If they could take the Suez and then move around the eastern end of the Mediterranean, and if Germany could take southern Russia and move around the east coast of the Mediterranean from the north, then that sea would become their lake. Big ifs, but not beyond the realm of possibility.

Oil was the key. Germany was already sending more troops into southern Poland, so they could move quickly to protect their Romanian oil supply should someone decide to try to cut that off. They wanted oil, needed oil. A modern army ran on oil. And if Germany and Italy eventually controlled the whole Mediterranean basin as well as Russia's Caucasus fields, they would control the bulk of the world's oil, ensuring their own supply of it and denying that same supply to everyone else.

Greece would have to be taken in sometime. Yugoslavia was already coming into Germany's 'sphere of influence'. And what would Turkey do this time? Stay neutral? That's what they said now, but how neutral could they afford to be if Greece were conquered along with southern Russia, and the Wehrmacht was poised along the northern border as well as just across the Bosporus, with the Italians coming up from the south? An accommodation? Probably.

He snorted a little laugh. He had just lost nearly the whole of the Western world except for North and South America in twenty minutes. And America was the big question, of course. What would they do? What would the United States do? Sit on their hands and say that this was a European war and they didn't want to get suckered in again? But if Churchill could get this stuff to Washington, it might, just might, shake them up a bit. And with Canada fighting for the 'Mother Country' already...

Enough of this. He had a job to do. Gloom and doom about the prospects for the world would have to wait. Forever, he hoped. He put each cartridge of exposed film back into the heavy dark paper that had originally protected it. Then he taped the paper shut and put the cartridges into his pocket. The camera was empty and ready to go into hiding again. And later, after Heinrich had made sure that the blackout shades had been properly adjusted, he'd go down to the drawing room and read some British papers before he went to bed, stashing the two cartridges when no one was around. Electricians tape was already holding the four spare cartridges to the underside of the right front corner of the chest that was covered by the window seat, the chest that held the British newspapers. There was plenty of room under the overhang, five inches at least on either side of the lid. The cartridges were small. The exposed film could go on the left side so that if he had to grab more in a hurry, there would be no mistake.

It ought to be alright. Who the hell would think of looking for anything there? The only problem was that the chest was getting full and would have to be cleaned out before too long. But all anyone ever did to clean it was to pull out all the papers, throw out the old ones and put the new ones back in on the bottom, so even that shouldn't be a problem.

Certainly no place in this room was safe. There had been neither the tools nor the time to hollow out a chair leg or some such. And now that Kramer had his suspicions about the film, he'd be going over the room with a fine tooth comb, if he hadn't done it already. The main problem now was how to get the film to England without it either being detected or ruined. It would have to be in something waterproof. If only he were learning how to operate the darkroom instead of Dieter, he could take care of it easily. Negatives were flat, safer the transport, and far less likely to be ruined than film which was always in danger of being prematurely exposed.

He sighed. There was no darkroom, and 'what ifs' were the stuff of which insanity was made. He had too much to do to worry about it now. Notes. Comments. Suggestions. Would the OKW ever decide on a plan? This was the fourth change to come across his desk since he'd gotten here.

He supposed he should be grateful that the OKH and the Kriegsmarine couldn't seem to agree, because until they did, there could be no invasion. But it made for one hell of a lot of extra work and it would be far better if he could take the final plan to England. How many more changes would there be after he left? Or before? If they left at all.

*    *    *

Kramer stepped back from the window and checked his watch. 0809. Richter and Bergmann were leaving early for a Saturday. And with a dispatch case and that damn fool machine pistol. Bergmann was thumbing his nose at the regulations, saying, "All right. You tell me that I have to carry a weapon, so I'll carry a weapon." But Minten didn't have the brains to see that. Bergmann was laughing at the rules while he was obeying them to the letter. It was infuriating.

And Richter had to be laughing, too. That idiot Hektor. Twenty-one film cartridges missing, for God's sake. No. More than that. And most of them still unaccounted for. Damn 'honor list'. Kramer's jaw tightened. The man should be sacked. If it were up to him... But Hektor was an institution. Bah! Not that sacking him would help this situation. Sacking Hektor would be locking the barn door after the horse was stolen in a big way. If Richter had even half that film, he had far more than he needed.

He had to have it. Kramer had seen Bergmann bringing in the dispatch case again last night. Working at home. Ha! Taking pictures where he knew he wouldn't be interrupted, that's what Richter had been doing. And he had every excuse to keep his door locked when he had those files in there.

He looked at his watch again. 0815. The girls wouldn't start cleaning upstairs for almost an hour, 0915 at the earliest. If he skipped breakfast... No time like the present. But where was that bitch of a girl? She hadn't gone out with him. Nevermind. He locked the door.

Kramer walked quickly down the hall and slipped into Hans' room. He locked the door behind himself before the force of the fact that it hadn't been locked hit him. It showed that Richter was confident. Then his smile was nasty. Careless at last? Richter was bound to slip up some time. Everyone did.

He started with the armoire. Nothing in the clothes and no false bottom. Very little on the shelves. Neat as a pin. Nothing underneath. It was the same with the desk. He even took out the drawers to make sure that there was nothing taped the underside.

And he checked the overstuffed chair, the crevices, the bottom, the buttons, each one with a quick pull. Nothing. He swore as he checked his watch. 0850.

None of the floorboards had been disturbed, and there were no cracks in the baseboards. He tapped the head and foot of the bed as well as legs. They were solid. By now Kramer was actively angry.

He hauled the feather tick onto the floor and got down on his hands and knees, patting across it, gently at first but finally all but pounding it into the floor. Nothing, nothing, NOTHING! Shit!

It had to be somewhere. Where else could Richter have put it? In a frenzy now, he tore the bottom sheet and the mattress cover from the bed and traced a shaking finger along the mattress seams. Nothing. He pulled each one of the buttons on the mattresses, tearing off a loose one. Damn. He threw the mattress over – it was half off the bed now – and repeated the process on the other side. Nothing. He pounded it in an impotent fury.

"Hans!"

Kramer froze. Had there been a knock? He hadn't heard one. He looked at his watch. 0910. Time to get out anyway. He pulled the mattress back onto the bed as quietly as he could.

"Hans, what are you doing in there?"

Kramer smiled. Fräulein Scheuermann. She could wait. There'd be no problem with her.

He dumped the bedding on top of the mattress. Let the maids take care of it. They'd think that Richter had had an active night. Who knows? Kramer smiled and turned to a leer. He might have.

There was a definite knock this time.

He strode to the door and threw it open. "Well, well, Fräulein. What an unexpected pleasure."

"Unexpected, I can believe, but I doubt that it's a pleasure since you certainly are where you shouldn't be. What are you doing in there and where is Hauptmann Richter?"

"Now, now." He stepped out into the hall and shut the door behind him. He had heard feminine laughter and there was the sound of footsteps on the stairs. "Is that any way to refer to your fiancé?" The word was a sneer.

She stared at him, disgusted.

"Nothing to say? Now that is an improvement."

"Usually when I have nothing to say, it makes you very angry."

Bitch. He reached for her arm and then laughed as she pulled back before he could touch her. The maids had reached the top of the stairs. With the 'American' group here, they were fully staffed again.

He glanced at them as he took hold of Annaliese's upper arm so tightly that she couldn't pull away without making a scene.

"Downstairs!" He hissed, then nodded politely as the maids brushed by. One turned back to stare after them but they didn't notice her. He was propelling Annaliese relentlessly toward the top of the stairs.

Annaliese glanced back briefly and tried to pull away when she saw that the girls had disappeared around the corner. Kramer took great pleasure in tightening his grip even further as he started pulling her down the stairs after him. Her foot caught and only the fact that she grabbed the banister saved her, but even after that he had to give her a jerk to keep her upright. "Just as well I didn't let you go."

"I wouldn't have fallen at all if you hadn't been dragging me after you like a poor imitation of a caveman." She was furious. "Now let me go! I am perfectly willing to talk to you but not while you're hurting me."

"Oh," he said, his voice full of sarcasm, "did I hurt you? I'm so sorry." He wasn't. He wanted to hurt her and hurt her very much indeed.

The bitch was lucky. He couldn't do anything here. He let her go.

"Thank you so much." She matched his sarcasm as she continued down the stairs, rubbing her arm, not bothering to notice whether or not he was following her.

She walked into the dining room and stood surveying the scene with considerable dismay. Heinrich looked up.

"Fräulein?" He and a man she had never seen before were waxing the floor.

"I was just looking for Hauptmann Richter." It was the only excuse she could think of. She looked back over her shoulder and saw Kramer standing in the hall, smirking at her. She felt her face reddening.

"Hauptmann Richter went out early with Lieutenant Bergmann. He asked that I tell you when you came down that he would be back at 9:30 to pick you up."

"Thank you."

She walked back into the hall, ignoring Lieutenant Kramer as she went through into the dining room, which was already being set up for a luncheon meeting.

By this time Kramer was laughing out loud, his vicious mood

gone. He loved seeing her so discomfited. She was afraid, actually afraid of him! Better and better. "The library, Fräulein. There's a meeting in the solarium."

She swiveled around, staring at him.

He laughed again. "No more closed doors, I promise."

She lifted her chin and swept past him into the library. "You'd better hurry. Hauptmann Richter will be back in a few minutes."

"No such luck. He and Bergmann went off somewhere over an hour ago."

"Didn't you hear Heinrich?" She looked triumphant. "I thought you made it your business to hear everything. He left a message saying he'd be back to get me at 9:30."

"My, my, isn't he the faithful one." His lip curled. God, how he hated that cool, level gaze of hers. "Then I'll be brief. I want Richter's schedule, his schedule for today and every day for the next week."

"I don't know it. Today is Saturday, and Saturdays have been the same from week to week. All of next week is chaotic."

"What are you doing this morning?" There was a nasty edge to his voice.

"Getting our marriage license." She glared at him.

"Well!" His eyes were glittering. "So he's going to go through with it."

"You told me that you had no doubt I would succeed. Are you starting to lose faith in your own judgment?"

"Never, Fräulein. Never." The edge was back in his voice. "For instance, my judgment tells me that you can tell me what his schedule is, even if you have to give it to me day by day. Where will you go after you get the license?"

If he wanted an account of Hans' time... Kramer was up to something. "He has to go back to his office," she said slowly.

"See how easy it is?"

She just looked at him.

"No lunch?"

"A brief one, if there's time."

"Not very romantic for a bride and groom just having gotten their marriage license."

"Have you forgotten where we're going to be in two weeks?"

"Scarcely. But I thought you might have." His eyes seem to be burning right through her. "If I," he amended that, "if we don't succeed, that's precisely where you will be going."

"We? You mean me. If I don't succeed and in the process pull your fat out of the fire... You. Needing a woman. If that isn't the living end." Her laughter was a bit wild.

Bitch. Laughing at him. At him. "Laugh while you can." His fury was barely contained. "When you're swinging at the end of a rope, you'll be laughing out the other side of your mouth."

"And if I am, as you say, swinging at the end of a rope. Laughing out of the other side of my mouth," a stab of fear clutched at her heart, "then I'll see to it that you're on the next rope, laughing with me."

He was maintaining only the barest threaded control over himself. "I will never hang." He spit out each word separately as his now red face loomed close to hers.

She took an involuntary step backwards, watching him, grateful that the door was open and that Heinrich was in the drawing room. Why was she needling him this way? She was courting disaster. But he was insufferable, an obscenity. He thought that he had her where he wanted her and, in a way, he still did. But she couldn't let him know the extent to which she had freed herself. It would be too dangerous. So she tried to make herself seem calm, be polite. "Did you want to know anything else?"

"Bergmann."

"What about him?"

"His schedule." Bitch.

"I don't know about that, either."

"Then make it your business to know."

"Lieutenant Bergmann is no part of what you asked me to do."

"He is now."

Kramer wanted a clear field for whatever it was. "Very well. I'll try."

"And I want your precise schedule, everything, every day, through Friday."

"A set up." Oh, why had she said that?

His smile was slow, secret. The bitch was bright. Very bright.

"Annaliese..."

They both turned, surprised by the voice from the doorway. Her face lit up as Kramer watched. My God, she was a good actress. He had to hand her that. Then he looked at her closely and there were faint stirrings of suspicion that it might not be an act. He laughed to himself. That was ridiculous. She couldn't afford anything but an act if she wanted to live. She was just... relieved – and women were superb actresses, anyway. He ought to know. He lived the bulk of his life with one of the best.

Hans had stopped in the doorway and was looking from one of them to the other. He didn't like it. There was tension in every line of Annaliese's body and Kramer looked annoyed. Being interrupted? Probably. If he had so much as laid a hand on her...

Kramer snapped to attention. "Herr Hauptmann."

Hans was surprised. What had been going on here? Kramer was rarely so correct and even then only in the presence of a superior officer.

"Lieutenant Kramer." He was wary now.

"My congratulations on your impending nuptials. Will your uncle be coming for the happy event?"

Happy event? "I hope so." What was this? He looked at Annaliese but her expression was unreadable.

Kramer's brain was racing. If the general came... It would have to be done before the general came. Richter had to be alone. Without reinforcements at hand. "When will he arrive?"

What the hell business was it of his? "Thursday evening at the earliest. Why?"

"I had the pleasure of seeing him again briefly, in Dunkirk. I hope that I shall have an opportunity to renew acquaintances."

"I'd forgotten you'd known him in Prussia."

Kramer waved a negligent hand. "I met him only in passing. Is the wedding to be an intimate family affair?"

Could he possibly be angling for an invitation? Was that what this nauseating sweetness and light was all about? If it was, think again, Kramer. "Yes, as matter of fact, it is." He held Kramer's eyes with his own. "And I'm afraid that Fräulein Scheuermann and I must leave. We have an appointment."

It was Kramer who looked away first. "So I understand." He walked past Hans, then turned. "Have a pleasant morning, Herr Hauptmann." Then, with a brisk nod and a "Fräulein" in Annaliese's direction, he turned on his heel and left the room.

Hans looked after him, still puzzled. "Why do I feel that I was being sneered at?"

"Probably because you were being sneered at," she replied wearily.

Damn Kramer, he thought and reached for her hand. Here they were about to get their marriage license, for God sake, and Kramer was managing to cast a pall over that as he had almost everything else. He'd have to see what could be done about that. "Come on," he said briskly, then softened it with a smile. "Let's go and see about getting married."

She held onto his hand tightly as they walked to the Kuebel.

It was only after they had pulled to the gate that she finally spoke, and then it was with a curiously flat tone. "I found him in your room this morning, searching for something. And he wants to know your schedule for the week. Yours and Dieter's."

"A set up."

She nodded. "I thought so, too. What was he looking for?"

Film. It had to be the film. Damn. He should have checked out the window seat this morning, but Dieter had been with him so there hadn't been a chance.

He braked at a corner, thinking that he was being ridiculous, a veritable Nervous Nelly. The last thing he should do was check out the window seat over and over, especially if Kramer were watching him. No. The more the film was left alone, the better.

"Hans?"

"Yes?" He looked over at her briefly before crossing the intersection.

"I asked you if you knew what he could be looking for."

There was an edge to her voice that he didn't like. Play it loose. The truth. Always the truth whenever possible. The truth was so disarming. "Dieter told me that Kramer was angry about the way Hektor was running the Supply Room. Some of the film for the miniature cameras is unaccounted for. Hektor's system, if that's what you want to call it, leaves a great deal to be desired. Maybe Kramer thinks I'm photographing everything I can lay my hands on so I can take it to England."

"Are you?" And she managed to keep it light, teasing? Oh, God, she hoped so. Whatever Kramer had been looking for... He was looking for something definite.

Hans laughed. "Of course!" Tell the truth, make it outrageous enough and no one would believe it. "I took rolls and rolls of film that I intend to develop in the Abwehr dark rooms. Then I'm planning to have one of the maids at the School House stitch the negatives into my shorts."

How could she have been so silly? Damn Kramer, anyway. She relaxed and played along. "But what if the sailboat tips over? Would they be ruined?"

"By no means. I shall be wearing waterproof pants – the new sort they have for babies – a very large size."

The picture of Hans in poofy waterproof pants flashed into her mind's eye and was too much to bear. She started giggling. How could she have let Kramer's ridiculous suspicions get to her? After all, Hans' mother was an American, so he would scarcely be betraying her. And it was war and he was German. Oh dear, oh dear. She'd been so silly!

Hans kept glancing over at her. It had been far too long since he'd seen her like this. Keep her that way. That was the important thing. Put on a stern face. "So you think waterproof pants are funny? And after all the trouble I went to get ahold of them!" How the hell was he going to get that film to London without being discovered?

She nodded and tried to catch her breath. It was such a relief. Oh, how she loved him.

She was still giggling intermittently as they walked up the steps of the town hall and there was nothing for it but for Hans to laugh with her.

The official who had all of the forms ready for them to sign was delighted to see a couple in such obviously high spirits. It was all too rare these days, with all the red tape that had to be gone through. But then, most of theirs had been cut. Perhaps that explained it.

*     *     *

"Captain Compton's office."

"Miss Trimby?"

"Mrs. Richter?"

"How good of you to know my voice."

"I'm sorry, but Captain Compton is not in at the moment."

"Never mind. Actually I wanted to talk to you, to tell you myself how delighted I am that you'll be at our wedding."

"I was pleased to be asked."

"My dear, I wouldn't not have you there. I'd want you if only because Michael is so fond of you. But since James will be there... I know he wants you to be, as well."

Annabelle sat there, not quite knowing what to say. "It... It will be good to see him."

"It will be for me, too." Anne became businesslike. She'd made Miss Trimby uncomfortable enough. "I do hope that you'll stay with us at the Watson's. There's plenty of room."

"Why, thank you! That would be a great help. I was planning to ask James where he could stay when he calls again, but I know it's difficult in Dover just now."

"Indeed." Anne's tone was dry. She cleared her throat. "It will be a great help to me to have you there. James is going to be Michael's best man and I was hoping that you would be willing to stand up for me."

Annabelle was floored. "Goodness, Mrs. Richter. I'd be honored." She hesitated. "Who's going to give you away?"

There was a moment of silence at the other end of the line before Anne finally gave a little laugh. "James is. I'd forgotten that. Never mind. We'll work it out. It's to be a very small affair. You and James, my Hannah and Max, and a friend of Michael's who's the Deputy Constable of the Castle. At least I think that's what he's called." There was a stab at her heart. If John were here, he could be Michael's best man and James, as her eldest son, could give her away. Damn you, John. Damn you to hell, my lovely son. But none of that was apparent in her voice.

Annabelle was smiling. Mrs. Richter didn't know about the honor guard. It would delight her soul. "It sounds perfect." She hesitated, not wanting to ask, fearing that she might be intruding. But there seemed to be nothing else for it since, if she went later, someone would have to meet her and take her out to the house. She took a deep breath and pushed the words out. "Would it be all right if I came down on the train with all of you?"

"By all means! It would simplify things considerably since we'll have a car meeting us there. It will be good to have you with us."

Bless her. "Saturday morning?"

"I think so. May I let you know?"

"Of course."

"I'll see you then. Two weeks from today. The seventh."

Annabelle's heart was pounding. James... Two more weeks. "I'm looking forward to it."

"So am I."

She sounded so definite that it was all Annabelle could do not to laugh.

"And would you please tell Captain Compton that I called?"

"The moment he comes in."

"Thank you."

"And thank you, Mrs. Richter, for everything."

*       *       *

It was late and Dieter was yawning as he walked to the window seat. He hadn't had time to read any of the foreign papers for days. The American ones had started coming in, and he was anxious to see if they were as good as the British, to say nothing about the different viewpoint they might have about the war. But even if they weren't as good, they would certainly be better than what passed for a newspaper in Germany these days.

He lifted the lid of the window seat. Crammed. It must be the sudden influx of American papers. Heinrich had fallen down on the job. He probably had too much to see to with this new set of agents, but still...

As he pulled out the top few papers, the very top page tore at the corner. Odd. A nail? No, a nail would've left a long slit. Curious now, he felt under the left side of the overhang all the way back into the front corner. A lump. Sticky. Curiouser and curiouser. He pulled on the lump and it came out in his hand.

Electrical tape. A corner of it must've come loose. He turned a lump over in his hands and froze. A film cartridge. 16mm. The size of film missing from the Supply Room. The film for the miniature cameras. What was it doing here? He looked at it closely. The film had been exposed and then rewrapped in its own paper. Was there more? He put his hand back in under the overhang and felt around. One more. He pulled it out. Now what would two cartridges of exposed 16mm film be doing in there?

He lowered the lid and sat down heavily in the nearest chair. 'I always try to be careful about things like that.' Why did those words of Richter's pop into his brain now? He sat absolutely still, knowing why they had. Damn Kramer and his insinuations. What he ought to do was hand the film to the Hauptmann and decide with him to whom it should be taken. Fuck you, Kramer, you and your damn sick suspicions. But if you're right... If you're right...

He took a deep breath, rose and went back to the window seat. There was only one way to be sure. He'd have to develop the film himself. And if it were the Hauptmann's? He refused to frame an answer.

The hinges complained as he threw back the lid so viciously that he had to catch it with one hand as he thrust the other under the right overhang. One, two, three, four. Four more film cartridges. Unexposed? Probably. Exposed on the left unexposed on the right. He left them where they were and lowered the lid. Then he put the exposed film into his pocket and bent down to pick up the papers he dropped to the floor.

Tomorrow was Sunday, and this Sunday was supposed to be a day of relative rest, a reward for all their hard work. He should be able to get into a dark room without any problem. If anyone asked he would say he needed extra work on his developing technique. God knows, that was true enough. The film had to be handled just so and it still took him longer than it should. His lip curled into a parody of a smile. Besides, it would present the perfect picture of the zealous agent-in-training, perfecting his skills on his own time. Too bad he didn't have some of those damn nature pieces they always had him taking to enlarge. But he was all caught up with that. He sighed. They weren't 'damn' nature pictures. Actually he had begun to enjoy taking them and was getting good at it, or so they said. It was one of the few things he did these days that gave him pleasure.

"Dieter?"

He swiveled around, startled, his hand hovering over his pocket briefly before he made it drop. "Just getting some bedtime reading." Hans was looking at him closely. "What's wrong?"

He shrugged. "Just tired, I guess. It's been a long day."

Hans nodded sympathetically. "Swimming can really take it out of you when you're not used to it."

"That must be it."

"How did it go?"

He shrugged. "How was dinner with your prospective in-laws?"

"Fine." What was it? Dieter looked positively grim.

"Where's Annaliese?"

"She stayed the night since we're supposed to have tomorrow off."

Dieter nodded and gave an exaggerated yawn as Hans moved towards the window seat. He'd wanted to get more film but he couldn't, not with Dieter standing there. Morning would have to do. But his alarm clock was on the fritz. It had been a rush this morning. There was a sucking in of breath as he lifted the lid and pulled out some papers. "Heinrich had better tend to this." He should try and find another place for the film. But where?

Dieter nodded again, not trusting himself to speak.

"The New York Times!" Hans crowed. "I haven't seen one in years!" Why was Bergmann looking at him like that? "More swimming tomorrow?"

"Bright and early."

"Get me up, will you? I have a lot of work to do so we can drive over there together. My alarm clock's broken."

"Sure."

And then, as if in response to some invisible signal, they turned together and walked out of the drawing room and up the stairs without saying a word.

# Chapter XVI

"No. I haven't forgotten!"

Kugelmann snickered as he watched Kramer's face darken into a dusky fury.

"I know it's been over two weeks since I told you about it, but you can't set up something like this overnight, for God sake."

Kramer's jaw snapped shut and he held the phone's receiver away from his ear. Kugelmann could hear Minten's squawking coming out of it, but it was impossible to understand what he was saying.

"But it's the perfect time, Herr Major."

More squawking.

"I know that you sent Kugelmann for the papers, but this is too good a chance to miss."

Kugelmann sat down to wait even though Kramer hadn't said he could. Just like that bastard not to think of it. He pulled his shirt away from his chest. It was a sticky day and the door to the office was shut. If it hadn't been for a fan stirring around what little breeze was coming in the window, it would've been unbearable. He looked at Kramer closely, surprised. The lieutenant wasn't sweating. He'd always suspected that there was something a little inhuman about Kramer, and now he was sure. Anyone who wasn't sweating today couldn't possibly be human.

Kramer was bearing down on the major, but for once he didn't seem to be getting angry. Probably because he felt that success was at hand, that Minten would have to give in and was objecting only on general principle. Minten was getting sick of this little game and Kugelmann didn't blame him. Having to placate a bastard like Kramer... But one of these days, and before too long...

Uh-oh. Minten was really giving him a bad time. "You just do it, dammit. Or... Listen, he's in here working and there is almost no one around. It is Sunday, for God sake. And you do need the papers."

A pause.

"Look..." Minten must have interrupted him, for there was another pause.

"I know that Hauptmann Kruger's here from Berlin, but you'll be back at the School House in plenty of time. He's not due here until five. I can take care of things afterward."

Kramer was clearly exasperated. "You have to open the safe! You're the only one with the combination!" He sucked in a breath. "Come in the back way. Then the guard at the reception desk won't know you're here."

"Just tell the guard at the back that you don't want anyone to know you're here. Make it an order. He'll have to do what you say!"

"No. No." His pencil was beating a tattoo on the desk. "I'll keep Richter busy while you're on your way in and then tell him I have to go to meet Kruger."

Kugelmann was watching and listening, wishing to hell that the major would give in so they could get this ridiculous business over with. He wanted a nap. Damn those visiting VIPs anyway. Hauptmann Kruger had been a pain in the ass last time he had been here and wasn't any better this time.

Kramer rose and began pacing the few steps the phone cord permitted. "I know I'm not meeting him," he snapped. "What's wrong with you? It's just an excuse."

He sat back down, triumphant now. "All right then. Kugelmann is on his way to get you, or he will be in a minute. When he gets back, he can go across the street to the gym to call Richter while you're opening the safe."

Kugelmann sighed. No rest for the weary. He could use the phone in the gym. There wouldn't be any problem since Dolph was on duty, but why couldn't Kramer have bothered to ask him first? He was sick to death of all these machinations. It would be such a relief when Kramer was gone. Literally gone. Safely gone.

He rolled his eyes. They were still talking. Unbelievable. Minten was difficult enough to handle, but add Kramer to it... Last night, for instance. It had been the one of those nights. At least Kramer had taken charge of Hauptmann Kruger. God knows where they'd been.

"Oh, he can arrange to use the phone in the gym office all right and without being disturbed. One of his 'dearest'," — the word was said with a definite leer – "friends usually manages to pull Sunday duties since it gives him time for his various... ah... pursuits."

Kugelmann glared at him.

"He'll leave right away." Kramer slammed down the phone before there could be any reply. "Go get him."

Arrogant bastard. "To whom are you referring, Herr Lieutenant?"

"Look. Don't give me any of that. I just had the course with that idiot you work for."

"You work for him, too."

Kramer looked at him for a moment before realizing what was amiss. "Stand at attention when addressing a superior officer! No one gave you permission to sit!"

Kugelmann stood slowly and put himself into the semblance of attention. "Always delighted to stand for an officer, but as for your being superior..." He let the sentence trail off.

Kramer rose, leaning over the desk on his fists. "Listen, you snot-nosed little prick, talk to me like that again I'll arrange to have your teeth shoved down your throat."

Kugelmann almost shook his head. The bastard couldn't even take care of that for himself. But he said nothing. What was there to say?

Kramer sat back down, composing himself. "This needs careful timing. It will take you twenty minutes to get Minten and come back. He said he'd be ready."

Ha! That would be the day.

"In fifteen minutes I should go to Hauptmann Richter's office and keep him busy so he doesn't accidentally run into Major Minten. Actually I'll give you five extra minutes. I'll go in twenty minutes. Don't let Minten enter the building before..." He looked at

his watch and considered. "1500. Then you go to the gym and call
Richter at 1510 on the dot. We'll tell him that the major left in a
rush after the briefing this morning and forgot that he needed the
American files for the dinner meeting this evening. There are three
files, and I'll see that they're on Minten's desk. They're what you
came for anyway. Tell him that you were to pick them up but that
the major had something else for you to do, that you caught me in
the office but I had to leave for an appointment and so couldn't get
them to the School House on time. But I left the office door unlocked
for him. Then he'll know he has to go right down because the door
shouldn't be left open at all. Tell him, too, that Minten wants him
at the School House with the files by 1615 so that they can go over
the agenda before dinner."

"There is no agenda." Kugelmann wasn't giving an inch. He was
disgusted. This was one big fat waste of time. And leaving the office
unlocked. Jesus!

"But Richter doesn't know that," Kramer snapped. "Just do as I
say and do it now."

Kramer's eyes were glittering dangerously and Kugelmann had
the sense to know that he had pushed him far enough. "Anything
else?"

"Yes." He reached into his desk drawer, pulled out a Luger and
shoved it across the desk. "Take this. I'll sign out another."

Kugelmann shook his head.

Kramer gave a harsh little laugh. "I'd forgotten your aversion
to pistols. Even so, you do know how to use it, don't you?" He was
sneering now.

"Of course," said Kugelmann archly. Small weapons were part
of the required training for Abwehr drivers, and he had done well
enough with it despite the fact that firing a gun always made him
physically ill.

"All right then, take it."

"Why another gun?" Kugelmann asked stubbornly. "You have
one and so does the major. And Richter never carries one."

"He just might this time, and I don't want to take any chances.

Since you'll be across the street, you can't come in until after we're in Minten's office with him. So if there is trouble and if he does have a weapon, you can be the cavalry, charging in in the nick of time." It was all Kramer could do not to laugh. The idea of Kugelmann 'charging to the rescue', waving a pistol, was ludicrous in the extreme.

Kugelmann shuddered.

"Don't worry." Kramer could hold back his laughter no longer. "I don't think he'll try anything."

The corporal flushed, knowing too well what was going through Kramer's mind. "I certainly hope not." For your sake and Minten's, you bastard. If you think I'm going to face a loaded pistol for the likes of you, you have another thing coming. I wouldn't do it even for Minten and he's done a hell of a lot more for me than you ever have. He picked up the gun and dropped it into the briefcase.

"Get going."

"Certainly, Herr Lieutenant." He snapped to attention. Might as well get the form right, if not the substance. He raised a stiff right arm and gave a rousing "Heil Hitler!" then turned on his heel and left, just as Kramer's surprised, "Heil Hitler" began.

*     *     *

Dieter put the first strip of negatives in the enlarger and snapped the switch that turned on the light. It had been a long wait to get into a dark room, something to do with a rush job on some reconnaissance films that had just come in. But now, finally, everything was ready. His stomach felt as if it was full of lead, but his hand was steady as he adjusted the focus to clarify the black and white blur on the base plate. Too much. Back a little. There.

He stared at the white words on a black background. Sea Lion. The sight of those words burned through his brain. Sea Lion. He slumped onto the stool behind him and let out a long breath. Sea Lion. Jesus.

'I always try to be careful about those things.' The words flashed through his mind's ear. Damn right you are, Richter. Careful about how many more film cartridges you take and you sign for.

'Are you a good liar, Herr Hauptmann?' What had his reply been? Something like 'I don't do it often, but when I do, I'm very good at it.' Yes. He was. Very good indeed. No wonder he'd said it would be relatively safe for him to go to England. There was no 'relatively' about it. He would be welcomed with open arms. But what was he going to do about me when he got there? And Annaliese? My God. Annaliese. He's going to marry her!

Suddenly bile rose in his throat and he just managed to reach the sink before his stomach heaved up what was left of his lunch.

It was a moment before he could reach into his pocket and take out his handkerchief. He went to the faucet and wiped his face, then turned on the water hard to wash the disgusting mess down the drain. When it was gone at last, he bent down to the faucet and managed to catch enough water to rinse out his mouth. He stood there for a long time, leaning forward, stiff-armed, on the edge of the sink, head down, mind numb. He shook his head to blot out the picture of those words, but it didn't work. They seem to be etched under his eyelids.

Finally, he gave it up, moved back to the enlarger and put the negatives through. One after another, strip after strip, until he'd seen them all. He was in a dead calm as he sat down to consider. It was incredible. Not only Sea Lion but the details of the proposed pact between Germany, Italy, and Japan, reports on projected Italian operations in North Africa, and unit by unit assignments for troops being sent into southern Poland, ready to move to protect their Romanian oil fields, should that become necessary.

The codenames of the operations matched those in the file envelope he picked up for Richter. What the hell kind security clearance did he have to be able to get hold of this kind of stuff? And why hadn't Minten had it lifted once it was decided to send Richter to England? Dieter's laugh was bitter. Minten and Admiral Canaris were sending Richter to England. That was rich.

What a patsy he'd been. If the film had been found by someone else, who would have believed he wasn't in it with Richter? He'd brought those files to him, at the School House. Jesus. If there had been anything left in his stomach, he would've been sick all over again.

There was a tap at the door.

Dieter looked up and growled. "Who is it?" The door was locked so a red light would be on, and whoever was there would think that he was still developing.

The voice was muffled. Dieter got up reluctantly and went to the door, pulling back the black curtain covering it so he could hear. "I'm sorry. What did you say?"

The man was speaking slowly and distinctly now. "Hauptmann Richter called down and asked if you would please meet him in his office at 1530. He said he'd be done by then."

Well, wasn't that nice of him. Done with what? Taking more pictures? Dieter would have staked his life on it. Sunday and almost no one around. He looked at his watch. 1435. He cleared his throat. "Tell him I'll be there." Be there. He dropped the curtain. This moment, he didn't want to be anywhere, let alone 'there'. Unless it was home. At the inn on the mountain and well out of it. Never in it in the first place. Richter. Jesus. The one man he had trusted in the whole fucking world beside his father.

What to do? Burn the negatives and have done with it? He couldn't burn them. Not here. It would set off every alarm in the place. And he was damned if he was going to carry them out, bad enough that he carried them in. Get caught with these and be thought part of it? Not bloody likely.

He opened one of the drawers of the counter and pulled out three small glazed tissue envelopes. Then one by one, he picked up the negative strips by the edges and slid them into the envelopes. He hated touching them. Get them away, out of sight. Leave. No. He had to make copies of the negatives he was supposed to be working on. Should have had all this finished up long ago but after swimming lessons, the whole damn morning had been taken up with an unscheduled briefing. A Hauptmann named Kruger had flown in unexpectedly from Berlin with the fake intelligence they were to take to England. Nothing like waiting until the last minute, but apparently they wanted it to be the 'latest' and 'logical'. Actually, it sounded real enough to him. But it was a big pain. Not only did they have to be generally aware of the contents, but they had to know where they had supposedly gotten them. He barked a little laugh. What a waste of time that was. With this stuff...

He searched the drawers until he found the manila envelopes, various sizes, for holding finished prints. He took the smallest one and slid the filled tissue envelopes into it.

Fingerprints. My God. His fingerprints would be on the envelope if it were found, and all the tissue envelopes. He reached into his pocket for his handkerchief before he remembered the sodden mess in the wastebasket.

It took too long, far too long, but finally the envelopes were wiped clean with his shirttail, and carefully taped under the drawer in the corner, the one with the most in it. 1450. He'd have to move fast.

He reached for the envelope containing the practice negatives and ripped it from the clip it hung from on the overhead cabinets. He had torn it. For some reason it gave him considerable satisfaction, especially since the negatives were undamaged. There would have been hell to pay if they had been.

He put the first one on the enlarger and set the big timer for twenty-five minutes. After all, it wouldn't do to keep the Hauptmann waiting.

\*　　\*　　\*

Hans bent the neck of the lamp back into the usual position and snapped it off before putting each of the three 'American files' back into the appropriate envelope and fastening the clips. Whitehall would be more than interested in dropping all of this into Washington's lap. Too bad the landing sites weren't definite yet. There were five choices on the east coast of Florida and six on Long Island. At least that would narrow it down. The files would tell what the agents would be after. They were to develop ties with the German-American Bund, find agents among the members and use that group to put out Germany's point of view most forcefully. Then there were the convoys and their departure dates. Most important of all was the American aircraft industry. Both intelligence and sabotage. Yes indeed, Washington would be most interested and, hopefully, appropriately grateful.

Minten's insistence that morning, during the break in the briefing, that Hans talk to the agents-in-training to go to America that evening had given him the perfect excuse to get at the files. If anyone questioned his having them, he could always say that he needed to know where the agents were going and what they were expected to do so he could organize what he ought to be telling them, right? Wrong. Nothing he could tell them would be any help with that. His knowledge of the United States was strictly general, 'life and times in the U. S. of A.'

Ridiculous that he should have been able to get hold of this, that he could still get a hold of anything, really. The security clearance should have been lifted the minute they decided to send him to England, especially for anything including Sea Lion. The only thing he couldn't get hold of was the planning briefing for Russia, and he doubted that there was a copy in Hamburg. It was still the deepest of dark secrets and not really Hamburg's concern anyway.

Annaliese had been wonderful about canceling their afternoon together, saying that after Friday they'd have a lifetime of afternoons together. My God, he hoped so. She was with her aunt and uncle instead. How many years would it be before she had another Sunday afternoon with them, if ever? Damn the war, anyway.

He'd had to tell her he couldn't see her after that God-awful briefing. Kruger was bright, very bright, but why the hell couldn't Abwehr have sent someone besides the top security aide, someone who could talk intelligently without putting everyone to sleep? At least Kruger was leaving for Dunkirk tomorrow, to check on the security arrangements there, so they wouldn't have to listen to any more of his dreariness. Except for the session tonight. Kruger was to give a pep talk to the American agents. 'Pep' wasn't the word for it. A lassitude talk. At least it would be if he talked to them the way he'd talked this morning.

Damn. He still had to check out the new reconnaissance films. Brighton was the prime landing area at the moment and Minten wanted to report on how the defense had changed. They ought to be in the file room by now. Take them back to the School House, along with the old ones for comparison? At least he didn't need to photograph those. If he were given a roadmap in London, he could explain it all easily.

And thank goodness. He had only two and a half film cartridges left. The half roll still on the camera had made it more than worth the risk entailed in bringing it in from the School House. Actually, it hadn't been that much of a risk. He'd brought it in the locked dispatch case, and he'd take it back the same way. So unless he was stupid enough to let someone look into the case and then into the locked bottom drawer of the file cabinet where he kept the one assigned to him...

He locked the case and stuffed it into the knee hole of his desk, then picked up the American files and started towards the door. He was startled by a loud knock as he reached for the handle and was barely able to hold back a curse when he saw who it was. "Oh, Kramer. What can I do for you?"

"You were expecting Marlena Dietrich?" There was a nasty edge to Kramer's voice as well.

"She'd be infinitely preferable."

"I'm sure." Kramer glanced down at the film envelopes in Hans' hand. "Taking them back, I see."

"Oh. Yes. Why?" He hadn't wanted Kramer, of all people, to know that he had them.

"The girl in the file room told me that you had them. I'm to put them on Major Minten's desk so Kugelmann can pick them up for him. I'd have taken them myself, but I have an appointment."

What was wrong with Kramer? He was fairly babbling.

"And just what are you doing with these files anyway?" In one way it had been a godsend that Richter had them. It was the perfect excuse to come to his office, but since these files were to have been part of the bait, they would have to think of something else.

"I'm talking to the American group tonight."

"Oh?" Kramer was looking at him with considerable amusement. "So you need to know what they are up to?"

"Exactly," Hans said drily.

Kramer saw the expression and burst out laughing. It didn't matter what Richter had been doing with those files. Nothing mattered anymore. It would all be over for the 'golden boy' Hauptmann, and within minutes.

Hans stared at him in disbelief as he handed over the files. Kramer took them and turned away without a word, hoping that Minten had been able to get into the building by now. He hadn't an excuse to stay any longer.

He was surprised to see Hans follow him out and turn to lock the door. "Where are you going?" He tried not to sound as frantic as he felt. Richter couldn't leave the building, not now!

"Down to the file room. I have to sign those files out to Minten if he's to have them, and I need to pick up some other stuff for a report that he wants me to do." Why did Kramer care and why was he telling him? Nervous? The camera... Thank God he had to lock the door when he left, even for a few minutes.

Kramer's brain had gone into high gear. That should be all right. Minten was coming in the back way. But he had to say something. "Why not send down for them?"

"It's Sunday!"

"Oh... yes... right." Kramer cursed himself for acting the fool. Of course it was Sunday. And it took ages to get files on Sunday. "I won't keep you." He turned and walked down the hall towards his and Minten's office, and once he turned the corner, he all but ran, bursting into the outer office to find Kugelmann standing there, staring at him, clearly startled. "Where's Major Minten?"

"In his office." Where else, you idiot?

"Why aren't you over at the gym, calling?" said Kramer.

"I was just about to leave."

"You weren't supposed to come in."

"I wanted to put my briefcase, with its contents," he emphasized every word, "under my desk."

"But you weren't supposed to come in!" Kramer repeated it, angry now.

"I'm so sorry that I inadvertently took the briefcase with me. But it's not time to call yet, anyway." Kugelmann was annoyed. It was 1502. Kramer ought to get his time straight.

"Now you have to wait."

"Why?"

"Richter just went down to the file room."

"Then isn't it lucky that I did come in? You couldn't have told me, otherwise."

Kramer flushed. Kugelmann was right, of course. But it wasn't so much what he said as how he said it. Rank insubordination, that's what it was. But there was no sense upsetting things any further. Not now. Not when victory was so close. "You'd better go, Kugelmann," he snapped. "It may take time to make arrangements, especially if someone else is using the phone. And go out the back way."

Did Kramer think he was stupid? "What time is it you want me to call now?"

"In ten minutes." He checked his watch. "1515."

Kugelmann's eyebrows shot up. "Ten minutes to get files out of the file room on Sunday?"

My God, was there no limit? "Ten minutes!" His heart was pounding. It had to work. And Kugelmann had damn well better not foul it up. The plan was perfect. Why was he standing there? "Go! The back way! Run!" His voice had risen to a shriek.

Kugelmann got out, not bothering to shut the door after himself.

Kramer galvanized himself, slammed the door to the hall, and fairly flew into Minten's office.

The major turned from the safe where he was standing. "Don't you ever knock?" Minten was furious. He had hastily shoved the envelope containing Schroeder's papers back into the safe, under everything, cursing the fact that there had been no time to hide it somewhere else, anywhere else where Kramer couldn't look. Part of Kramer's idiotic plan involved leaving the safe unlocked and that wouldn't do, not with Schroeder's papers in there. True, they were in a plain buff-colored envelope now, but still, it wouldn't do.

Kramer just stood there, looking at the disgruntled major and then he started to laugh, quietly at first, and then so hard that there were tears streaming down his face.

"Get a hold of yourself, man!" Minten was furious.

Kramer spoke in bursts as he struggled to contain his laughter. "Here we are... about to find the leak... that has had Berlin frantic for weeks... And Kruger, the one who told us about it," Kramer collected himself, "Kruger is here to see us pull Berlin's fat out of the fire. And all you can worry about is whether or not I knock at your office door?"

Minten glared at him without speaking.

Kramer slapped the American files onto the desk. "You'd better get another set of files out. I got these from him so there's no temptation there. It will have to be something else, something really good."

Minten turned back to the safe and riffled through the files, careful to keep the buff-colored envelope covered. "Here. The perfect one."

"Which?"

"Kruger brought it with him. The plans for the occupation of England."

"That should interest him."

"If he is what you think he is."

Kramer ignored the sarcasm in the major's voice. "Actually even if he's not. After all, his mother lives there, and his brother, to say nothing of that precious godfather of his. He'll want to know what's in store for them."

Minten nodded vaguely as he shut the door to the safe, aware of Kramer's eyes on him. He had hoped to lock the safe after all, without Kramer noticing, but apparently there was no chance of that. It should be all right. Richter would be alone in the office for only a few minutes. Besides it wasn't Richter who was the snoop. "Let's get out of here." He came out from behind the desk. "All I want is for this farce to be over. I need to meet with Kruger." Because Minten was keeping his eyes on Kramer, he bumped into the heavy leather-covered wing chair in front of his desk. He stopped and swore.

Kramer was standing by the door. "What are you waiting for?"

Insolent shithead. Minten sailed past him and out the door as Kramer glanced back, making a final check. Everything looked as it should. "The safe is unlocked?"

"Of course it's unlocked! God Almighty, Kramer!" Minten was agitated. He had to get out of this without that safe being opened. "If you want to have any trap left to spring, we had better get into your office, now!"

They went. Kramer opened his office door and allowed Minten to precede him through, after which he locked it carefully behind them.

Minten squeezed himself into the only chair in the office other than the one behind the desk, wondering why the hell his was the only office with chairs that were large enough. He mopped his brow with a none-too-clean handkerchief, bitterly regretting giving in to Kramer over this. Why had he? Kramer had to be kept calm, unsuspecting, that's why. But this... did he have the faint suspicion the Kramer could be right? Ridiculous.

"Is your gun loaded?"

Minten looked up, angered by the imperious tone, as Kramer sat down behind his desk and pulled out the bottom drawer. But he forgot his anger as he saw Kramer put a Luger on the desk. "Going to do battle?" The sarcasm was inescapable.

"Trying not to. I want him all in one piece. Is that fancy pearl-handled piece of yours loaded?"

Minten glared at him and nodded slowly. The pearl-handled revolver he had acquired on the beach at Dunkirk was the pride of his life. He'd had to have a special holster made for it.

"Then you had better unsnap the holster cover."

"Kramer," Minten was spluttering, "this is quite intolerable. Your gun should be more than enough."

"Not just mine, Herr Major." There was a sly smile playing across Kramer's face. "Mine, yours, and the one I've given Corporal Kugelmann. Not that he's worth counting. That Kugelmann of yours is a real weak sister."

Minten's face turned a deep purple. Kramer was not the least bit intimidated

"I said, unsnap the cover."

Minten felt a cold chill running along his spine as slowly, reluctantly, he unsnapped the holster cover. "Kugelmann hates guns, you know. Especially pistols. It's foolish to involve him."

"He'll do what I tell him to do." That deadly quiet quality was still there. "He knows what will happen if he doesn't."

"And just what will happen if he doesn't?" Minten was trying to sneer.

Kramer just looked at him and what Minten saw in his face made him very glad that his holster flap was unsnapped.

*     *     *

The timer rang itself all the way down before Dieter looked up. He stood there, staring at it for a moment before he put down the tongs and looked at his watch. 1515. At least he had just pulled the last print out of the hypo and was putting it on the wash line when the damn thing went off.

He put the practice negatives back into the envelope, folded it over where it had been torn, and fastened it with a clip. The pictures looked all right, but Rausch was fussy. Too bad he didn't have more time.

The funnels were already in the bottles, and he was careful to put the developer and the hypo into the right ones. Fussy details.

Were they fussy about things in England? England. He gave a short bitter laugh. If he ever got to England. And if he did, Richter would probably arrange for a proper darkroom for him, right inside British intelligence headquarters. Oh, God.

He rinsed the pans and looked around. Everything was in order. Chemicals replaced. The darkroom looked just as it had when he'd come in. He slid the drawer in and out experimentally. Fine. Everything was fine. That was rich. Nothing was fine. Nothing would ever be fine again.

He hooked back the black curtain, then unlocked the door before switching off the lights. It was impossible to know what he would do when he saw Richter, and he wasn't anxious to find out. So he didn't hurry as he shut the door after himself and started down the hall.

*       *       *

Hans was sitting tipped back in his chair, hands clasped behind his neck. He stretched. It had been a long, hot day and all he wanted was time to sit under a tree in the garden and relax with a cold beer before dinner. What time was dinner? Minten hadn't said.

He leaned forward and pulled the dispatch case out of the knee hole, unlocked it and put in the reconnaissance photos, old and new, along with a few quick notes he made, carefully holding the camera to one side.

The phone rang. What now? Dieter was due at any moment, and he wanted to get out of here. He snapped the lock shut and picked up the receiver. "Hauptmann Richter."

"Herr Hauptmann." The man was speaking quickly and he sounded a little nervous. "This is Corporal Kugelmann."

Grand. Just grand. "Yes, Kugelmann?"

"Major Minten left in such a hurry after the briefing that he forgot he needed the American files for this evening. I had planned to pick them up myself but the major has something else for me to do. He suggested I call you to see if you'd be willing to bring them along to the School House when you come. He'd also like you to be there by 1615, if possible, so that he can go over the agenda with you."

Agenda! Minten had told him was going to be an informal dinner! Visions of beer and trees vanished like the dreams they were. It was already almost 1525. "Where are they?"

"In his office on the desk."

Right. Kramer had said something about leaving them there for Kugelmann to pick up.

"Herr Hauptmann! Are you there?" His voice was anxious.

"Sorry. Sleepy, I guess."

"I'd hoped to have a nap this afternoon, myself."

His peevish tone made Hans smile. "After the war, Kugelmann."

"Then I hope it's over soon."

"Amen!" And Hans had a thought. "How will I get into the major's office?"

"I caught Lieutenant Kramer just as he was leaving and asked him to bring them down to you, but he said he was in a hurry and had to go out the back way so he didn't have time. I'm afraid he simply left the office unlocked for you, which means" – Kugelmann coughed delicately – "that you'll have to get them right away, if you don't mind."

Just like Kramer. But to have to go to Minten's office? Minten's unlocked office? He remembered all too well the last time he had been alone in Minten's unlocked office. Kramer had come barging in with a lot of nasty insinuations. The fact that they happened to be true was beside the point. But there seemed to be nothing else for it. He couldn't very well refuse. "All right, then."

"Thank you, sir. That will be a great help."

"No trouble. Lieutenant Bergmann will be meeting me here in a few minutes and we plan to go straight back, anyway."

"Even so, thank you, Herr Hauptmann."

"You're welcome."

Kugelmann hung up the phone, thinking as he did that it was too bad that Kramer had such a bee in his bonnet about Richter. Richter was a good sort, the type of man Kramer would never understand. Richter never pulled rank or tried to make anyone feel stupid. Then he laughed to himself. He couldn't afford to think that way about anyone, not these days.

And he'd better get going or Kramer would have a fit. Kramer would have a fit anyway. But it wasn't his fault that the damn phone had been tied up for five minutes after he got there. An oberst... He sighed and opened the office door, a cold chill running down his spine at the thought of the pistol waiting for him.

*       *       *

Hans reached for a piece of paper and scribbled, "In Minten's office picking up files. Have dispatch case. Be right back.

He left the note propped up against the gooseneck lamp where Bergmann would see it the minute he walked in. As he picked up the dispatch case, he caught sight of the machine pistol standing in the corner. That was overkill if anything ever was. No one even looking at Bergmann would want to tangle with him, machine pistol or no. In fact when he had first seen Bergmann, he hadn't relished the prospect of having such a tough-looking customer around. Funny how rarely he thought of that anymore. Still, it was an odd face for a doctor. That is if he ever got to be one.

Sobered, Hans walked out the door, careful to leave it unlocked. Dieter would be right up, and with the dispatch case gone and the file cabinet locked, it should be safe enough for the moment.

*       *       *

As he came across the entryway, Dieter saw Hans walking away down the hall. Where was he going and why the dispatch case?

He walked on slowly, nodding briefly to each of the guards as he watched Hans turn the corner. Minten's office? Probably. Anyway, he'd be back soon enough or he'd have called down to the darkroom and left a message. Dieter found the note on Hans' desk and settled down to wait, not at all happy about it. Gave too much time to think. He wasn't anxious to face Richter, but he was even less anxious to think about facing him.

Hans walked into Minten's outer office, Kugelmann's domain, and looked around. The door to Kramer's office was shut and everything was quiet. Just as it should be. Then why did he feel uneasy? Principles, probably. This office was enough to give anyone the creeps. Minten, Kramer, and Kugelmann. Now that was a three-horse parlay if there ever was one. Actually, Kugelmann wasn't so bad, once you get to know him. Then he thought of Dieter's experience and grinned, deciding that it must depend on how Kugelmann felt about you.

He turned the knob and the door to Major Minten's office eased open noiselessly. My God, Minten had left the safe uncovered. But Kramer had been in here since then, and he would've locked it even if Minten had neglected to. Hans was not at all anxious to be in Minten's office with an open safe. Once had been more than enough, and so close to the end...

He unlocked the dispatch case and put in the files. Only then did he notice the other file at the far corner of the large desk. He stared at the number, reading it upside down. There wasn't a code name on it yet, so it had to be new. But the number made it part of the British series. Could Minten want that, as well? After all, it was on the desk. He really should check it, shouldn't he?

He was smiling as he pulled the file from the manila envelope but it died as he skimmed the front page. Plans for the occupation of the British Isles. He turned to the next page and one line leapt out at him, striking him like a physical blow. 'All able-bodied males between the ages of eighteen and forty will be evacuated to the

European continent to be used as part of the labor force of the Third Reich.' It put him into a fury. They were planning to enslave the bulk of male Britons!

'Britons never, never, never will be slaves.' That line from *Rule Britannia* roared through his brain like an express train, over and over, and almost before he knew what he was doing, he had walked to the other side of the desk, turned on the lamp, slid out the first few pages, and grabbed the camera from the bottom of the dispatch case. Two minutes. It was all he'd need. He couldn't get it all but he could finish the roll. Just that one sentence was more than enough. He raised the camera and focused carefully.

*       *       *

Minten tried to shift in the chair. "What's keeping him?" It was a harsh whisper. They had been in there for hours.

Kramer consulted his watch, trying to look casual. Damn. Richter should have been here five minutes ago, at least. If Kugelmann had fucked it up...

"And what's keeping Kugelmann?" Minten's voice was slightly louder this time.

Kramer moved next to him so he could whisper in Minten's ear. "Keep your voice down, for God's sake. Do you want to ruin everything?!" Damn Richter. Damn Kugelmann. "I told him not to show himself until he knew we were in your office." Couldn't the idiot remember anything?

"How will he know?" Ass. Richter would undoubtedly shut the door to the hall. "I thought you wanted the whole arsenal in at the same
time. Got your courage up, have you?"

Kramer flushed and opened his mouth but just then there was the sound of the door opening. They both froze and stayed in strained silence, listening to the footsteps crossing the outer office. A pause and then footsteps again. The door to Major Minten's office had to be opening and then... Silence.

After what seemed like an eternity, when Minten could stand it no longer, he said, "Let's get this farce over with or he'll be long gone." The words came out as a croak.

Kramer snapped himself erect and glared at Minten briefly before beckoning imperiously with his pistol and tiptoeing toward the door. Minten struggled out of the chair and tiptoed after him. Kramer made the mistake of glancing back at him and it was all he could do not to laugh.

He slid the bolt back carefully. Not a sound. Then he began on the doorknob, willing not to make a fatal click. It didn't and the door swung open noiselessly on well-oiled hinges. He moved quickly across the outer office and through the door into Minten's office. What he saw filled him with fierce joy.

Hans was poised over the open file, snapping the last picture on the roll. He looked up, the camera in midair. It was a moment before he lowered it without saying a word.

It was with great satisfaction that Kramer heard Minten's wounded roar, almost in his ear. "God dammit all to hell. The bastard was right!"

Dieter stood and looked around. He was damned if he was going to wait any longer. Richter had the dispatch case. They could leave straight from Minten's office.

He grabbed the machine pistol and slung it over his shoulder, hating it suddenly, remembering Richter with it in his hands, using it to such good effect in Boulogne. He felt like throwing it out the window but instead he went through the office door and made sure it was locked behind him. That almost made him laugh. He was locking the barn door after the horse was stolen, in spades.

As he rounded the corner, he saw Kugelmann push open the door to Minten's office and go in. He swore under his breath. Kugelmann was the last thing he needed right now. So he stopped just short of the door that Kugelmann had left open and peered around the jamb just in time to see the corporal, Luger in hand, rush into Minten's office. Startled, he pulled back. Richter was in there and Kugelmann hated guns. What the hell...!

He peered in again. Minten's office door was open as well and he could see Kramer's back. Kramer? A real convention. He didn't like it. Kramer in there and Kugelmann with a gun...

And, my God, Minten. What the hell...? The major was almost shouting, his voice so strident that no one heard Dieter as he crossed the outer office and slammed himself against the wall to the right of the door, out of the line of sight.

"Get him out of here!" Minten sounded vicious. "I can't stand the sight of him!"

"With pleasure, Herr Major." Dieter grimaced at the jubilation in Kramer's voice. Had Richter really been taking more God damn pictures and been caught dead to rights? Jesus. Served him right if he had.

"Get going, Richter." Kramer again.

Dieter's reaction was immediate and almost without volition. "Herr Hauptmann?" He stepped into the doorway, holding the machine pistol easily in his hand. The safety was off. "I... Oh... Excuse me. I got your note." His eyes took in the scene. Richter was behind the desk opposite the doorway. He'd been hidden by Kramer's back. Kramer had moved left, startled by Dieter's arrival, but the pistol leveled at Hans didn't waiver. Minten was just to the right of the desk, his pistol in his right hand, and Kugelmann was close behind him, pistol held in a gingerly fashion also in his right hand. It was pointed at nothing in particular, and he looked very uncomfortable.

Dieter was cradling the machine pistol now, as if it were heavy, his finger loose on the trigger, the barrel pointed in Kramer's general direction. Kramer was the most formidable of the three by far. Would he shoot Kramer? Could he? He didn't know. And anyway, why should he? Richter... Then a vision of his father's face flashed before him, as if he were trying to tell him something, but Dieter pushed that aside, making himself concentrate instead on the room and everything in it.

Kramer recovered first. "Well, well, Bergmann." The pistol still hadn't wavered. "Just in time to help haul your precious Hauptmann off to the pokey. Be glad they're not doing this for you, and in England. That's what would've happened, you know."

Dieter was careful not to look at Hans. "Quite an arsenal for taking in just one man."

"We weren't taking any chances." Kramer was sneering now, confident.

"What's he supposed to have done?"

"He's a spy." Minten spat out the words as he lowered his pistol. "We have a great fucking bastard of a spy on our hands." He laughed bitterly. "We caught him red-handed. I really do hate having to admit you were right, Kramer."

Kramer snickered. "That I can believe." Nothing could destroy this moment for him. "Move, Richter." He waved the pistol imperiously. "Let's get this over with."

Hans just stood there, a little smile flickered across his mouth from time to time. Dieter was watching him closely now, deadly calm, waiting. Waiting for what? A denial? His lip twitched. Caught red-handed. Twice today the Hauptmann had been caught red-handed. No. There could be no denial. Not this time.

"I said, MOVE!" Kramer was the picture of menace now. "And you damn well better move because there's nothing I'd like better than to shoot you right here, right now." His smile was sardonic. "That is, unless it's watching you hang." He considered that briefly. "In fact, I'll make sure I'm there."

"Hanging and assaulting women. Two of your favorite entertainments." That odd smile was still coming and going, but Hans' eyes were flashing dangerously.

"Ah, yes. The lovely Fräulein Scheuermann. So you heard about that. I'm surprised. But I'm not surprised that you didn't do anything about it." Kramer's lip curled into a sneer. "She was asking for it. But she'll have to be even more... ah... amenable now that she won't have you around to look after her interests."

"But she'll have me," Dieter snarled.

Kramer turned, staring in surprise, and for a moment all eyes were on Bergmann as he stood just inside the doorway.

The moment was long enough. Hans tore the pistol from Minten's unresisting hand. He swept it around and fired at Kramer before crouching low, below the level of heavy oak desk to point the pistol at Kugelmann. Hans' bullet had grazed Kramer's shoulder as his finger tightened on the trigger, making his arm jerk, throwing off his aim. The bullet caught Minten in the neck just as he lunged for his pistol. He fell toward Hans like a stone, blood spurting in an intermittent fountain from a hole just above his collar.

But Kramer saw none of this because he had dived behind the heavy leather-covered wing chair off the front left corner of the desk. Neither did Dieter who had leapt back through the doorway into the outer office.

Hans had to fall backward and to one side to avoid being pinned down by Minten's falling bulk, and now he struggled back to his knees, shoving the desk chair on its rollers, back into the corner. Watch Kugelmann. Watch Kugelmann. Where's Kramer?

Then blessed detachment descended over him as it sometimes did in battle. He welcomed it as he watched himself, up on one knee, just beyond the length of Minten's outstretched body, with his head still below the level of his desk, the pistol pointed at Kugelmann. The little man was hysterical, screaming obscenities as he began firing wildly in all directions until bullets from two pistols slammed into him at the same time.

Dieter risked a quick look around the doorjamb just as Kramer came out from behind the chair in a crouch, heading for the desk.

Without realizing he had moved, he found that the machine pistol was chattering, jumping slightly in his hands. He saw the armchair disintegrate and what was left of Kramer slam into the bookcase. Even then he couldn't seem to stop. His finger was still hard on the trigger when the weapon finally clicked empty. He threw it to the floor and stood there, chest heaving. Jesus. Oh, holy Jesus.

"Bergmann?" The voice was cautious.

"Yes?" It was an angry hiss.

Hans rose slowly from behind the desk, pistol still in hand.

"Kramer?"

"He's dead."

Dieter looked as angry as he sounded. Hans was grateful that the machine pistol was empty and on the floor.

There were footsteps pounding down the hall. They both turned as an armed guard, who had obviously flattened himself against the wall in the outer office, peered around the doorjamb, rifle at the ready.

Hans was careful to keep his right hand down inside, the pistol below the level of the desktop.

"What the hell is going on here?" The voice was gruff and a little fearful, and the face had disappeared.

"Three men have been shot. We need a doctor and an ambulance at once." Hans snapped it out as a command.

The guard reappeared, all of him this time, and he stood looking around, slack-jawed.

"Move!"

"But what...?"

"They're dying."

The guard moved, his footsteps pounding back down the hall. He was shouting as he went. Hans was grateful that it hadn't occurred to him to use the phone in the outer office.

But he had to work fast. Seconds counted. "Dieter, check the major and Kugelmann. If there's anything to be done..." His mouth tightened. They had to die. Pray God they already had.

He grabbed the camera from the desk and knelt by Kramer's body.

Dieter leaned over the major. There was no blood flowing from the wound in his neck. A bad sign. No pulse either. Minten was done for.

Kugelmann was lying half on his side. Dieter sucked in a long breath. There was a faint flutter of the eyelids and a pulse visible at the carotid. It was something short of a miracle that he was still alive, but it wouldn't last. Not with the wound like that. The bullet had gone through the right side of his forehead and torn away part of the top of his head as it came out. It was Richter's bullet because of the upward slant. And there was another hole in his gut. Kramer's. The pulse in his neck was weaker now and even as Dieter knelt beside him, it stopped altogether. He put his fingertips on the spot to make sure that there was nothing. Nothing.

Three men were dead. None of them worth mourning, not even Kugelmann who was relatively harmless, but still ... they were dead.

He stood, and looked over at Richter and gave a bitter little laugh. And then he moved toward the door, his eyes never leaving Hans, even as he lowered himself to the floor where he sat, leaning on the wall, watching.

Hans had wasted no time. Kramer was dead. There was no doubt about it. And he was lying on his back which made things easier. As he knelt there, trying to avoid the blood that seemed to be everywhere, he pulled out his handkerchief and wiped the camera clean, thanking God it was the one from the School House, the one he had stolen from the supply room.

Then, fighting down the bile that was rising in his throat, he held the camera with the handkerchief and placed the fingers of Kramer's right hand on it in what he hoped was the proper position. Then, still holding the camera with the handkerchief, he rose, gingerly stepped over the body and did the same thing with Kramer's left hand before pushing it into the left trouser pocket.

"So he's going to be a fall guy."

Hans looked over at Dieter briefly as he stood and dug into his pockets for the film cartridges. "Any other suggestions for getting us out of this in one piece?"

"No."

"How are..." He waved toward Minten and Kugelmann, then started wiping off the film cartridges.

"Dead."

He nodded and knelt, pushing the cartridges into Kramer's right hand trouser pocket. Too bad about the film but there was nothing else for it. At least he had the sense of what was on it.

"What's the story to be?" Dieter sounded inexpressibly weary.

Hans listened carefully. No footsteps in the hall. He moved towards the safe. Stupid. There should've been hordes of guards pounding down the hall by now. The handkerchief was still in his hand. He tested the door to the safe. It was open. Plenty of bait in the trap.

"The exact truth, for the most part. That I came to get the files for Minten after Kugelmann called and asked me to. But instead of me... I found Kramer here taking pictures of them. He got the drop on me since I don't carry a gun, and Minten and Kugelmann came barreling in. They'd set a trap, the two of them, thinking they catch me. Didn't tell anyone... Afraid of a scandal? But they got Kramer instead, and he turned the tables on them."

He was riffling through the files with the barrel of the gun he picked back up from the desk.

"Kramer was trying to set me up, make me his fall guy. He'd laid the groundwork carefully... Look, I'll take care of that part. You came down here looking for me – I did leave a note for you – and walked in without realizing what was going on. It distracted Kramer enough so that Minten could go for his gun and Kramer shot him. I got Minten's gun when he fell. Except for those details, tell the truth. Tell the truth unless you absolutely have to lie and then make the lies as close to the truth as you can. It's the easiest way to remember..." What's this? He had lifted the whole pile and saw a buff-colored envelope lying on the bottom of the safe. He took it out.

"You do lie very well, Herr Hauptmann."

Hans stopped. The contents of the envelope were in his hand. "Would you rather I didn't?" Dieter shook his head slowly, his face a mask.

"Not at this point."

Then he saw that Hans was transfixed, staring at the papers in his hand. His curiosity got the better of them. "What is it?"

"What Kramer had on Schroeder. It has to be. But how the hell did it get here?"

As Dieter shrugged, they both heard the sound of feet running down the hall. Hans shut the safe and twisted the dial to lock it.

Fortunately the handkerchief was still in his hand. Where to put the papers? He looked around wildly.

"Your boot."

Hans nodded gratefully and stuffed the sheets down his boot just as two men rushed into the office. Fortunately he was partially hidden by the desk and they saw only a figure, apparently leaning over the prostrate form of what had to be an officer, judging from the boots. Hans came to a standing position slowly. It was the same man back again along with the Sergeant of the Guard, Braun. That must've been what took so long. He had waited for Braun. Heads would roll over that.

"There's an ambulance and a doctor on the way." Braun was breathless. Then he saw Kramer in his jaw went slack. "Who...?"

"Major Minten, Lieutenant Kramer, and Corporal Kugelmann. And I'm afraid that an ambulance won't help now. They're all dead." Dieter's voice was curiously flat.

Braun paled visibly. "What happened?"

"That's what I'd like to know." They all turned at the sound of a deep voice from the doorway. It was the Hauptmann in charge of security. Goebel. The guard snapped to attention.

"As you are, and then. Now what is all of this." He looked around briefly. "God!" Then "Who?"

It was Hans who repeated it this time.

It was a sharp intake of breath as Goebel checked for himself. My God, the shit was going to hit the fan over this. It had to happen on a Sunday when there were so few people around and he was across the street in his rooms, sleeping. At least he had had enough sense to stay dressed. He looked at the two guards ominously. "Have you touched anything?"

"No, sir." The men answer almost in unison.

"You, Richter? Bergmann?"

"We just checked the..." Hans gestured helplessly.

Goebel nodded, then turned to Dieter. "Lieutenant Bergmann,

would you mind going to my office with Private Felzer? I'd like to talk with Hauptmann Richter here first. I'll come up when I'm finished."

"Certainly, sir." Dieter rose. Hans caught his eye briefly as he turned to leave but could read nothing in his expression. Private Felzer followed him out.

"And wait there with him, Felzer," Goebel bellowed after them, "until I come, or someone comes to relieve you."

Felzer's face re-appeared in the doorway. "Yes, sir."

Then the Hauptmann turned back to Hans. "Now. Into the outer office. No one comes in here, no one touches anything until after the ambulance has been here, the doctor," he amended. "Not that it will do any good." He looked away with anguished distaste. "But the forms have to be preserved."

Hans moved past him and through the doorway gratefully and stood, looking around, seeing nothing. Though his knees were shaking, somehow he couldn't seem to make himself sit down. Ready to run? He would have laughed if it weren't so ludicrous. Where to go and how to get there?

"Braun. Shut the door. Find some paper and take notes," Goebel was saying as he picked up the phone and asked for his office. "An ambulance is coming," he barked into it. "The minute it leaves, I want a photographer up here. And meantime, get a hold of Bodenbender tell him to get his ass over here." A pause. "No, I don't know where the hell he is and I don't care. Just find him and get him over here. Tell him we'll need the fingerprint kit and everything else he can find." Another pause. "Three men shot. ... Yes. ... For God sake get some more men in here. Two at least. One posted outside the door to Major Minten's office and the other outside the door to mine. Stay there yourself if you can't find anyone else. Feltzer is coming up there in a minute, bringing Lieutenant Bergmann with him. They are to stay in my office until I get there. ... Without talking to anyone. But send down for coffee or anything else Bergmann needs. Right. Yes."

The voice turned testy. "I won't forget about calling the commandant." With that he slammed down the phone. "Damn old maid," he muttered and there was a snicker, quickly suppressed, from Braun.

"Now," Goebel asked briskly, rubbing his hands together nervously as he looked around. "What happened?" He slid into Kugelmann's desk chair and gestured for Braun to pull another up to the end of the small desk.

Hans looked back at him and took a deep breath. No one had suggested he sit down and suddenly he badly needed to. "Corporal Kugelmann," he began slowly. "He called me about 1520 and asked me to pick up some files from Major Minten's desk. Apparently, he needed them for a meeting at the School House. I had checked them out myself earlier, but Lieutenant Kramer had come and collected them, saying he was to leave them on the major's desk for Kugelmann to pick up."

He stopped. He was sweating and his knees were shaking. "Look, I'm not doing this very well. Do you mind if I sit down?"

Goebel looked at him closely. He had seen the same signs in Poland. Men would go to battle and do superbly well, only to collapse once it was safe to do so. Richter had gone chalk white. "By all means. I should've thought of it myself. It's just that…" He gestured towards the four chairs that line the longest wall.

Hans sank gratefully onto the nearest one. He was shaking all over now. Steady. Steady. This isn't time for you to lose your head. He took some deep breaths.

"Are you all right?" Goebel was looking at him anxiously. "Some brandy?"

The thought made him gag. He shook his head. "Where was I?"

"Lieutenant Kramer had come to collect some files from you, files that you had checked out, to put on Major Minten's desk for Corporal Kugelmann to pick up?" Confusing, but that seemed to be the gist of it. He glanced at Braun who gave a faint nod of agreement, and then bent his head to the pad of paper again.

"I gave Kramer the files and he left. Then I went down to the file room to sign those files over to the major" – and thank God he had – "and pick up some other papers I needed."

Braun was scribbling furiously, the stub of a much-chewed pencil dwarfed by his ham-fisted hand.

Hans went on, telling exactly what happened, Kugelmann's call, the unlocked office, which raised not only Goebel's eyebrows but his hackles. Still, there was little he could say. It was Major Minten, and the good major was dead so there was little that could or would be done. But still... Appalling from a security standpoint.

"I took the dispatch case with me," Hans was saying wearily, "and went right down to pick up the files."

Goebel saw in his mind's eye what he hadn't even realized he'd noticed, a dispatch case just visible on the floor beside the desk, files spilling out.

"When I got there, I found Kramer behind Major Minten's desk taking pictures of some files he had spread out there. One of those miniature cameras..." Had the timbre of his voice changed? He made himself pause, rubbed the back of his neck, and look around. They were both sitting there, frozen, waiting.

"He was so engrossed in what he was doing that he didn't hear me open the door. But I wasn't carrying a weapon and before I could do anything, he picked up a pistol he had sitting on the desk. It was then that Major Minten and Corporal Kugelmann came barging in."

The thought came. Goebel sat forward, eyes mere slits of steel, voice hard. "What the hell were they doing here? They'd sent you to get the files for them, for God sake!" It was odd, very odd indeed and he didn't like the sound of any of it, not in the least.

"Because there is an information leak somewhere in Abwehr and I think they thought it might be me." Hans paused. The silence was electric. "It had to have been a trap to see if it was, apparently without telling Lieutenant Kramer, since he was the one who fell into it. The lieutenant and I have never gotten along." It was hard not to refer to Kramer in the present tense. He had been omnipresent for so long. "I think Kramer had picked me to be a fall guy."

"Fall guy?"

"I mean that he was getting worried. They were probably close on his trail and he decided that I would be a good one to take the blame for him, since my mother lives in London and my brother is in the Royal Navy."

Goebel nodded slowly. He had heard that rumor, so it was true. My God.

"Anyway, Kramer knew he was caught and because he had a gun on me, he had the drop on them, as well, even though Corporal Kugelmann had a pistol in his hand. The corporal hates guns." Present tense again. Hans saw Braun nod his head in agreement as he wrote.

"Lieutenant Kramer came out from behind the desk and had us all move away from the door. I managed to get behind the desk. Major Minten and Corporal Kugelmann were to the right of it, where they are now.

"Then Bergmann came looking for me – I'd left a note telling him where I was and that I had the dispatch case. He probably had the machine pistol with him so we could leave straight from here – anyway, when he came in, Kramer was surprised and made the mistake of looking around at him. I was able to drop behind the desk. The major went for his gun, and Kramer shot him just as he got it out. He nearly fell on top of me and I managed to get ahold of his pistol. After that, it's not too clear what happened. All I know is that Corporal Kugelmann went berserk and started shooting wildly. I had to shoot him when the gun pointed in my direction, but Kramer must've got a shot off at him, too, because I heard a single shot before the machine pistol went off. After that, it was all over."

"If that's so… Where's the camera?" Goebel's voice was a mere rasp.

Hans' reply was calm, even. "He stuffed it into his pocket."

Goebel turned to Braun. "Check his pockets, but don't get your paws all over it."

He nodded and rose. "Yes, Herr Hauptmann."

Goebel went to the door and watched him in silence.

"There's something in his right pocket, sir!" Braun was excited now. He held up one of the film cartridges. "And there are more."

"Leave them."

Braun hurriedly stuffed the cartridge back into Kramer's pocket and moved to the other side of the body. "I think this is it, sir. It's small, steel..."

"Don't touch it!"

The sergeant pulled his hand back as if he had been burned.

There was a scuffling in the hall. "Keep those damn stretcher bearers out, Richter, if that's who it is." Goebel growled, eyeing Braun as he rose carefully and all but tiptoed away from the body towards the outer office. Only then did he back Hans up by placing his bulk squarely in the doorway.

The white-coated doctor stopped, looking at Hans briefly before squeezing by Goebel, who turned and indicated the way into Minten's office, then turned back and glared at the stretcher bearers who were standing in the hall, each leaning on their respective still-rolled up stretchers as if they were shepherd staffs. Either they didn't notice the look or they didn't care, because they looked both bored and tired.

It was at that moment that two more guards arrived. Goebel ordered one to stay with the stretcher bearers and take them off when the doctor was finished. The second man was simply to stay by the door and keep everyone out. Then he gestured Hans back into the office angrily.

The doctor was just standing, his stethoscope loose in his hand. "What the hell war were you fighting in here?"

"All dead?" Goebel asked gruffly.

"All dead," the doctor said, shaking his head as he looked down at Kramer again.

"And if they'd been alive," said Goebel, angry suddenly, "they'd still have been dead by the time you got here! Where the hell were you?"

The doctor looked annoyed. "I could have been here when they were shot and nothing would've changed." He gestured towards Kramer, then pointed at Kugelmann.

"Half his brain was destroyed almost at once, and the major

there was shot through the carotid. He bled to death immediately."

He stuffed the stethoscope into his pocket. "This has been one hell of a busy day, and I've been out on emergency calls, one after the other, since about six this morning." He was glaring at Goebel. "I still haven't had breakfast and it's well past lunch." He started out and stopped again. "You'd better look after that one." He jerked a forefinger at Hans. "He's pale as a ghost. Incipient shock, I'd say."

Then to Hans. "Are you all right?"

Hans nodded.

"For God's sake, sit down at least before you fall down." Then back to Goebel again, still angry. "I don't know what went on in here and I bloody well know not to ask. And you better know that I have brains enough not to talk about it either unless I'm asked at an official inquiry. And," –- he went on before Goebel could say anything – I shall see myself out, thank you."

With that he was gone.

Goebel wiped his forehead with his handkerchief. Thank God for a sensible doctor. He had to keep this under wraps until he could get to the bottom of it, and beyond that, until the official story could be decided upon because – his heart sank – he had the feeling that no matter what the truth was, the truth was the last thing that the powers-that-be would want known.

A peculiar business. A very peculiar business indeed. He stuffed the handkerchief back into his pocket. Richter seemed to be telling the truth and he hadn't tried to run. He could have. Not that he would've gotten far. The exits were sealed at once, the minute the shots were heard, thank God. Braun had done that much right, at least. Still, if they had run and been caught, all this would have been far less complicated. As it was... Who the hell knew who was telling the truth or would tell the truth about anything?

And now that the doctor had come and gone... Shit. He'd forgotten to get his name. That meant a trip over to the hospital to find him. He couldn't very well ring up and ask for the doctor who had come over to military HQ just now. The less said about this whole mess, the better. Would he really keep his mouth shut? Probably not entirely. Who would? And there were the fool stretcher bearers. How much had they seen? Or heard? God, what a mess. And on a Sunday. And where the hell was Bodenbender?

And the commandant! Jesus. What was wrong with him? He should have called the commandant at once. But he'd been asleep when the switchboard had called him. Maybe that was the problem. Damn Sunday, anyway. This was a mess for Berlin. After Richter went through everything again, that's who he'd call. Berlin. Meantime, heat or no heat, the bodies would have to stay where they were. Until the photographer and the fingerprints... Where was the photographer?!

He reached for the phone. "Get that photographer up here right away," he snapped without realizing he had only the switchboard and not his office on the line. He slammed the phone down.

"All right, Richter," he said grimly, leaning the chair back and lacing his fingers across his ample belly. "I want to hear it all again, and from the beginning. Ready, Braun?"

The Sergeant nodded, biting back a hiss of exasperation.

Hans sank into a chair and leaned his head against the wall, closing his eyes, knowing that he was exhausted and knowing too that Goebel was going to be looking for discrepancies. Not a healthy combination. Well, he just had to make sure that there weren't any. That was the advantage of sticking so closely to the truth. There weren't so many extraneous details to trip you up. He had trod the fine line once. He would just have to keep doing it over and over until this was done.

Then something occurred to him. "You'd better call the School House and tell Hauptmann Kruger that the major and I won't be able to make the dinner meeting. But I warn you, he won't be pleased. That meeting was part of the reason he flew in from Abwehr headquarters in Berlin."

Goebel's ears perked up. From Berlin. Abwehr headquarters. This was an Abwehr mess. Let this Kruger take care of it. Let him deal with Berlin. Let him make the decisions about the bodies. Having Kruger here might be the only piece of luck in this whole rotten business. And Bodenbender could arrange for whatever Kruger wanted done. But where was the commandant? Why the hell hadn't he called back? Never mind. It didn't really matter. The commandant wasn't the man to deal with this. He wasn't the man to deal with much of anything outside military strategy and tactics. The thing to do was to get ahold of this Kruger.

Fortunately Kruger had just walked through the School House door, and Heinrich was able to put him on the line. What he had to say made Goebel wince more than once. Why hadn't Richter mentioned that Hauptmann Kruger was Abwehr's Assistant Chief of Security, for God's sake? But at least he would be coming right over. Whatever this meeting at the School House was, it would have to wait.

He had no sooner opened his mouth to ask Richter to start again when the call came through from the commandant. He was horrified by what Goebel had to tell him but relieved that Hauptmann Kruger was coming in to help. And he said that he'd be right in. Goebel grimaced. He had to, of course. There was nothing else for it. But the commandant was the last thing he needed.

It was a relief to hang up the phone and say, "All right, Hauptmann Richter, please begin at the beginning."

The photographer chose that moment to arrive.

*       *       *

Dieter stood up and started pacing. It was good to move. He'd had it with lying down or sitting still. He wished that he could do some deep knee bends or push-ups, but not with the guard sitting in the corner reading a magazine. An hour and a half of sitting across Goebel's desk from Hauptmann Kruger while he asked and asked again all sorts of questions in all sorts of ways. Different questions and then the same questions made to sound different. He wished it had been Goebel on the other side of the desk. Goebel would have been a breeze. But Kruger was a very different proposition. Long-winded but tough and bright while Goebel was a fuss-budget, all bluster and few brains. Thank God he'd been able to tell the truth. Well, almost. Richter was damn clever and he could think fast. He had to hand Richter that. But then, he couldn't have survived this long if he wasn't. Just how long had he been at this? And how had he managed it?

Sweat was pouring off him now despite the open window. The light was fading outside, but he'd asked the guard not to turn on the lights. It would have meant putting up the blackout curtains, and that would have only made matters worse.

Had he seen Hauptmann Richter doing anything unusual?

"What do you mean by unusual?"

"Going into odd places. Talking with people that neither of you had reason to know?"

"No, sir. And I was with him almost twenty-four hours a day until he got that cast off."

Kruger nodded. He must have remembered the cast well. "But why were you taking care of him?" He eyed the Iron Cross First Class on Dieter's uniform curiously.

"I was his tank driver through Poland and France and we were used to each other. Also, I had two years in medical school before I enlisted, and so I was better able to deal with him than most people would have been."

"When were you commissioned?"

"Several weeks ago. Major Minten and Hauptmann Richter both felt it would be better if I were an officer. It has to do with an assignment, sir."

"Just so. Just so." Kruger had nodded.

Did he know? Dieter couldn't be sure and felt that it wasn't his place to tell him if he didn't.

After that, Kruger had changed his tack and started on Kramer, and Kramer and Richter. That had been easy. Kramer was a trouble-making bastard... had been a trouble-making bastard. He stopped pacing. The vision of the hideous mess that had been Kramer had appeared and wouldn't go away.

Then he started pacing again, faster now, as if that could wipe it out. Everyone would tell Kruger what a bastard Kramer had been. All that he had to do was stick to the facts as he knew them from day one in Dunkirk.

But then Kruger had started asking questions about Hans again, about Poland and France and the time between. He wanted to know what they had done here in Hamburg, as well, how Hans had spent his time, and about the correspondence with England.

Dieter didn't know why that had surprised him, but it had. With the correspondence having been arranged by Major Minten and undoubtedly going through the censors as well, it wouldn't be a secret.

Fortunately, he could tell Kruger all he knew without hesitation, and when he'd finished, Kruger had nodded his head in a way that told Dieter that he'd only confirmed what Kruger already knew.

Funny that they hadn't asked him more about himself. But then, his smile was sour, maybe they didn't need to.

He flopped down into the chair, exhausted, and looked at his watch. Only 2130. Six hours since he'd gone to Minten's office. It seemed more like six weeks.

If Richter was sending information to England, and he had to be, how was he doing it? The letters would seem to be the only way, especially when he was in the cast. There had been no one else, nothing for over a year. He would have known, especially since Dunkirk. And knowing what he knew about letter codes now, it would be entirely possible, even with a careful censor. His mother? Unlikely. Still, Kugelmann had said that Richter's godfather was in British Intelligence . But to involve his mother... No. It had to be the woman. Julia Henderson. Richter had never mentioned her before Hamburg. And not to mention a woman that gorgeous... It had to be her.

But what on earth book could he have used? One of the mysteries? Unlikely. They seemed to come and go. The only book he had that had enough words and page numbers was the German-French dictionary. That? But he must have been writing in English. It would have been an awful pain and there was a built-in chance for error with the translation involved. Still, it was possible, especially with someone as bright and painstaking as Richter. And Richter certainly had been glad to see that book when he'd given it back to him in Dunkirk. It had barely been out of his sight since. True, the Hauptmann had let him use it in France, but only when he was with Madame Richard, at the house.

And the time involved in working out that sort of letter... Where the hell had he found the time, especially when he was in that cast? It had to have meant losing a lot of sleep. Good. He deserved to lose sleep, at the very least. In fact, may he never have a peaceful night's sleep again.

So why did you do it, Dieter? he asked himself. Why did you save Richter's hide? With your family, if you were caught out...

He rose abruptly and went to the window, staring out, seeing nothing.

The vision of his father's face came again, the same vision he'd had in Minten's office. He recognized it now. The day of the Anschluss. Father in an impotent fury, hating what was happening, hating everything the Nazis stood for, but powerless to do anything to stop it. Was that why he'd done it? Because for once he hadn't been powerless? Because for once... For once what? Kramer had wanted Annaliese. Just the way he looked at her, the way he'd treated her in Fenstermacher's office. The thought of that still made his skin crawl. So maybe if Kramer hadn't mentioned Annaliese, it wouldn't have happened. But the gun had been ready to fire. Safety off. Why had he taken off the safety?

Nothing made sense. That is nothing had made sense until the shooting had started. When the shooting started there had been no thought, no need for sense. He had just reacted. Maybe he and Richter had been through too much together. Maybe because of that he couldn't just let that bastard shoot Richter down, no matter what he'd done. Who the hell knew? He'd just done it, and now he was stuck with what he'd done. Stuck with playing along. Stuck with going to England and stuck with having to look at Richter again. And they'd have to seem to go on as before. There was no choice,

no-God-damn-choice. Not about that, not about anything now. He
was trembling as he jerked
himself around. "Soldat?"

The man looked up. "Sir?"

"What's your name?"

"Schell, sir."

"Do you play scat?"

"Yes, sir." Schell grinned.

"Have cards?"

"Yes, sir."

"Let's get the guard from outside and get on with it."

*    *    *

A man he'd never seen before ushered Hans into the front seat of
the Kuebel and another stranger – obviously a guard – got into the
back.

Where was Dieter? House arrest for them both, Goebel had said.
Just a temporary measure. They didn't want any questions asked. It
was all to be very discreet. If the Hauptmann would simply stay at
the School House and not discuss the situation with anyone...

At least he'd be able to see Annaliese and get rid of those papers.
Thank God when they'd searched him they hadn't searched his
boots. And thank God, too, for the little toilet rooms in the loo, with
floor to ceiling doors. There hadn't been time to tear up the papers
nor could he have taken the number of flushes necessary to get rid
of them. A wisp of a smile appeared as he envisioned flooded loos,
water pouring down the halls and through the ceilings, the oaths
as the clogged plumbing was dealt with. It certainly would have
enlivened the day. Not that it needed more enlivening. God...

He'd been able to stuff the pages of flimsy under the sole of his
foot. The boot was tight, but the papers were safer there. And after
he'd done that in the loo, it had been easy to roll the heavy envelope
up tight and hide it in his hand, shoving it into the wastebin

by the sink when the guard had turned away. Even if someone was suspicious enough to go through the trash, there was nothing written on the envelope to tell where it had come from.

What was he going to say to Bergmann when he saw him? What could he possibly say? Bergmann had known when he walked into that office. So why, with everything he had at stake...

"He'll be sent along presently," Goebel had told him when he'd asked about Dieter. And he'd looked at Hans, hard. "You realize that this situation must not be discussed, even between the two of you."

"Of course," he'd said, without comprehending. Bergmann had been there, after all. Not that he wanted to talk to him about it. He was surprised to discover just how much he didn't want to talk to him about it.

"We don't want any discussions at all," Goebel had gone on to say, "not until after we've completed the investigation, and not even then. We'll have an official version, which is the only one that can be discussed, and you both must go along with it, whatever it is. It shouldn't take too long. The facts seem to be as you presented them."

It had been hard to hide his relief. "They are as I presented them."

Goebel had just nodded.

"Must I stay in my room?"

"No! I thought I'd made that clear. Your staying in your room would excite more comment than anything else, except your... ah... disappearance. We don't want any speculation. Arrange to have your work brought into you... Do that. You could say that it was a quieter place to work, and it would give you an excuse to stay clear of people much of the time, without exciting comment."

"The official version had better be established soon." House arrest... Well, it could have been worse. Far worse.

Goebel had given a wry smile. "The grapevine?"

Hans had smiled back, surprised. Goebel had some sense, after all. "The grapevine." It was going to be all over HQ by morning, no matter what anyone tried to do about it. And the story was bound to grow with the telling. But the fact that Goebel had talked to him that way was most encouraging.

"Herr Hauptmann!"

Hans sat up and looked around. They were in front of the School House and the driver was standing beside him with the passenger door open. "Sorry. Tired, I guess." He got out. "Thank you."

The driver gave him a smart salute that he returned. The extra guard Goebel had sent along must have jumped out at the gate.

Annaliese had obviously been waiting, watching for him from the landing, for as he came down the hall, she started down the stairs, her face white and strained.

Hans went to her, thinking that he wasn't ready for this, that he might never be. But he was especially not ready now, not after everything that had happened during the past few hours.

"Are you... Are you all right?"

He nodded.

She kept her voice low, looking around anxiously, "What happened? I came back and you weren't here and the meeting was over. Or maybe it was never held. I'm not sure. All Heinrich would tell me was that neither you nor Major Minten is here and that Hauptmann Kruger had torn out of the house as if a million devils were after him."

"Annaliese..."

But she was too upset to stop and kept prattling on. "No one knew anything."

"Come upstairs, Annaliese." It was a command. He moved past her and went up the steps.

She had been about to ask again, but her jaw snapped shut and she turned to hurry after him. What was wrong? He was never like this. What could have happened? And where was Dieter?

Hans was at the door to her room. It was unlocked. He went in, and waited, holding the door open for her. She snapped on the light as he shut the door and slid the bolt with a loud click.

Her heart was pounding wildly as he turned back to her. Something was very wrong. He looked exhausted and so grim. But she could read nothing in his expression. It was as if he had closed a set of shutters over his face.

Neither of them said a word.

Finally he turned away, sat down in the chair by the window and began struggling with his boot.

She was staring at him in disbelief. Could he want... now... before he told her? She couldn't possibly. Not now.

She was even more puzzled when he didn't start on the second boot but reached down into the one he had just taken off to pull out a thin packet of papers that looked considerably the worse for such wear.

He held the papers out to her with the same shuttered gaze and she moved slowly toward him, somehow not quite able to hold her hand out for them. Was that what it had been all about? And why had he been hiding them in his boot?

"Take it." He sounded angry.

"What is it?"

"Take it!" He thrust out the packet emphatically.

She took the papers, finally, still staring at him.

"Open it." He turned away and began pulling his boot back on.

She turned the packet over slowly and began unfolding the flattened wrinkled sheets of paper. Evidence of embezzlement by Kapitan-zur-See Friedrich Schroeder. She looked up, and when she spoke, her voice was barely above a whisper. "Where did you get this?"

He sat there looking up at her, his forearms on his knees, his hands hanging loose between his legs. It was a moment before he could bring himself to say it. "Minten's office."

She stumbled backward, hitting the bed and sitting down on it abruptly. "How did you... Major Minten's office?"

He didn't cushion the blow. "He's dead. Minten's dead. Minten, Kramer, Kugelmann. All dead."

"How?"

"Shot."

"Shot?"

"In Minten's office."

"Who...?"

"Dieter and I."

It was as if he'd hit her. Her mind went blank and he saw her sway slightly. It was well she was sitting down. "How!? When!?"

He leaned his head against the back of the chair and looked at the ceiling as he told her the story precisely as he had told it over and over, first to Goebel, then again to Kruger. He was careful to keep his voice low.

She sat there in silence, staring at him, not quite able to believe what she was hearing. And even when she began to, there was the sense that there was something very wrong with what he was saying. Something she couldn't quite put her finger on. "What about these papers?" She asked when he finally gave her an opening.

"They were with some papers on Minten's desk, in an envelope. Kramer must have had them with him. After the guard left to call an ambulance, I took a quick look to see what was there."

"But why would Kramer have them with him? They were his hold over my uncle and me. He would have kept them well hidden!"

Hans shrugged. "Maybe he was moving them from one place to another. Who knows, but whatever the reason, be glad. When he gets them, maybe your uncle can do a better job of covering his tracks."

"He paid it back."

"I'd be surprised if he hadn't. He's that sort of man. In fact, I'm surprised he took it in the first place. He must really have been up against it."

"He was." She was watching him carefully, beginning to have an inkling about what was nagging at her brain. If she could just put it all together... "I know." And suddenly she did.

"Know what?" He was really looking at her, at last.

"It wasn't Kramer, was it."

"What do you mean?"

"He was obsessed with you."

"That was just to throw everyone off the track."

"No, Hans." Her voice was firm now.

"If it wasn't that way, suppose you tell me how it was." He had a trace of a sneer in his voice.

"Kramer set a trap for you. It explains everything. Especially why he was so confident that day in Hauptmann Fenstermacher's office."

Hans just sat there looking at her.

"The trap was far more Kramer's style than Minten's. Minten was clever, but if it had been his... He wouldn't have been in that office himself. And even if he had decided to be, he would have had real gunmen with him, several gunmen, not Corporal Kugelmann." She gave a nervous little laugh. "Certainly not Corporal Kugelmann. No. I'd say that Lieutenant Kramer came in and found you, and that he had Major Minten and Corporal Kugelmann with him because he wanted to prove it to the major, wanted him to be in on the kill." She shuddered at the word. "Only they were killed, instead."

My God. She had it all. Hans just hoped Hauptmann Kruger wasn't that perceptive. Attack was the best defense. "If that's the way you feel... You have what you need to make your uncle safe. You can back out of this trip anytime you want, possibly make a heroine of yourself in the bargain by telling Kruger this fairy story of yours. The only trouble is that he might believe you and then where would Dieter and I be? Of course, if you weren't believed, you'd be laughed out of town. Why not plead insanity, or just get sick? That would get you off the hook."

She was angry now. "And am I to back out of the wedding, too?"

"If you wish." He was glaring at her, but his heart twisted in anguish.

Annaliese went to the door and switched off the light. It was stifling in here and in more ways than one. "You are such a fool."

It took a moment for her eyes to adjust to the darkness. When they had, she went to the window, careful to stay away from the chair and raised first the blackout and then the window. She was still angry.

"First I'm a spy and then a fool. A marvelous combination."

"I told you a long time ago..."

"Keep your voice down!" He hissed. "There's a guard in the garden."

She spoke more quietly. "I told you a long time ago that I didn't care if you were what Kramer said you were. That's not quite true. For a while I did care. It worried me. And he was so persistent. The day we went for the license... But you were so... I thought Kramer was crazy!

"Now it really doesn't matter. I just don't care. I love you. That's all that matters, that and the fact that I have to go to England. There would be too many questions if I backed out, especially now. And if I'm right, and it's the only explanation that makes sense, then you can't afford any more questions than are already being asked. And if we don't marry, it's the same thing. So unless you can't stand the sight of me, you'd better marry me and take me to England with you, just as we planned. I know that even if you don't trust me, you won't let them hurt me, or Dieter either."

He couldn't look at her, even in the darkness. The trust. Oh my God, the trust.

"And if you don't love me, you can always divorce me when we get there. You could say that you had to marry me to be sure of getting out, to avoid suspicion. I'd back you up, if that's what you wanted. It would be a fraudulent marriage. That's grounds for divorce anywhere isn't it? Or is it for annulment? It doesn't matter. Either would do."

And the love... But he was full of bitterness as he said, "My, my aren't we getting technical suddenly?"

Her heart was breaking. She was right. She had to be. But if she weren't, how could he stand her suspicions, her willingness to believe that he was a double agent?

Oh, dear God, what if she were right and the only reason he was marrying her was because he felt sorry for her, because she had to go and he wanted to make sure she wasn't hanged? After all, she was the one who had suggested it. No. No. He loved her.

He had to love her. No man could... Could he? And he couldn't tell her. It wasn't safe. Even now. It was like standing on quicksand. No matter which way she moved, it would make her sink faster. But if she stood still, she'd sink anyway, just more slowly. Better to get it over with. She kept her voice flat, devoid of emotion. "You know I have to go, unless..." She looked away. "What do you intend to do?"

"If I were what you say I am, I should be sweeping you off your feet onto the bed, protesting my ardent love for you, telling you that all I want in the world is to marry you. Then I would prove my point by making violent love to you."

"Is that what you want to do?"

"Yes." His voice was weary. "It's what I always want to do."

Her voice was strained. "Do you love me?"

"Yes. But feeling as you do, you ought to forget about me and stay here."

His outline was clear in the darkness. She walked over to the chair, still without touching him. "No. That's not what I ought to do. Because I love you, what I ought to do is what I want to do and that is to marry you and go with you. And what you ought to do is what you want to do." Her voice had turned into a harsh rasp. "Why don't you do it?"

He rose slowly and stood looking down at the white shadow of her face until finally he began doing precisely that.

Later, as he lay with her on her narrow bed, almost asleep, she smiled to herself and brushed the hair back from his forehead, whispering, "Sleep, darling Hans. I won't talk about this again, not to you, not to anyone. And I won't ask any more questions. It's better if you don't tell me. That way I won't really know. Tell me in England, when it's all over and we're all safe, because we will be safe there, won't we." It wasn't a question.

She felt his small nod as he drifted off to sleep. Unseen, she nodded her satisfaction. But it was a long time before she slept.

# Chapter XVII

Wednesday. Hans looked at the calendar on his desk as if he could make the pages turn, the days pass, by sheer effort of will.

Only an hour's worth of questioning this morning, but how many more mornings? Did one hour mean that things were winding down, or to be strung out? Oh, God... He stretched.

At least the wedding hadn't been canceled. Aunt Karin was going full steam ahead, oblivious to everything else. And their Sunday departure for Dunkirk hadn't been canceled, either. But they were living in limbo.

Not that that seemed to be bothering Annaliese. She was almost...serene. And the way she'd handled things had been nothing short of brilliant, twisting things just enough, telling Kruger that Kramer had been after her and in his fury over her engagement, had hauled her into Hauptmann Fenstermacher's office to try to convince her that Hans was a British spy so she'd break it off. And when she'd laughed in his face, he turned vicious and physically abusive. No, she hadn't told Hauptmann Fenstermacher that part of it, because she didn't want Kramer's idiotic story repeated to anyone else.

He shook his head in admiration. The story not only covered all the bases and stuck very close to the truth, but it reinforced his own story, that Kramer was trying to make him his fall guy. Because she'd figured it out, she'd done it all on her own, without asking him anything. First Bergmann, then Annaliese. If anyone else had figured it out...

There was a tap on the door and he looked up, exasperated. What now? He had too damn much to do... "Come in!"

The door opened and Hans burst out of his chair. "Uncle Karl!" A visitation of the gods? No one could be more welcome.

Karl grinned and shut the door behind him before coming across the small office toward his delighted nephew with his hand outstretched.

Hans scrambled out from behind the desk and shook the proffered hand warmly. "I thought you weren't coming until tomorrow night. Is Aunt Gretl with you?"

"No, no, my boy. Gretel is still in Prussia. This wedding of yours came up at such short notice that she wasn't able to tear herself away. It seems we have a wedding of our own in the offing."

"Which one?" The bane of Karl's existence was that he had never had a son. The eldest of his three daughters, Dorothea, must be what? Twenty-one?

"Dorothea."

"You're pleased?" He certainly looked pleased.

"Very. The son of an old friend. Don't think you've met him. Fine boy. A real comer. Good family. He's out there now. On leave. That's why Gretel stayed, to chaperone and see he doesn't get away." Karl roared with laughter at what he must have thought was a good joke.

Hans smiled. "If Dorothea looks as much like Aunt Gretel as she used to, there's no way she could get rid of him."

Karl beamed. "You're right, my boy. She does. And she's just as sweet as she always was."

Hans didn't quite know what to say. Dorothea had been a real tomboy as a child and sweet wasn't exactly the word he would have applied to her. Still, she was a good sort. Maybe that's what he meant.

Karl didn't seem to notice his silence but sat down brusquely without waiting to be asked and said, "None of this is why I'm here today instead of tomorrow. Actually, I got in last night."

"Why didn't you call me?" Hans was half-sitting on the edge of his desk, his arms folded.

"More to the point, why didn't you call me? I had to hear about your... ah... present difficulties from Admiral Canaris."

Hans frowned. God knows, he'd been tempted to call Karl, but...

"Because it's very touchy business and the investigation has to stand on its own merits. I didn't want anyone to think I was calling you in because I needed reinforcements. And besides, you have enough on your plate without my getting you involved in this mess."

"You need reinforcements?" Karl was looking at him hard.

There was a little trickle of sweat running down Hans' back that had nothing to do with the weather. It was relatively cool for once.

"Who doesn't, anytime? But if you mean, was I worried about it? I'd be a fool not to be. The head of station, his assistant and his driver are shot in the head of station's office, and I was there and not only survived but shot the driver? And in the bargain, it was my assistant who came in in the middle of things and not only survived as well, but shot the head of station's assistant. To top it all off, the head of station's assistant is accused of being a spy for the British, and was trying, apparently, to set me up to take the fall for him. It boggles the mind. Someone has to be blamed. I just hope they are not trying to stick us with it."

"Why should they?" The voice was casual enough but the eyes were steely.

Hans didn't like it. He had never seen Karl this way. "Because Kruger is probably going to be stepping into Minten's shoes. It would be a big promotion for him even though he considers Hamburg the boondocks since it isn't Berlin, and he's going to want to show everyone that he's the best there is. He'll want everything tied up in a neat bundle. I just don't want Bergmann and me tied up in it." It should be all right -- the trickle of sweat had turned to a stream – especially since the camera he left on Kramer had been discovered to have 'gone missing' from the supply room, something Hektor had neglected to mention in the wake of the flap about the film. Bad luck, Hektor, but then you make your own bad luck. Stupid way to run things.

Karl had relaxed and was sitting back in the chair, nodding in agreement. "Very astute of you, my boy." And at that moment Karl wished, and not for the first time, that Hans really was his boy. Astute, perceptive, brains, savvy, and a great deal of courage. He had shown that in Poland and undoubtedly again in France, and he was showing it even more right now. He wanted to fight his own battles. A boy to be proud of, Anne.

And he was doing superb work. Admiral Canaris had several analyses he'd made in hand. Said they were brilliant, even said Minten had tried to take credit where no credit was due for one or two of them. Yes, a good boy.

Karl had to be sure, and now he was. He had told Admiral Canaris and Hauptmann Kruger he was, even without seeing Hans, but still, he had had to be sure. Hans wanted the case settled on its own merits and that was wise. Kruger was a power-hungry bastard and he'd investigate the hell out of this, not wanting any storm clouds hanging over his new fiefdom. So Hans was wise to be worried about Kruger, or he would have been if the evidence against this Kramer weren't so overwhelming. Odd that he'd turned out to be Hilde Flade's nephew, Birgid's cousin. The mother a selfish, self-centered, grasping woman. Gorgeous. He'd have to hand her that. But going through life leaving scandal after scandal in her wake. And now the son. A first-class prick, apparently. No one had anything good to say about him. The only loose end left was how he had managed to get the information to London. But with him dead, that would have to remain a mystery. Anyway, good riddance.

"Uncle Karl?"

He looked up. "Sorry, Nephew. It's been a long two days." He shifted in the chair. "But I have had one consolation. I managed to get Georg's Birgid to come along and keep me company. Charming girl."

"Indeed, she is. That was really good of you. Georg misses her."

Karl chuckled. "She all but fell on my neck. Too bad I was sure it was because she wanted to see her husband. Would have been enormously flattering otherwise. Silly business, their not being able to live together here. I intend to look into it when I get back."

"I'd be careful about that."

Karl snorted. "I know all about Georg's father. You forget I've known Wolfe for years, since we were boys. Always was a radical.

But he's kept his nose clean since they sent him home. Horrible thing. Good German. Don't know what the hell we're coming to. Just shot off his mouth when he should have kept quiet. But he paid. Oh, he paid. Looked like hell. Still doesn't look right. Never will. And the sins of the father shouldn't be visited on the son, especially sins of idiocy."

Hans smiled. "If you're not careful, you'll be shipped off for those same sins yourself."

Karl looked surprised, then he laughed. "I shoot off my mouth with calculated care. Always have. That's the better part of valor, especially in the military. If I'd always said what I thought..." He roared with laughter and was still laughing when he said, "You must know all about that, especially here."

"Too much to suit me." Hans was grinning, thinking that he'd almost forgotten how fond he was of this man. Straight. You knew where you stood with him. A good ally.

"I can imagine." His tone was dry. "Give me fighting men every time. But even they're not immune. Especially these days." Karl leaned forward, slapping his knee for emphasis. "Now, about this mess you're in."

"And it is a mess." But it was amazing how much better Hans felt about it suddenly.

"Not any more."

"Really? Who says?"

"I say and so does Admiral Canaris."

Hans' eyebrows flew up.

"He got the preliminary report by courier Monday afternoon and called me in. He was most impressed that you hadn't let me know about it." Karl hadn't been impressed, at least not at the time. He'd been mad as hell.

"Then I'm doubly glad that I didn't."

Karl stiffened slightly. "Clever of you."

Hans shrugged but he didn't like the sudden change. "It just didn't seem to be the thing to do."

"That's what I mean. Clever."

"I wasn't trying to be clever, Uncle Karl."

"Didn't you need to be?"

"No. Just honest, fortunately." That trickle of sweat was there again.

"That's what I told Admiral Canaris." His voice was hard. "I told him that you'd never been devious." He paused, studying his nephew carefully. "Your story is the truth."

"Of course!" Hans managed to sound surprised.

Karl was still looking at him. But finally he relaxed again, smiling slightly. "I told him that, too. I just had to be absolutely sure in my own mind."

"Can't trust anyone these days?" His voice was full of bitterness.

Karl sighed. "I'm afraid so. Don't like it. Hated having to sound you out. But I had to. Had to be absolutely sure. Just heard something in your voice back there... Silly. Hard time for you. Everyone on your back. Had to be sure."

"And are you?"

"Yes. You aren't Anne and Gerhard's boy for nothing. Shouldn't have doubted you, even a little."

"Forget it, Uncle Karl." Hans was hating this himself. "As I said, it's a touchy business. Especially with Mother and James still in England. Even more since James is in the Royal Navy."

"James should have come back. But he was born there. Not the same thing. You were born here. James was a problem for you. Can't deny. That and the letters you were writing that girl. Canaris had copies. Said some of them were pretty torrid." Karl chortled. "Read one. Hot stuff. A phrase or two I'll have to remember to use myself. But no code. They tried everything. Kramer put them up to it. Backed up your story of his being out to get you. How he took in Minten I can't imagine. Minten was a pig but sharp, shrewd, and amazingly good at his business. Only met him once, but the admiral thought highly of his work. Laughed though. As I said, he'd tried to pass off some of your work as his. Shows you do good work when your superior tries to steal it outright.

"But those letters." He shook his head. "Proud of you, my boy.

Didn't know you had it in you. Still waters run deep. She must be something."

Hans actually blushed.

That made Karl laugh again. "Is she?"

He nodded, laughing a little himself. "Spectacular looking. Delightful. But she's no Annaliese. I broke it off when... when I knew that I loved Annaliese."

"So I heard. That was the other thing that made the admiral feel that Kramer was throwing dust in our eyes. If you were sending information through her, you would scarcely have broken it off at such a critical moment. Wouldn't have been wise of you to fall so much in love that you'd be willing to lose your only contact, especially one that had been so conveniently arranged through channels for you."

Thank God Minten had been so drunk that night.

Karl went on. "There was a bit of a flap when the news came through about your godfather."

Hans's heart was beating fast. "What about him?"

"He's an officer, a high one, in British Intelligence."

"Jeezus." It came out as a sigh. So they did know what Michael was. Kramer wouldn't have kept that quiet. If Kugelmann knew...

"You didn't know?" A brief remnant of his previous look flashed back and then disappeared.

"How could I?"

Karl nodded. "How could you indeed? He scarcely would have advertised it. What did you think he did?"

"He said he was in the Foreign Office. That's where his office is, or was when I last saw him. But he was never very specific about what he did. He traveled occasionally. I just never paid any attention to it."

"When was the last time you saw him?"

"The summer my father died."

"No time for you to have been recruited and trained. You were lucky in that, too. Your time for the last four years has been very well accounted for. Kramer looked into everything. Big file. A help now, actually. He was having you followed. You kept your nose clean." Karl shook his head. "Especially here in Hamburg."

"Not much choice. You saw the cast."

Karl chuckled. "Didn't give you much room to maneuver."

Hans smiled back and nodded.

"Good thing Minten set that trap for you without telling Kramer. Must not have trusted him. Good thing," he repeated. "From what I hear, Kramer wouldn't have been above framing you."

"Why are you telling me all this?"

"Because I spent the morning and half the afternoon with Hauptmann Kruger going over everything. Canaris suggested it. Wanted to make sure I didn't think my nephew was being rail-roaded. You are my nephew, after all, even though it's only by marriage. Always have been a little in love with your mother." His laughter was a bit forced.

"You have good taste."

"Indeed!" Karl looked relieved.

Hans smiled, amused suddenly. Better get Karl off the hook. "And are you satisfied?"

"That you aren't being railroaded? Yes. And I'm satisfied, too, that Kramer was doing precisely what you said he was doing. It all fits. Kruger thinks so, too. Would have thrown you to the wolves, my boy, if I thought that you'd done it." His voice was hard, bitter. "Nothing else for it. And Admiral Canaris knows that. That's why he let me come. Germany has too many vipers at her bosom as it is. Would have hated it but would have done it. Glad you didn't."

Uncle Karl wasn't always the easiest person to follow when he was in full flow but his meaning here was very clear. The trickle of sweat running down Hans' back had become a stream. He didn't dare turn around. "So am I!" Had he kept it light enough? Apparently.

"Guards have been pulled. Goebel called while I was there."

"I hadn't heard." It was all he could do to suppress a sigh of relief.

"Told Kruger I'd tell you. You've been told." He grinned.

"Many thanks." Hans grinned back.

"Calls for a celebration. Get your jacket and that man Bergmann of yours. Good man. Saved you in Dunkirk, too."

"And once before that."

"Deserves a good dinner. And a medal. Did he get one?"

Hans shook his head. "Only for Poland."

"Too late now. Too bad. Can't over this. Can't even mention it, you know. All hush-hush. Official release will say it was a car accident."

Hans snorted. "Will they be dumped off a cliff? I'm afraid that Kramer would never pass inspection as a car crash victim."

"Car burned."

He winced. "Convenient."

"Very. Tomorrow."

Hans nodded heavily.

"Let's forget it, if we can. You, Bergmann, me, and good lord, almost forgot that fiancée of yours. Dying to meet her."

"Then you shall. I'll call her. It will be quite a celebration."

"A lot to celebrate. Georg and Birgid, too."

"Better and better!" He paused. "But this report..."

"Finish it tomorrow."

"But there's so much else..."

"Leave it. You're human. Someone else will finish what you can't. Life's too short. Planning's chaotic anyway. No one can settle on anything." Karl sounded disgusted. "Never get there at this rate. No secret since you're working on it. Third report or fourth?"

"More like the fifth or sixth." He was laughing as he picked up the phone.

*     *     *

The night threatened disaster. Dieter had come, but reluctantly. He wasn't the same and, of course, things between them weren't the same. But then, why should they be? The way he'd used Bergmann, without a thought to the danger to his family. As a screen. To carry files. Playing on his trust. And the film. He shuddered. The day Dieter had brought out the film, saying he didn't dare leave it in the darkroom and he damn well wasn't going to get caught burning it himself. He'd simply thrown the envelope onto the desk and walked out. God. So he had to have known before he walked in on that scene in Minten's office. Known! So why had he done it? If Bergmann had an answer to that, he certainly wasn't giving it. Again, why should he?

But then Annaliese had gotten him out onto the dance floor and they had danced, were spectacular together in fact, had people watching, clapping. Annaliese was laughing and Dieter was laughing with her. But then the music had slowed and they had stayed on the floor, dancing slowly, talking hard. Whatever it was they had talked about as they danced, when they finally sat down, Dieter seemed more like himself than he had since before the shootings. Hans asked her about it when they were dancing later, but she just shook her head, saying it wasn't a night for questions, that it was a night to celebrate, especially since Georg and Birgid were able to be together, as well, and what a pity it was that she couldn't live here with him and someone ought to do something. Maybe Uncle Karl? And wasn't he a delight!

He didn't pursue it. It was his turn for acceptance.

They ate, drank, laughed, danced, and enjoyed. Uncle Karl had the time of his life. They all did.

*     *     *

"And do you, Johann Michael Richter, take Annaliese Scheuermann to be your wedded wife, to have and to hold from this day forth, for better, for worse, for richer, for poorer, in sickness and in health, to love and to cherish, 'til death do you part?"

She's so beautiful. And, dear Lord, she looks so happy. Please let me keep her that way. She knows. Let her accept me when I tell her what she already knows. "I do."

A haze of sight and sound. Words heard and responded to. Flowers. Faces. The man reading the ceremony. Imposing. A judge? It didn't sound like a civil ceremony but he wasn't wearing a clerical collar. Never mind. It wasn't important, nothing was important except that it was Annaliese standing beside him – always and only Annaliese – and she was marrying him.

Annaliese on one side, Dieter on the other. Fitting. The three of them...

His conversation with Dieter picked a strange moment to come flooding back..."You know if you go" – his own words to Dieter came back to him – "you'll have one hell of a choice to make. Either you work for the British, sending messages they want to send and have Abwehr delighted with you, or you'll probably be regulated to the hinterlands under close guard with both your parents and Abwehr thinking you're dead."

Dieter had sucked in a deep breath.

"You hadn't thought that far ahead, had you? The return I'm giving you for having saved my life... How many times?" The question was rhetorical. They both knew.

"Three times." It was a growl.

"Three," repeated Hans softly. "So you'll have your life, but either you turn traitor to Germany..."

"I'm an Austrian!" His head had come up and his eyes were flashing. "And don't you forget it. If I'm going to be a traitor to any country, it will be to Austria, thank you."

"Are you being a traitor to Austria?" Hans' voice was vicious. "I thought that was the point. Why you refused to be an officer, because somehow you'd be a traitor if you served in the German army, in Hitler's army, as an officer. Splitting hairs, damn you. Sitting in harsh judgment..." He looked away.

"And I don't have a right to?" His face was vermilion, the cords were sticking out on either side of his neck and the scar made his face a twisted wreck. "At least I was honest about it with you. But you... A friend? Jeezus," he muttered and stuffed his fist into his pockets, his eyes seeking something, anything but Hans, and finding nothing. "A 'friend' who uses people. The ultimate contradiction in terms. God deliver me."

"I hope He will."

"Because you won't be able to?"

"Oh, I'll be able to, as promised."

"Annaliese and me both?"

"Of course." His voice was hard and controlled. It would be both. It had damn well better be both, or they would have nothing from him.

"My, my, aren't you the all-powerful one. Is that why you're marrying her, to confer on her your all-powerful living grace?"

"Of course." He was matching anger for anger. "What else? Except for the fact that I happen to love her."

Then something triggered in his consciousness and he heard with wonder, "... I now pronounce you man and wife together. Whom God hath joined together, let no man put asunder." And then he was kissing her, having to make an effort not to kiss her too hard or too long. England. She was going to England with him. Going home. Oh, God... He was still holding her, whispering in her ear, "I love you."

She smiled up at him then, that wonderful, dazzling smile of hers, and laughed when he still didn't let her go. "I'm so glad."

The music had started again, a harp that Aunt Karin had hired for the occasion. Heavenly music? Just Aunt Karin's style. For some reason the thought amused him, and he laughed back at her, utterly happy. Then, finally, he let her go, and as he turned, she slid her arm through his.

Dieter came around and kissed Annaliese soundly on the cheek, then shook hands with Hans, a tentative shake, almost wary, but a handshake all the same. "You're a lucky man." His voice was a bit grim, but Dieter was looking him in the eye, at last.

"I know. On all fronts." His hand tightened briefly around Dieter's before he let go. "And you know I'll do my damnedest to keep her... safe and happy."

A sharp nod, a curt, "I know," and then he was gone, leaving

Hans staring after him in surprise, but not for long. Aunt Karin was swooping him into an all-encompassing hug, gushing into his ear, "We're so glad to have you in the family."

He had barely begun his politic, "I'm glad to be in the family," when she was off, in full sail, heading for the commandant. Aunt Karin had no doubts about where her priorities lay.

"Do you know what a good girl you have?" Hans turned back. Kapitan-zur-See Schroeder - could he ever bring himself to call him 'Uncle Friedrich'? – and there was the trace of a tear in his eye.

"Yes. You know I do. And I hope you know, too, that I intend to take very good care of her." Please, God.

He nodded solemnly. "As you're taking good care of us all."

Why the hell was he bringing that up now? The scene in his office after the investigation had been completed had been painful in the extreme, for both of them. The kapitan had been mortified and grateful at the same time, babbling that he had paid it all back, wouldn't have taken it in the first place if his wife hadn't been so desperately ill and if the Kriegsmarine hadn't refused to pay for the special treatment at a private sanitarium. Hans had done everything he could think of to convince him that didn't matter, that he understood, that it had just been a great satisfaction to know that he'd never have to be under anyone's thumb about that again. But nothing had helped and he had the feeling that if they hadn't been going to England, the burden of Friedrich Schroeder's gratitude would soon become onerous in the extreme.

But before Hans could say anything else, the Kapitan had to give way to an ebullient Uncle Karl, who was hugging both the bride and groom at the same time. "Don't know how this boy got so lucky!" He was beaming down at Annaliese. "And if he doesn't treat you the way he should, let me know!"

"And just what would you do about it?" Annaliese was looking back at him with a faintly malicious twinkle in her eyes.

Karl burst out laughing. "Hans, my boy, you are going to have your hands full with this one!" And then he was gone.

Georg had greeted Annaliese formally. "Frau Richter." But it was

Hans who was startled by that, which set them all to laughing.

Birgid had simply hugged her and wrinkled her nose at Hans who was having none of that. He grabbed Birgid in a big bear hug, whispering in her ear, "Be happy yourself."

When she looked up, her eyes were shining. "I already am. Your Uncle Karl is seeing to our housing problems."

His cousin, Gunter, was wringing his hand, then Hauptmann Kruger, the commandant and on and on. There weren't more than twenty or thirty people at the wedding, but before they'd all finished giving their congratulations, it seemed more like a hundred.

There was a light supper and then a cake to cut, with champagne for toasts and more toasts, including a rather bawdy one by Uncle Karl, which had the bride and groom laughing through their blushes and everyone else roaring with laughter, including Aunt Karin.

When it was all done, Hans retired to the loo to collect his thoughts while Annaliese went upstairs to change. His head was spinning with the effects of the champagne and all that had happened. Dangerous, even today. Perhaps especially today.

He smiled as he remembered Uncle Karl and Kapitan Schroeder ensconced in a corner. They had understood each other at once. Odd, because they were so different. Uncle Friedrich. He tried it out but it still didn't work.

Hauptmann Kruger had been quite a surprise. Had Aunt Karin heard that he was to be head of station? The announcement hadn't been made yet. Or had Kapitan Schroeder suggested that Kruger come, as a gesture of 'solidarity?' In any event, Aunt Karin had moved quickly. Kruger hadn't even mentioned it yesterday when they had talked after the 'official results' of the investigation had been made known. Thank God they had to leave for England, and at once. Given time and a more thorough investigation... As it was, everything had come out even better than he dared hope. Kramer had been named the leak and everyone had been satisfied, especially Kruger, whose promotion was assured. It had been a convenient resolution for everyone. Even Berlin was happy. And if Berlin was happy, then so was everyone else.

There had been a momentary confusion before the public announcement of the 'car crash' when it was discovered that the Kramer listed as the next-of-kin wasn't kin at all, but just a Hamburg lawyer. That had been shrugged off, however, since the lawyer had his will, and it was felt that the lieutenant didn't want his mother notified directly.

There was a vague rumor floating around that there were some secret papers of Lieutenant Kramer's missing from the lawyer's office, but this had not been confirmed. As one of the HQ men who was always in the know had said to Dieter with a wink, 'Why would a lawyer advertise a lack of security in his own office?' Was that where Minten had gotten the evidence that Kramer had against Kapitan Schroeder? But how would he have known about it, let alone where it was, and even if he did, why would he care enough about it to have stolen unless he wanted Schroeder under his own thumb? It was a puzzle. Probably always would be.

He looked in the mirror and grinned at himself ruefully. This was no time for Hauptmann Johann Richter, husband, to be standing in the loo trying to solve the unsolvable.

When he walked out the door, it was to find his Uncle Karl standing there, ashen faced, apparently waiting for him.

"What's wrong, Uncle?" What on earth could have happened?

"I just heard where the three of you are going."

Hans didn't know what to say.

"It worries me, my boy. How can you possibly carry it off? Your mother..."

Hans sighed. "The only part that worries me is Mother."

"I should think so! That woman is no fool."

"We shall have to live somewhere else."

"And your godfather being in British Intelligence..."

Hans's mouth tightened to a grim line. "If I play it right, that should be a help."

It was Karl's turn to sigh. "So you're learning to be devious after all."

"I shall have to be or we won't survive."

"But to take your wife and best friend..."

"At least we'll all be in it together, and I'll be with people I know I can trust."

Karl brightened slightly. "True enough. I wish I could ask you to give my best to your mother, but that would scarcely be wise. I wish she could have been here today."

"So do I. That's the only good thing about all of this, our going, I mean. I'll be seeing Mother. Actually she's going to be married soon herself. I hope we're in time for the wedding."

"Are you pleased?"

"Ironically enough, she's marrying my godfather."

"God! Then you had better find some other place to live."

Hans laughed, a sharp little laugh.

"At least he'll be more than ready to believe that you're really defecting. He wouldn't want to believe anything else."

Just as you wouldn't, Uncle Karl, Hans thought. It made him profoundly sad. "How did you find out about... England, if you didn't know before?"

"Kruger let it slip. I guess he thought that Admiral Canaris had told me everything. I really gave him hell. I'm not in Abwehr, but I know enough not to talk about things when the other person has no need to know, whether he actually knows about it or not. And when it involves such very sensitive information...!" He shook his head angrily.

"You'll have to be properly appalled when the news comes out."

"If it comes out. I don't think that the powers-that-be are given to advertising defections, even when they're not real. Maybe especially when they're not real. Does her family know?"

"Just her uncle."

"And what does he have to say about it?"

"He's not happy, but there wasn't much he could do."

"What's he going to tell his wife?"

"Probably that we're going to Warsaw. I don't know."

"Warsaw?"

Hans just looked at him. The word 'Russia' could not be mentioned. The planning for it was just gearing up and Warsaw would have been a logical Abwehr posting.

Then Karl was nodding slowly. He understood. Hans knew he would.

"Hans?" It was Dieter coming into the hallway. "Good." Then, "Excuse me, sir," to Karl.

"That's all right, Bergmann. The bridegroom takes precedence today."

He smiled briefly. "Thank you, sir. Are you finished with him?"

"Yes."

He nodded. "Frau Schroeder asked me to find you, Hans. Annaliese is ready to go."

"I'll be up in a minute."

"I'll be out in the Kuebel. It's ready to go."

"Fine. Thank you."

Hans thrust out his hand toward his uncle. "I'm glad that you could be here. You're the only member of my family who is."

Karl took his hand, shaking and warmly. "You've forgotten about your cousin, Gunter."

"I'd like to."

"Don't blame you. Could never figure out where he came from except that poor Hilda would marry that fool husband of hers. Knew he'd come to no good. The son certainly hasn't. Impossible."

"Makes money, though."

"Probably prints it. How anyone has the patience to do business with him..." Karl shook his head.

Hans laughed. "I'll tell Mother I saw you and you asked me to send your best when I wrote next."

"Good. Good. That ought to do it." He shook Hans' hand again, almost wringing it. "Be careful, my boy, and take care of that wife of yours." He gave a bark of a laugh. "But I have the feeling she can take good care of herself when she has to."

Hans was smiling as he turned and made his way to the back staircase to go up to get Annaliese. Karl looked after him, wishing that he hadn't known. It would have made life much easier. He shook his head. No, that wasn't true. He would have heard about this supposed defection eventually from someone. It wouldn't be possible to keep it totally under wraps. And if he hadn't known the facts, he would have felt that he had helped a British spy, that Hans was indeed what Kramer had tried to make him out to be. He shuddered at the thought. Take care, my boy. You'll need to. All of you will.

He walked slowly out into the front hall, just in time to see Hans and Annaliese come down the stairs and rush out the front door into a hail of confetti.

*     *     *

"Michael, darling!"

He pulled the receiver away from his ear. She was all but shouting into the phone. "Anne, dear love," he spoke cautiously into the mouthpiece, the receiver still well away from his ear. "If you want me to hear what the minister has to say eight days from now..."

She laughed. "I'm sorry. It's just that I have the most incredible news. I've had a letter from John. He's getting married. He is married. Yesterday! A girl named Annaliese Scheuermann. Her parents are dead. He didn't say how. And she was raised by an uncle who is a Kapitan-zur-See. This damn war..." Her voice had taken on a bitter edge but it disappeared as she said "He sounds blissful."

"As well he should!"

"Oh, Michael, I wish I could have been there."

"So does he, darling."

"Damn this war. I haven't even met her! And it's so sudden!"

"Are you sure?" John had said something about a girl in his last letter to Julia.

"He says that he met her when he got to Hamburg last June. He sent a picture of them together. He looks wonderful. She was smiling. A lovely little thing. He says that in some way she reminds him of me."

"Then she's bound to be perfect."

"A lot you know."

"You mean there are things I still have to find out about you?"

"You'll just have to wait and see."

"You're not going to give me the bad news ahead of time?"

"Not on your life!" She was most emphatic.

"Then I'll just have to take my chances."

"Yes, you will." She paused. "There is one thing, though." She paused again. "I'm not very well organized and you are so efficient."

He laughed.

"Don't laugh. It really intimidates me at times."

"My laughing?"

"No. Your damnable efficiency."

"My darling, I have every faith that if it became necessary you could run the war single-handed."

She snorted to the phone. "If I were running it, our straits would be desperate indeed."

They already are, my dear, he thought. At least they are right now. Give us a few more months... But all he said was, "Nonsense. You'd be our best secret weapon. Turn that bewitching smile of yours on der Fuehrer and he'd forget everything else including the war."

"Shall I try?"

"Not on your life. Some sacrifices are too great, even for Mother England."

"It's just as well. He's not my type."

"That reassures me more than you can possibly imagine."

She laughed. "Roll on the peace."

"Amen." It was a heartfelt reply.

"Has Carter left yet?"

"Yesterday."

"I don't think he approves of me."

"Oh, I think he does, but I also think that he knew he couldn't cope with a full household."

"Will you miss him?"

"In some ways, very much. He had been with me for a very long time. and he's a good man. But somehow I think you'll find ways to console me."

"When?"

He smiled, utterly happy. How could he not love someone who made him so happy? "Tonight?"

"Of course! Would you like dinner... too?"

"Please." He was laughing into the phone.

"When will you come?"

"Eight too late?"

"No. That's fine. About eight." She paused. "Michael, are they as happy as we are?"

"I devoutly hope so."

"So do I. But I don't think it's possible. No one could be as happy as we are. Especially over there."

His smile faded. "Until eight. Bye, darling."

*      *      *

It was a moment before Hans realized where he was. He turned his head to look at her as she slept but he could see only her profile. Room to maneuver. He smiled. The Panzers always like to have room to maneuver and he and Annaliese had it at last. That bed of hers at the School House had been far too narrow. All this room and yet they had gone to sleep together, in the middle of the bed, like two spoons in a drawer. Somehow in the night they had separated, but she was there and she always would be there.

He moved toward her and raised himself on one elbow, looking down, memorizing her face until he could stand it no longer. He brushed a tendril of hair from her forehead, then leaned down and gently kissed each of her closed eyes before pulling back to watch her wake up. She did it gradually, staring at him for a moment with heavy-lidded eyes. Then she smiled up at him, a slow, luxurious smile and it was the end of sense and finally wakefulness until well after noon.

# Chapter XVIII

Dieter glanced up as the small sailboat gave a lurch to starboard and bumped against the jetty. "You're late."

Hans was balancing himself against the sway, up near Annaliese, who was sitting in the bow. His face was grim. "It's on for tonight."

Dieter looked out over the wreckage still cluttering the Dunkirk Harbor without seeing it, as Annaliese wrapped her arms around herself and shivered slightly. "Is it supposed to clear?" It was a cool morning and there was a haze hanging in the air.

Hans looked around. Visibility was what? Three kilometers? Four at the most. "The meteorologist says clearing today, then more of this tonight. First quarter moon, so no moonlight by the time we're scheduled to land. High tide at Dover about 0300 but that won't matter unless the E-boat dumps us so far off the mark that we have to land on the beach. Even then... We'll be landing in broad daylight and with low tide at 0930; there'll be plenty of beach almost anywhere." Despite the damn cliffs. And despite the minefields. Thank God it was a wooden boat.

*     *     *

"I don't know why Michael wouldn't let me tell John when we were getting married or where. It's ridiculous." Anne was positively grumpy. "And why he had to go tearing off to Dover almost the minute we got here is beyond me!"

Annabelle had to look away to hide her smile. This was indeed a woman in love. She couldn't bear to have the captain out of her sight. And as for him... Her smile broadened. It had to have been urgent or he would never have left her alone, especially within half an hour of their arrival. Not today of all days.

Still, it was hard to believe that after all this time Mrs. Richter didn't at least have an idea of what he did, that she'd have to wonder why an MI6 section chief would be unwilling to advertise his precise whereabouts on any given day to anyone in Germany, even to his godson, especially to his godson. John Richter's letters were certainly being monitored by someone over there, and if that someone knew who Michael Compton was... It was especially bad because they were in Dover, only 20 miles from the French coast and within a range of the long range German guns on Cap Gris Nez. "He probably wanted to take care of whatever it is today, so that nothing can possibly interfere with tomorrow, Mrs. Richter."

"Nothing better had," she snapped. "And call me Anne." Then she stopped, aware of how that must have sounded. "I'm sorry, Miss Trimby. I really am. I don't know what's wrong with me."

"Pre-nuptial jitters? I've heard they're very usual. And I'd be pleased if you would call me Annabelle."

It was a lovely day, or it had been. It was getting hazy again. They'd been walking the downs for almost an hour and until now, Anne Richter had set a brisk pace and said very little.

"I don't think that's it," she said softly. "I don't know what it is. All I do know is that I want Michael, right here, right now. I can't... not have him here. I'm just being silly, I know. And poor Michael has enough on his hands without having to deal with a silly woman, too."

Annabelle didn't know what to say, but fortunately for her, Anne didn't seem to expect her to say anything.

"And John," she said bitterly. "I want John here, too, instead of somewhere over there" – she made a sweeping gesture in the vague direction of the Channel – "with the German army. What do they call it this time? The Wehrmacht. Last time it was the Reichswehr. Why can't they just pick a name and settle on that? Idiotic. And Hitler calls Germany the Third Reich. The Third Empire. With what he's conquered, it is a bloody empire, for the time being at least. So why why not call the army the Reichswehr? At least it would be consistent. But no. The Wehrmacht. Probably because the

Reichswehr lost the last war and he doesn't want anyone to think about that. So change the name. Good psychology. I wonder what they'll call it the next time, after they lose this one?"

She was in full flow, talking almost to herself. "I didn't understand it when John stayed over there long enough to be called up. And he should have run, even then. If not right away, at least after Poland, when he could see what was coming. I didn't understand it then and I don't understand it now, because it doesn't make any sense. He's not that sort! Not their sort. And he always hated fighting. Do you know..." – She turned on Annabelle and there were tears glistening in her eyes – "that he has a Ritterkreuz, one of the highest decorations Germany gives for that. Fighting. A Ritterkreuz! And he never told me about it. I had to hear from someone whose Dutch nephew saw him in Berlin. Last February." Then more softly. "He never told me. And he didn't tell me because he knew I'd hate it, just as I hate everything he's doing over there. The cost to James alone!" It was almost a wail.

She jammed her fists into her jacket pockets and lengthened her stride as she struggled to control herself. "He didn't tell me because somewhere inside he's still a good, kind, thoughtful boy. And he's not a Nazi. I keep telling myself that he can't be, that he couldn't be, no matter how hard they might try to make him one. Even Karl can't have become a Nazi. Karl is as Prussian as they come and a thoroughgoing man of honor."

She gave a quick little laugh. "Well, for the most part he is. A bit of a womanizer, our Karl. But he is a Prussian, and not one of those Nazi gangsters!

"I'm sorry." She had stopped again. "You have no idea what I'm talking about. Karl von der Greif is a general on the German General Staff and he's John's and James's uncle by virtue of the fact that he married Gerhard's younger sister, Gretl. Gerhard was my first husband. Oh dear." She gave a helpless little laugh. "He's my only husband until tomorrow. I can't very well have had a first husband until I have a second." She took a deep breath. "I certainly am running on today." Then she was walking again, more briskly this time back toward the house.

Annabelle moved to catch up with her. "You have every right to run on today. I'm sure that if I were getting married tomorrow, I'd be a complete babbling idiot."

Anne stopped again and looked at her, thinking that James was so lucky. "If that boy had any brains, he'd club you over the head, throw you over his shoulder and cart you off to the nearest preacher the first chance he got."

"Goodness! He wouldn't need a club." Then Annabelle realized what she'd said and her face reddened.

Anne smiled, a slowly growing smile. "You have no idea how pleased I am to hear you say that. And don't worry, I won't breathe a word to James. That boy has always taken his own sweet time about things, and he can't be rushed. The few times I've tried, he balked like a mule. But, oh my dear, he has such a good heart." Her eyes filled with tears again. Ridiculous. Silly, weepy woman.

Annabelle saw the change, and for the first time she understood something of what the war had to be doing to Anne Richter. It was her own personal war. A son on each side. By God, how could she stand it? Captain Compton, she thought, you damn well better be there when we get back. She was surprised at the fierceness of the thought, suddenly realizing that she had grown very fond of this woman. How nice. Especially if she and James did... She didn't dare put it into words. Time. Patience. But it was so hard. She loved him so much and just wanted to be with him.

"There you are!"

Annabelle looked up and smiled. Captain Compton was coming towards them through the garden, and it was obvious that 'you' was singular, rather than plural. His eyes were on Anne and Anne's whole face was alight as she stopped to wait for him.

He was beside her now, smiling down at her before he turned to Annabelle. "Did you have a good walk?"

"Yes, sir. Thank you. Is there anything I can do for you?"

"No, Miss Trimby. Not at the present. But thank you for asking."

"Then I think I'll go and finish unpacking." She smiled at Anne.

"I enjoyed our walk."

"So did I. It's been ages since I had a good walk in the country."

Annabelle was at the French doors before Michael thought to shout after her, "Dinner at eight!"

She turned back and gave a little wave to show that she'd heard, then frowned and looked up. That sound. She knew that sound. Oh, God. That faint drone. Planes. She stepped back onto the patio, craning her neck. There. Just there. Specks in the sky. German. They had to be since no planes had gone toward France earlier.

The drone was louder now and the specks larger. Two sizes. Bigger ones flying unsteadily with smaller ones flitting around the edges. And there were masses of them. They seem to cover the sky up to the horizon. The first ones were almost overhead now. Us. Oh, God, please not us.

Her heart seemed to stop as the planes started to fly over, and then she gave a choked little laugh. All those planes to bomb the Kentish countryside? Not bloody likely. And there was no need to bomb Dover, anyway. Not with those long-range guns pounding the town periodically.

But then there were tears in her eyes as she saw other planes coming, the RAF, their contrails high in the sky, coming from the north and west, converging on the Germans. She tried to keep track of the contrails, to see how many there were – knowing there were too few – but tears blurred her vision, and soon there was no use even trying as the German fighters rose to intercept and the contrails twisted and turned into confused patterns.

Two puffs of explosions high in the sky. Whose? Whose? "Oh, God," she said it ferociously, "let it be theirs!"

Michael was holding Anne to him tightly as they walked in silence.

"Where are they going?" she asked finally, but Michael didn't answer. He was watching the planes closely as they came on and on, trying to judge the direction and numbers. They weren't splitting. One huge formation, all heading for the same target, and there was only one target in that direction that was large enough to warrant that many planes, only one target in all of Britain that was large enough. London.

There was a fierce ache in his heart. London. A terrible price to pay, but if it were London, London just might save them all. Two more weeks of concentrated bombing of the RAF fighter fields and the radar stations and the war might well be lost. A mobile radar station had already had to replace the one at Ventnor, and several others were held together by spit and baling wire. Without their radar 'eyes', any air defense would be close to impossible.

And the airfields. Conditions at some of them were close to impossible. Especially at Manston. And if the fighters couldn't land to refit and refuel at those fields, they'd have to move farther north, away from the channel coast, and then...

"Where are they going?" she asked more emphatically this time.

Michael looked down at her, hearing the tension and aware suddenly that she was shaking. Should he? She'd know soon enough anyway.

"London." Poor London. One hell of a trade-off, even with what was at stake.

He heard her gasp, "Oh, God." It was a tremulous oath. But then her voice firm. "We are all here. Together. Safe. They're not bombing the ships in the channel, so even James is safe for the moment. If the house goes, then it goes. But damn them all to hell!" Her face was full of fury. "At least John isn't up there. If he were... If he were bombing London... Oh damn him, Michael!"

There was a choking sob as she tore herself away from him and all but ran into the house.

He looked after her, his heart twisting. Was it worth it? Was anything worth hurting her like this? Making him live a lie to her? But if he told her... how could he? It wasn't safe to tell her. Not for John. He smiled grimly. Not for himself, either. Anne was right. Damn them all to hell.

It was a long time before he turned and went into the house.

\*       \*       \*

"Supper ready?" Hans came into the living room of the small seaside villa that had been assigned to them and stood, looking out the window at the sun setting beyond the dunes. Unfortunately a battery of eighty-eights blocked their view of the Channel.

"If it's not, it will be soon." Dieter yawned elaborately and stretched.

"A short one then, while we're waiting."

Dieter nodded, thinking that Hans had had more to drink these past few days in Dunkirk than he'd ever seen him have. 'Hard on him, going home, encumbered as he was with a wife and a friend?' he asked himself, not without bitterness. Then he sighed. That was one thing Annaliese had tried to make him understand, how hard all this was for Hans, that he wasn't the sort, that it was taking a toll, had always taken a toll.

He shifted around in the chair and watched him pour out two small glasses of schnapps, studied his face as he handed over one glass, then turned away to pick up his own. She was right. He hadn't been the same, not since the shooting. He had thought about it afterward, that day in Hans' room when he thought his anger would never go away. But, oddly, it was beginning to. 'Are you being a traitor to Austria?' Hans his voice in all its viciousness came back to the as it had too often.

What would being a traitor to Austria be? Not the Austria that was part of the Third Reich, but the real Austria, the one he grew up in, whose mountains he had trod since he was a child. The Danube running through Vienna and the parks. He grimaced. Waxing sentimental. Shit. But it wasn't Austria that had stuck him in the army, was it? Hauled him out of medical school, put his whole family under a form of house arrest, hostage to his father's silence, to his silence now.

No. It was Germany. Adolf Hitler's God damn Germany. And because Hans had been fighting that Germany all along... Who the hell was the traitor? He, because he'd given into the system, went along with the perpetuating of the Third Reich out of fear, or Hans who risked life and limb and friends and everything? He looked down at his glass in silence.

"Hazy again."

He looked up, saw Hans staring out of the window again, and followed the direction of his eyes.

"Better for us if it's not a clear night." Hans drained his glass and turned back to pour more. "Just as long as it doesn't turn into a fog." The words were barely more than a mutter.

"Confusion to our enemies," Dieter said loudly and raised his glass.

"That's already taken care of," said Hans slowly. He was eyeing Dieter with something akin to wariness. "At least as far as the immediate ones are concerned."

Dieter rose and came toward him.

"Bon voyage," Hans said as they linked elbows in the age-old German fashion and with a formality that almost turned it into a rite. After a long swallow Hans cleared his throat and asked, "Scared?"

"Shitless." Dieter sank back into the chair. "You?"

"Equally."

"And Annaliese?"

Hans smiled. "I really couldn't say. She seems totally unruffled. Reminded me that it was my mother's birthday tomorrow and that we hadn't a present for her and then said that we would have to do something about making out a budget."

"A budget?" Dieter had to laugh. "Jesus." He shook his head and mumbled it this time, almost to himself. "A budget."

"My reaction exactly."

Dieter lifted his glass. "To your fair lady and her budget," then tossed down the rest.

"To my fair lady and her budget," Hans repeated and raised his glass towards the ceiling and their bedroom.

*       *       *

A church bell was ringing in the distance and it was scarcely a slow, solemn knell. Michael looked over at Charlie Fitzhugh with concern.

Charlie shrugged and took another sip of wine. An excellent vintage, one to be savored, especially these days. He put down the glass. "A fire somewhere?"

Anne shivered. It was London that was burning, the docks in flames. Any fire here would be nothing in comparison. "If it is, I hope they put it out quickly."

Charlie looked over at her, admiring her once again, thinking that Michael had been right when he said that a book could be made on the fact that she was beautiful. Exquisite was a better word for it. And the tall, slim, elegant Miss Trimby. What an office decoration she'd make. Could she possibly be a good secretary in the bargain? Probably one of the best. Michael would insist on the best. "A veritable feast, Mrs. Richter." Damn that church bell. But if it were anything serious, he would have been contacted. "How did you manage it?"

Anne smiled." I haven't the faintest idea. I think we can consider this dinner a wedding present from Hannah and Max."

"A handsome present, indeed. So your Max has hidden talents, Michael. Every household has need of a scrounger these days."

Michael laughed. "Max has outdone himself this time, even for Max."

The phone rang.

Michael frowned and Anne looked fixedly at her wine glass, turning the stem to allow the candlelight to catch the facets of the cut crystal. Annabelle's hands were clenched tightly in her lap.

After a moment, Max appeared at Charlie's elbow. Anne suppressed a sigh of relief. "There's a telephone call for you, Colonel Fitzhugh."

"Max, will you please tell whoever it is that I am at dinner." Charlie just refrained from snapping. Idiots. He had told them not to disturb him unless it was a real emergency. His heart fell. What could he be thinking of? Of course, it had to be an emergency. And the church bell...

"Excuse me, please," he said to Anne as he rose and carefully placed his napkin beside his plate. "I think I'd better take it."

"Of course."

Max was just coming back into the dining room. He stepped aside to allow Charlie to precede him into the hall. He indicated the phone and kept his voice low.

"It's a Captain Hedges, sir, and he asked me to tell you that it's a very urgent matter."

He nodded. "Thank you, Max," and picked up the phone.

*     *     *

"Is it likely to be something serious, darling?"

Michael shrugged. "Everything's serious these days." The church bell. He should have realized at once. Church bells were to be rung only to warn of invasion. But the Germans weren't coming. At least not tonight. It couldn't be. The latest reconnaissance photos and all of their intelligence sources indicated no unusual activity. And to mount an invasion on the scale of the one that would be required... And the planes had bombed London, not the coastal defenses, and on far too massive a scale for it to be a diversion.

"It would be too bad if Colonel Fitzhugh had to leave," said Annabelle soberly.

Michael looked at her and smiled. "It would be indeed. Especially before dessert. He's good company."

"Yes, he is."

At that moment Charlie reappeared, clearly agitated and trying valiantly to hide it. "I'm very sorry, Mrs. Richter, but I must leave."

"I'm sorry, too, Colonel Fitzhugh, but of course you must."

He turned. "And Michael, I'm afraid that you'd better come with me."

Michael gave him a hard look, but Charlie's face told him all he needed to know. He nodded, took a sip of wine, dabbed his mouth with his napkin and rose

"Darling, I'm sorry."

"I know you are. Just come back as soon as you can."

"I'm afraid he may be quite late, Mrs. Richter."

"By noon, please, Colonel Fitzhugh."

Charlie laughed. "I wouldn't like to have to try to keep him that long."

"You couldn't." Michael grinned at him then leaned down to kiss Anne's cheek. "I'll be back as soon as I can."

She nodded. "If it's too late, sleep there and come back in the morning, or Max can bring your things in to you. You'll need all the rest you can get."

He started laughing. It was contagious. Soon they all were laughing, and Anne could do nothing but join in helplessly.

Michael was still laughing as he said, "Miss Trimby."

"Captain Compton."

"Miss Trimby, it was a pleasure meeting you. I'm sure I'll see you tomorrow."

"I'll look forward to that, Colonel Fitzhugh."

Anne was trying to look serious. "We all will."

That's set them off again.

Charlie was grinning and shaking his head when he said, "I'm really sorry to have to cart off your bridegroom."

"All is forgiven." Her smile was brilliant. "And I will see you tomorrow."

"I hope so." His voice was grim suddenly as he turned to follow Michael out.

Anne and Annabelle looked at each other, neither wanting to say what each was thinking.

Finally, Anne sighed and said, "Let's have our coffee and dessert in the drawing room and enjoy the fire."

Annabelle nodded as she rose. "An excellent dinner, Mrs. Richter."

"Anne, please, yes. Yes, it was."

She drew in a deep breath as she led the way into the drawing room. Suddenly she was quite sure of something she'd suspected for a long time. Michael was not simply in the Foreign Office.

*      *      *

Michael leaned back in the rear seat of the staff car beside Charlie as the driver concentrated on staying on the road. The faint beams of the blackout headlights were barely adequate to the task. And even then only at very slow speeds.

Charlie leaned over and spoke, almost in Michael's ear. "It's Cromwell."

He stiffened. Codename Cromwell. Army and Home Guard at full readiness. Danger of imminent invasion. Why? It couldn't be. Someone had just got nervous. Too bad there wasn't some sort of intermediate order, something between business as usual and all out alert. But there wasn't.

"Damn fools spent nearly half an hour checking before they called me."

"At least that explains the church bells."

"Do you think they'll come?"

"No, but I think conditions are right for them to. We knew they would be about now."

"Better to be safe than sorry," said Charlie gloomily.

"Are we safe?"

"God, no. I wish we were. Just whistling in the dark, I'm afraid. Turn Jerry back with scythes and pikes? Not bloody likely." He sighed. "It's better than it was three months ago but we need the winter. By spring we'll be ready for them, but not until spring."

"Don't worry; they won't come."

"How can you be sure?" There was only one safe answer. "Anne said so."

"Anne said so?" Charlie gave a little laugh "Remarkable woman, and that. Wish I'd found one like her." He sounded wistful. "Worth hanging onto."

"Damn right."

"Lucky sod."

"Damn right."

They lapsed into silence, each wrapped in his own thoughts.

\*     \*     \*

Lieutenant Commander Fredericks came out onto the bridge and stood looking around. Damn haze. Visibility down to what? Next to nothing in the darkness. Supposed to clear but there were no signs of that yet. One hell of a night for this Cromwell business. Maybe it was clearer off the suspected landing areas? Probably, or the signal wouldn't have been sent out. At least the cliffs made the whole Dover area into a fortress, so they wouldn't come here. Thank God. Dover had enough to cope with without that.

If only the ships had radar. It would make life so much simpler and them far more effective. But radar would be a long time coming to destroyers. It was too bulky. And when it finally did get small enough, the old V and W's would probably be the last on the list.

An eastbound convoy was due off Dover between 0230 and 0300. He hoped the haze had cleared by then. A convoy, by God, crossing the path of the invasion force? He chuckled. That would be a first-class mess if there ever was one. He brightened at the thought before coming back to the present and looking around again. Rank doth have its privilege. He hadn't spoken, so he hadn't been spoken to; they had come to know him well.

James' watch. Too bad *Vectis* had to be out on patrol tonight. It was his mother's bridal dinner. At least they were patrolling just off Dover so they ought to be back in ample time for the wedding. Should be fun, being part of the honor guard. He smiled.

"Wish it would clear."

Fredericks saw the gleam of James's teeth through the darkness. "All the better to see you with, my dear?"

"Exactly."

"Let's hope that we are cast as the woodsman and not the wolf."

"Amen to that."

"Think they'll come?"

The captain shrugged. "Who knows? But there must be at least a chance of it or the army and the Home Guard wouldn't have been put on alert."

James' voice was hard. "Well, we are as ready as we can be."

"At this point. But next spring..." His voice trailed off.

"Guns. We'll have more guns by then, and tanks."

"We sure as hell haven't much now," Fredericks tried not to sound gloomy. "When I think about everything we had to leave at Dunkirk..." He shook his head.

"They're taking the field guns out of the museums, for God's sake," James said.

"They work, but that's about all you can say for some of them," Fredericks sounded actively gloomy now. "Still, Jerry will have one hell of a fight on his hands. We haven't had foreign invaders on our soil since 1066."

"We'll have to do a bit better this time around."

Before Fredericks could reply, a voice rang out, "Captain!"

He all but sighed. "Yes, Number One?" What was he doing up here anyway?

"Do you hear it, sir?"

He listened, but it was a moment before he could hear it. Planes. A steady drone. From the south. High level. Bombers. The Luftwaffe. London again? London was already burning. The docks. What a fire that must be. The perfect target beacon. Poor London. "Yes, I hear it."

The sound was louder now.

The planes came on and on and it was quite some time before the sound disappeared as the planes swept north over the coast. Fredericks shivered. At least it wasn't Dover. Then he smiled a very good smile. One hell of a note to be wishing Dover's disasters on someone else, especially London. But Dover had had about all she could take.

\*     \*     \*

Hans looked back toward the harbor, which was already swallowed up in the darkness. He was glad the planes had gone. They had heard them in the west as they assembled over Calais, huge numbers of them. London again? Mother... Where was Mother? And Hannah. Michael. James was at sea. At least he should be. And the docks were a long way from Eaton Square. Still...

The docks. He had been almost physically ill when he'd heard they were burning. Father had often taken him down there when he had to oversee loading or unloading of special cargo. He had loved it. The huge ships from all over the world. The smells. Men bent nearly double under their loads. The cranes. Gone. All gone. Where would it end? No sense thinking about it. Not now. There was too much else to think about.

He slapped the belt under his sweater nervously, just to make sure it was still there. He had managed to exchange the real negatives for the same number of fakes before they were sealed in the small waterproof pouch that now was snug against the small of his back, held there by the web belt to which it was attached.

The E-boat was really moving. He looked back at the foam of the wake, grateful that the rise of the cabin sheltered them from the force of the wind the E-boat was creating. Testing the engines? He hoped so, because at this rate they would get to their station far too soon. They would have to stooge around, waiting for the star shell that would be the signal for the E-boat to run in and drop them off. As if in response to his thoughts, the engines were throttled back. Good.

At least this time the powers-that-be weren't taking any chances. An eastbound convoy was due in the Dover patrol sector shortly before 0230, and a squadron of E-boats would be lying in wait, well inside what was thought to be the western boundary of that sector, ready to attack the convoy and draw off the patrol ship. But the sector boundaries were changed at irregular intervals, so it was impossible to be absolutely certain that the E-boats were attacking in the right place. But even if they were close to the line on the wrong side, it should be close enough.

The time of greatest danger would be when the E-boat was unloading the sailboat. Not that it was difficult. This was one of the E-boats that had been modified to lay mines, and the sailboat would simply be slid down the rails and into the sea. But the E-boat would have to stop to do it. Not for long, but it would have to stop. When an E-boat was underway, it could outrun even a destroyer, and once the E-boat was gone, it wouldn't matter if they were found. But for those few minutes when the E-boat was dead in the water...

They were getting closer and closer every moment. He clenched his fists and his legs automatically adjusted to the pitch and yaw of the boat. England. He wanted to shout it. England! The word screamed through his brain.

Dieter was looking at his boots, even though all he could see was the dark shadow of his feet against the lighter deck. It was hard to believe. He really was going to England. It had all the qualities of a bad dream. But this time he wouldn't wake up. He'd never considered going to England. Vienna had been far enough from home, thank you. Would he ever get back there, get back to medical school? Or to the inn? The mountains. Father, Mother, and Sabina. His heart seemed to weigh a ton. What was it to live if he couldn't go back? Hans had said that he'd have to make a choice, defect or live in some sort of isolation under a fake name. Isolation where? The north of Scotland on a farm? That wouldn't be so bad, on a farm. But to have his family think him dead... One hell of a choice.

He hugged himself and shivered. He was going to have to go into the cabin. It was getting cold out here. He gave a small bitter smile.

How the hell could he possibly be cold when he was wearing a uniform jacket on top of a wool sweater with a life belt on top of that? Clever of Richter to insist that he wear his uniform jacket. No chance of being accused of being a spy no matter what happened when they landed. But then Richter had always been a clever bastard. There was a sick feeling in his stomach as he felt a hand on his shoulder and heard Hans his voice in his ear. "We are on our way!"

Dieter shook off the hand. Hans could afford to sound happy. He was going home, for God's sake, and bringing the spoils of war with him.

Hans stood, looking down at Dieter's shape in the darkness. He should have thought. He'd been so full of going home, of it nearly being over, that he'd forgotten what this was for Dieter. "I wish..."

"Don't we all," Dieter snapped. "I'm through wishing. Wishes never come true." He subsided into silence.

Hans turned and went to the rail, watching the E-boats wake.

Annaliese had heard the exchange from where she sat, on the other side of the cabin door, well out of the wind. Dieter had sounded horribly bitter just now. But then, why shouldn't he?

He'd finally told her about his family just the night before when Hans was off tending to something or other. It was a time for confidences, sitting on the dunes, out of the line of sight of that infernal coastal gun, watching the sun set. She had let him talk on and on about home. It was almost as if he needed to have someone to know that he was leaving and why. It was monstrous.

And to have done what he did for Hans, despite the dreadful risk to them... And then to have to pay such a terrible price for having done it. He was leaving everyone and everything that meant anything to him for exile in a strange land where he would know only Hans and her. It would be Hans saving Dieter this time and Dieter had to trust that he would. He had been forced to turn his life over to Hans, hand it to him on a plate. It was what she had done, too, but she and Hans were married. The trust...

Then she remembered Hans's slight nod as he was falling asleep. He wouldn't betray that trust. He couldn't. They'd be all right.

It had been hard not to ask questions, but she hadn't. He loved her. That had to be enough. And once they got to England, this stupid charade would be over. Hans would tell her everything.

"I'm going back to see how the sailboat's riding." Hans' voice broke into her thoughts, startling her.

She nodded and watched him move aft in the darkness. It wasn't easy to walk on the deck, and she was glad to see that he was being careful. When he had disappeared, she looked across at Dieter. Even his outline looked dejected.

She moved over next to him, making sure she was leaning against his arms slightly. The muscles twitched and she heard him ask, "Worried?"

"Only about you."

A grunt of surprise. "Why about me?"

"Because it's hardest for you."

Dieter just nodded slowly because he didn't know what to say. Hans was lucky. He had Annaliese with him. But maybe that would make it even harder. He'd have someone else to worry about, and God only knew whether they'd be able to stay together once they got to England. To have someone and then not to have her, that would be hell. It was all right for Hans. Hans was going home. But for him... It was better that he was alone.

They sat there in silence, and after a time he was surprised to realize that he felt better about things. He couldn't have said why.

*       *       *

James yawned. The convoy should be coming through any time. At least the haze had cleared, for the most part anyway. Orders were to sweep ahead of the convoy, turning back for nothing except a formal distress call, sweep ahead to the eastern perimeter of their sector and then back again, covering the same ground twice to try to catch any E-boats that might be trying to sneak in ahead of the convoy to lie in wait for it. That had happened before. He shuddered, remembering the convoy, what, three weeks before? E-boat attack after E-boat attack by night and then Stukas by day. God. It had been hell. The Channel was strewn with wrecks for miles. Those bastards hadn't missed a trick.

At least this was patrolling in the grand style, back and forth. Not one of those damn boxes with nothing in it. And if Jerry were up to his old tricks... The line of his mouth was grim.

"Object. Red 4-5."

James' head turned in time to see the challenge from the oncoming ship.

"Reply!" It was Fredericks. James hadn't realized that the Old Man had come onto the bridge.

*Vectis* signal lamp flashed and, without needing to be asked, James stepped off the compass platform and, as the captain stepped on, retired to the port railing. He didn't even think about it, didn't stop to realize that they were able to perform the intricate movements of their shipboard ballet instinctively, confident that each performer would be where he should be when he should be there. They all knew the choreography by heart.

"Twenty degrees starboard."

They were turning to run ahead of the convoy. Nothing to do again. James yawned elaborately.

"Cocoa, sir?"

Rigby. Bless the boy. "Indeed. Thank you." Something to do and the warmth of the mug felt good in his hands. It was a cool night.

"Meet her. Steady on Oh-8-5."

How long would the Old Man keep the con? It varied. He hummed to himself, a nameless little tune, then took a cautious sip. The cocoa was hot. It was turning into a nice night, after all. Were the Germans on their way? Too early for it, even if they were. They'd want to land the first wave when it was just light, so they could see where they were and what their ships' guns were hitting, if they had any ships to have any guns to hit anything.

He looked back and took another sip, less cautiously this time. Fortunately, the cocoa had cooled. The convoy had been left behind, invisible now in the blackness but certainly still steaming along at a steady seven knots as all convoys did, come what may.

"Star shell! Dead astern!" Both lookouts had called almost in unison. And there was the sound of distant gunfire. James grimaced. Where the hell had the E-boats come from? They had just come through that area and had seen nothing. Trouble was the damn things were so low in the water that they were all but invisible at night unless they were moving. Then the bow wave was a clear white line. Miserable to have a dust-up back there just within their sector and not be able to be in on it. Sweep on, McDuff. He sighed and wondered if the patrol ship west of them was taking care of any E-boats to the stern of the convoy. Probably. Lucky bastards. Still, *Vectis* had had a dust-up of her own last night. Couldn't hold them all.

"Somebody's getting what for!" Rigby sounded excited.

"Looks that way." Something was on fire. They were about four miles ahead of the convoy and all the action seemed to be to the stern of it.

"Wish we were there."

"Don't we all."

"Guess we had ours last night."

"That we did, Rigby. And there'll be more to come."

"But not tonight."

Rigby sounded so crestfallen that James had to make an effort not to laugh. "You never know."

"You think we might run into something, sir?" He sounded eager again.

"As I said, you never know."

Rigby sighed. "You finished, sir?"

"Yes, thank you."

Rigby took the mug and disappeared.

James looked over the rail, watching the bow wave break. The rigging was singing and the deck fittings were vibrating. Yes, a thoroughly lovely night, despite the damn Germans. Where was Annabelle? He yawned. Ridiculous to wonder that. She was at the Watson's, asleep. He hated having to miss that dinner. Hannah would have outdone herself, and Annabelle by candlelight... She had looked marvelous enough this morning, in the Dover station. Just holding her... Damn.

Mother getting married. Odd thought. But she had looked so happy. Michael, too. Mrs. Compton. He tried it out again. Mrs. Compton. Much as he liked Michael, that was going to take some getting used to.

"Bow wave. Green 1-Oh."

James swiveled, staring just off the starboard bow.

\*       \*       \*

Hans had seen the star shells and felt the E-boat gather speed. His heart was hammering. This was it.

And then there was no time for thought. They checked everything again, struggling to keep their footing as the boat raced through the water, making doubly sure that the gear lashed down in the sailboat, which lay half canted on its side, was still in place, duffel bags along with a bag containing half-empty canteens, the remnants of a picnic Abwehr had sent along and a packet containing maps and a compass, all designed to convince the British that they had really sailed across themselves.

When Hans was finally able to rise, he found Annaliese's hand and squeezed it. She was shaking.

He had to shout over the roar of the engines, though Dieter was only a step or two away. "Ready?"

"As ready as I'll ever be," he shouted back.

"Lifejacket?"

He just barely heard Dieter's "right," for a violent movement of the boat had thrown Annaliese against him. He grabbed her and leaned against the rail to keep from falling, all but shouting in her ear, "I love you!"

She tightened her arms around him briefly, then pulled away and reached blindly for Dieter, hugging him as well. She felt his grunt of surprise before he held her back, so hard that she needed a moment to catch her breath after he abruptly released her. There were tears in her eyes.

They stood there side-by-side, leaning against the port rail, not minding the spray, saying nothing until at last the E-boat started to slow.

An agonized shout from Dieter. "A wake, Hans?"

Hans searched through the darkness and then he saw it, a faint white 'V' with the far side abbreviated. "A ship! To port!" but Hans' frantic shout came too late. The engines had slowed to an idle and the E-boat was sliding across the oncoming bow wave on her own momentum. Before the boat could gather speed again, a star shell lit the night.

*     *     *

"E-boat estimation point dead ahead!" the lookouts shouted almost as one.

Fredericks' "Star shell! Guns, fire as you bear! Starboard twenty!" began even before they finished. Got her dead to rights, by God, sandwiched between *Vectis* and the shore, and they were passing her to the E-boats stern so her torpedoes were useless, for the time being. She'd have to turn to run and meantime...

"Don't let her get away!""

The crack of A and B guns was music to Fredericks' ears. But the E-boat was far from helpless. Her own forward gun was firing back as the water under her stern churned to a foam and she began to pull away. He felt a shudder. Damn! Hit *Vectis* would she? By God, she wouldn't get away with that!

A straddle. He was elated. Their gunnery had improved markedly in the past few months. Plenty of practice helped, he thought sourly. Lines of tracer from the port Oerlikon were raking the E-boat's stern, hitting something sitting there. What the hell was that?

She was moving away fast. Damn. Damn. Damn. At least the X and Y guns were able to fire now, as well. And then, at what seemed to be the last possible moment, the E-boat stopped suddenly and he saw flames.

"Port twenty." A hit! A hit! It was all he could do not to jump up and down.

"Got them! Got them!" Rigby wasn't so restrained. "On fire! Good-oh!" Then he remembered himself and snapped his jaw shut, wiping his hands nervously on the seat of his pants. He heard James laugh and turned, grinning apologetically, "Sorry, sir."

"Not necessary to be sorry. My sentiments exactly."

The now-all-too-familiar black figures were leaping into the sea, silhouetted against a range of orange flame. The fuel tanks? And what was that on the stern? A mast. A mast? James saw it just before the flames got to it. A sailboat, by damn, canted over on her side.

They were still turning to port, circling around to come up west and slightly south of the wreck so they could drift down toward it on the wind and pick up any survivors. Fredericks was watching the dying flames carefully to fix the spot. "James."

"Sir?"

"Go down and see to rigging the nets." Number One was attending to the damage in the port bow. It couldn't be too serious or he would have had a report by now.

"Aye, aye, sir." James disappeared down the ladder.

"Away whaler's crew!"

Finally, after what seemed like an age, he was able to say, "Slow ahead together... Midships... Meet her. Steer 1-3-5." The coxswain echoed every order.

"Lower to the waterline."

And at last, "Stop engines." *Vectis* was sliding to a gradual halt.

"Away whaler!"

There was the slap of the whaler hitting the water and then *Vectis* was drifting. The silence was deafening.

\*　　\*　　\*

"Dieter!" Hans's shout ended in a sputter as he took a wave in the face. He shook his head and turned his back to the wind, motioning for Annaliese to do the same. He'd managed to hang on to her when they'd jumped over the side, but where the hell had Dieter gotten to? And he was hurt. Hans had heard a sharp cry of pain just before he hit the water.

He tried again. "Dieter!" There. That was better.

"Here!" The reply was strangled but definite.

"Where?" Hans turned his head sharply towards what he thought was the direction of the sound.

"Here!" It was almost a grunt this time, but at least he had the direction. Annaliese's hand came out of the water, pointing toward the sound.

"Come on! Can you move?"

"Of course." She sounded indignant.

He struggled to move against the chop of the waves, toward the sound of Dieter's voice. Damn life preserver. It was almost as much hindrance as help, to say nothing of a wool sweater and a uniform jacket. He stopped for a moment. Boots. Get off the boots. It was an enormous effort for Hans to bend enough to grab and tug at first one then the other. But at last they had fallen free. "Talk, Dieter!"

"Don't... know... if... I... can..." And there was a choking cough.

"Back to... the wind." Hans was breathing hard with the effort of moving against the waves. He had to stop again. It was just as well. Annaliese's head was bobbing towards him. She was barely making a ripple. How did she do that? He had been wallowing around like a whale in distress while her arms never cleared the water.

"Okay?"

"Yes." But she was gasping for breath.

"Dieter!"

"Here, damn it."

At least he wasn't coughing now and he was closer. But his voice sounded strange. Whose wouldn't? He began moving again with Annaliese close behind. He was trying it her way and it was easier. "You okay?" He managed to call.

"Leg."

At last Hans saw a black blob bobbing in the dark of the waves, and finally he was beside him, and turning to shout, "Annaliese!"

"Coming!" The reply was a grunt, breathless, but finally she was there, too, turning her back to the wind, lying back as far as she dared, to let the life belt hold her while she caught her breath.

Hans was floating next to Dieter. "Your leg." Economy of words. There was no breath or inclination for anything else.

"Broken. Boat lurched. Hit rail."

God. "Bad?"

"Hurts."

If Dieter admitted that it hurt, then it hurt like hell. "What can I do?"

"Nothing. What's there to do?"

He was right. There was nothing to do. The ship? He looked around. There were anxious cries off to his right. Where was the ship? There was no sign of it. Would they leave them here? Not bloody likely. But where were they?

When he looked back it was to see that Annaliese had worked her way around to Dieter's other side.

She put her hand through the strap around Dieter's life belt. They had to stay together. Keep Dieter in the middle. Oh, God – it was a plea – keep us together. She remembered Uncle Friedrich saying that it was easier to find groups in the sea than individual men one by one. Besides, they had to stay together because they had to stay together.

"Okay, Dieter?" Hans asked again.

"Okay." But his voice was weaker.

"Ship's gone." It was Annaliese.

"They'll be back."

"You sure?"

"Gentleman in the... Royal Navy... pick up the survivors." He gave a choking laugh. It had just occurred to him. "We're safe."

"Safe?" Annaliese couldn't believe what she'd just heard. "Sea? Broken leg? No ship? Safe?" She had to get the words out between breaths.

Hans had finally gotten into a position where he was riding the waves more comfortably and found that he could talk. "We'll get caught on the high seas, and in uniform."

"Unless they don't come back." Dieter sounded profoundly weary now.

"They will." Hans was serenely sure.

"How can you... be sure?" Annaliese sounded worried.

Time for a little humor. "I was worried... But here I am... damn bullets missed by a hair's breadth. But I must be a cat with nine lives. I survived. We all did and we all will."

"Twenty-four lives."

Hans made the mistake of turning back towards Dieter and he got slapped in the face by a wave for his pains. He had to turn back. It was a moment before he was able to ask. "Why twenty-four?"

"You saved twenty-seven in Poland. Used three. Twenty-four left."

"So how many does that give you? You saved twenty-seven with me plus the three I nearly lost."

"Only two. Bauer saved one."

He had Dieter's interest. He was talking now and his voice sounded better. "Two and eight then. You saved my arm. Glad to have it right now." And he was. More than glad. "Was getting sick of it anyway."

"Your arm?" It was Annaliese who asked.

Hans snorted and shook his head, trying not to laugh, not wanting another mouthful of seawater. "Dieter saving me. It should be my turn to save him." He paused and took a deep breath. "But I can't. Even here. Damn Royal Navy will save him. Not me. Shit!" He managed to sound disgusted.

That made Annaliese giggle, and he was glad to hear it.

"But they'll be saving you, too!" Then it struck her so funny that she laughed, which was a mistake. A wave hit her open mouth and she wound up choking and coughing.

"Forgot about that." He sounded very disgusted indeed. "Hate it. Somebody's always saving me. Want to save somebody!"

"Twenty-seven," Dieter reminded him. He seemed amused.

"All of us did that. It doesn't count."

"Then you're back to nine lives."

"Twenty-seven then. Shouldn't cut it down to nine. The way things are going… That's shaving it too fine." He was tired now. He wanted to go to sleep. Think. Think. Keep talking.

"Captured on the high seas." Dieter was trying to think about that, but his leg hurt so much that it made thought difficult. Why did it seem important that he was going to be caught on the high seas?

"You'll be an ordinary prisoner then."

"Grand!" Dieter's head was spinning. He shook it but it only made things worse. "Not ordinary."

"Right. Extraordinary." Hans spit out a mouthful of seawater. He felt as if he'd swallowed half the Channel. "Your parents will know you're alive." He floated again, holding onto the strap of Dieter's life belt. "And where you are." He just managed to shut his mouth as a wave hit him in the face. The wind must be shifting. "Turn."

"Can't." It was barely a whisper. Dieter's ears were ringing. Then he was being turned and there was an exquisite pain from the torsion it put on his leg. His head slumped forward.

Hans saw what was happening, released the strap and grabbed a handful of Dieter's hair, using it to pull his face out of the water. "Dieter!"

There was no answer.

"What is it?" Annaliese had been floating, listening. She was upright now and terribly afraid.

"He's passed out." Hans was working his way around Dieter, holding up his head, until finally he was in a position to act as a breakwater for him. He wished that he had thought of that sooner. Dieter was floating almost straight up and down and it was hard to keep his head back far enough to keep his mouth out of the water. They had to get some weight off his bottom half. Bring up his legs.

But one was broken. Which one? He hadn't said. "Can you... Check out his legs?... Which one?"

Annaliese didn't bother to answer but struggled to get under-water. At once she came up and went down to try again, sliding her hand down each leg. Oh, God. It really was broken. The left one. As she broke the surface and gasped for air, a wave hit her full in the face and she was choking. It was impossible. She couldn't seem to get her breath.

"Turn! Turn!" She heard Hans shouting at her through the haze but she couldn't seem to make herself move. Another wave hit her. She couldn't breathe. Then there was a fearful tug at her life belt and she was being turned and held, right next to Dieter.
"Get your head up!" He was yelling at her ear.

She barely managed, but when she did, she found she was floating a little again, chest heaving, riding the waves, the life belt and something else holding her up. Hans? How was he doing that? She turned her head slightly and saw that she was being partially supported by Dieter's shoulder. Hans must be holding her there.

He was just barely managing that, and he couldn't keep it up for long. Dieter's head was against his chest and he had the back of Annaliese's life belt in one hand as he worked to keep the two of them together. It had been a near thing. He was shaking.

After what seemed like an eternity, when he thought that he couldn't hang on for another moment, he heard her voice saying, "I'm all right. You can let go."

He did so, gratefully, and they rode the waves, side-by-side in silence, until he felt he could speak. "Got to get... his boots off."

She heard the distress in his voice and she was afraid again. But she knew too that he had enough to contend with without her being afraid. "Can't. Leg."

"Which?"

"Left."

"Right boot, then."

"I'll try."

"No!" He couldn't go through that again. "Can you... take his head?... Make breakwater?"

So that was what he was doing. "Yes."

She pulled on Dieter's shoulder to slide herself around, then grabbed his hair to hold his head back, shielding him as Hans moved away, protecting his head from the effect of the waves with herself. She could feel the problem at once. Would one boot be enough? And could he get it off?

'I can do this,' Hans thought. He gritted his teeth and went under, feeling along Dieter's legs. Damn life preserver. Hard to stay under. God Almighty. The left leg was broken. He gave a quick pull on the right boot. It gave, but only a little. He surfaced, then went down to try again. It took three tries but finally, as he gave a last, desperate tug on the heel of the boot, his lungs bursting with the effort, he felt it slide off, and let it fall away. Dieter's body rose, but only slightly.

He was on the surface again, gasping for breath, his back to the short breaking waves. Was it enough? It was going to have to be. There was no way to get his pants off without taking off that other boot, and with that leg...

"Hans."

"Yes." It was all he could manage.

"Why... would Dieter's parents... think him dead?"

Hans rode the waves. He simply couldn't tell her. It took too much energy to talk. He was riding a bit better. She had to be getting tired. He almost laughed. He was beyond being tired. Slowly he worked his way around beside her. "Take him?"

"Yes."

They made the switch in slow motion.

"Why, Hans?"

Hans jerked his head around toward the sound of a splash off in the distance. What was it? Another sound. Oars? Whatever it was, it was going away from them. But there was a dark shape moving up into the night. How far away? It was impossible to tell. He could hear the cries in the water, renewed now that there was someone to hear them.

"Here!" he shouted. It was almost a scream.

Annaliese shouted with him.

There was no reply. Had they not heard? But at least the ship was coming closer.

"Here! Here!"

They were shouting again as a searchlight stabbed a finger through the night, finally finding and holding as they continued to shout and give sporadic waves.

But then they were content to wait as they saw that the ship was drifting towards them on the wind. It seemed to take forever.

A voice drifted across the waves. "Nets. Ready?"

"Yes!" He shouted the word. Nets. But they must have some other way to get Dieter up.

The ship was closer still, drifting right down on him, the spotlight out now. But it didn't matter.

Then another voice came booming through the darkness, speaking in impeccable German. "There are boarding nets."

Hans was puzzled. There was something about that voice, that accent... It took all his strength to shout back in English, "Man hurt!"

"Repeat!" The word came back in German.

Ass. If he was determined to speak German, so be it. Hans shouted it again, in German this time. The ship was only about 30 yards off now. The sea was a little calmer. The ship must be cutting the effect of the wind and the waves.

The searchlight stabbed a finger at them briefly again and went out.

"Can't hear!" The voice was inpatient now, still speaking German. "Can you board?" What was it about that voice?

"Man hurt!"

This was met with silence.

Thanks a bunch, thought Hans. He waited. There was nothing else for it. The ship was only about 10 yards away. Searchlight. They weren't taking any chances. He couldn't blame them. At least the sea was calm, and that was an enormous relief.

Then that voice came again. "Sending down a bowline. Put it around the injured man, under his arms. We'll haul him up. Can you climb?"

Hans looked towards Annaliese. "Can you climb?"

"Of course."

"Yes!" He shouted up toward the deck of the ship looming over them.

"The line!" came the shout and there was a splash beside him. He grabbed the loop and struggled to get it over Dieter's head, thinking that it was well that Dieter had on a life belt. The pull of that rope against his back and underarms would have been hell otherwise.

He was grunting with the effort. Dieter still hadn't moved, and now they were being nudged along by the ship. It was an oddly frightening sensation.

"Need help?" Annaliese his voice was close to his ear.

"Bend his arm and lift it."

He could hear her labored breathing as she struggled to help him. It took every ounce of strength he had, even with her helping, but finally they managed it.

"Climb!" His voice was harsh. She had to do it on her own. God, help her. It was a prayer. She was climbing.

He shouted up, still in German, "Done! Mind his left leg! It's broken!"

"Right!" came the answering shout. "Climb!"

But Hans waited, hanging onto the net until he saw the line was tightening and that Dieter was being lifted out of the water.

Only then did he begin to climb, looking up to see Annaliese being helped over the rail. Thank God. At last he could concentrate on himself. It was just as well, since it was a real effort to climb with the slack of the horizontal ropes each time he put his weight on one. Good thing these ships were low to the water, or at least this one was, by the stern. What was it? A destroyer? Probably, with that low stern and so much higher by the bow.

Finally, he was being unceremoniously hauled over the rail and dumped onto the deck. He was tripping as he rose slowly, legs

shaking a bit with the effort. Annaliese came to his side, followed
by a few stares, but most eyes were over the side, on Dieter as he
was being hauled aboard.

Hans took her hand.

"Mind his leg."

"Which one?"

"Left, damn it."

"Weighs a ton."

There was a responding grunt as Dieter's head appeared.

Hans was squeezing Annaliese's hand so hard that it hurt, but
she said nothing. Dieter. He was so still. At least they were being
careful as they hauled him over the rail.

"Ought to break the other bloody leg for him," came the angry
growl.

"Briggs! None of that."

Hans swiveled and stared, but the officer who had spoken was
hidden in the shadows. Then he switched on a hooded flashlight as
he moved towards Dieter who was being lowered to the deck.

"Mind his leg," followed by, "his leg, dammit"

Hans couldn't move. His eyes were riveted on the officer as he
bent over Dieter. The man stood back to give him room. "Murphy,
get Doc and a stretcher. Briggs, keep an eye on these two."

There was the sound of footsteps pounding away on the iron
deck.

The officer was slapping Dieter's face likely now, watching for
any reaction by the light of a hooded flashlight. There was no
response.

As he rose, Hans was able to see the line of his mouth, grim
now, and the set of a bold jaw as the light went out.

Annaliese felt the sharp intake of his breath.

"What is it?"

Her whisper was urgent, but Hans didn't hear her. He had
dropped her hand, but she could sense the tension in him. It almost
crackled in the air.

Feet were pounding on the iron deck again.

"He's here, Doc."

"Right, James. I'll take him." Another man was with him, carrying something. A splint?

"What about these two?"

She was startled by the voice almost in her ear and glanced back. The man seemed enormous. She shivered. It was the man who had wanted to break Dieter's other leg.

"Get them below."

"Please." She was summoning all of her English. "Let us wait and go down with him." Briggs' hand was rough on her arm.

"Let them stay." James' voice was harsh. "When the whaler comes back, they can all go down together. The woman goes to the captain's harbor cabin."

"Aye, aye, sir," Briggs grumbled, letting go of her arm and moving back a step. She was grateful. She didn't like being touched in any way by that man.

As two men came up with a stretcher, the sounds of the whaler returning could be heard in the distance. A group of sailors moved toward an upright structure which she realized must be used for hauling in the boat. The doctor was still bent over Dieter, putting on what had to be a splint.

"Lieutenant Richter, sir!" The voice was young.

"Yes, Rigby."

"The captain said to tell you, sir, that he would appreciate your staying with the prisoners until they're sorted out."

"Thank you, Rigby. Tell him I'll see to it."

"Aye, aye, sir." Message delivered, the boy was off from whence he came. But Annaliese didn't notice that. Her head was spinning.

Lieutenant Richter? That couldn't be a common name in England. It wasn't all that common in Germany. And the doctor had called him James. James Richter. Oh, God. It couldn't be. But if it were James, that explained Hans' behavior. She looked over at Hans but all she could see was his profile. He hadn't taken his eyes off that officer.

The whaler was alongside now, and there was another voice, a nasty supercilious voice. "Let's get this mess cleared up."

Annaliese was puzzled. What mess could he mean? The water she was dripping on the deck? She couldn't help that. Or Hans either. Dieter? What?

"Damage below taken care of?"

Hans gave a wisp of a smile. He recognized the veiled sarcasm in James' voice.

"Yes. A lucky shot. Well above the water line. Let's get this going."

The gunner was seeing to the hoisting of the whaler with its crew while the German survivors came up the nets.

James was disgusted. What the hell else was there to 'get going' until the rest of the survivors were on the deck?

"I'm doing just that, or will be as soon as Doc is finished and the prisoners are on board. Captain's orders."

He glanced towards the rail as the survivors came over. Not many. Four. No, five. With these three, that made eight. Eight out of how many? Nineteen? Twenty? And one a woman. A woman on an E-boat. What the hell were they doing with a sailboat? Planning to sail into Dover harbor? "Coxswain?"

"Here, sir."

Good. No time would be wasted then. "Sort them out. Ratings to the mass deck for'ard. The captain, if he's here, to the wardroom with any other officers. And the woman to the captain's harbor cabin."

"Shall I take the woman down, Coxswain?" Briggs' voice was a low growl. Annaliese shivered at the thought of his taking her arm again, but he hadn't moved. Hans was still just standing there.

James winced. Briggs was a thoroughly nasty customer. He'd probably scare her to death. God knows, she was safe enough, under the circumstances. Even so, he wished he thought to assign one of the other ratings to see to her. He smiled bitterly. Why the hell was he worrying about the niceties of dealing with a German spy, woman or no?

"Well, well. A woman."

James sighed as Stillson moved toward Annaliese. Damn fool should be making his damage control report to the captain. But he couldn't bear not being in on it when something was going on. Number One was a real nosy bastard.

Stillson was looking down at her. "Jerry seems to be dropping them all over the Channel these days. Don't see what they expect to accomplish with a bedraggled little bitch like this one, though. Let's get her out of here."

"She stays with me." Hans' voice was low, menacing, and he had spoken English. Damn bastard.

Now it was James who froze.

"And just who the hell are you?"

Stillson was sneering. He really enjoyed dealing with prisoners. Everyone was watching them now, including the prisoners and their guards.

"Her husband." Hans' fists were clenched. This ass wasn't going to take her away from him. No one was. He'd gotten her this far. He was going to take her the rest of the way himself.

"Too bad, you twit. She goes." Stillson shoved her against Briggs even as he leaned towards Hans, sneering again, triumphantly this time.

Unfortunately Stillson leaned a bit too far. His jaw was sticking out. If it hadn't been, Hans might not have hit him. But the target was just too tempting.

This... person wasn't going to take her. And on the 'her,' the haymaker landed. All sense of fatigue was gone as he grabbed Annaliese away from a startled Briggs and shoved her behind him, against the rail at the foot of the stretcher, just as Stillson fell to the deck.

Briggs recovered quickly and grabbed for Hans, spinning him around to get a hold on him from the rear. But as he did, he got a ferocious elbow in the stomach, which doubled him over.

Hans sidestepped and raised his hand, giving Briggs the edge of it on the back of the neck. It was only Briggs' heavy muscles and the

fact that the blow was not well aimed that saved him. He dropped
to the deck with a giant grunt and was still.

There were angry mutterings and a semi circle of men closed in
around Hans.

"Get the other prisoners below!" James' tone was stentorian as
he shone the light into Hans' face to blind him, not noticing the
face for a moment. He glanced around, reassured by the sound of
the coxswain's voice as he heard the same thing echoed from him
in none too gentle tones. It could have become nasty in another
minute or two.

There was a reluctant shuffling of feet behind him and mutters
of "Move on there." They moved.

Then, finally, James took a moment to look at that face as the
semi-circle of men closed in once more. The circle was smaller now.

"Wait!" James' voice was strangled. The man stopped.

The eyes were screwed shut against the light, but there was no
mistaking that face or the fury in it. Little brother.

Jesus. Well, he had learned how to fight after all, hadn't he.
And there was a twinge of grudging admiration. He had got that
bully Briggs and that shithead Stillson in the bargain. James almost
laughed before he remembered where he was. When he spoke, his
voice was rough, controlled. "Murphy!"

"Sir?"

"You and," he stabbed the light toward another man, "you, take
the stretcher down to the wardroom." Doc had departed before the
mayhem had begun, to get things ready.

"Henderson, tend to Number One." He risked a glance in
Stillson's direction and saw that Henderson was already bending
over him. The first lieutenant was groaning and moving a bit. There
was someone else with Briggs, who was on his hands and knees,
shaking his head like some sort of giant bear.

"You." There was another gesture with the light.

"Sir?"

"Help that man get Briggs down to the mass deck for'ard. And
you," the finger of light hit yet another face, "help Henderson get

Number One to his cabin when he can go."

"Aye, aye, sir."

As he clicked off the light, he caught the sight of Rafferty. Just the man. "Rafferty, take the woman to the captain's harbor cabin."

Then, "Coxswain, we'll need a guard in the wardroom flat, as well."

"I've already seen to that, sir. Need any more help here?"

"No, thank you. I'll tend to this one myself."

Hans was still standing there with Annaliese behind him. The stretcher was gone.

Rafferty moved toward them.

"No!" Hans put a hand back to keep her from moving. His legs were shaking with fatigue and his ears were buzzing in a most peculiar fashion. He said it again as Rafferty paused. "No!"

"No, what?" James was furious but he managed to get it out in German. He didn't want anyone to know just who this was.

Hans replied in kind. "She stays with me and we go where Bergmann goes."

The coxswain was moving toward Hans from the other side. James glared at him through the gloom. "I said I'd handle this."

He took a step back and waited.

"Who the hell is Bergmann?"

"On the stretcher." It was an effort for Hans to talk now and he was shivering.

"The doctor has him. He's a good doctor. The woman..." He couldn't bring himself to say 'your wife'.

"The woman will be safe in the captain's harbor cabin. There will be a guard outside and the man who's taking her there is an incurable romantic. The only danger she'll be in from him is that he'll fall in love with her before he gets her there."

He had to get the deck cleared. This couldn't be allowed to go on. There were angry mutterings.

Hans managed to step aside. "Go." It was in order. He didn't look at her.

"Hans!" She was pleading with him.

"Go!" It was an exhausted rasp.

She took a step towards James. "He'll fall. He's exhausted." She had felt the tremors running through his body as he pinned her to the rail.

"Go," said James, still in German. "I'll see to him."

Rafferty's hand was on her upper arm and his voice was oddly gentle. "Come on, ma'am. You'd better come with me and get out of those wet things before you catch your death." He gave her arm a little tug, and she had no choice but to go with him.

"My husband..." Right now it was a struggle to speak English.

"Lieutenant Richter will see to him. But he looks as if he can see to himself." It had been a sheer pleasure to see Briggs laid out like that. Time someone did it, even if it was Jerry. Briggs was never going to get over that. And that ass of a first lieutenant... He chuckled to himself.

Annaliese was too tired to wonder why.

"Want him in irons?" The coxswain sounded almost hopeful.

"No!" James could barely control his anger. Of all times... Why the hell couldn't he have shown up on someone else's ship?

"Just see that the men get back to their stations. He won't give us any more trouble." He could hear Stillson being led away along the iron deck.

Hans was sitting now, his back supported by a stanchion.

The coxswain moved off. There was no arguing with that tone and besides. Jerry did look about done in. Still, you never know. He'd stay around, out of sight, just in case.

James was almost spitting out the harsh German gutturals. "Get up! And don't you give me trouble..."

"No."

His voice was profoundly weary.

"I've given you enough trouble." James had said that Annaliese would be all right, so she would be.

And Dieter was with a doctor.

"I said get up!" James reached down and grabbed Hans' arm, hauling him to his feet.

"Damn right you've given me trouble. Four fucking years' worth. I wish to hell I'd left you out there."

Hans struggled to stay on his feet as James pulled him across the iron deck towards the after superstructure.

"Where are we going?" It was odd to be talking German with James. The only place where they'd ever talk German regularly was in Prussia.

"The wardroom. You're an officer, aren't you?" The word was a sneer.

"Annaliese!"

That was her name. Mother had said that just today. Yesterday. It seemed like last month. "I told you. She's alright. And your... friend is in the wardroom, with the doctor. He'll check you out when you get there. Mother would kill me if anything happened to you." And she would. Her precious younger son. James was very angry indeed.

Hans stopped and leaned against the after superstructure, bracing himself against James' pull. How could he have forgotten. Mother. Michael. James could get word to Michael.

"Come on!"

James was trying to pull him to the door. Hans lost his footing and would have fallen but for the wall.

"You've got to ring up Michael."

"Why the hell...?!" James had to loosen his grip to open the door. Hans stayed leaning against the superstructure.

"Tell him I'm here. Otherwise, it could be days before he knows."

They were inside now, and James was shutting the door behind them. "So?"

"I've got to see him!"

"Why the hell have you got to see him?"

They were facing each other in the dim light coming up through the hatches in the floor.

"Because..." He paused. Old habits die hard. And he he'd had four years of silence, only recently broken and then only because there was no other choice. Was there a choice now? There was if he were willing to wait to get to Michael. But this was James. Still...

"I just have to. That's all."

His legs were shaking again, but he was damned if he was going to sit down and let James know just how tired he was. He was sick of being the little brother.

"He's a busy man these days." James was over by the hatch, which led down to the wardroom flat.

Busy. God. A lot you know. Hans was angry himself.

"If you don't want to tell him I'm here, then tell him his precious Siegfried is back."

He gritted his teeth. He shouldn't have said that. Showing off to big brother? Hell. But he did have to see Michael and as soon as possible. Still, he shouldn't have said it. Abwehr mustn't know. No one must know. Abwehr must think he'd simply been captured by the British and that the British thought that he was delivering the plans to someone, that they were real. Or possibly that he had pitched them. They mustn't even suspect what he was really doing, let alone that he had the real plans with him. Those plans could still be changed. Probably would be anyway, some. But the outline was there. James could save him days and it was James. James had always known when to keep his mouth shut.

"What are you talking about?"

Jesus, James could be infuriating. Didn't he understand? "Code-names, you idiot. Haven't you ever heard of codenames?"

"Of course." The words hadn't sunk in yet. "But Siegfried, for God sake. Just the idiotic, dramatic sort of code name a little brother would think up."

"We never thought of that." Hans was controlling himself with an effort. "Besides, it was Michael's idea."

James just stood there, staring at him.

A head came up through the hatch leading to the wardroom flat. The man looked from one of them to the other, curiously. "Need any help, sir?"

"No. No," said James absently, switching back to English without even thinking about it. He was still staring at his brother.

"We were just going down. He wanted to go to the wardroom with the injured man, but he's going to my cabin. He needs to be kept separate from the rest."

The man nodded and his head disappeared.

"Wait!" It was Hans who shouted after him. The head reappeared. "How is the wounded man?"

The sailor looked at him warily, then at James. James nodded.

The answer came slowly. "He's conscious. But Doc says they'll have to set the leg in Dover. He's leaving the splint on."

James nodded slowly. "Thank you, Murphy."

"Is that all, sir?"

James nodded again.

Murphy's head disappeared.

James gestured towards the other hatch, the one leading to the cabin flat. Hans looked at him closely for a moment. Then, as if he'd made up his mind about something, he moved to the hatch and started down the ladder.

The guard watched them come down, nervously fingering the pistol hanging in a holster from a web belt around his waist. James was brisk, business-like. "I'm going to see to this one in my cabin. He needs to be kept separate from the rest." He opened the door and Hans went in.

James looked back. "Everything under control?"

"Yes, sir. The first lieutenant is... ah... resting."

"And the woman?"

"She has some tea, and Rafferty rustled up some dry clothes for her."

Leave it to Rafferty. He'd moved quickly. Where on earth had he found anything small enough? "Good. I'll be out in a few minutes."

"I'll be right here, sir, if you need me. Did he really knock out both the first lieutenant and Briggs?"

News had traveled fast. Rafferty probably. "Yes."

The guard, Cross, shook his head and fingered his pistol grip again. "Doesn't look the size."

"He must be bigger than he looks. They'll be all right."

"Even so, sir." Cross shook his head again. "Be careful with him. I'll be right here." He didn't like the lieutenant being in there along with a man who could do that. Look like a drowned rat, he did, that Jerry. But you could never tell with them

James nodded and went into the cabin, shutting the door behind them. John was sitting on the deck, still in his wet clothes. "Get out of those things." He pulled out the drawer under his bunk, throwing out clothes. Underwear, a sweater, socks. Pants. Pants. His would go around John twice. Colin would have some. Too tall, but he was thinner. A blanket, meantime. James was trying not to think.

Hans was pulling on the sweater. The belt with its pouch was under his sodden clothes on the deck. There hadn't been a towel. "Can you let him know?"

"Who?" James sat on the edge of the bunk.

"Michael."

"He's in Dover." What could Michael have to do with any of this? That job of his... What did Michael do, really?

"Then radio him. Can you?" If Michael could come straight to the ship, or send someone...

"Don't know. The captain would have to."

Hans was shivering and sweating at the same time. "Can he keep his mouth shut? My name can't be mentioned."

"Of course!" James was angry again and confused.

"Then ask him. Tell him if you have to. Michael will want to know what I have for him and right away. But for God's sake, don't tell anyone but the captain. Abwehr can't know. Understand?"

"What the hell do you mean, 'Abwehr can't know?' What can't Abwehr know?"

"About my seeing Michael."

Hans dug through the pile of wet clothes and pulled out the belt. "About what's in this."

"What's in it?" A web belt? Oh. Some sort of packet attached.

"I can't tell you. I wish I could. It's for Michael."

"What's he got to do with it?"

Michael. Oh, God. He really shouldn't know about Michael. Too late now. James had better be able to keep his mouth shut. "Michael sent me."

"Where?"

"Back to Germany." Jesus. Couldn't he understand anything?

"When?"

"After Father died."

"Michael sent you back to Germany after Father died."

Then finally it all came together and he was all but shouting, "Michael sent you to Germany? Four years ago? Four God damn years ago? And all this time... All this time you've been..."

His voice trailed off as he slumped back against the bulkhead.

"A spy." Hans' voice was dull. He'd said it. Out loud.

James started to laugh. "Oh, God. Oh ... my ... God." A spy. John was a spy, a British spy. Michael was his spymaster. Oh, my God. There was more to Michael's job than met the eye.

Hans just sat there staring at him, the belt hanging from his hand. He hadn't known what sort of reaction he'd expected but this was scarcely it.

Then it hit James full force and the laughter stopped as abruptly as it had started. He was furious. "Why the hell didn't you tell us? Do you know what you've put Mother through? And Michael! How in the name of sweet heaven could he do that to her? He's marrying her tomorrow. Marrying her! That bastard!" James had stood, was in front of the door now, glaring at his brother.

"It wasn't safe to tell her, or you either. Don't you see? It had to seem that what I was doing was real."

"Real, shit! It's been real for Mother all right. And for me!"

"That part of it was hell. I hated that and so did he. But I was the only one he could send. Don't you see?" He was pleading now. James had to understand. "I'm a German citizen. I have a degree in mechanical engineering and an uncle on the German General Staff. It had to be me. And Michael didn't tell her because he was keeping me safe. It was my life, for God's sake. Do you think it's been easy for me?"

"Was it worth it?" James was still glaring at him, his mouth a hard line.

"I don't know." Hans lowered himself onto the bunk. All he wanted was for James to understand so he could go to sleep. He could sleep for a week. The belt dangled between his knees. "I really don't know. No. Well, yes. Sometimes." He sighed. "I just don't know. Michael could tell you, but I doubt he would. You shouldn't know about him, either."

Shouldn't know about him either. The words echoed through James's brain. John looked so... tired. Four God damn years. Four... goddam... years. If the past four years had been hard for him, for Mother, what must they have been for John? Looking over his shoulder all the time. Not being able to trust anyone. And the danger. By God, the danger. It was James who was shaking now.

There was a rap at the door. "You all right, sir?"

"Yes!" It was a snarl. "I'll be out in a minute." He switched back to German without thinking. "I've got to go. Get some sleep. You look like hell."

"What about this?"

He gestured with the belt.

"What about it? Give it to Michael."

"And you'll radio him?"

"I'll ask, but if I can't, I'll ring him up first thing."

"He's the only person who can have it. If he can't meet the ship..."

James grabbed it and stuffed it under the mattress. "There. If you can't give it to him, then I will. No one will look for anything there."

John was crawling under the covers before he remembered, "Annaliese."

"She's just across the way. There'd be hell to pay if I put you two in the same cabin, married or no. She's fine. Dry clothes and some tea. Probably asleep by now."

"Tell her I'm all right." He was half-asleep already. It was wonderful to lie down. Just wonderful.

"All right. I'll tell her."

"Married tomorrow."

"What?"

"Mother and Michael. Married tomorrow. Is she happy?" He knew that Michael had to be. Michael had always loved Mother.

"Sublimely."

"And on her birthday. Quite a day for Mother."

A load had dropped off him. Here was someone he could trust at last, at long last. James would take care of things. He had said that he would and he would, and keep his mouth shut in the bargain. James knew what was at stake, at least part of it. Enough. Hans couldn't have moved if he tried.

James smiled. "And you're going to be one hell of a present for both of them."

He heard a sleepy chuckle in reply as he switched out the light and put his hand on the doorknob. "Sleep well, little brother." He couldn't go on. There was a catch in his throat.

The voice was thick, sleepy, but the words were unmistakable and in English, at last. "Cut out the 'little brother' shit. Annaliese says that I'm just the right size."

James was laughing as he shut the door after himself. The guard was staring at him. "Cross, please tell the lady," he waved toward the Captain's harbor cabin, "that her husband's all right. That he is sleeping."

James wanted to see her, wanted badly to see her, but there wasn't time. He had to get to the captain at once. He bounded up the letter without waiting for a reply.

Cross looked after him, and shook his head in wonder as James' feet disappeared. Officers were an odd lot. He'd never figure them out, and there was no sense trying. Lieutenant Richter had been in there with that prisoner for a long time, far too long if you asked him. But he was rarely asked about anything. There had been loud voices at one point, the reason he knocked. That one was dangerous, if the story could be believed. Incredible. But the lieutenant said it was true and Lieutenant Richter didn't go around talking through his hat. But he'd come out laughing. Laughing, for God sake. What could Jerry have said, especially that one, to have made the Lieutenant laugh?

He was still shaking his head as he tapped on the door to the captain's harbor cabin.

# Chapter XIX

"Where are you, darling? It's 10 o'clock!" Anne was almost shouting into the phone. Michael pulled the receiver away from his ear.

"I know. I know. But wait..."

"I was worried sick when I got up and you still weren't here. Did you get any sleep?"

"Yes. Some. But..."

"Shall I send Max for you?"

"No. No. Will you..."

"Where are you?"

"Anne!" He bellowed her name into the phone. "Please be quiet!"

There was dead silence on the other end of the line. He waited. "Are you still there?"

He heard a giggle and sighed with relief. Most women would have been furious. "Look. Have Max bring in my clothes. He knows what I need. And get yourself together, and fast, and come in with him. I have a present for you." He was grinning. By God, he did, and what a present.

She didn't say a word.

"Did you hear me?"

Still there was nothing.

"Anne!"

She gave in, laughing. "You told me to be quiet. I was practicing to be a dutiful wife."

"That'll be the day!" Before she could say anything he rushed on. "Can you come? And right away? I got the wedding put back half an hour, but it was the best I could do."

"Michael!"

"I know. I didn't mean it that way. But you're going to be glad I did when you see what's here."

"Where are you?"

"At the hospital."

"James? He's not…"

"Good grief, no. He's fine."

"Then why are you at the hospital?"

"The present is here. In a manner speaking, it can't be anywhere else, at least for the time being." John had refused to leave until he knew that the other man – Bergmann wasn't it? – was going to be alright. The leg had to be set and he wasn't out from under the anesthesia yet. Nasty break, but the doctor had said that he would walk again. And that wife of John's… The two of them were in the tiny back office, out of the way. Thank God it was Sunday.

"What on earth sort of present could you have for me at the hospital?"

"You'll just have to come and see." He was grinning again. He couldn't seem to stop grinning. And those negatives. By God, the boy had come through again. They were already on the way to London in two packets, real and fake. "I promise you it will be worth the trip. And oh, could you bring a complete change of clothes from the skin out? Something simple." Anne and Annaliese looked about the same size. The shoes might be a problem, but any port in a storm. She could get the right size tomorrow if Anne's didn't fit.

"Shoes, too?" She was being sarcastic. It was almost as if she could read his thoughts.

"That would be helpful."

"You know how utterly maddening you're being, don't you?"

"Yes, dear." He did. But he was almost laughing as he said it ever so sweetly.

"It had better be worth it, if it means our wedding's been pushed back for even half an hour," she grumped.

"It is, darling, and it's the only thing that possibly could be."

"You're being so mysterious. All right." She sounded resigned. "I'll tell Max and we'll be right there. Annabelle, too?"

Annabelle. He'd forgotten about her. Thank God it was Miss Trimby. Miss Trimby could keep her mouth shut.

"She had better come with you. And drop Hannah off at the

church. There won't be time to go back for either of them anyway, James should be here by then."

*Vectis* was being repaired, minor repairs, thank heaven. Holed above the water line. It might even mean that James could have a day or so off.

"Have Max call me when you're ready to leave, so that I can be out front to meet you." He gave her the number.

"Is James in on this, too?" She was writing down the number.

Michael gave a little laugh. "You might say that. Actually he was the one who picked it up for you." He was absurdly pleased with that remark.

"Maddening! Maddening. You are positively maddening!" With that, she slammed down the phone in his ear.

He winced and sat there, receiver in hand, laughing uproariously.

Forty minutes later Michael was waiting in front of the hospital as the car screeched to a halt. He opened the door and Anne all but leapt out. "Now, what is it?"

"Patience. Patience." Patience wasn't Anne's strong suit. "Do you have the clothes?"

"Yes. In the case in the boot."

Max was standing at the driver's door, watching them. Then he remembered himself and opened the back door so Annabelle could get out.

"Get the case, will you, Max?" asked Michael. "Then park the car. We may be in here for some time."

Max nodded, relishing the exasperated expression on Mrs. Richter's face as he opened the boot and took out the small case. Whatever it was, it was bound to be good. The captain was exceedingly pleased with himself. He certainly had Mrs. Richter going, and that took some doing.

"Miss Trimby. I'm so glad you're here. I'll need your help with this."

"Of course, sir." She was looking at him, puzzled by his whole manner. What on earth was going on? He looked like a schoolboy about to play some marvelous prank.

Michael took the case from Max and waited for Anne and Annabelle to precede him into the shadow of the doorway. They were no sooner in the reception area when he said, "Darling, I'm afraid that you'll have to wait here for a few minutes."

"Oh, Michael!"

He looked at her, smiling at her annoyance. Then he really saw her at last, and his heart was in his throat. It was her wedding day and she looked every inch the bride. She was wearing a wonderful floppy-brimmed hat. Smaller than most of that sort and a perfect frame for her face. And that dress. A pale yellow, matching the hat. He didn't know one material from another, but it was soft, filmy, and the skirt fell in deep folds.

She was looking back at him and her irritation evaporated. He didn't need to say a word. What he was thinking was written all over his face.

He leaned down, his voice almost a whisper in her ear. "You are beautiful and if it's bad luck to see you before the wedding... I don't believe it. There is no such thing as bad luck. Not today. And when you see... Darling, wait. It won't be long." He straightened up, his eyes almost pleading with her.

She nodded, content to wait at last. It was Michael. There had to be a good reason for all of this. And he was so pleased with himself, or he had been until this moment. "Of course I'll wait." She smiled up at him, happy. "Just don't take too long."

He squeezed her arm before he turned, businesslike now. "Come with me, please, Miss Trimby." And then they went off down the hall, Michael, Miss Trimby, and the small case.

She settled herself carefully in a chair, nodded pleasantly to the nurse behind the desk and prepared to wait.

It was almost ten minutes before he came back when he did, he was oddly diffident. He just stood by the chair, looking down at her. She rose, still calm. "Is it ready now?"

He took her arm and led her down the hall. "Yes. Yes, it is. I... I'm going to take you to the administrator's office. He's not in today, and he said that I might use it. I want you sitting down when I bring... it in."

"All right." She wondered at her own composure.

Then they were at the door to the office. He opened it and pointed to a wooden armchair. She went over and sat down.

"I'll be right back."

She waited, her heart racing. Why did she have the feeling... This was going to be something important. Every line of Michael's body told her that this was very important indeed.

Finally, he was back but he was empty-handed. And he was shutting the door after himself, leaning against it. Why did he look like that? So upset?

"Where is it?"

"Outside. Listen, Anne." He was speaking rapidly. The words came tumbling out as if a dam had broken.

"I had to tell you first. I took him away from you. I did. He was willing to go, but it was I who sent him. I hated it. I have hated it for four years. But it's been a special kind of hell for the past few months. He has served Britain brilliantly. And you can never tell anyone that he has. Things have to go on as before. I wanted to tell you before this. And I might have told you this morning, anyway. But it was too dangerous for you to know. Dangerous for him. Not now, thank God. But you can't tell anyone. Do you understand?" He was sweating.

Her mind was blank. She couldn't seem to take in what he was saying. It was a him? What him? What him could put Michael in such a state? And then her jaw dropped slowly and her eyes filled with tears as she stared at him in total disbelief, her heart pounding wildly. She knew. She knew who it had to be.

"You do understand, don't you, Anne?" His voice was hoarse with anguish. "You can't tell anyone that he's been working for us. You'll want to. God knows. I want to. But you can't."

It seemed to her that it was someone else's voice saying first, "Yes," and then, "No, not entirely. But you will explain it later, won't you?" Oh, God! The tears were spilling over now, just a few. She didn't wipe them away because she didn't know they were there.

"Yes. As much as I may tell you. I love you."

Anne rose. She couldn't stand it any longer. "Where is he?"

Michael opened the door and he was standing there. John was standing there. An older John and he looked so tired. "You're so thin!" And why was he wearing a British naval officer's uniform? She couldn't seem to move.

And then he was smiling at her and it was her John smiling, laughing now as he engulfed her in such an enormous bearhug that her hat fell off. "Happy birthday, Mother."

Michael heard it as he left the room and shut the door and leaned his head against the wall. It took some time for John's words to sink in. It was Anne's birthday, and he had forgotten all about it. He hadn't even wished her happy birthday. But what difference would that make now that she knew what he had done to her, had been doing to her for the past four years. Could she ever forgive him? Even with her son back safe and sound?

He looked up and had to smile in spite of himself at the sight of Annaliese as she came around the corner followed by Annabelle and, good grief, James. He'd forgotten about James. Anne's clothes fit her perfectly, and she'd done something to her hair. It was hanging loose about her shoulders and curling slightly. She really oughtn't to wear those braids. This way she looks bloody marvelous. Why? She wasn't pretty exactly but there was something about her that made you think she was. Something better than pretty. She caught sight of him and her smile was dazzling.

Just then the door to the office burst open and a disheveled, glowing Anne appeared, hat in hand, her son at her side.

"Happy birthday, Anne."

She flung her arms around him, laughing. "Thank you, darling. Did anyone ever have such a birthday?" And then she was looking up at him, smiling, hugging him again. "I love you so much."

His arms tightened around her, holding her to him as if he'd never let her go. It was a long moment before she managed a breathless, "Darling?"

Reluctantly, he released her and she took his hand.

"My dear," he said, breathless himself, "I have another present for you." She hadn't seen the others yet.

Anne gave a little groan. "I don't know how much more I can stand!"

They all laughed at that and she turned. Her eyes met Annaliese's and she knew who it was, even as Michael said, "May I present your daughter-in-law, Annaliese Richter."

Their hug was brief and after the slightest hesitation on Annaliese's part, quite mutual. She had been so afraid of what her mother-in-law might say, what she might think of the girl who had married her son. Thank heaven for the clothes. Odd that they fit so perfectly, even the shoes. No one had bothered to tell her where they'd come from, and she had been too flustered to ask. Everything was happening so fast. She was lovely, Mrs. Richter, exquisite, just as Hans had said.

Anne had stepped back and they were looking at each other again. She heard her mother-in-law gasp and then burst out laughing. "The clothes. This is what my clothes were for!"

Annaliese's cheeks were burning as Hans slipped an arm around her and bent down to whisper in her ear. "You look wonderful."

She looked up at him anxiously and said in German, "Do you think she minds about the clothes?"

He grinned down at her, and said loudly in English, "Do you mind about the clothes, Mother?"

Annaliese was mortified.

"Oh, my dear... I can't think of anything I'd rather do with them." She studied her daughter-in-law critically. "And I can see precisely why John married you. Welcome. Oh, welcome."

Annaliese leaned back against Hans. John. That was going to be hard to get used to. She'd never heard anyone call him John before.

"James!"

Annaliese watched as Mrs. Richter hugged him, too. James had come to see her shortly before they'd docked in Dover. He'd been shy, not quite knowing what to say. He looked better now, far better.

Big. A nice looking face. Not handsome, really, but very masculine, and very different from Hans. And he looked so happy. She thought that Miss Trimby, Annabelle – such a funny name – had something to do with that.

Anne was looking at her elder son. "Thank you for bringing him home."

James made a wry face. "There was nothing else to be done. You'd have had my hide if I left him out there."

That made them all laugh.

It was a moment before Anne could ask, "Annabelle, have you met my son, John?"

"Yes." Hans admired her cool, level gaze as she put out her hand. He took it and shook it formally. "Just once. Four years ago."

Anne drew in a sharp breath before she looked up at Michael. "Can we see John's friend?"

Michael shook his head. "No, darling. Not now. But you can see him tomorrow."

"He will be alright?"

"Yes." It was Hans who answered. "The doctor says that he'll be fine, but he's weak and terribly tired. No one can see him until tomorrow. They just let us look at him, but he was barely conscious and couldn't talk." Even that had been difficult to arrange and he blessed Michael for it. The doctor had been told that Dieter was Annaliese's brother, a refugee from Alsace. And he'd had to put on this fool Naval uniform before he went in so that there wouldn't be any questions.

Anne nodded. "All right. Tomorrow." She brightened. "Then everything is settled except for one thing."

"What's that?" Michael thought that he had thought of everything.

"We have to get married."

He grabbed her and hugged her hard, laughing with the joy of it. And it was only ten minutes later, after he'd had a quick wash and change, thanking heaven that he had thought to shave earlier, and Anne had restored herself to a vision of cool elegance, that they piled into two cars, the second courtesy of Charlie Fitzhugh, and, with a befuddled Max leading the way, went up to the church within the castle walls to do just that.

*   *   *

It was the happiest of weddings. Charlie Fitzhugh never quite got over it. Later that night when he was about to give it all up and go to bed, he poured a dollop of whiskey into each of two glasses and squirted in a splash of seltzer before he handed one to his adjutant. "You could have cut the happiness with a knife, Henry. She even laughed after he kissed her at the end of the ceremony and hugged him. And then everyone was hugging everyone else, including me." Charlie sounded positively gloomy. Henry hid his laughter well.

Then Charlie brightened. "She was enchanted with those crossed swords. It was worth the trouble ten times over. Funny thing, though. Another couple was there. Didn't expect them. A Navy man. He was the best man. Wife had a funny accent. They went straight to Michael's car after the ceremony, and Max whisked them off somewhere. All very strange. He was a relative of Mrs. Richter's. Mrs. Compton's," he corrected himself. Odd to have a Mrs. Compton after all these years. "The wife's a refugee from somewhere. Must have gone down to the hospital to be with her brother. Some sort of injury. Had to be operated on this morning. Too bad. She was an interesting looking little thing. Very attractive." He grinned. "Always enjoy an attractive woman."

Henry nearly choked. One thing the brigadier's wives all had in common was that they were uncommonly attractive women.

"Good day. Caught three more spies in the Channel. Radioed in about it, I guess, because they were whisked right off the ship to God knows where. Those boys from MI6 were right on it." Poor Michael had been hauled out of bed before dawn. It was a wonder he could stand after having so little sleep. Seemed to be bearing up well enough. Henry didn't know about Michael. That pleased Charlie. There were very few things Henry didn't know about.

The whiskey was gone. He handed the glass to Henry who did the honors for them both this time.

Charlie raised his glass. "Confusion to the Hun and ecstasy to the newlyweds."

He and Henry drank deeply.

# Epilogue

MOST SECRET 30 October, 1940
To: Michael
From: Hogan

Very many thanks for your protégé. A good man. He has unusual abilities re: analyzing raw data.

Suggest his being seconded to Tony from time to time for training others to do his former work, if a suitable disguise can be arranged.

\*    \*    \*

12 November, 1940

Dear Mother and Michael,

The weather is lovely here as is the countryside. And they're keeping me very busy. A., too. She's translating newspapers and magazines, etc. Becoming quite fat and happy.

Actually, the 'fat' part is going to get worse, before it gets better. It seems that she is to make me a father. Whoopee! (That means – are you ready for this, Michael? – that you are going to be a grandmother, Mother!)

Love, John

\*    \*    \*

1 December, 1940

Dear Captain Compton,

I feel free to write as I want because the lieutenant said he would deliver this to you by his hand.

My leg is out of the cast since last week but I still limp. I may always but it means nothing since I am where I am.

I don't know enough words in German, let alone English, to thank you for everything you have done for me. It is all very hard to believe after everything that has happened in the past year and a half, that I could ever go on with my medical studies; I had despaired. And that it could come by the hands of those I had been told were my enemies makes it more than I can believe.

Everyone here is very nice and help me in every way. I work hard with my English and it gets better. And I am tutored to remember all that I have forgotten from my medical school, which is a great deal. Captain MacDonald says I will be ready to start at the next term in February. It will be repeating part of what I have already done, mainly because of my English being bad, but also because it is different here. And that is the right thing, I know.

And I thank you, too, that it is possible that I write my family and they write me. They think I offered to work in hospital as an orderly because I want to even though I am an officer.

My sister marries a fine man on the day after Christmas. So my mother says she is happy. They are all happy. And they are happy that I am safe and well. They would be even happier if they knew what I was really able to do.

I thank you for everything.

Give all my best to your lovely wife and of course to my friends.

Heartfelt greetings,

Dieter (now Bachmann)

\*     \*     \*

HMS VECTIS
24 December, 1940

Darling Annabelle,

By the time you receive this, we will have left. I know I can't have your reply for some weeks, but I want you to have time to think about it.

I told you once that war was no time to fall in love, that there was no time for love or any other sort of personal consideration, but I'm afraid there is no help for it. Seeing you-know-who so happy with his wife, to say nothing of Michael and Mother. I just love you and I hate the bits and snatches of time we have. Granted, naval life isn't conducive to anything else right now, but when we can be together, I want to see you properly. All the time. Night and day.

What I'm trying to say is – Will you marry me? As soon as it's practical? No. As soon as it's possible.

I love you with all my love,

James

\*       \*       \*

Friedrich Schroeder looked up from the Red Cross lettergram. There were tears in his eyes. "So. She is to have a child." Our Christmas present, he thought. She says it's our Christmas present since she has nothing else to send. And what more appropriate present could she give?

"Yes, poor lamb." Aunt Karin was angry. "Why couldn't you have told me where she was really going..."

"Karin," he said warily, "why did you have to bring that up again?"

"Because... you never tell me anything! But to let her marry him and to go off to that horrible place... And when I think that she could have married that fine Ernst Hoffer. If you hadn't objected so violently, hadn't sent her to that naval friend in England... None of this would've happened if you hadn't done that!"

He turned away and poured himself three fingers of schnapps, his hands shaking with fury. It was amazing how Karin rewrote history into what she wanted it to be.

\*       \*       \*

Anne looked around the small cottage dining room, relishing the sight of three dear faces in the soft candlelight. Michael was across the table from her, with Annaliese at the foot and John at the head standing over the roast wild duck, carving tools in hand, smiling at his wife and then bowing his head.

"Dear Lord..."

\*       \*       \*

29 December, 1940

Signal to HMS *Vectis*, somewhere in the North
Atlantic

To: Lieutenant James Richter

From: Admiral Thomas Markham, 2nd Sea Lord

A.T. says emphatic yes.

*   *   *

MOST SECRET 15 January, 1941

To: Michael

From: Tony

Training program greatly helped by new addition to
the staff. Am protecting his identity as requested
using an executioner's hood. He says he hopes it's
not a prologue… Bless him.

*   *   *

17 February, 1941

Dear Mr. and Mrs. Trimby,

I want to thank you for your kind hospitality,
especially on such short notice. But I know you
understand that naval life rarely permits anything
else these days. Still, it was more than gracious.

It was, of course, wonderful to see Annabelle, and
I very much enjoyed meeting the whole family. Mrs.
Kirby looks a great deal like her sister, and your
grandchildren are charming.

I am grateful that Annabelle and I have your
blessing, especially since it was so happily and

generously given. I do love her with all my heart
and shall do my best to be a good husband. I ask
nothing more than the privilege of sharing my life
and my substance with her, because without her
life would have no meaning.

I was touched to know that the banns are already
being posted so that we can marry as soon as the
Navy permits.

Thank you again for all your kindness. My mother
and step-father are looking forward to meeting you.
They love Annabelle already.

Most Sincerely,

James Richter


                    *       *       *


Office of the Dean
Edinburgh, Scotland
30 March, 1941

Dear Michael,

Hope you can read this. Preferred not to have my
secretary type it.

You asked me to keep you apprised of the progress
of young Dieter Bachmann. I must confess that
I had serious reservations about taking on a
refugee, especially since his records are totally
unavailable, understandable as that is these days,
and despite your strong recommendation. But my
fears were groundless. In fact if you have any
more like him, please send them along, at once.

His attitude is superb and everyone sings his
praises. One of our plastic surgeons was longing

to have a go at that cracking great scar on his cheek, but he just laughed and shook his head in an emphatic no. Finally told the surgeon that women are fascinated with it! They certainly are with him. I think he'd charm the birds out of the trees in that department, scar or no scar.

That leg of his has healed well, and the limp is barely noticeable unless he's tired. But I doubt the calf muscles will ever be the same.

His first exam results are only slightly above average but I'd be very surprised if, once he really gets the language down, he didn't wind up either at or very close to the top of the class.

I know enough to know that you haven't told me the truth about his background and neither has he. 'Nuff said. Doesn't matter. He's a first-class boy who'll be a first-class doctor.

Best to Anne, and of course to you.

Mark

\*       \*       \*

*The London Times*
Sunday, April 20, 1941

The Honorable Angus and Mrs. Trimby of Harrold, Bedfordshire announced the marriage of their daughter Annabelle Louise to Lieutenant James Paul Richter, RNVR, in Harrold on April 14th.

Mrs. Richter is a secretary in the foreign office and Lieutenant Richter, in private life, was the manager of Richter and Company, an Import-Export firm. He is the son of Mrs. Michael Compton of Eaton Square, London and the late Gerhard Richter.

The couple will honeymoon in the Lake District until the
lieutenant is required to return to his duties.

*    *    *

```
MOST SECRET 3 May, 1941
To: Michael

From: His penultimate employer

H.M. wishes to decorate your protégé. Realizes it
must be done in secret but despite that wishes to
show his appreciation. Since he is not British it
will be the highest possible award, but an honor
still. Arrange when his work permits.
```

*    *    *

```
To: P.M. 20 May, 1941

From: Michael

End of June, perhaps early July the soonest. He
is in the north and there is a confinement in the
offing, so he feels he must not leave. He is very
honored, of course, and looking forward to meeting
H.M. as well as yourself.
```

*    *    *

```
20 May, 1941

Dear Michael,
```

Just a note. Dieter Bachmann made top marks in the latest round of exams.

He says you intend to see him soon. Plan to have dinner with Mary and me when you do.

All the best wishes to you and Anne,

Mark

\*    \*    \*

June 7th, 1941

Dearest Annaliese,

My thoughts are with you so close to your confinement. I know how hard it is to wait. I shall be there on the 15th and plan to stay as long as you need to have me there.

Annabelle has moved in with us since their block of flats was bombed in the last big raid. She misses James dreadfully and says she couldn't survive if she weren't working for Michael, whom she still calls Captain Compton since she feels nothing else will do in the office!

Give our love to that scamp of a son of mine and an abundance for yourself.

Anne

\*    \*    \*

"Stalin still doesn't believe you, sir?" Michael was incredulous.

"No." Churchill looked even more like a bulldog than usual. "We've had to be very careful, of course. Wouldn't do to compromise Ultra, but dammit Michael..." His face turned pinkly pained. "What could we possibly have to gain if this were a lie?"

"A wedge driven between the Russians and the Germans," said Michael drily. "The Russians have always been highly suspicious of our motives."

"So they'll sit on their arses and let the German juggernaut roll right over them, and all because they don't trust us." Churchill's neck disappeared. "Damn fools."

"Let's hope they are able to swallow the Germans the way they swallowed Napoleon."

The prime minister harrumphed. "It took their winter to do it. We've bought them some time by heating up the Balkans, and at a terrible price, not that they'll ever acknowledge that we have, the ungrateful bastards. But if it's just enough and winter sets in before the Hun can get to Moscow..."

"You think they'll get to Moscow that fast?"

"Don't you? Stalin almost destroyed his armies with those damn senseless purges a few years ago. Always did think the Germans were behind that."

Didn't we all, thought Michael.

"In fact, they could easily get further than that if the Russians don't get help when it happens."

"And will we give them that help?"

"Of course!" Churchill's eyebrows flew up. "Any enemy of the German is a friend to us. Now," he leaned across the desk, his manner confidential, his voice low, "that... person of yours. He's to have lunch with me after he sees the king."

"Very well, sir. I'm sure he'll be quite pleased."

*     *     *

19 June, 1941

*Manchester Guardian*

A lying-in hospital in the area experienced some minor damage in a Mosquito raid. There were no deaths, but a delivery room was damaged and a woman in labor slightly injured. The baby boy was safely delivered.

*    *    *

20 June, 1941 – Headline of *The London Times*
 GERMANS INVADE RUSSIA

*    *    *

26 June, 1941

Dear Uncle Friederich and Aunt Karin,

I have tragic news. Annaliese was safely delivered of a boy on June 18 but died of a severe infection on the 24th. A bomb caved in half of the delivery room as the baby was being born, and it was all the plaster dust that caused infection, despite the doctor's efforts to keep her covered. He was shielding both her and the baby with his own body as he completed the delivery.

Everything possible was done for her and when it was seen how ill she was, I was taken to her. And so I was able to be with her when she died.

It was her wish that the baby be named Gerhard, for my father, -- Friedrich, for you, sir -- Otto for her father -- and Dieter for our dear friend Dieter Bergmann.

He will be with my mother and stepfather when he leaves the hospital, which he may have done

already. He is fine and they will take good care
of him.

I am sorry for everything, especially for bringing
her here. I loved her better than life itself, and
I only wish it had been me instead. Without her,
life is nothing. I am sorry for you because I know
she was as a daughter to you and she loved you so
much.

Love,

Hans

\*       \*       \*

July 2, 1941

Hans stood looking at the king, thinking that he looked tired,
exhausted really. But oddly, despite that, his stutter had been barely
discernible. A good man. It was written all over his face. The direct
antithesis to the portrait of Dorian Gray. Certainly not the king
of his childhood dreams and games, which were highly colored by
the legends of King Arthur, when a king always wore his crown
and carried a sword. But perhaps this one was even better. He
was simply a good man in a naval uniform who took on a duty
for which he had been prepared. A shy man with a stutter, forced
to speak and speak again in public, and all of this because a self-
indulgent, self-centered ass threw everything up to follow a siren's
song. He smiled at the thought that maybe, just maybe, that siren
had served England well when she took off their man who would
be King Edward the 8th.

"Well, young man?" The voice was gruff. The bulldog face of the
prime minister was looking at him curiously. He was seated again
after seeing the king to the door, in the simple wooden armchair
at the head of the green felt-covered horseshoe-shaped table in the

War Cabinet Room under Whitehall. "You asked to see me alone before we have lunch with Michael?"

"I want to go back to Germany."

\*     \*     \*

July 3, 1941

"Michael didn't..." Anne's eyes were glittering dangerously.

"He doesn't like this any better than you do," Hans snapped. "That's why he insisted I tell you myself. So you'd know it was all my doing. I did it myself, arranged it through the prime minister himself. Michael has his orders."

"Then why are you bothering to tell me at all?" she asked acidly. "You certainly didn't the last time."

"Mother..."

"Why?"

"Because you'd guess, as soon as you found me in a German POW camp."

"Why on earth there?"

"So it will look real. I'll be escaping. It's the only way I'll be safe and accepted back in Germany."

"Hail the conquering hero?" she sneered.

"Exactly."

She turned away. "Your son has lost his mother and now..."

She heaved a great shuddering sigh. When she went on, her voice was flat, controlled. "You'll be killed."

"No, I..."

"Oh, yes!" She had swiveled back to face him. "And that's what you want. To be gunned down assassinating Hitler or someone. In a great dramatic act of vengeance. You blame yourself and you blame that baby." He opened his mouth but she rushed on. "Don't deny it. You haven't touched him, haven't even looked at him. The big hero-spy with a Ritterkreuz and whatever the king gave you hasn't the courage to face his own son, to see those startlingly blue eyes of his mother's looking out at you from that baby's face. So you'll run away to lick your wounds by taking vengeance on the Germans and yourself!

"You're such a fool! She adored you and you loved her. And she loved that baby so. You saw her, holding him, loving him, almost to the moment she died. She was ecstatic about him and the fact that she had given you a son. To her, he was the living fact of your love for each other. And you, you stupid sod, are turning your back on all that she gave you and are running away. God, I hate it!" She was standing, fists clenched, looking up, tears streaming down her face.

"And I don't think I can bear it again."

*      *      *

SECRET

5 July, 1941

To: Colonel Riddely Ross, DSC

Commandant
Camp Staunton
Near Ashford, Kent

From: General Harold Chalmers, CBE, DSC, Commander of Prisoner of War Camps for all of Britain

You will receive orders of transfer to your camp for one Johan Richter, Hauptmann, Captured 8 September 1940. You will note there is no record of the place from which he was transferred or for any of his movements during the past year. He has been held in close confinement and has no idea where he's been. But it has been deemed that there is no further need for this and so he has been sent to Staunton.

This is for information only. Please do not file. Destroy.

Personal note enclosed: Sorry, old son. I know you'll recognize him when you see him. He's Anne-now-Compton and Gerhard Richter's boy.

Amiable but tough. Good luck.

HW


\*      \*      \*


July 25th, 1941

Darling John,

I'm glad to know at last where you are when you get my letters. I hope that the camp is a good one, as such camps go, and that you're getting enough to eat.

Punch -- Max, Michael's driver and man-of-all-work, who was once a prizefighter, started calling little Gerhard that -- because of the way he waves his fists- and I'm afraid it's stuck. I hope you don't mind. Speaking of Max, he and Hannah are in love and there may be a wedding in the offing. What a meeting of the minds that will be! Anyway, Punch is growing like the proverbial weed and is such a good baby. Everyone is mad about him. Hannah is devoted to him but we've had to get in some extra help in the form of a delightful French refugee girl who lives here with her brother. So it's a full house! Thankfully happily so. Punch is in your room, surrounded by your pictures and baby things. He's safe and we will try to keep him happy

until this world madness is over and you can be
with him.

Despite the insanity of your German ventures, I do
love you, though as always these past five years,
I cannot agree with what you do.

Mother

                    *        *        *

20 September, 1941, 0500 hours

Emergency bulletin to all military and civilian
police units and all military commanders in Kent
and East Sussex

From: Colonel Maximillian Hartfield

Chief of Military Police for Kent and East Sussex

24 German prisoners tunneled out of Camp Staunton
just southwest of Ashford this night. 9 recaptured.
Specifics and orders follow.

‹

                    *        *        *

21 September, 1941, 1600 hours

To: General Randolph Merriman-Walker, Chief of
Military Police for all Britain

From: Colonel Maximillian Hartfield, Chief of
Military Police for Kent and East Sussex

21 prisoners recaptured. None is John Richter, who
has eluded roadblocks (before his picture could
be fully distributed) and seems to be heading for
London with impeccable papers which say he is RAF
Wing Commander John Goodwin or Goodman.

\*     \*     \*

Sunday, September 21, 1941

"Well, Michael," the smugness in the prime minister's voice was apparent, even over the scramble phone, "I'd say congratulations are in order. You managed it all beautifully. I just got the report that the Germans are ecstatic, trumpeting the news everywhere, that three of their lambs have escaped from the British wolf, picked up by one of their 'craft' somewhere off the coast of Britain. It was a submarine, wasn't it?"

"Yes, sir." Michael was exhausted, and it was difficult not to snap. He was relieved that John was safe, but he was scarcely delighted by where he was. And it had been very difficult to keep the Royal Navy out of the way. That was a headache he was still having to deal with.

"The boy's a wonder." Michael could almost see Churchill shaking his head in admiration. "If anyone can succeed with this, he can."

"Yes, sir. You're right about that." Provided that they don't send him to North Africa or Russia, Michael thought grimly. Russia. Oh, Anne...

Michael had handed her the letter unopened without comment. The only thing written on the envelope was the single word 'Punch'.

\*     \*     \*

Dear Punch,

This has to be made into a better world for you than it was for your mother and me.

Just never doubt that you are loved by

Your Father

\*     \*     \*

Punch sat soberly in Anne's lap while she rocked and read it to him, his expression unchanging even when her voice broke.

It wasn't until she was finished and had put the letter carefully on the table beside him that he finally looked up at her, sober still, until finally and gradually his face brightened into the very first real smile of his life.

# About the Author

**AJ Hodges** was a wife, mom, and driver of tanks. She raised three fine children and lived in Plymouth, MN with her husband of over sixty years. AJ passed away in 2021 after a long, full, and wonderful life.

Thank you for reading **That Mad Game**. It would be very helpful and much appreciated if you would leave a review of this book on Amazon and Goodreads. We'd be most grateful.

# Coming Soon

## The sequel to That Mad Game
## The Winter Soldiers

Sign up at http://thatmadgame.com[1] to be notified of its availability.

---

[1]http://thatmadgame.com

www.ingramcontent.com/pod-product-compliance
Lightning Source LLC
Chambersburg PA
CBHW030536020726
47494CB00005B/1397